The Fall of

Clearwash City

Book 2

Timothy J Waters

Copyright Notice

- -

Book Dedication

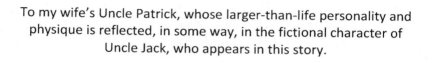

To my wife's Uncle Patrick, whose larger-than-life personality and physique is reflected, in some way, in the fictional character of Uncle Jack, who appears in this story.

"It's never a good thing to journey hastily without knowledge, otherwise your steps will lead you astray."
The Book of Proverbs 19:2 – The Bible

Thank You and Contact Details

My thanks to everyone who has helped me with this book – to those who have chatted with me on many an occasion about the contents and to those family and friends who have proof read the book with me,
you know who you are.

Contact the author using the following address:
Email: authortimwaters@gmail.com
You can find out more about this story on the website:
www.clearwashcity.com

This book is available in a variety of formats. You can find all purchasing and any other details on Amazon.

- - - - - - - - - - - - -

After reading this book it would be a great help if you left a review on Amazon from where you purchased it.

If you liked this book then please consider supporting the author by purchasing an extra copy for someone else who you think will also enjoy reading the story.

A Note from the Author

Even though this is the second book in the series, the story is a prequel. It goes back in time to look at the roots that brought about the initial downfall of Clearwash City and the rise to power of Mr E.

It should be possible to read this book as a standalone story, i.e. you don't need to read "The Waterworks of Clearwash City" first to enjoy this book. However, knowing what happens in the first story would be a help to any reader.

The Clearwash City Chronicles
Volume I

TIM WATERS

To any young people reading this book,
the prologue and introduction sections are perhaps a little difficult to understand. (They're mainly for adults like me who like to think a lot!) You don't actually have to read either of them as the story stands by itself. If you really want to know the background ideas behind the story, have a good browse through and see what you can pick up. If you're not into prologues and introductions, then just turn to chapter one and begin reading and enjoying the tale; you'll quickly find out what's happening and soon see what it's all about. I hope you enjoy reading this story as much as I did writing it.

Tim Waters.

- -

Contents

** Initial Notes about the Preface **

The preface on the next page contains vocabulary that you may not be familiar with, all to do with the process of weaving on a loom. So that you have a better understanding of the text, here are those words and their meanings.

yarn – a spun thread ready for use in weaving

loom – a framed mechanism for making textile cloth by weaving

reel – a tube or cylinder on which thread can be twisted and wound

warp – the selected yarn threads which are preloaded by the weaver and made ready to be woven to make the fabric.

weft – the crosswise threads which are woven over and under the warp threads to form the textile material

shuttle – the holder that carries the weft yarn as weaving takes place and which is shot from side to side as each row is created

beating – the action of pushing the weft into place on the edge of the weaving

fell – the very edge of the weaving where the last yarn, called weft, was beaten in

treadle – a series of foot pedals used to mechanically lift the loom in the process of weaving

- -

Preface

Unlike our 'Waterworks of Clearwash City' story, this book's unfolding narrative does not weave the threads of a happy tale. History reveals that some of life's most captivating and vivid garments were not sourced from a pleasant yarn, but fashioned on a woeful loom; their design unfolding from an ill-fated reel where the strands selected, placed and pulled, were not those that anyone would wilfully choose for themselves. Sometimes it's the blending of the darker threads, the disdained colours of dread, fear and dismay, intertwined with the blood-stained strands of betrayal, duplicity and disloyalty, which catch the eye. Together they form a stunning textile of wearable art, not normally found amongst the more conventional, bright colours which pamper to and indulge our more common desires for general, standardised optimism.

Finding yourself dressed in such a garment can be a shock. If it does happen to you then remember this, the answers as to why it is yours to wear are not found within the patterns of weaving. Instead, look at the intent expressed within the warp – those predestined strands which form the givens within your tale. Until you see the reasons for the threads selected, you'll never comprehend the path you have to follow. It is said that character and destiny are fashioned in the furnace of adversity; a flying shuttle experience where life seems out of control, random, chance driven, without context. Yet it is in that very place of mere accidental opportunity, repeating itself over and over, where each thread is purposefully added onto life's loom. Row by row it grows and the firmly chosen threads are combined to form a pre-set picture, as you complete each fallible run.

This book looks at both our threads and our failures, the latter being the so-called meaningless blotches that we leave behind in the wake of our daily meanderings. Often we run from them, pretend they're not there or imagine them someone else's deeds. But we forget that the place where we fell is always the edge of the weaving where the weft, the crosswise threads on the loom, have been beaten into place. It is in the threading, the beating, the treadle treading and the shuttle shooting that causes us to become the people our yarn provider has always desired us to be. All of these teach us to never despise the product or the process, together they work to produce the core of our final, woven prophetic form.

Introduction

NOTE: If you are a young reader, just miss this part of the book out and begin reading from chapter one as this section is for adults and you'll probably find this bit really boring! ;-)

Have you ever been squeezed? I don't mean physically. I mean, have you ever been intellectually, emotionally pressed upon; such as being offered a job you don't want whilst under the threat that, if you don't take it, your current employment may well be terminated? Sadly, it's more common than you think. That type of unseen burden, that weighty atmospheric heaviness, brings about an unsettling feeling that you're being 'moved' in a certain direction – like a chess piece in a strategy game, pushed on by an invisible hand into what seems like 'the place of no return', the middle of the board. Upon arrival, you find the adjacent squares occupied with strong, fully armoured, battle-ready rooks, knights, bishops and queens; all eager to make their next step and geared up for the kill. As you stand in the shadow of their overbearing presence, in every way your pawn like status continually proclaims, even shouts out, its feeble inadequacy, no matter how much you try and tell it to be quiet.

Coming to terms with your new surroundings, it slowly, and most uncomfortably, dawns on you that you've actually got no idea how you got into such a place – or what further measures have already been calculated in the coming moves by the player who's playing you. On this occasion the normal 'mind reader' superhero ability, so often given to the great heroes in fictional tales, hasn't been offered and all that's left in this *out-of-depth* and *I'm-so-dead* environment, to aid your survival against this onslaught of the will, are the feeble workings of your own fragile humanity. You feel 'out of options' – that somehow life has been deliberately stacked against your freedom to make choices and the fountains of turmoil within register an alarm that your very personhood and rational choice-making credibility has, in some way, been marked as absent.

When such an event occurs, it's not the 'Way Out' exit sign or even the "Help, Get Me Out of Here!" symbol you initially look for. Rather, it's the 'Jump First and Think Later' survival square; often immediately available but rarely the right choice to make. For you, getting out from under the shadow of the greater figures is the most important thing; let them get on with the job of slugging it out. This seems to be the best and most sensible option. For when did one so little as *you* ever achieve anything in the shade of those who are so mighty? You're not a warrior king or a mighty man of valour or even a brave, young hobbit! You're just you. But what if someone whispered in your ear and told you a secret or two – that in this world of the bold and the brave, it was actually the delicate and very breakable *you* who could make the difference in this wild game of move and counter moves? What if it was *you* who now held the keys to how each player played out its part?

Holding the destiny of all in your hands will most probably not have been on your personal life agenda as you grew up. Trying to find yourself in this strange world is difficult enough without bearing the burden of everyone else's wellbeing and destiny. So when the question was put to your young mind of what you would one day be, your response would very likely *not* have been, "To hold in my hands the fate of my city in a time of crisis!" Now there's a response rarely heard! So when you find, in reality, this very weighty option presented to you, it's not surprising to find yourself completely unprepared for both the office and its burden. Schooling does not offer a 'How to Respond when Everyone's Fate is in Your Hands' course. It's only then that your gullibility and naivety shines through; your artlessness in the dark arts, your lack of ability to engage in underhand deception.

"Be as wise as a serpent and innocent as a dove," the old saying goes. But serpent wisdom, whilst in the time your of innocency, is a difficult thing to come by in a fallible and imperfect world. Gaining the first whilst retaining the latter is not an easy thing to do. Often you just find yourself swept along, not knowing what's happening, who's doing it, why it's being done, who holds the strings to make it happen and how it's all going to end. It's only after the disaster has taken place that reflective wisdom comes, but by then your 'innocent as a dove' status has been shattered and you mourn for a world that once was and now is not.

So too for the people of Clearwash City, who, in the time of their innocent and naïve timidity, find themselves caught up and carried along on the tides of emotional persuasiveness and underhand intimidation. We see the people swayed, controlled, manoeuvred, picked up and put through the political and philosophical clothes wringer. Once made impotent by the squeeze, they're intellectually pulled, pushed, pinched, punched, panicked and partitioned; being tipped up and dropped into a melting pot of therapeutical persuasion, stirred in with a good dose of broad promises and vague vocabulary; who hasn't heard that before! Together these produce a potent brew. As a result, in their time of dulled enlightenment and social crisis, they quickly find themselves driven to a collective dead end, a cultural cul-de-sac of hopelessness based on misinformation coupled with aggressive idealism; a constant attempt to make them fit an ideological future none saw or understood, except those who played out their agenda on life's theatrical stage.

With political leaders who are more concerned with their own ideology or their place in public office, the people lose both their sense of place and home. The only alternative is a cultural wilderness wandering which makes even the most familiar locations feel like a foreign land. Once all is said and done, however, the survivors of this great upheaval come to see that their final destiny is not for others to choose on their behalf, no matter how manipulating their enemies have been. For when life has delivered her final disciplinary blows and reflective wisdom seeps into the depths of their bones, they perceive with renewed eyes that the pre-given task to overcome the evils in this world are not just still at hand, but *in their hands* to face and deal with in whatever ways they can.

I wish I could say that every story ends happily ever after, but it doesn't. However, no matter how difficult the outcome, there is always that little word called 'hope'! Little it may be, but that which this small seed produces grows into a tree that can house the 'nest sites' from which dreamers can spread their wings and soar into the heights. For hope leads to stirring, stirring to awakening, awakening to commitment, commitment to determination, determination to steadfastness, steadfastness to persistence, persistence to devotion and devotion finally leads to a thing called freedom; that wide open space of dancing delight shot through with the thrill which none can enjoy except those who have passed through the years of turmoil and now see the fruits of their painful and heart-breaking labour. Who would have thought that such a small thing as 'hope' could do all of that? Who would have thought that *little you* could bring about such change? Faith, hope and love are said to be the greatest things, but in that mix, *little you* has its part to play too. Now there's a thought to think about!

- -

The Book's Characters

3

Chapter 1 – A Scarcity of Sound

Clearwash City sat in the middle of a most inhospitable desert and shimmered in the baking heat. Basking in the sun's dazzling brightness, she momentarily roused herself from her deep slumber, stretched out her stone limbs in lazy surrender, and yawned; relaxing her rock-like members in the brilliance of the morning light. It was hot! The oven dial pointed to a fiery roast and all around the air was a-stir; a moving, swaying, rippling mass that wobbled in the scorching breeze, stimulated and enthused by the engulfing temperature. Sitting beneath this blistering hotness the city closed her tired eyes and dozed. All seemed peaceful and very quiet. Having dissipated the night-time chill with her radiant, fiery beams, the great golden globe looked down from the firmament above and smiled. It gave her great satisfaction to see every part of the wide blue expanse saturated with her goodness; to see once again her dominance established in the heavenly realms and her reign unchallenged. Now she poured out from on high her sweltering kindnesses onto the many houses, streets and market squares below that belonged to the great metropolis. Like a weaned child under the care of an attentive mother, the city mumbled a half-hearted greeting to the world and then, after muttering something briefly under her breath, rolled over to continue her slumbering. Relaxing in the muggy warmth, she felt safe in the overbearing caresses of temperate, affectionate cordiality.

To the baked streets that were used to this kind of extreme heat, all seemed comfortable, agreeable and most satisfactory. To the human eye, looking on at the many dwellings and habitations scattered across the city, all was in place, an environment that was both neat and correct, kept with an immaculate fine-tuned efficiency, micro-managed down to the smallest detail. The city buildings were clean, well-ordered, and the many parks and open spaces showed off a landscape that was lush and green. The historical turnaround looked complete and at last sustained. No smog, no smoke and dirt it seemed was a thing of the past. Cleanliness was the word that came to mind, shouted from the rooftops even, and if cleanliness (which is next to godliness) was the aim of the day, then this was a successful city; a locality that fulfilled its divine call and put into practice that which it vigorously and religiously preached.

Looking across the skyline at the houses, parks, market squares, malls, mills, hills and canals, you could see that it was a place of no nonsense and no compromise. It was as if a dedicated army of fanatical cleaning technicians made sure that every spot of every surface was washed, polished and shone. Purity was now the new romance. For those in charge it was the latest and greatest expression of heart-throbbing eye-candy; a coalition of habitations, industrial workshops and public spaces that together cast a charismatic allure, hypnotising the visitor with its perfect edifices, shapes and architectural masterpieces. A wonder to behold, it all worked like a neatly fitted jigsaw to form a seamless and impeccable picture. If it were an anthem, then it would sing out its tune in perfect harmony. If it was an engine, then it would have purred with pleasure; a perfectly balanced, precision

5

made, well-oiled machine. This was success on a scale rarely imagined, let alone realised. To any that saw the big picture, who understood the grand utopian plan, they could feel nothing but the tingling satisfaction of a romantic and idealistic vision fulfilled.

This too was the perspective of the burning sun who watched from on high in the expanse of the sky and followed each day her faithful course across the heavens. But this champion of the heights lived so far above the capital that her distant evaluations and assessments were obviously limited. Just as a dictator only sees the broad picture painted before him (standing on his balcony to overlook the cheers and applause of his troops, officials and specially selected populace; not seeing those places off limits to the dictatorship's propaganda machine, the realities of poverty and starvation, oppression and fear) so too it was from the bright shining sun's standpoint as she daily watched the scenes unfold in Clearwash City. "All is well," would be the sun's repeating mantra from her far-off vantage point – but these things can only be clearly seen from the ground. As always the 'devil was in the detail' and this 'devil' had run riot in the city streets for many weeks and months, perhaps years.

One of those 'on-the-ground' details lay just outside the city's front gates. There the historic remains of a great riverbed ran its deep channel into the hardened rock where a gushing waterway had previously carved out a passage of life years before. Now only trickles of water meandered and tiptoed over those smoothed pebbles and rounded stones where once a torrent had flowed. The eminent and illustrious river was subdued. The thirsty desert had drunk for so many-a-season of the river's great banquet of abundant supply that at one time it was actually rumoured to be ready to yield up its territory to the continuous flood – but now the sand was back and the ground panted for just a sip of water.

Back in the city, blubbering pools of wet mud briefly appeared each morning throughout the streets and lanes where once fountains of water had spouted and flowed (these ever-emerging muddy overflows were quickly cleaned up by an army of volunteers nicknamed the S.P.L.O.D.G.E. team, 'splodge' meaning the 'Sanitisation and Purification of Leaking and Oozing by Disinfecting with Germicidal Engineering'). Memories of those crystal-clear powerful and gushing sprays were now faded, and perhaps it was just a dream or the beginnings of a legend that they once fed the city with fresh, vibrant and clean water. It was so sad to see such strong springs of life reduced to a mere whimper. In their place large industrial pipes had been used to cap these untamed sources and the water was now restrained and piped in a more civilised way that allowed the population to control their flow; though the water pressure was not what it used to be and sometimes a mere dribble was all that they gained from their new business venture. This wasn't, however, the most disturbing thing about Clearwash City. Disappointing might be a word chosen to describe the lack of bubbling brook and absent watercourse but 'deficient' would be a better word to describe the derelict human life that existed within the confines of the city walls.

It was rush hour, time to be busy, but instead of hustle and bustle a muted noiselessness draped itself over the subdued capital. Like a miasma of gloomy desolation, this heavy silence splayed itself across the airwaves like a saturating and polluting smog that would not shift or move, even though it was a bright and hot spring morn. Amidst the great heat, you could still feel the chill of the quietness and hush as if it were an eerie calm preparing the way for a great thunderstorm, a tempest or typhoon. So invasive was this hush and stillness that it pervaded not only the parks, canals, avenues and gardens, but the back alleys and market squares too - everywhere where humanity should be, and yet was not.

Even the wind was lost. Normally this rousing gust of activity found its blustery bearings by passing in-between and around a busy humanity. It loved to run from person to person, from child to adult, from families and friends to groups of boisterous teenagers. All together they created a variety of gaps and narrow spaces that forced the breeze to squeeze here and there as it made its daily journey across the city. Human bustle made life in this place interesting, colourful and fun to navigate. Now, chasing its echoes down the winding lanes and cobbled corridors, the solitary breeze whistled its way through the streets looking and searching for signs of life. No coats to tug, no hats to blow off, no children to laugh and play with – it tarried for a moment on its broken hearted and lonesome path to cast a glance at the disappointing emptiness. Then on it continued, finally reaching the outskirts of the city walls, untouched and unmoved by those it sought out.

It wasn't that the absence of any noise itself was a problem or that the stillness and quiet was somehow unexpected, it was something else; this peculiar, subdued tranquillity, that now hung in the atmosphere, showed a locality holding its breath. The city suffered not so much from a shortage of noise but rather a scarcity of sound. The lack of clamour from workmen and the non-existent din of a crowd revealed a city in starvation; a famine of racket, uproar, tumult, shouting, agitation, hubbub and hullabaloo.

This strange singularity of deprived commotion gave off a silence that was so deafening it demanded being listened to, so loud that you had to strain your ear to hear anything at all, for there was indeed nothing to hear. Nothing, that is, except perhaps the odd chirp from the early morning bird who sought to tell everyone that he'd been up for hours and that, if they were not very careful, he would be the only one to show his face that day.

Sound had packed its bags and left, a withdrawal of noise that was the embodiment of abandonment. Where it had gone and why, was a question anyone could ask, but there wasn't anyone to ask. Perhaps the answer lay in the presence of a corpulent, portly, invisible lady, a woman of drunken pleasures, called 'motionlessness' who sat in the main square. Next to her was her sister called 'dearth'. Together they made up the new ideological order of the day and their presence ensured that all hopes and dreams that would normally stir the human soul to life on such a fine morn were dulled and sedated. Noiselessness now ruled over the activities of what might be called the 'living humanity' that existed throughout the hours of daylight. Living the population might be, but 'human' or indeed 'humane' is not a word that should be used to describe their deeds. For the citizens of Clearwash City were all dreamily shut away behind closed doors. Cosy, clean, contented and chilled, the good life was here and no-one was going to take it from them. Like a mind drug, shrouding vision and insight, the silence that had infiltrated the lives of these people, the general populace, was comforting.

They slept so peacefully and every morning it was the same. It didn't matter that your sleep had been slightly interrupted at dawn when doors were kicked in and soldiers made their arrests and those few voices of dissent were marched off to who knows where. Betraying others the night before, to prove your loyalty to the new regime, would guarantee a supply of food, unlimited exclusive commodities and entertainment for hours; followed by a sleep-in that subsequent morn which imitated the life of a spoilt millionaire. Party, sleep, rest and more perpetual play to follow, a cycle of quick immediate pleasures, exhilarating and thrilling, bringing instant gratification to the soul. The body, however, worn out by this constant activity, could chill and find its rest throughout the following hours of daylight, getting ready to do it all over again when evening came. So the night life was found to be better than the day, for it held the keys of happiness and contentment; strange that this had become the final conclusion of the city's enlightened citizens. Education, it seemed, didn't hold the keys to wisdom and insight, just to a dictatorship of what is called 'current thinking' which pays no homage to the realities of the life that surrounds us. Now, for the people of Clearwash City who were drenched in the new ideology, the day had nothing to offer them but the song of blank vacancy that played itself out to the background beat of snores from an exhausted people.

There was a sound, however, that did sometimes slip into this blank space of empty life. It meandered its way on the breeze, across the open air, in what was once a more affluent part of the city (now considered a little old fashioned and frumpy); a cheery tune, highly at odds with the rest of the dulled quiet that surrounded it. The city's stillness tried to suffocate this irritatingly happy intrusion but the melody persisted, undeterred and unrepentant – despite the strong disapproval and protest from its surroundings. The tune's delightful message leaked into the atmosphere from the back of a grand mansion. To be precise, through an upper attic window, left slightly ajar. Behind the window, a small room, and the source of the charming jingle, a horn of an old and rusted record player that magnified and fed the agreeable sound into the air. The player's receiver head floated gracefully along its prescribed path on the grooves of the vinyl disc like a beautiful skater performing a well-rehearsed routine; that is until it bounced up and down where the record had warped slightly and the tune being played wobbled in protest. The lively notes that did manage to get played correctly, however, soothed their way through the room's stillness, leaving it enriched by its joyous sound.

The furnishings within the converted attic space were comfortable enough, two leather backed armchairs facing each other opposite an open hearth that hospitably housed the remaining embers of a night-time glowing fire. If there had been a normal peacefulness in the air you would have thought the environment homely, sociable and even jolly. Indeed, to the stranger's eye, the first impressions of the room would bring ideas of sweet friendship and cordiality. Outside, however, the descended silence had nothing to do with serenity.

At a table, set to one side of the armchairs, sat a lady of the realm. The sharp and pointed expression etched across her face hid her normal gentle features that were so familiar to the people amongst whom she lived. She was a woman with a task before her, one that she would rather not do.

Taking a few moments to mentally prepare herself for the job at hand, she briefly stilled her mind and then picked up a silver quill, dipped it into a small bottle of ink, and penned the following:

"Lady Georgiana, daughter of Lord Stephen Pluggat and Lady Melanie Lynette,
To the people of Clearwash City, set free and made clean by the King's liberty and grace. To those whom I love, who have so grown in my heart and who I now hold with such tender care and great affection.

My dear friends,

It is with great anguish and turmoil within that I write for you this short account of those things that have so recently been fulfilled amongst us. I do this now so as to not lose my voice in the midst of this present chaos. In writing this, I am very aware that it is not only a short history of a season past that I record, but also my personal farewell to those of you that remain once I am gone. For I sense and feel that my time here is drawing to an end and that I shall soon pass through and beyond the veil that separates our world from the next."

Chapter 2 – The Beginning of the End

Lady Georgina's silver quill scratched the ink across the page as she continued to write. Her manner of authoring was harsh, almost severe, holding the quill's spine tightly to scrawl each letter, each word, as it came to mind. The duty set before her wasn't easy. No-one likes to write about any measure of failure, let alone one that stems from a fortune lost, but this assignment had to be completed. So, forcing the inked nib to move on the paper, she mentally stamped onto the tea-stained parchment the story she had to tell.

"I want you to know," she wrote, "that I have spent myself for you and the good cause of our great and noble city. Yet, before this silver chord is severed and I step into a more eternal place, whilst I am still in this human tent of a body, I wish to continue to pour out that which remains of my life; in so doing I hope that you may all drink well and deep from our communal cup that was passed onto us by the good King himself, to carry on in his name.

The silence, as it is now commonly called, is here. I can almost feel it in this room as I write. Its gentle quietness lingers and lurks at the doorways to each of our houses and homes and even now, after all this time, few heed its arrival. Perhaps one day there may be a time when we can all sit back and reflect, to consider that which we should have done to prevent its entry, so that never again will we make the mistakes that have so clearly been made amongst us. I fear, however, that I will not be one of those few who have the privilege to partake in such an occasion, if any such occasion is to be found. Victims we all are, and victims we will remain.

For when those most culturally refined and gracious wolves recently entered our land, we welcomed them with open arms and paid no heed to the rattling and tugging of our consciences that sprang to life as we followed in their wake. Now today, that which once was so glorious, being restored to us by royal command, is again fallen and gone. A city lost in itself and broken through misguided desire and perverted intent. Such a depth of agony and despair fills me now when I reflect upon this glory so departed; lost and forgotten by those to whom it should have stayed and remained with forever.

Wisdom, it seems, does not belong to the philosopher or the scholar: not to the intelligent or those adept at attaining success. Nor does it belong to those who busy themselves with the many matters of life's callings. Wisdom is a small, gentle voice that speaks quietly and persistently. It does not bow its knee to the human soul or chase recognition from culture or power. It will not fall subject to a false smile or a handshake from those who deliver rewards. Wisdom never changes, and those who embrace it find themselves kept safe; and so indeed we would be today - if we had but listened to its call.

Yes it is very true that for many a year we enjoyed a great peace and prosperity under the rule of our wonderful King, and to this recent past I will initially refer as I write. He had saved us from a slavery to which none of us had the answer and brought us into a spacious place, full of good things, which in turn gave a joy that tasted of eternity itself. Our victory had been won for us, the weak rescued from the strong and an opportunity for us to enter into it ourselves. Yet I began to perceive

11

that, despite our freedom, the people took little opportunity to grow. I now understand that victories not only have to be welcomed by those who are rescued, they have to be received, grasped and made their own. Yet we, disturbed by ancient flaws, quickly gave way to being fat with wealth and so deluded with self-honour that we forgot the one from whom it all came. Before long we were nothing but a delusionary drunkard, gazing over his sparkling bottle of addiction and kissing it, as if it were life and freedom itself. Reason was dead, wisdom departed and confusion held the keys of opportunity and decision.

However, before I talk of such things and bring them into clear view, I find I must step back a little and prepare the ground; for our failings in this matter do not originate from the time of our recent straying. The roots of our current sufferings run much deeper, and it is these that need our attention. I have often found that the roots of our beginnings point us to where we should finally go. It is the roots that hold up the tree and, once they are corrupted and compromised, it's only a matter of time before the great oak begins its fall.

Our ruin began early in my childhood but was made manifest several years later in my youth. I remember it well. The culmination of which was to be found in the last day I saw my city in its former glory. On that day I held in my hands both my innocence and childlike trust. It was also the last day I saw, face to face, my most honourable father. The sun had risen that morning amidst a dusty, dirty haze, as unnatural as breathing the polluted air that surrounded us. Upon first seeing it, I knew we faced difficult times. Something was coming, though I discerned not its substance. As I stood, looking out across the skyline of our homes, I perceived we were at a doorway, an opening, a gap in our monotonous history; one that presented itself at the end of a long and narrow one-way street – a destination that we had long chosen, and from which we could not return."

Lady Georgiana stopped writing and laid down her quill for a moment. Her will was set, this task she now performed had to be completed, but it was almost impossible to continue without taking a breather. Eventually she picked up her quill again and wrote some more, detailing how the war broke out that morning. She recalled how a war of words had been raging for many a year, but on this day weapons of war were added to the argument and many lives were lost.

"What I didn't know," she wrote, "was that the sunrise I beheld that morning, would be the last I would see for many a day, if not many a week."

Down went the quill again and she closed her eyes. There she could see painted pictures, scenes of devastation imprinted on the canvas of her mind; vivid images clinging to her imaginations – flowing from a place that was deeply embedded in her soul. She could see the tumbled down walls of buildings and the rubble that lay scattered across the streets. The shouting and bellowing, the cries, the tears and she could still hear the boom, boom, boom of shells that were fired across the sky. She drifted into a semi-sleep and everything from the past became very clear.

- -

"Hold the line! Hold the line!" a voice shouted through the dust filled air.

The empty spaces in streets and communal squares where people normally walked were now occupied by thick clods of choking fumes. Once busy with friends saying their 'hellos' these same marketplaces, courtyards and malls were now filled with a haze of turmoil and destruction. Between the floating and drifting smog, shadows of figures dashed and darted from hiding place to hiding place, seeking refuge and a space where they could perhaps remain alive for just a few more moments. Ducking here and darting there, they made their way across the maze of streets to places where they could find sanctuary. It had been like that for several hours now, a stream of scurrying refugees all running for their lives. Only recently had they found solace when the shelling slowed to an occasional boom rather than the regular pounding that had been the drum beat of the day.

Among them the wounded, the disheartened and the emotionally damaged - they sought the haven of medical staff or the advice of newly elected military leaders who knew nothing of war. You could see them, the scatterings here and there of moaning individuals or groups or pairs of comforting friends, each trying to find their way down unfamiliar streets that they'd walked on for many a year, picking their way through the holes and debris that were scattered across their paths; a bedazzled humanity, wandering targets, stupefied by deafened eardrums and minds filled with images that the eye should not see.

There were many heroes that day. Not the kind often celebrated in action films who are expert at killing others, filled with a rage and madness that somehow passes itself off as an accomplishment to take multiple lives. No, the saviours of the day were actually the quiet ones who herded the weak into safety or those people who found themselves out of their depths - who did jobs that they did not understand and yet, whilst not knowing what to do or what would happen next, still stuck to their tasks until they were somehow done or someone else turned up to take over from them. Each of these did their duties amongst the lives of so many broken people and kept going till they could give no more.

One such person was a middle-aged man; at least you thought he was middle aged. When needed, he could run fast enough (to dodge the shots that were fired at him) and he could lift up those who were wounded in his arms and carry them to where they needed to be. But once the day was almost over he walked with a stupor that conveyed the look of someone twice his age; a man on whom the world had driven over, ploughing deep its furrows into his very bones.

Sitting down and putting his head in his hands, he thought there was nothing else he could give. A seasoned politician and Doctor of Science by profession, he had spent much of the day either searching for survivors or playing the role of a Doctor of Medicine. Person after person he had treated till he was numb with grief and tired beyond exhaustion. Giving relief and strength to the wounded and comfort to the distraught, he felt that he'd handed his life over many times to those who grieved around him. It was only moments later, however, that the sound met his ears of another body dropping and thudding onto the ground nearby. Against all his emotions, he stirred himself to action, dragging his heart back into place to get up and deal with his next patient. Walking over he saw the frame of a young woman, perhaps a teenage girl, slumped in a heap. There she was, her clothes blackened and her face and hair covered with dust and debris. Despite the dirt that plastered her face, however, the man immediately recognised her and his heart broke all over again.

Taking her hand gently in his, he checked her pulse and then the rest of her for wounds. To his great relief he found that she wasn't dying, though he was greatly concerned about two deep gashes which ran across her left hand and arm. Taking a small bottle of water from his jacket pocket, he washed the lacerations and then dripped water onto her forehead, gently wiping her face and brow. Slowly she came round. Sweat poured from the young lady whilst her mouth ran dry with dehydration. After a few sips of water, her face twitched nervously and the tension she felt caused her to grind her teeth together, as if to stifle some great discomfort. Gradually her sluggish mind came into focus and her surroundings became familiar.

"Oh Dad!" she said, once the haze had gone a little from her eyes and she could see who was attending her.

"Steady," he said, in a breathless tone, trying to sound as if he was in control for his daughter's sake.

"Oh Dad!" she blurted again, but she either couldn't find the words to say or was unable to speak.

"Stay calm," replied her teary-eyed father, giving her a quick peck-of-a-kiss on the forehead. "You must stay calm."

The girl tried to speak again but she was either overcome by some kind of fear or doubt or perhaps just the pain that she currently felt.

"I'm going to give you something to take away the pain and it may briefly put you out," her father said. "This will hurt only for a few moments. Then you'll see me again when you come round."

The girl shook her head.

"Must listen," she said trying to sit up. "You don't know…" but the words still didn't come out.

"Stay still," he replied. He placed his hand behind the back of her head and, with his other hand under her chin, helped her to rest her head back onto the grassy bank upon which she lay.

She breathed in some quick short breaths, coughing out some dirt from the side of her mouth. Her eyes flickered and spun upwards, gazing almost into the top of her eyelids, before closing them to breathe a little more easily. The man fumbled through his jacket pockets, searching frantically for something. Eventually he located a syringe and a sachet of liquid. With trembling fingers he opened the packet and began to suck the watery solution into the needle's cylinder.

The girl came round again and noticed her father preparing her injection.

"No," she whispered through trembling lips, her throat still hoarse with thirst.

Her father ignored her and continued to finish preparing the needle. Seeing that she didn't have much time, she shook her head from side to side as if to try to overcome the pain that shot through her body. Her efforts finally brought forth a burst of tears, but crying was also too painful to endure.

"Stay still," her father said, a little more firmly this time as he took hold of her arm.

There was panic in the girl's face.

"You don't know what's coming," she finally said, in great anguish; just getting the words out brought another overflow of tears.

"Georgiana," the man said. "You must stay still."

The girl was determined, however, not to do as she was told.

"I have seen it," she blurted out. "Dad, I have seen it with my own eyes."

More tears streamed down her cheeks.

"You must get away from here, right now," she said. "There's no time…" but the sentence wasn't completed.

The man finished giving his daughter the injection and seemed to be relieved when she was out cold.

"I need a stretcher!" he bellowed over his shoulder.

A few moments later two men appeared carrying a stretcher between them.

"Dead or alive?" asked one of them, in a manner too casual to be polite.

The girl's father just stared at them and, when they recognised him, dropped their flippant stance and almost stood to attention.

"This one is very much alive," he said, in a purposeful tone. "Take my daughter to the nearest pod or bunker and make her comfortable."

The men, slightly stunned by the news of whom they were to carry off, hurriedly set the stretcher by the girl and carefully placed her twisted frame onto it. After they had lifted her up from the ground her father briefly leant over his daughter.

"Goodbye my sweetheart," he said, and kissed her cheek. Then he whispered something into her ear, ran his fingers through her hair, and stood back to watch her being carried off.

The stretcher bearers disappeared over a fresh bank of earth, recently created by an exploded shell. Once they were gone, the scientist/would-be doctor sat down and bowed his head again between his knees. Shells began to be fired but he didn't move. He'd reached the point where he felt so hollow that caring about himself seemed of little consequence. Fortunately, he still had friends nearby that were able to take charge of him, to lead him by the hand and take him to a place of apparent safety.

"Hold the line! You hear me! Hold the line!" a voice shouted.

Almost immediately the fresh firing of multiple guns rang through the air and the familiar noise of the day started. Boom, boom, boom, the shells dropped out of the sky and scattered across the ancient city's streets. Within moments, however, and to everyone's surprise, the pounding stopped. All was still, nothing moved and no-one spoke. The ragged band of soldiers who still protected that part of the capital cast glances at each other, looking for enlightenment or an order saying what to do. Silence whispered something sinister whilst everyone waited for the next assault to begin.

Then it started, a noise, a sound. Wailing, it came to life and filled the air with a lonesome and heartless melody; it gave the impression of something being awakened in great distress. The droning, tormenting hum rose and fell on the heavy afternoon air, like a military warning siren, unsure whether to sing its woeful howl or not. From afar, to their right, other engine sounds joined in, the kick-starting of many machines. More and more commenced and now there seemed to be fresh noise from every part of the horizon.

15

Off in the distance something stood up. As tall as the buildings that surrounded it, its frame was long and thin. Perhaps it was being supported by long legs, you couldn't see, but its head was like a brown box covered with indentations. This object was joined by another and then another. They kept popping up till hundreds of them could be counted on the skyline. Slowly the heads of these machines split open and each one released thousands of buzzing insects into the air. Gathering and gathering, the creatures rose in swarms and congregated in their localities, clustering communally as one, till they looked like a mass of teeming hornets or an army of shining locusts.

The small creatures all looked alike; about the size of a man's hand and coloured a silver-grey. Covering their bodies were a series of metal plates which ran from tail to head, culminating in a single helmet at the front; shielding the creature's skull and resting on top of a pair of metal tusks that protruded from the sides of its jaw. Each insect had three pairs of legs and a swaying, swishing tale, like that of a scorpion. The buzzing sound emanated from four delicate, almost transparent, wings that flapped and fluttered at a tremendous velocity. As they flew, their bodies snaked from side to side, clicking and clacking as they went.

Slowly they moved forward, several mountains of fluttering, glistening steel, rising higher into the heavens as if finding their rightful place in and amongst their horde. Then across the city they came, like flocks of birds preparing for a great migration – but this collective of buzzing hymenopteran wasn't going anywhere.

After spiralling high in great circular routes, they finally dropped down - flooding the streets and driving out the populace before them. People yelled and screamed. Desperately they tried to get away as the air became thick with the insect's whirring, humming bodies - but alas, there was no-where to run. The people found themselves covered with the creatures and then, after a quick scan, they were either stung, from which the person collapsed to the ground, or were lifted into the air and taken away.

Out from the horizon, troops made their way down the streets of Clearwash City, following the hymenopteran and capturing anyone driven out of their hiding place. At the rear of this military parade smaller groups of workers followed, not to conquer, but to process the captives and 'tidy up' (as the practice was termed) after the insects had finished their work. It seemed as if this would be the end for the people who now fought for their lives. Strangely enough it wasn't. It would later be recorded, however, by those who write to tell the tale of history, that this certainly was the beginning of the end.

Chapter 3 – Solitude & Lonely Company

The record head stroked the vinyl disc back and forth, back and forth. Lady Georgiana jumped, she had slipped into a sleep she had not expected. Coming back to herself, she saw the hearth fire was dead and the sun at high noon. There wasn't much time for personal reproach, so her immediate feelings of disappointment with herself didn't get chance to sit in her emotions. The record was quickly picked up, placed back into its white sleeve and the player turned off. Casting her gaze up and down the long driveway that led up to her mansion, she remained stationary until satisfied that danger wasn't lurking nearby. Returning to her desk, she read the last few paragraphs to refresh her mind, then picked up the quill and began to write.

"The consequences of war that met my eyes have never left me, not for a single day. How you can measure such a thing as grief is beyond me. All you can do is taste it and let it live inside you till somehow it is lessened in some way by other things. It would be good if schooling or childhood enabled and prepared us for disaster – but sadly that is not possible. I came round that fateful morning to solitude and it would have been better for me if I had chosen its lonely company."

- -

The young Georgiana startled herself out of her sleep. It was those few moments of not knowing where she was, and in fact who she was, that caused her initial panic. The light was dim, the stretcher bed on which she lay unfamiliar, and the utter silence that surrounded her (except for the echoes of her first calls for help that bounced back off the metal walls) was cold and unwelcoming. It took a while for her to see clearly. One of her eyes wouldn't open. The mud on her face had dried her lid shut and she had to spend some time peeling her eyelashes apart before she could ease the rest of the dirt away and so see again. The lack of vision, the cold, the damp, and the gloomy darkened space she found herself in, brought severe feelings of abandonment and vulnerability.

"Hello?" she ventured again, sending another cautious call into the darkness – but still no response. "Hello!" she half shouted, hoping to hear some footsteps coming in her direction – but none came.

Her legs felt stiff and her knees and side ached from what she thought must have been her long sleep. She reasoned that she'd slept so heavily, she'd been a dead weight; only supported by the stretcher she'd been carried on and, underneath that, a shallow mattress with its superficial padding allowing the bed's springs to poke into her side, shoulders and thighs. The discomfort, however, grew with each moment that passed and it soon became obvious to Georgiana that the pain she felt was still primarily from her injuries. Her exhaustion, however, got the better of her. Within moments, without knowing that is was happening, she rested her head, closed her eyes, let her mind drift and quickly fell into another sleep.

Hours must have gone by, or that is what Georgiana figured. Her drowsy eyes reopened and were now greeted by a room that, though dull, was not as dark as before. Small shafts of light dropped down from multiple points across the ceiling. It wasn't artificial light either, more like redirected sunshine from somewhere outside the building. Looking at her surroundings Georgiana at least now understood a little more of where she was. She had been laid to rest in an underground pod, typically used by horticulturalists. These places were created for the growth of delicate foods or plants that grew well in controlled environments, such as rhubarb or mushrooms, where too much light would spoil the crops and just enough illumination could deliver great results. The pods were also used to carefully grow the groceries for some of the finest local restaurants in the city – who boasted an exclusive menu made up from hand-picked, premium ingredients.

Pod cuisine was famous for texture and taste and it was always a treat to eat at such a food outlet. However, this wasn't the sole use of the pods. They were also utilised to nurture and sometimes house rare plants too. No wind to disturb them and no pests or blazing sun, there was many a rich naturalist who had invested in a pod and kept his prize plant collection safe and sound underground. Georgiana had visited a couple once when she and her father had thought about investing in some rare flora, but the only ones available at the time were in a part of the city which her father said was "off limits" for her – which meant it was just that little bit too far away for him to keep an eye on what she was doing; she loved her father very much but sometimes he could be a little too overprotective, or so she thought.

Many pods were shallow structures, sitting side-by-side in long lines like caravans in a holiday park. This pod, however, belonged to a wealthier owner. The room was underground and seemed to be set apart for specialist herbs. There weren't any rows of bedding tubs where food crops could be harvested, just a few tables with assorted pots and the odd shrub scattered across them in no particular order.

Whoever ran this pod was either a lazy gardener or too busy to tend to his hobby. Perhaps the other rooms adjacent to this were full of well-tended cuttings and seedlings and this room was just a "potting shed" or storeroom? Either way, Georgiana had seen enough to stir herself to get back onto her feet. She hadn't moved or walked, however, for a good while and getting up proved to be more of a challenge than she'd expected.

It didn't take too much time to discover which parts of her hurt the most. She soon learnt which limbs she could move and how to move them without wincing too much. Eventually, by placing one arm across her rib cage and the other down onto her hip, she found she could steady herself a little and so reduce the pain. This way she was able to manoeuvre her body into a sitting up position. Dizzy from the effort and legs dangling over the side of the bed, she eased her right leg down onto the floor to take the weight before delicately placing her left foot on the ground next to it. Once done, she had to take a few sharp intakes of breath to compensate for the twinges in her left ankle. A crutch would have been welcome but all she could do was take a single hop towards a chair and grip tightly onto its frame to steady herself. The single leap was most painful and she immediately wished herself back onto the bed again.

Next to the chair, however, was a table, and on the table a couple of plates with bread, biscuits and what looked like a bottle of water. She reached out for the food and for the first time remembered the damage done to her left arm. The deep scarring on it seemed, however, to be healing but a more thorough examination would be required in full daylight to ensure the wound was not going septic. Hurriedly she consumed the dried bread whilst swigging back what she hoped was just stale water, in order to generate enough moisture to swallow. Finally the biscuits went down and she felt a little more normal. Now it was time to find out where everyone was and, more importantly, to locate her father. She stumbled towards the doorway, one hand on her hip and the other moving the chair by her side so she could put her weight on it rather than her left leg. Each step became an accomplishment and she looked forward to being able to lean on the door frame with her other arm when she finally got there.

Time went by and she made good progress. Having passed through the doorway her confidence grew as she learnt how to use the chair effectively. Down three corridors she went and then found a set of steep steps going up into the open air. Even before she placed her foot onto the first step, however, her nose turned up at what was outside. The smell, wafting in on a sudden breeze, caught her by surprise. Stale and sulphurous, the mixture of burnt buildings and perhaps burnt flesh caused her to hesitate on her mission of discovery. It was not something she was used to and did she really want to know what would cause such an odour? Nevertheless, her hands gripped the iron rail and, placing her left foot onto the first step, she hopped her good leg up next to it. This motion repeated itself until she could feel the odorous breeze blowing almost onto her face as the top came into sight. The opening was not large, this main (vertically unlocking) door to the outside world was being kept only a-jar and she would have to heave herself up and squeeze through the top gap; not a prospect that was particularly inviting in her current condition. One last time her hand gripped the top of the rail and then, with eyes tightly shut from the strain, she forced her legs up the last steps, thrusting her head and torso through the gap and then, with a final pull from her arms and a push from her good leg, she flopped out onto the outside earthen ground.

After wincing for a few moments, knowing that she'd pushed her shattered body too far, she opened her teary eyes to look at her surroundings. Moments later she was bent over on all fours trying to gather her retching stomach. Everything was burnt, blended together as smouldering piles of charred debris from fallen and flattened buildings. It was something the young Georgiana hadn't imagined before let alone seen with her eyes. Devastation was something found in history books and story tales, not on her doorstep. Reality kicked in and childhood was over.

Some of the sky had cleared from whatever had happened days earlier and there were only signs of the fires that had once raged here. This section of the inner-city circle was completely devastated and all resistance dealt with in a manner that showed no restraint. Off in the distance balloon ships sailed here and there with loud speakers squawking out commands or commentaries at the people below – but they were too far away for the words to be clearly made out. Georgiana sat and wept. There was nothing else to do.

"Oh Dad!" she murmured.

Despair and desperation sat with her, companions you'd rather be without but somehow they're difficult to get rid of once they've arrived. She stared across the skyline, hoping to see her father walking here and there amongst the debris, but this part of the city seemed abandoned. Minutes went by and Georgiana's gaze turned from a systematic scan of her surroundings to become more of a lost stare into nothingness. Eventually her steady flow of tears increasingly blurred her vision and she dropped her head and let them run down her face into the fresh puddle that they collectively made on the ground. She didn't get up and explore, in fact she couldn't – it was beyond her physical capacity, so she just sat in a helpless state of shock.

The breeze suddenly picked up and the dust and the flaky, charred materials that covered the ground swirled about in great clouds. They eventually settled again spreading these burnt-out flakes-of-war further and wider across the city. Multitudes of these fragments and specks settled and rested on Georgiana's clothes, face and hair. Again the wind blew and the process happened all over again. Within minutes she began to look like a statue, painted grey from head to foot. Breathing in this mixture of carbonized death began to bother her. Putting her long sleeve over her mouth and nose, to try and filter out some of the stifling, gagging material that clogged in her throat, she choked and wheezed.

Her coughs, however, were interrupted by an abrupt eruption of airship engines nearby. They fired up from somewhere just behind the nearest set of buildings, about a quarter of mile away to her right. A coalition of around twenty ships appeared and sailed into the sky, making their way towards the centre of the city. She hadn't realised that other people were so close by and the sudden noise of their mechanisms coming to life startled her. Perhaps if she hadn't been covered with burnt materials she might have been seen, but now she looked as grey as the ground about her and her camouflage was as good as that of any chameleon.

The ships flew in formation, in the shape of a crescent moon. Using this configuration they methodically worked their way down each section of streets to scan the area below. As they went, soldiers would occasionally drop overboard, using long wires to quickly descend to the ground. Moments later shots were fired and more fighting took place.

"They still haven't won," Georgiana thought to herself, and some measure of hope rose within her. She understood perfectly well, however, that she may be just observing a 'mopping up job' after the war, where the new city authorities were dealing with any final bits of resistance or loiterers who had not yet been caught.

Alarm sirens wound their droning noise up from somewhere across the other side of the city and one by one, more airships ascended into the sky. They too began searching the streets, steadily making their way towards the devastated area where Georgiana was and where the other ships were close by. Instinctively she knew it was time to move. Shuffling on her bottom back towards the stairs, she tried to get through the gap and into the pod. In her hurry, however, she misjudged her last move and tumbled down the stairs, grasping at the rail towards the bottom to break her fall. More tears flowed as she howled with the pain. She jumped as a pair of hands took her by the shoulders and this was followed by an unexpected hug. Then a face, a concerned look with tender eyes and, "Now then, now then," came a voice from a mouth that was almost shrouded by a large over-grown gingery-brown moustache and beard.

Georgiana found herself quickly comforted and then picked up and carried back into the pod. This time, however, she wasn't taken into the room where she had slept, but another side room where there was plenty of light and many home comforts. She was placed on a large leather settee, which felt more than comfortable. In her tiredness and pain she couldn't remember much of the following conversation.

"What's your name?" was the first question.

"Georgiana," came her reply.

"Your face looks familiar," the man had said.

"My father's Lord Stephen," she said.

"So he is, so he is," came his reply. "And what are you doing in this part of the city?"

"I don't know," she said. "I passed out giving a message to my father and woke up over here. Do you know where my father is?"

The gentleman ignored her question.

"Well you're quite lost," he said. This part of the city has been burnt to a frazzle and there's no-one here."

"What happened?" she asked.

"Big fire," he replied, stating the obvious and adding nothing to his answer.

Georgiana found his limited responses to her questions a little frustrating. He surrounded her, however, with words and deeds of kindness and gentleness which she found soothing. After a warm drink and more food she rested her head on the arm of the sofa and soon felt a cushion pushed under her for more comfort.

"Thank you," she said, in a tired tone.

"You're very welcome," came the reply.

"Who are you?" she eventually asked.

"Rupert," he replied, "though most of my friends don't call me that anymore."

"What do they call you?" she enquired, in a dozy tone.

"Basil," he said, with a laugh.

Georgiana meant to be polite in her reply saying, "That's a nice name," but what came out was, "That's a strange thing to be called. Why call you that?"

"I love growing Basil," he said. "That's what I do."

"Why?" Georgiana yawned.

"Ocimum Basilicum, or Basil, is the greatest of the garden herbs," he replied. "The word Basil literally means 'king' and so it should do with the number of varieties that can be grown."

Georgiana knew she'd pressed a button in him and this man was now going to talk about his plant passion. Her mind began to fade as he went on and on.

"It is also considered as the king of herbs by many a cook or restaurant chef. My personal favourites are African Blue, Genovese Basil, Siam Queen, Lemon Basil and Red Rubin Basil – also known as Opal Basil. Add excellent taste they do and never fail to bring a strong flavour to good food. My personal ambition is to grow at least ten new species over the next few years and to make a name for myself..."

He stopped when he saw Georgiana's eyes glaze over.

"Oh I am sorry," he said. "Get very carried away with myself on certain subjects I do."

"That's ok," she replied. "I'd love to hear more when I'm a little better."

Basil, however, wasn't convinced by her last statement but carried on the conversation anyway saying that he was sure it would only take a short time for her to recover and then they could talk about Basil as long as she wanted. With that, the general chit-chat went on between them for a brief period but Georgiana's replies got more and more muddled as she became overwhelmed with tiredness.

"What happened out there and where's my father?" was one of her last questions as she tried again to get some sensible information out of him.

"Now Georgie," came Basil's voice in a gentle but firm manner. "You have a good sleep and we'll talk some more once you're rested."

"Georgie!" she thought to herself, as her last tired thoughts went through her mind. "Where did that name suddenly come from?" She didn't like the nickname that he'd so quickly given her, especially in such short a time of being acquainted, but his friendly compassions and gentle affections overrode any of her immediate emotional objections. After Basil had poured some fresh water on her deeply grazed left arm, a blanket and pillow were quickly provided and these comforts helped her slip into a deep sleep.

Chapter 4 – Beer, Beards and Broth

Hours later the young Georgiana came round to find herself staring at a man fast asleep. He was a little tubby around the edges and had a good start on a well-developed stomach. His intakes of breath were deep and after each gasp he blew out a draft of air that made his moustache flutter in the breeze. This ridiculous repeating motion she found strangely reassuring and she gave a little giggle as she watched him. Slouched back in his chair, his droopy limbs sprawled out in all directions. He wore a tweed jacket and baggy brown trousers that were badly in need of pressing. At the bottom of his flaccid legs was a pair of well-worn wellington boots that hadn't been cleaned in years. Here was a man without ceremony. A 'take me as you find me' gentleman who wore his heart on his sleeve. She thought him a nice, rounded teddy bear, whose frame and stature reminded her of a jolly fiction character from her childhood storybooks. One who bumbled through life and meant well, spreading good cheer everywhere he went, but one who wasn't too efficient at communicating or getting things exactly right. She felt quite safe. This gentle, almost comic-like man, was a good person to be around; despite his inability to have a deep conversation - remembering her brief dialogue with him when they last spoke a few hours earlier.

She watched him for a while before casting her gaze around the rest of the room. The environment matched the man, friendly, practical but quite unkempt. The raggedy surroundings needed a good clean and the tat clearing out. He was obviously a hoarder as well as an investor in plants – the far side of the long room showed a stockpile of miscellaneous junk (bric-a-brac the likes of which Georgiana hadn't seen before) gathered and piled up against the wall like a squirrel's stash of winter nuts; one item on top of another, a collection of probably useful items, all tangled up in each other with bits and parts scattered across the floor. Nice as this gentleman may be, Georgiana wasn't sure that in the long run he was going to be of any use to her in finding her father or influencing the city. This was a man wrapped up in his own life and interests and who obviously needed someone to take care of him, let alone be of any use to anyone else.

There was something about him, however, that kept her heart not entirely closed. Perhaps it was his soft and persistent kindnesses she had experienced before falling asleep. Whatever kind of person he was, he was a little too trusting. There he sat, fast asleep, with a stranger in his room and a city outside that was in the middle of civil war. No alarms on the front door, no locks on the room they were in and an easy chance of being found and arrested by the authorities. No, he wasn't very good at doing other things in life except that which was his hobby, Georgiana reasoned.

She was just mulling this over when Basil began to stir. He snorted a couple of times and then jerked into a sudden, awakened state. His first stare was straight into her eyes. Georgiana briefly dropped her gaze, so as not to alarm him in his waking moments, then lifted her eyes again and smiled. Basil seemed momentarily befuddled and took a few seconds to gather his thinking before remembering where he was and that he had a guest.

"Hello Georgie," he said, rather embarrassed at finding himself splayed in his chair in what must have been a rather indiscreet way. He quickly pulled himself up to sit correctly, wiped his eyes and mouth with his green-fingered, soily hands, and bumbled straight into a conversation.

"Good morning," he added, rather hastily. "I hope you haven't been awake too long?"

"Only a few minutes," she replied.

"And are you feeling any better?" he enquired.

Georgiana hadn't thought about the question much.

"I think so," she cautiously responded. She turned her attention to herself and after wiggling her toes, fingers and limbs a little she added, "Better than I was, thanks, but it still hurts quite a lot when I move my left leg."

"Not to worry," came Basil's yawning reply. "You rest up now and we'll have you better in no time I'm sure."

A few more pleasantries were exchanged between them and Basil got busy with food.

"There's not much to eat," he said. "Well," he added, "by not much I mean not much choice. I've got a broth continually on the go in the next room, just keep it gently boiling I do. There's plenty of it but not much of anything else I'm afraid."

"Anything would be nice," Georgiana replied, hoping that she meant what she said.

A few minutes later Basil reappeared from the next room with a tray. He put it on a coffee table and then dragged the table and tray over to where Georgiana was sat. On the tray, a couple of bowls of steaming broth, each of which sat next to a tall glass of yellowy brown liquid with a foamy white top.

"Beer and broth," said Basil.

"Oh, thank you," said Georgiana.

"Not much I know," continued Basil, "but it's the best I can do in the circumstances. I hope you like beer, brew it myself I do in my spare time."

Georgiana had never tasted beer before and the smell of the hops already turned her nose. She was hungry and thirsty, however, and did her best to engage with what was before her. The broth was surprisingly nice, and reminded her of a story about a ship's cook who kept his simmering casserole cooking the full duration of the voyage – putting the leftovers from other meals into it to make the tastiest of stews. The beer, however, wasn't pleasant but she hid the gut feeling she had by putting the broth spoon quickly into her mouth after each sip.

Basil sat next to her and tucked in too. It wasn't long before his beard and moustache had a good dose of beer foam and broth in and amongst them. His loud sipping on his broth spoon and slurps on his beer glass at first irritated Georgiana a little, but it wasn't long before she was laughing at his generous conversation and jolly mannerisms, which ended in both of them laughing when Basil missed his mouth with his drink and spilt the liquid down his chin and front. Georgiana picked up a napkin and handed it to him.

"Sorry," said Basil, wiping himself down.

"Beer, beards and broth," said Georgiana in reply. "Who could want for more?"

"Beer, beards and broth," echoed Basil, as if making a celebration toast, and so the meal went on and the conversation continued.

Basil finally added a question into the chitchat that had been puzzling him.

"So why did you come visiting my pod? What brought you to try and climb down my stairs?"

"I didn't come visiting," Georgiana replied. "I was put here by whoever carried me on the stretcher that I woke up on."

Basil looked a little confused. "But yesterday you fell down my stairs when you came visiting," he said.

"I was coming back into the pod," she replied. "I woke up here yesterday in one of the back rooms on a stretcher. I shouted out but no-one came to help me. I got up and made my way down your corridor using a chair and then went outside. Then the sirens started across the city and I tried to get back into the pod again and fell."

Basil sat for a few moments to take in Georgiana's short account.

"So, so you're telling me that you've been asleep in one of my potting rooms?" he finally said, a little speechless.

"I suppose so," said Georgiana. "I really don't know how long I've been asleep but I must have been here for quite a while, before the fire at least."

Basil looked stunned.

"I am very sorry," he finally said. "If I had known you were there then I'd have made you more comfortable and got you some food and drink."

"You mean the bread, drink and biscuits that I found on the table weren't there for me?" said Georgiana.

"No," came the reply, "but I'm glad you found them," he added.

The conversation carried on for a little while and, when enough had been said, Georgiana tried again to retrieve the information from Basil that she had not managed to get the previous day.

"What happened out there, in the city I mean?" she said.

26

Basil's relaxed frame immediately changed and the tone of his voice tightened.

"I'm sure you saw enough when you went outside," he said. "Not much more to say really."

But that wasn't good enough for Georgiana. This gentleman, nice as he was, needed to be pursued till she had the answers she was seeking.

"I need to know," she said, rather abruptly.

"No you don't," he replied.

"Why not?" she said.

"Because you don't," came the reply.

A little quiet passed between them and Basil got up from his seat. Georgiana knew that if he began to potter about she'd quickly lose the flow of the conversation, so she spoke up as Basil walked down to the other side of the room.

"Basil, I can't hide from what's happened out there and I need to find my father, my mother and sister-in-law. I will be leaving this pod as soon as I'm able and the more I know now the better it will be for me to do what I need to do."

Her words didn't sound very refined, polished or mature, but that wasn't the point. Her request for information was out in the open again and an awkward few moments followed.

Basil tried to pretend she hadn't spoken and made several attempts to start other lines of chatty talk. Each time, however, she asked the same question, repeating herself again and again.

"Basil!" she finally said, in an almost cross tone. "I need to know where my family is and I will not shut up till I have the answers I need!"

"I'd heard you were a feisty one," he said, almost to himself.

"But what has happened?" she pressed.

"Who knows," came his quick reply.

"Do you know?" she persisted.

"Why would I know?" he said, irritated by her persistence.

"Well, do you?"

Silence.

"Basil, do you know what has happened to my family? Do you know what has happened to the city?" she almost yelled.

"They're all dead!" he shouted back, dropping his guard for a moment. The ferocity of his reply surprised even him, and he showed immediate embarrassment at his outburst.

"Dead, the lot of them," he then said, very quietly.

He looked across at Georgiana. His brief stare met hers and she could see the pain in his eyes. Then he looked away, as if he could not bear anyone looking into his soul.

"Heard them all burn I did," he said, with his back turned to her, "every single one," he added, then his gaze dropped to his feet. "Never heard a sound like it before. The sound of so many voices all crying out together and a raging fire that was so hot it drove me out of my spy hole and back into this room. But even from here I could still hear them; crying out together and no-one to save them."

Georgiana realised that he hadn't been trying to protect her from the information that had just spilled out of him. Her questions had forced out a memory that he himself was desperately trying to forget.

"I'm sorry," she said in a quiet tone, tears running down her face. "Must have been a terrible thing," she added.

He nodded. "It was," his eventual whispered reply drifted out of his quivering lips on the breath of heartbreak.

Georgiana sat on the sofa and her tears began to turn into a stream.

"I'm sure there was nothing you could have done," she said, wiping her eyes and trying to talk in a tone that would make him turn around so that she could gain his gaze again.

Basil didn't reply.

"So they're all dead?" she finally said, wiping her eyes. "Even my father?"

Basil said nothing again.

"Did any get away?" she enquired.

Basil walked over to her and sat on the opposite edge of the settee, just near where he had been sitting when they had enjoyed their meal together, but a little further away and put his hand onto the arm rest as if to search for some comfort. His stare was set squarely on the wall opposite. Perhaps he wanted a little relief and emotional ease himself but didn't' know how to get it.

"Some may have," he said, "but I didn't see any. Perhaps there are other parts of the city that are not burnt like this is. I don't know."

She shuffled over to him, put her hand under his elbow, and rested her head on his shoulder. The two of them sat together and wept.

- -

Back in her attic, Lady Georgiana wrote some more about how she and Basil were a comfort to each other over those next few days.

"Understanding that you have lost everyone makes anyone left your closest relative," she penned. "That day, Basil became a good friend of mine. One who would continue to be so through thick and thin for many years to come. In the future he would share some of my most difficult times. Today I miss him so much and, despite his many bumblings," she added, "I would so love to have him here with me right now, rather than this solitude and silence."

She stopped writing again and checked her pocket watch. Footsteps were heard on the stair outside and the door to the attic opened.

"Here you are m'lady," said the maid.

A small tray of tea and cakes were placed on the edge of her writing table.

"Just thought you might need some sustenance to keep your strength up," she said.

"Thank you," said Lady Georgiana, with an attempted smile.

With that the door opened and closed again and the housemaid was gone. Lady Georgiana settled herself into one of the armchairs and lifted a cup of tea to her lips. It was refreshing. She was glad of the thirst-quenching beverage.

"Beer, beards and broth," she said to herself, in memory of her friend, and sipped her drink.

Chapter 5 – A Party Celebration

Lady Georgiana wiped her mouth with the napkin provided and went to sit back at her writing desk. It wasn't long before the events of the past were flowing again and unfolding on her page.

"I must," she wrote, "now jump back to a few months earlier to tell the full tale of how our city fell. Sometimes hardship is not our enemy. It's easy to be on the lookout when things are going wrong; easy to keep a keen watch when you're struggling, to look for the best solutions and the traps when so much is at stake. Sometimes the real enemy is disguised as a comrade called 'achievement' or 'winner', someone who is meant to be your companion and friend. It's hard to recognise, especially when it comes in the guise of success. Success is like a drug that provides a stupor, an incurable numbness to danger. Success and accomplishment are imagined as a high wall that cannot be scaled, a fortified castle that you believe impenetrable or a great dam that cannot be breached. Success, I have found, is a liar, and will say anything to keep itself from falling off its pedestal. So let me begin at a time when our city was indeed a great success, a place that had attained fame and fortune. It was a sensation and triumph both materially and socially. It was a time when we lacked for nothing and I personally had never felt so secure, so loved and so much at home." Lady Georgiana paused. "Home," she wrote again with a pause. The word had been written on the page so quickly, so easily. "It's a funny word," she penned. "It's a place that you think will never change, will remain forever, and is always available to you. Then, once you lose it, you spend the rest of your life looking for it again." Lady Georgiana dipped her quill into her ink well. "So here we go," she wrote. "I'll start my account with a meal and show how home turned into heartbreak, success into suffering, perfection into perdition and affability into an anguish that is still with me today."

- -

The room's atmosphere was a delight. A candle lit table decorated with evergreen shrubbery, elegantly strung across and in-between dishes of steaming soups, broths and beverages. Around the table, a family party that showed a household at ease with itself. The food was excellent and the conversation flowed with cordiality and affection. At the head of the table, Lord Stephen. To his right sat his wife, Lady Melanie, and opposite her, their daughter Georgiana. Next to Georgiana sat Emma (her pregnant sister-in-law) and then, Richard - Emma's husband and Georgiana's slightly older brother. Opposite Richard a blank space at the table where a place was set but not taken up. Then down the table a variety of guests who knew the honour of being invited to the house where they dined and who relished the food and good friendships that they had so suddenly found.

"Your very good health," said Lord Stephen, his toast was acknowledged by many courteous replies or with nods of appreciation.

The conversation continued around the room with well-mannered laughter breaking in from time to time to punctuate the lively chit-chat. Everyone seemed engrossed until the doorbell rang and one of the employees of the house went to answer. Georgiana's face briefly scowled when a self-assured and buoyant voice greeted the attendant at the doorway and engaged in a lively dialogue as this new visitor strode down the corridor. Then in came a young man who navigated the room's perimeter, as if a member of the family himself, and sat down in the empty seat opposite Richard.

"You're late again," said Lady Melanie. "I do hope your mother is recovered?"

"Almost," replied the young man, as if not quite interested in the question. He settled down in his place, dropped the napkin over his lap, and lifted the lid on his dish to be met by the aroma of the soup.

"Almost?" she enquired. "I do hope she is getting proper care?"

The young man nodded and sipped his soup.

"I would have thought proper care would require constant attention from those you love," added Georgiana, in a tone colder than her mother's.

The young man looked up at her and gave a brief smile before breaking the small loaf of bread in half and dipping it into his soup bowl.

"We all need our space and a bit of a break from caring for others," Lord Stephen added, trying to lessen the tone of Georgiana's last comment. "Even the best of us, when we're ill, can be tiring at times," he added.

A gentleman down the table joined in the conversation.

"So young Erepsin," he said. "What is the forecast for your mother's recovery? Will we be seeing her back at the heart of the city's political and social calendar any time soon?"

"Not sure," came the young man's quick reply, between sips and chewing his bread. "The doctor's last words were a bit unclear on the matter; to be honest I don't think he knows himself."

"Shouldn't you have pressed him a little more to find out?" enquired Georgiana, who got a cough and glance from her father that was more than a polite correction.

"Leave him alone," said Richard. "Can't you see the poor man is in need of sustenance himself?"

The young man took another sip of his soup and smiled at his friend opposite.

"Thank you Mr R," he said to Richard.

"You're welcome Mr E," replied Richard.

"Would Mr R like to engage in a game of cards once the meal is over?" enquired Erepsin.

"Well, that would depend on whether Mr E is able to play this time without..." Richard paused for a moment to carefully choose his words, "...without having a tantrum when he loses."

Emma politely giggled at her young husband's response, but kept her laugh muted.

"Oh I wish you two would give up this 'Mr R' and 'Mr E' silliness," said Georgiana.

"Sorry sis," came Richard's nonchalant reply. "School day habits die hard."

"Well we're no longer at school," she carefully pointed out. "The days of being 'school chums' is thankfully over and gone."

Erepsin glanced over to Georgiana, gave her a quick wink, and carried on with his meal as if it were a serious task at hand. Georgiana felt her insides churn at his attention and she quickly glanced away to escape the inappropriate eye signal. The different courses were served like clockwork that evening and Georgiana's father was, as usual, the life and soul of the gathering.

He was a man of wide reading and very up to date on matters that concerned the city – though not so much taken up with his knowledge that he didn't have time to listen to the viewpoints and information that came from the people around him. Georgiana found her mind wandering after a time. She had participated in this social scene before and she knew exactly what her father was doing; feeding up different people from all kinds of backgrounds in the city with a most generous meal and at the same time feeding them with his vision for unity and constraint on difficult political matters. He somehow managed to do it in a way that no-one felt put-upon and at the end of the meal all believed themselves edified, educated and all-the-better for it. To him it was his duty to put together their ideological future in a lively, jovial setting and by so doing ensured that, to a certain measure, people were asking the right questions, seeking the right answers, and hopefully being kept safe by doing so.

"Nothing is worse than ignorance," he had once told Georgiana. "But someone who has only a little knowledge on a subject can also be equally dangerous. God save us from the well-intentioned actions and activities of the semi-educated and the ignorant," he would add.

It wasn't long, however, before Erepsin (having had his fill of good food) was gently undermining her father's statements by passing jokes between himself and Georgiana's brother Richard. Richard joined in the light chatter, often unaware of the implications of what his friend was saying, and laughing wholeheartedly at the

31

witticisms of his once school-mate friend. Lord Stephen, however, wasn't thrown by any of it. He had a great skill that Georgiana admired of knowing where the conversation was going, how it was being steered by Erepsin in the wrong direction, and how to bring it back into focus with very little effort. Often it was with a quick question to someone else in the room, perhaps someone who didn't know much on the subject. He would help them with their answers by engaging with them in the conversation, passing quick thoughts to them that they could say "Yes" or "No" to and then agreeing or disagreeing – even supposedly wrestling with his own thoughts out loud (as if working them out in his own mind) and then coming to conclusions that they could all agree with. In this way everyone felt a part of the meal and the general discourse, even when they had very little to say themselves. Georgiana thought at the time that the occasion was wasted on these people and didn't see the full implications of her father's efforts. Years later, however, once it had clicked what he was doing and how well it worked, it was something she adopted as a method of her own.

"So, to the matter in hand," said Lord Stephen, as the mealtime conversation began to draw to a conclusion. "Can we not see that the historic and communal King's Law that underpins our city is the very foundation of our freedom? Constraint is not only a barrier that goodness itself should not cross, otherwise it ceases to be good, but it is also a wall of defence against an outside enemy. Constraint allows freedom to live in safety within the confines of those walls where values are not compromised and the wolf, which prowls outside, is not able to get in. Without limitations we are not truly free. Freedom always comes at a price, but when you think about it, it's not a price at all. The hefty fine of lawlessness and self-rule always brings with it a wage that culture has to finally pay and, in the end, we're left penniless, all because we wanted to see what throwing off constraint could achieve."

Nods appeared around the room as the words went in.

"This is why King's Law is and still should be the foundation of our living. Any city that shakes off the wisdom of the past to experiment with the new, that which sounds so broad and enticing, will find itself entangled and ensnared. There is no reward for journeying to a far-off land whilst neglecting home. Anyone who lets their eyes roam to the ends of the earth to find fulfilment forgets that prosperity does not exist on the horizon, but in the tasks that are at hand. The chores of everyday goodness demand a living that is careful, where the barriers of constraint allow normality to be great and constancy in living to be glorious, not only for the current generation but also for the generations to come."

"Greatness is seduced by the laws of the timid," Erepsin coldly chipped in.

"And wisdom is proved right by her children," said Lord Stephen, in an abrupt manner that he had not used with Erepsin all evening. "The generations that have already gone by have proved to us beyond doubt what is good and right and true. History is on the side of the peacemaker and the constrained. Prosperity and liberty stays with those who do not stray into the land of the self-egoed and the highly notioned, who want to pursue a dream of humanity without limits where no-one is able to pull back the behaviour and ideas of the culture to a safe standard, because there is no standard anymore – just an open space to nothingness that provides no guidance or rule to which society can be pinned and therefore kept safe. It is our limitations that make us great and keep us secure."

Erepsin shrugged his shoulders, knowing that to say any more would be disrespectful to his host, but at the same time he made sure that his demeanour displayed his objection.

The meal finished and after an hour or so of social discourse the guests knew it was time for them to go. When the house was finally cleared, and all who had been invited were on their way home, the family relaxed in the lounge. As usual Erepsin was still with them and he had enjoyed listening in on one of the families favourite games of verbal banter; a game where each in turn quoted a proverb, spoke a riddle, a ridiculous rhyme or gave a self-contradictory statement for everyone's general amusement. The object of the game was not just to entertain, however, but to make your words or comment on a shared theme add to or contradict the words of the pervious speaker. It was the perfect tool for sharpening the mind and the Pluggat-Lynette family were well practised in this verbal art. As a new family member, Emma sat completely fascinated by the quick thinking of the group. Every now and again the family gave her a word or phrase to say that would add to the repartee and then off they went again, seeking to outwit each other with their verbal jousting and so to be the last person standing who had something quick and smart to say. Normally it was Lord Stephen and Georgiana who would end up doing battle as the wordplay came to its speedy climax.

For much of the game Erepsin was only able to chip in here and there as the talk was too fast for him. Once it was over, however, he took the opportunity to tell Richard and Emma about his latest wheeling and dealing that could possibly make him a fortune, if his schemes came off. Georgiana chose to sit by herself, with a book, not at all interested in Erepsin's 'blabbering' as she would refer to it after he had gone. Tonight, however, seemed a little more tiresome than usual; Erepsin didn't leave at his normal time and he seemed to waffle instead - his extended conversation looked as if it was an excuse for lingering, perhaps loitering, for some kind of purpose of his own. Lord Stephen and Lady Melanie saw it too, but kept the matter just between their shared eye glances, making very polite dialogue between themselves and Georgiana - when they felt she was getting too engrossed in her reading.

"Well I think I'll be off," exclaimed Erepsin, after finishing his tale about his latest balloon race exploits and his monetary vision for turning it into a citywide sport.

"Thank heavens for that," said Georgiana, under her breath. "Safe journey home," were the matter-of-fact words she spoke out of the side of her mouth, not even glancing up from her book.

"As always, Mr R, your sister is the height of concern for my welfare," Erepsin said to Richard.

"As usual," replied Richard. "But then again, sis looks out for everyone."

Erepsin was just in the motion of turning round to leave when something popped into his mind, or that was the way he wanted it to look.

"Err, Lord Stephen," he enquired. "May I have a moment or two of your time before I leave? There is something that I would like your advice and guidance about. It won't take long."

Georgiana immediately felt a bloating, guttural unease which swelled and flowed through her veins; her sharply frozen exterior being the only visible guide to what to she felt, but she didn't move her face from behind her book.

"Yes of course," replied Lord Stephen, turning his chair to face the young man.

Erepsin hesitated, "The subject," he continued, "is of a rather delicate nature. I was rather hoping to talk in a more private setting."

"We can chat in the library if you like," Lord Stephen responded.

Erepsin nodded. "That would be good," he said.

"Shall I come with you?" Georgiana enquired.

"We're fine," interrupted Erepsin.

"I'll be back soon," Lord Stephen smiled, aiming his attentions at Georgiana as he and Erepsin went off to the library for a short chat.

After Erepsin had gone, and the family had talked for just short of an hour, all went to bed except Lord Stephen - who spent a little time in his study as he liked to do. Georgiana took the liberty of waiting for him there when everyone else thought she had retired for the night.

"So what did he want?" was her first question.

"I thought you were in bed," replied her father.

"You shouldn't give him your time like that you know," said Georgiana. "He'll just take advantage of you in the end; misrepresent you in some way to others and say that you've said something that you actually haven't. He twists everything that people say, for his own gain. You shouldn't trust him as you do."

Lord Stephen sighed, "You can't just block people out," he replied. "Erepsin's a person too, no matter how much you dislike him, and everyone should have our attentions, no matter how deserving or undeserving they are."

"He's unstable and irresponsible!" Georgiana almost snapped. "We shouldn't even let him in the house."

Lord Stephen sat down in his armchair and picked up a book from the coffee table next to it.

"My dear daughter," he began. "You and I know and understand that Erepsin is not a man to be trusted. He is brash, rash, wild in his imaginations, impatient, at times impertinent and has a natural talent at getting on everyone's nerves - altogether he's a badly assembled personality. But if we push him away he'll just become worse still. Whilst he's around us, there's a chance that he'll pick up at least a measure of sound advice and perhaps, just perhaps, that might steer him away from too great an error in the future."

"He'll use us for his own ends," replied Georgiana, "I know he will."

"If he tries, then so be it," said her father. "I won't, however, be giving him reason to resent us."

"You're afraid of him?" enquired Georgiana.

"No," said Lord Stephen, in a tone that showed he was a little tired of his daughter's misunderstanding of his meaning. "I'm concerned at what might happen if he's left to himself. Even though everyone talks about our current prosperity, I say that the city is not in a good place right now. Politically it's weak, its vision is blurred and the fabric of society unstable. Erepsin isn't a game changer. He's not a person to hold high office but he is the kind of person to throw a spanner in the works if he's left unguided and unwatched. I don't want to turn round in the years to come to find an unnecessary mess that needs cleaning up."

Georgiana still wasn't convinced by all that her father said but she was a little more comforted after hearing his words. To her, however, Erepsin was a time bomb, a tick, tick, ticking clock of destruction - as unstable as a drifting mine, all at sea and not knowing what he will collide with next. He was without conscience, short fused and driven to devour anything that fed his ego in order to fill some kind of gaping hole in his self-serving soul. "He'd devour the world if he could", she thought, "and still be unsatisfied." She instinctively knew that somewhere along the line he'd ruin himself and anyone within close proximity – which is why she didn't want to be around when it was time for him to self-detonate.

Once the subject of Erepsin was dealt with Georgiana and Lord Stephen talked for a good ten minutes more. Without getting into too much of a discussion, they chatted about the immediate concerns that her father had about the city and the potential political ways forward to solve them.

"I still can't see why you waste so much of your time inviting unimportant people to eat with us," came one of her final statements. "Who was there tonight who could do any good for anyone?"

"Don't look down on the naively upright," came her father's reply. "Most people are not born politically savvy, so sometimes we have to spend time teaching them what the conversation is that they need to be engaging in, in order to keep themselves free. The dark arts often found in the political arena, and the seductive talk that flows from it, can weave a deadly and destructive web into any culture. It can happen so quickly and, before people are aware of what's really happening, they find themselves trapped in a closed system that's full of control. It often happens to the simple man who is left clueless as to what is really happening behind the carefully chosen rhetoric until it's too late. But once an honest person gets a whiff of what's up, you never know how strong they can be to overthrow those who call themselves the political elite."

"That's not much good if those in power have the law behind them," replied Georgiana.

"An oppressed people are only as weak as they corporately allow themselves to be," replied her father. "And a government over a nation is only as strong as the people allow."

"That's not what I see," said Georgiana. "I see people intimidated and thrown into confusion. I see people sold false hopes and dreams that they can never have and right now I can't see any end to the wrangling and infighting until something very strong takes the side of the weak. The weak are always what they are, weak."

Lord Stephen leaned forward in his chair and eyeballed his daughter.

"Any culture that is in conflict and crisis comes to a point when they have to ask themselves questions about their own future and freedom; whether they are willing to play a part in making that future possible for themselves and for the generations to come. It is the place where the average 'nobody' in the culture becomes part of a corporate giant, someone who can make anything happen. That's why I do what I do. The weak made strong are stronger than those who strut with power. The love of life is stronger than the love of oppression. Those who chase freedom pursue it in a way that makes those who pursue power look half hearted. A person will lay down their life to be free, but a person who loves influence will slink off when the heat is turned up in order to live another day."

Georgiana pondered this for a while but was still not fully persuaded. Finally she had had enough and went to bed; still a little uneasy at the evening's events but more settled now that she knew more of her father's mind over Erepsin and the direction he was trying to steer city life. She still felt, however, that they were missing something, but couldn't quite put her finger on it. Having tucked herself up in bed, she wrote briefly in her diary and then dropped off to sleep.

Chapter 6 – Uncle Jack

The next day saw the city all astir. The whole population were to gather for an extended time of fun and entertainment that lasted throughout the day and into the early hours of the following morning. It was the annual celebration of the city's freedom given, according to legend, by an ancient and long forgotten king. Even though the full meaning of the event's historical root was now shrouded in the distant past and had been taken over by numerous modern traditions, (introduced and celebrated over recent decades to give it a new financial identity) the people still looked forward to the occasion with great anticipation and awe. Something of the original mystery still hung in the air and the day always brought out the thrill of life's spiritual unknown. So, despite the confusion over its origins, the day was always a highlight of the city calendar.

Stalls lined the streets with honeyed beverages tasting of sweet heaven or baked breads covered with extra syrupy coatings. In fact, by the time you'd travelled along the main avenue and sampled less than a tenth of that which was on offer, you could be on a super sugar-high that would last for hours and into early next morning. It wasn't the food, the games and general frivolity, however, which attracted the buzz of excitement to the event. As the calendar date approached there was one person's name on everyone's lips. To the children he was more important than Santa and to the adults he was a laugh that would last for many a day after he'd performed for them. There were even rumours that an underground betting culture had been set up for those people fool hardy enough to wager their hard earnt cash that the event would be a disaster - placing odds on the 'fat joker', as they called him, not surviving the occasion.

The gentleman they all talked about was commonly known as Uncle Jack. 'Uncle' because his persona was so huge that he came across like one of those awe-inspiring, larger-than-life relatives that you only saw twice a year, but who always left you speechless after his visit, and 'Jack' because that was the friendly name that he allowed everyone to call him. His full name was actually Jacob McArnold Crispus Ken-Worthington-Brown, a name showing his pedigree as one who came from a long line of gentry and nobility, if you traced his ancestry back far enough, and who had a rich cultural heritage to share with everyone. His personality, however, was bigger than his name. He was both a gentleman and loose cannon. Jacob McNutter was the name that his competitors called him, or rather Jacob McNutter Crackpot Kettle-Worty-Boom to be exact - but the last person who called him that to his face quickly found himself travelling at high speed; strapped face down onto a small wooden cart and being pulled by a group of highly-strung and manic greased pigs, to which the cart had been harnessed.

This example of being dragged like a sack of potatoes through the streets of Clearwash City soon made the point and the insulting nickname was now only whispered in conversations behind closed doors. Uncle Jack had a reputation for not having much patience, especially with "insolent vulgarians" as he would call anyone being rude about his person or his activities.

Some called Uncle Jack a 'friendly giant', others a 'blundering idiot' and still others an 'unbridled, experimental genius of alternative engineering and entertainment'. Whichever way you saw him, he left an impression that could never be erased. Rumours had been building for the past few weeks about 'the event' as it was called that Uncle Jack was to put on for them. Whatever happened, good or bad, everyone knew they were in for a treat. Georgiana remembered the first time she'd ever met him when she was just a little girl. Her father had taken her over to a large house, almost as big as their home, situated on the outskirts of the city. Upon arrival they had been shown into the main lounge. A commotion from the back of the house, however, caused her father to leave the room and explore what was happening.

"Daddy," Georgiana had whispered. "It's rude to go around someone else's house uninvited."

"Shhhh," her father had replied. "I just want to see what's happening."

"But Daddy, it's rude," she said.

"Only in normal people's houses," came his reply. "This is Uncle Jack's house and everything is different here."

"Why is it different?" she had enquired, but her father just put his finger to his lips and then beckoned her to follow him.

After going through a couple of rooms they entered a large kitchen. There a great big wobbly-bellied, fat-necked, bushy-bearded gentleman strode up and down whilst poking a stick into the gaps between the gratings under his feet. On the far wall was the butler who had seen Lord Stephen and Georgiana into the house. Lord Stephen caught the butler's eye and tipped his hat as if to say, "How do you do," and "I'm just looking so don't mind me."

The butler didn't seem too put out that he was there but just kept his eye on what was going on.

"I have you now you vulgarian varmint!" bellowed out the fat man's voice, shouting between the gaps in the metal plated floor. "Vermin, that's what you are. A scoundrel if I ever saw one. Not a rascal but a rat. Not a cheat but a crook. A villain, a robber, a burgling blaggard with thief printed right across those grubby, guilty fingers."

Turning to the butler of the house he called over his shoulder, "The rascal won't last long," he said. "Caught him, in his own villainy; the little wretch."

"He's too quick for you, your Lordship," shouted the butler. "The child moves too fast for you sir."

"Nonsense," came the fat man's reply. "This little vulgarian savage can't get away this time. His insolence and bold treachery have brought him into my trap and I don't intend to let him out till I've got him by the scruff of his scrawny little neck."

"Let me out!" shouted a boy's voice. "You'll not get any protection from further raids if you don't."

"Protection!" the fat man replied in protest. "As if I needed protection from your little gang of boy scouts. Transgression, my lad, is a crime and the misconduct of breaking and entering a private pantry is an offense that violates all decent society. Any such felony and breach of good common law is indeed a slur on our respectable neighbourhood's name. Don't you think for one moment that this sin, this infraction, this infringement of honest trust, is going to go unpunished? You're an insolent little vulgarian!"

"'Vulgsarious, insolenticus' I believe is the correct way of saying it m'lord," replied the butler. "It's a state of mind common in the young, especially when they're hungry."

"This little pest is too skinny to be hungry," the fat man replied. "And by the time I've finished with the squirming little toad he'll have wished he'd never heard of food."

"You're a blockhead," came the child's voice in protest.

"Barbarian!" shouted the fat man back at him, who for some reason seemed to be enjoying himself. "I'll have you for sneaking into my food store you lazy layabout. You should be working for a living, not spending your time pocketing other people's hard-earned wares."

"I'm not a Barbarian," the child called back. "Barbarians are hairy people, like you. You need some education you do."

"Why you impertinent little brute," the fat man called down, waggling his stick between the cracks in the metal framework beneath his feet.

"I'd rather be impertinent than a great big blockhead," said the child nonchalantly, as if not caring that he was in a trap. "Nincompoops like you are always trying to throw their weight around," the boy continued to shout, "...and, from what I can see, you've got too much weight to throw around in my opinion."

"Then I shall personally sit on you when I get my hands on you," said the fat man. "Then you'll know what it is to have a man of weightiness deal with you, and I can tell you from my experience of twenty years in the wrestling ring, that when I sit on a man, he doesn't easily get up again."

"Birdbrain!" the boy shouted back, now enjoying every moment of the conversation.

Uncle Jack winked at his butler who pressed a switch on the wall next to him and a door to the room in which the boy was trapped slipped slightly a-jar. Immediately the young lad took advantage of this, made good his escape, and moments later he could be seen running across the back garden and onto the moorland waste near the city walls.

"I shall be after you, you trespassing little weasel," called Uncle Jack through a window after him.

The boy shouted something over his shoulder and was gone.

"I don't know why you do it m'lord" said the butler, a few moments later.

"Did you put the extra bread and cheese in there?" Uncle Jack enquired.

"Yes," replied the butler, with a sigh.

"Good," said Uncle Jack. "At least it will help them for a few more days I suppose."

"You're too soft on them m'lord," said the butler.

"Yes," replied Uncle Jack, watching the boy's silhouetted figure run across the heath and disappear into the early evening shadows. "But as long as no-one else finds out, then my reputation for being a selfish and mean-spirited brute is intact."

With that Uncle Jack turned and saw the young, wide-eyed Georgiana watching them and Lord Stephen by her side, leaning on the wall and smiling to himself.

"Oh, and who might you be?" asked Uncle Jack in a kind-hearted voice to the little Georgiana.

"I'm Georgiana," she replied, "...and this is my father," she added, holding onto her father's leg for a little comfort whilst talking to this huge man.

Uncle Jack raised an eyebrow at Lord Stephen as if greeting an old friend but kept his focus on Georgiana. "And have you come to visit us or have you come to spy on us, like the naughty little boy that we've just let out of the pantry?" he asked.

Georgiana thought for a moment. "We've come to visit," she finally replied, with a smile.

"Well that's very nice of you to do so," said Uncle Jack, sending her smile back at her. At least she thought it was a smile that he was giving, his eyes were shining but his big bushy beard got in the way of whatever else was happening on the surface of his face. "Tell Mrs Ken-Worthington-Brown that we have guests and bring us some tea and cake," he said to the butler.

"As you wish m'lord," came the butler's reply.

Georgiana didn't in fact get to see this very mysterious 'Mrs Ken-Worthington-Brown' on any of her visits to see Uncle Jack. She only heard the lady of the house from a distance. She would hear her calling loudly from another room or hear her shouting things across the corridors of the great house. Whenever she walked her footsteps would give a thump, a thud and a stamp as she moved from place to place. Her voice wasn't nasty at all, just loud. Lord Stephen whispered in his daughter's ear that Mrs Ken-Worthington-Brown was a nice lady but also was a bit of a battle axe as well. Little Georgiana wasn't sure what a 'battle axe' was but it didn't sound too good, so she was content to know this mysterious 'Mrs Ken-Worthington-Brown' from a distance. Her voice and footsteps brought wonderful imaginations into her mind of who she might be or what she might look like, and they seemed to be more than enough to keep her thoughts most entertained.

The second time that Georgiana met Uncle Jack was nearly four months later when she and her father had again been travelling through the part of the city where Uncle Jack lived and her father had decided to make an unannounced stop on their way home. Lord Stephen must have known Uncle Jack very well or he would not have made an unannounced call; it simply wasn't done in their social circle. Having gone up the long driveway, they got out of the carriage by the main gates and were quite taken aback to see that Uncle Jack and his butler were both sitting on the steps that ran up to his house. Getting closer, it became obvious that Uncle Jack had a large amount of what seemed like custard and cream on one side of his head and shoulder. When Lord Stephen enquired as to why this was the case, the butler simply replied, "That would be the lady of the house."

Mable Ken-Worthington-Brown, or the 'boom-woman' as many people in the city called her, had a reputation for being someone that you did not mess with (and that included her husband). She had a very small circle of loyal friends and was rarely seen out in public during the day. She was almost as fat as her husband and had a voice and temper to match.

Lord Stephen, trying to be as tactful as possible, then asked if the lady of the house was in good health.

"As well as can be expected in the circumstances," replied the butler.

"Ah, I see," said Lord Stephen, though that wasn't enough information for him to figure out what had happened.

"Just trying to help," muttered Uncle Jack from under his breath.

"Sorry, I didn't quite catch that," said Lord Stephen, still fishing for more information. Normally Lord Stephen would have tipped his hat by now and walked away from the situation and Georgiana wondered why her father was still standing around. He was determined, however, to get more news, so kept his gaze on the dishevelled pair. She thought she saw her father's lip quiver, as if he were trying to control some kind of emotion that was stirring within him, and his voice, though full of concern, didn't seem as genuine as it normally was.

"You were *trying* to help?" he said again, wondering if any more words would come out to illuminate the situation.

"Her ladyship is on a diet," added the butler, "and is not in the best of moods. At least, she was in a good mood till his lordship here tried to encourage her in her quest to lose some more weight."

Lord Stephen cast his glance at Uncle Jack with a 'Well, what have you done now?' sort of expression on his face.

Uncle Jack stirred himself. "My good lady," he replied, "was telling me that she had lost some weight. I personally couldn't see any improvement so I just tried to be nice and keep the conversation going. She'd been looking in the mirror and had called me over. 'Look,' she had said. 'Look, I'm losing my double chin.' I had a good look and I can tell you that, as far as I could see, there was plenty of neck fat left for her to lose. So, trying to be polite and agreeable, I simply said, 'Yes, I see you've lost weight from around your gorgeous, delicate neck.' Then I looked again and said, 'Yes that extra chin is disappearing nicely.' Well she seemed very pleased with the comment, so I decided to venture some more words of encouragement – to butter her up, if you follow me."

"And what did you say?" asked Lord Stephen, seeing that the information he was after still wasn't quite complete.

"Well," sighed Uncle Jack, "as there was still plenty of fat and double chins left around her neck, I just simply added, 'One chin down, three more to go!' I thought it would be an encouragement to be honest!"

Lord Stephen stood motionless for a moment, trying to take in the dialogue that he'd just heard. "And the custard and cream?" he eventually enquired.

"Her ladyship took offense at his lordship's mention of the multiple chins that were still left around her neck and made good use of the nearest bowl of trifle from the kitchen."

"Oh I see," said Lord Stephen, his lip quivering. "Well," he finally said, in a resigned tone, complemented with a cough. "I think we'll leave you both to it and perhaps we'll drop in when things are a little more settled at home."

Uncle Jack shrugged his shoulders whilst the butler said that a visit at another time would be most welcome.

Into the carriage Lord Stephen and Georgiana stepped and on they went towards home. They hadn't been travelling for more than a few seconds, however, when Lord Stephen began to shake.

"Are you alright Daddy?" the young Georgiana asked, concern etched across her face.

No answer came but the shaking and the juddering got worse.

"Daddy, what's the matter?" she asked again, beginning to feel very uncomfortable about her father's health.

Lord Stephen shook his head and soon Georgiana's concern waned when she saw that he was in fact laughing to himself and trying not to be heard, as they were still obviously in ear shot of Uncle Jack and his butler.

"Ha, ha, ha!" cried Lord Stephen, in a sudden fit of laughter that literally snorted out of him as he exhaled.

"Shhhh, Daddy, they'll hear you," said Georgiana.

It was no good, however. Lord Stephen trembled with laughter and then let out a loud burst of hooting hilarity that echoed down the street they were in.

"One chin down and three to go!" her father eventually blurted out between gasps for air. "Ha, ha, ha, ha, ha!" he chortled.

"Shhhh, Daddy, they really will hear you," said Georgiana again.

"One chin down and three to go!" Lord Stephen cried out again. "Ha, ha, ha, ha, ha!" he hollered, holding his sides, as if they would split with his hilarity. "Talk about putting your foot in it! She won't be speaking to him for a month! Ha, ha, ha, ha, ha!"

His laughter became so ear-splitting, that it rang out across the city and everyone at the roadside turned their heads as the carriage passed by.

"One chin down," he cried again. "Three more to go!" he yelled out, amidst his continuous merriment. "Oh I'm going to wet myself," he bellowed.

Thankfully, this was just an expression rather than a reality. Eventually Georgiana couldn't contain herself either and spent much of the time on the way home laughing with her father, though she wasn't quite sure if she was laughing about Uncle Jack or just finding her dad's fit of laughter contagious. One thing was certain; he'd better give Uncle Jack a wide berth for the next few months because she was sure that he had heard all of her father's merriment at his expense. Now, years later, Uncle Jack had become a good friend of all the family, not just a personal friend of Lord Stephen. He had made several visits to their home, all without his wife (I don't think he actually told her that he was visiting) and they had had great evenings of good conversation and laughter. He was a great storyteller and, though you would guess that most of his stories were made up or grossly exaggerated, you still enjoyed listening to his adventures.

So this night of festive entertainment, where they would only see him from a distance performing his annual display as the climax for the city's freedom, was something that Georgiana looked forward to with an inner delight. Mysterious Uncle Jack might be to so many people, but she personally knew the man behind the celebrity image.

Chapter 7 – A Peg for the Nose!

Georgiana made her way down the main road that ran through the heart of Clearwash City. The smells from the stalls filled her senses with a child-like excitement, which she kept hidden deep inside now that she was an adult; a young adult she might be, but she was determined to be one in every way that she could. Richard, her slightly older brother, walked with her. In-between him and Georgiana, linked arm in arm with them both, was Richard's young wife Emma; clearly enjoying the first months of her pregnancy and proud to be part of the Pluggat-Lynnette family. The three were all smiles and gentle laughter as they talked, tasted drinks, sampled pastries or small pies along with cheeses, boiled sweets and, on one occasion, Emma picked out a large ice-cream Sundae; which Georgiana greatly desired to eat but at the same time she thought it might be a step too far, if she wanted to maintain her figure!

There seemed to be something new to do, taste or watch every few steps. Their outing had been a mixture of delights and everywhere they went, people tipped their hats to this new generation of high society. Georgiana loved the recognition she was now being given. Adulthood could not come too soon and she relished the attention.

Their walk finally took them into the great market square that sat in front of the presidential palace. Lord Stephen met them as they entered and guided them to where Lady Melanie was waiting. Together they stood in a huddle and looked up at the palace clock tower to see if midnight was upon them. By now the rest of the city had also assembled in front of the great palace to see Uncle Jack's show and the chanting had already begun.

"In the fullness of time, the clock does chime..." many were shouting. Over and over again those two lines were repeated. Some sung it and others just hollered it. Some just shouted, "Fullness of time..." in long drawn-out calls whilst others clapped out a beat and almost drummed the phrase like a rapper on stage.

"Why do we say it Daddy?" Georgiana had asked Lord Stephen when she was a little girl.

"It's tradition," he would reply.

"But why?" she would respond (this was when she was going through her 'why' stage where everything around her was a question).

"Well, we just do it every year," he replied.

"Why?" she answered.

"Just because," he replied – and that was the best reply she got in her childhood years. Further reading as a teenager revealed that it had something to do with a king who had once reigned over the city and legend had it that one day the king would return, but even this interpretation of the rhyme had been confused over the generations.

The crowd all looked up towards the clock tower where Uncle Jack would normally make his appearance.

DONG! went the clock. DONG, it went again. As each chime towards midnight rang out, a roar and cheer from the crowd went up into the air. Then, after the last ding-dong peal, they all chanted together:

"In the fullness of time,
The clock does chime,
Ding, dong, clap, clap, clap.
Tick-tocking a mechanical rhyme,
Ding, dong, clap, clap, clap.
Time is ticking, nearly gone.
Who will you be hiding from?
See the hands move to and fro,
Hear the silver trumpet blow!"

From somewhere in the crowd a single trumpeter sounded out a long blast and everyone cheered. The great illuminated clock face on the palace tower turned from white to a deep red and finally to a burning orange. The stage was set, and all eyes were on the clock, waiting to see when the fireworks would start and from which part of the clock's face Uncle Jack would appear.

"Have we missed anything?" came a voice to the right of Georgiana's ear.

Georgiana's spine shivered and Lord Stephen discreetly took and squeezed the hand of his daughter who was standing next to him.

"Ah, Mr E, Mr S, Mr P and Mr J" said Richard, to Erepsin and his friends. "No, you're all on time."

"Good to know Mr R," Erepsin replied. "Wouldn't miss this for the world."

Erepsin and his school-chums stood on the edge of the Pluggat-Lynette family huddle, next to Richard, and watched with delight as vapour began to flood out from the palace clock tower. From all around the clock's face, hot white mist shot out like jets of fine steam escaping the lid of a pressure cooker, whilst from small holes in the tower brickwork, thick clumps of heavy white smog leaked and spewed into the night air; as if the clock were an old grandad puffing on his pipe, discharging his fumes from his steam filled lungs.

From a series of small holes that ran right up and down the tower's external masonry, fireworks rapidly ejected one after the other into the night sky. They whizzed, whistled and whirled their explosive array of dancing fiery lights over the heads of the onlooking people. Once this initial multi-coloured display had finished, the crowd peered through the smog, trying to see from which part of the clock tower Uncle Jack would appear, but he didn't emerge as they expected. As time went by a rumble of murmuring confusion passed between the people, thinking that something had gone wrong. The crowd's gaze shifted skywards, however, when high up in the firmament an engine noise made it clear that something was moving directly above them. Out of the night sky an airship descended, initially at great speed but in its final moments of decent it slowed to a gentle glide. Its sides and underside were made from numerous metal panels. Down it came till it rested perhaps forty metres above the gathered people.

"This is a little too close for comfort," Lord Stephen commented to his wife, whilst suspiciously eyeing the ship above them.

"Awesome," said Erepsin, his mind ticking over at the spectacle in view.

Musical notes began to be blasted out from a large horn set-up at the ship's stern. The music was like that of a great brass band playing a merry tune. With every note played, a different metal panel on the ship's sides and keel momentarily lit up to accompany it.

As the music carried on its cheery melody, this multi-coloured flashing accompaniment was also complemented with more fireworks, sent out into the heavens from the ship's deck. It was as if the music, the fireworks and the ship were one instrument of lights, colour and small exploding bombs; a musical extravaganza with flashing illuminations, beams and radiances all blazing in melodic time and all perfected by the 'wows', 'ooohs', 'ahhhs' and the continuous clapping of the city people.

After a few minutes of this display, a brief halt in the music was rewarded with another round of applause and whoops and whistles from the crowd. Then the panels on the ship's underside flickered for a few moments and the projected face of Uncle Jack appeared across them. He smiled and, as he spoke, the music horn blurted out his words so that everyone could hear.

"Greetings to you all!" he shouted. "Welcome to my little show. I hope you like my new boat from which we will conduct our merry performance. This year, like every year, we start off with the candy crackers!" and all the children cheered, as if they knew what was about to happen. Along the sides of the ship, small holes appeared and the nose of many canons poked through each gap. A quick blast from each and a whizzing firework shot out over the heads of the crowd. The fizzing, crackling, streak of flame sparkled and hissed till it exploded. Down came tiny bits of fire and all around dropped small packets of candy balls. Children scrambled to pick them up to either shove as many of them in their mouths, before anyone else got to them, or put them into bags for later. Later, that is, to either eat or more importantly to use them as 'kid currency' (as many people called it) when wanting to purchase

46

either things or people's services later on in the year. Lady Melanie took a lone sweet that had landed on Lord Stephen's shoulder and popped it into her mouth.

"Nice?" enquired Lord Stephen.

"Delicious," she replied.

Georgiana held out her hat and caught a few that fell near her. She shared with Emma and her father whilst Richard, Erepsin and their friends lifted their heads up and moved from side to side; seeking to catch the candy directly into their gaping mouths, pushing each other aside in order to be the first to get at the falling confectionary.

"Will you all behave!" exclaimed Georgiana.

"Sorry sis," replied Richard, without taking his eyes off the incoming candy balls. "But I'm determined to beat Mr E's and Mr P's record of twelve full catches from last year."

"Well you all look a bit gormless to me," said Georgiana, "...standing there with your mouths wide open, we're meant to be setting an example, not making a spectacle of ourselves."

"Right you are," replied Richard, whilst he and his friends continued their game, eyes fixed on the small, edible treasures that were dropping out of the sky.

"Fizz bombs!" came the next announcement from the ship's music horn, and moments later the candy was accompanied by what looked like squidgy balloons that were sent into the air from slingshots set on the ship's deck. As the balloons were launched into the sky, umbrellas went up across the crowd. Lord Stephen and Lady Melanie shared one whilst Georgiana and Emma shared another. Many huddled together in groups whilst some turned their umbrellas upside down to catch the new incoming 'bombs'. Teenagers and brave children rushed towards them, trying to make the perfect catch. However, as each balloon was caught, the impact burst the flimsy exterior and a fizzy drink exploded over the person. Everyone laughed to see their attempts, each one getting thoroughly wet. The first properly caught balloon was by a gentleman who clasped his hands around the balloon's sides and changed the balloon's trajectory before redirecting it into his arms. This tactic stopped the balloon from bursting and he held it high, like a trophy, to everyone's applause. Having pinched a hole near the balloon's neck, he took a sip. The look of delight on his face encouraged many a person to put aside their inhibitions and try and get one too, despite the great possibility of getting drenched.

After a few more minutes of candy canon crackers and fizz bombs, where Richard and his school chums got themselves wet from failed catch attempts, the music from the ship changed and the great big projected face of Uncle Jack smiled and said,

"Now it's time for flowers for the more genteel folks who are amongst us."

From the ship's underside masses of sugary flower heads were released, blowing here and there on the night breeze, gently floating and fluttering down and onto the crowd. Everyone wanted to catch one, to taste the delicate flavours that lived in each petal. Down they came in their hundreds of thousands, like a snow fall on a winter's evening. Capturing them with cupped hands, many people took the time to look at the delicate blooms before eating them. Georgiana kept a few in a handkerchief so that she could press them. Like real preserved flowers, she had a book full from previous years. Lord Stephen caught one and put it into his wife's hair, which, to his displeasure, she immediately took out again and ate.

"It looked so nice," he gently protested.

"I don't like sticky, sugary hair," she replied. "Besides, they taste too good to wear."

After an assortment of sweets and drinks had been dropped from above, the entertainment moved to its climax. This part of the show was different every year. An attempt would be made by Uncle Jack to either break a world record of some kind or to do something that had never been done before. It was this part of the show where the bets were placed that Uncle Jack would, one day, eventually kill himself by one of his tricks going wrong.

"And now," came a pre-recorded voice through the ship's megaphone, "it's time for the main event. We're happy to reveal that this year, the most honourable Jacob McArnold Crispus Ken-Worthington-Brown has agreed to not only set off the final super-firework in a most daring and dangerous way, but that this year our brave and daring hero *is going to be* the world's first human firework! He will achieve this amazing feat by using the freshly discovered qualities of 'bounce power' which will hurl him across the sky with a giant Catherine Wheel attached to his back!"

A gasp of astonishment rose from the people as they began to imagine what those words might mean in reality.

"Bounce power?" enquired Lady Melanie. "Whatever is that?"

Lord Stephen's clueless expression showed he had no idea what was about to happen.

Moments later, great semi-transparent balloons began to inflate on the palace grounds near the tower. They were huge and, as each one rose into the air, it was held in place firstly by a rope with several people hanging on the other end and then, once each balloon got much bigger, it was attached to a metal chain that was anchored to the ground. The first set of balloons were clustered together to form a curved wall. Once in place, another curved wall of balloons was assembled opposite. More balloons were added to the sides of each wall so that by them a chamber was formed, with small gaps in-between allowing the audience to see inside. At both the back and top of the balloon chamber was a hole. To the top hole was fitted a wide rubber funnel, ready to catch anything that fell in that direction and to feed it into the chamber below. Attached to the hole at the back of the chamber was a spiral tube which wound its way upwards, finally pointing its head out towards the sky and in the direction over and above the gathered crowd.

"What on earth is he going to do?" asked Erepsin, more to himself than anyone else.

"In order to do this most incredible thing…," continued the megaphoned voice, "…we've had to combine a special mixture of gases, a blend of helium and extractions of concentrated methanthiol. Then we've had to super heat them before injecting them into each balloon. Each balloon also contains a powder that will change colour as energy is transferred into it.

"Oh dear," said Lord Stephen, with his Doctor of Science hat on. "I do hope that none of those balloons burst, or we're all really in for it."

"Why my dear?" asked Lady Melanie.

"It's the concentrated methanthiol," he replied. "If I remember correctly, it will smell a lot like rotten eggs, especially with it being super-heated. He could stink the whole city out for weeks if a balloon pops."

"Excellent," exclaimed Erepsin, rubbing his hands together and eagerly hoping for the worst.

His group of school friends exchanged eager comments on how they might help a balloon 'accidentally pop' whist Richard commented,

"You'd better put one of your business investments into a clothes peg factory."

"Really?" replied Erepsin.

"A clothes peg for the nose," Richard replied. "You'd sell loads of them, make an absolute fortune. If this goes wrong you could sell them left, right and centre. Get them stored in every inn across town. After people have finished their meals and drinks, before they go out onto the smelly streets, will they really want to taste their puddings and smell the outside air at the same time?" he said, in a friendly, sarcastic tone. "The ideal object to fix this problem would be a clothes peg on the nose," he said, tapping his young wife's nose and giving her a smile.

"One for the road and one for the nose," Erepsin added.

Everyone laughed, even Georgiana.

"Well, if one does burst, we're not staying around," added Lord Stephen. He looked over his shoulder in order to figure out the quickest route from the market square so that they could speedily get away before everyone stampeded. Then he signalled to his carriage driver to have it made ready in a side street around fifty steps from where they stood.

"You seem pretty sure that something *is* going to go wrong this year," Lady Melanie commented to her husband.

"I know how volatile that stuff is," he replied.

"My money is on disaster, as usual," said Erepsin. "The odds are quite good this year."

"Mine too," said 'Mr P' and 'Mr J' at almost the same time.

"He's been successful for the last seven years..." commented Richard, "...which is why I've given up wagering against him."

Lady Melanie glanced over at her son, who suddenly realised what he had said, so he pretended that he hadn't said it – though his stance for the next few seconds was quite awkward.

"Less talk of money and bets please," Lord Stephen added, seeking to guide the conversation into a better place.

The airship now moved from being directly over the crowd to hovering above and just to the side of the giant inflated balloon chamber. Out from the edge of the ship a timber beam was extended, as if someone was about to walk the plank. A few moments passed and then appeared the figure of Uncle Jack. Well, at least you assumed that it was Uncle Jack. He was wearing what looked like a camouflaged, army body suit, which was almost hidden underneath what can only be described as a personalised bubble suit; making him look as if he'd been covered from head to toe in giant oversized bubble wrap. On his head was a helmet, also covered in the same bubble wrapping, and the only distinguishing mark that told you it was really him was his beard that stuck out from underneath his chin. On his back was a huge disc

49

that you assumed was the mechanism for the Catherine Wheel and also attached to his back was a long cable that itself was attached to the top of the ship's main mast.

Waving to the crowd, who all gave him a great cheer, he walked confidently to the edge of the plank and looked down at the giant funnel that fed into the bubble room beneath him. You'd have thought that he was about to jump right down into it but instead he positioned himself sideways so that he stood with his back to the balloon chamber, facing towards the other end of the ship. Then a whole extra series of planks extended from the ship's sides in front of him. They were as long as the plank Uncle Jack stood upon, around a foot apart from each other, making what looked like a series of wooden steps. Uncle Jack readied his stance like a sprinter about to run a race.

"Ladies and gentlemen," the voice boomed out from the ship's music horn. "The brave and daring Jacob McArnold Crispus Ken-Worthington-Brown is now going to use the sling-shot method to launch himself into the bubble chamber!"

Chapter 8 – The Human Firework!

A huge cheer rose up from the crowd. Lady Melanie looked at Lord Stephen who raised an eyebrow at Uncle Jack's recklessness.

"I do hope he's going to be alright," Emma whispered to Richard.

"I'm sure he will, my darling," replied Richard, kissing her on the forehead and holding her close to give her a little comfort.

Uncle Jack's ship started playing some drumming music, as if to get the man ready for his leap of faith. The crowd joined in the beat with a steady clap and everyone focused on the man and his attempt at being the first human Catherine Wheel firework in history.

Clap, clap, stamp, stamp, stamp,

Clap, clap, stamp, stamp, stamp,

went the crowd. The musical drum beat got faster and faster. Uncle Jack purposefully bounced his weight on his timber beam in order to prepare himself for his run. The panels on the ship's underside started to pulse different colours as the moment of launch came closer and closer. Then appeared the image of a bright shining number in the midst of the ship's metal panels. It was the number ten, which turned into a nine, then eight, seven, six, five...

Emma buried her head into Richard's chest whilst Georgiana exchanged a quick glance with her brother and then her father. Four, three, two, one, went the countdown and then a huge 'boom' from one of the cannons on board ship.

Uncle Jack ran from plank to plank till he reached the last one and, deliberately bouncing off it like a high-jump athlete, he launched himself into the air. Up he went for a moment and then down, down, down he plunged towards the crowd below. It was only then that the onlooking crowd realised that the line which was attached to Uncle Jack's back was not a rope or a wire, but a piece of very strong elastic. Under the force and pull of his weight it stretched and stretched as Uncle Jack's figure shot towards the ground below. Those 'on-the-ground' members of his staff, who had assembled the balloon chamber, shrank backwards, thinking he was about to squash them with his fall – but the elastic quickly reached its limit and for the briefest of moments he was suspended around twenty feet above their heads. Those at the ship's mast, to which the elastic was attached, pulled a lever which, like a slingshot, whiplashed Uncle Jack back up into the air. A gasp and a 'yeah' went up from the crowd as Uncle Jack's figure zoomed away from them in what looked like a skywards arc.

Whoosh, he went, his body almost spiralling out of control and at the mercy of the laws of physics. The ship's mast bent slightly again as the elastic stretched in another direction with Uncle Jack's high-speed body attached to the other end. Uncle Jack had again fallen towards the ground, but this time on the other side of the ship. At the last moment another lever on the ship jarred the mast and, pulling him back again, propelled him high over the top of the ship and then straight down he plunged, right into the heart of the funnel which in turn plunged him into the waiting bubble chamber. If you thought that he was travelling quickly up to that point, then you were mistaken. The spectacle of speed was actually just about to begin.

I wish I could accurately describe the events that took place in the next few moments, but I can't. The blur of Uncle's Jack's almost fluid body as he bounced in the chamber from balloon to balloon is something that only the eye can understand. Indeed, you could not even trust your eyesight. For one moment you thought that Uncle Jack was in one part of the chamber when actually his bouncing form would briefly appear at the other side. All you knew was that, as each bounce took place, the powdery substance inside each balloon shook in some way to show that impact had been made. The different bodies of what looked like Uncle Jack's multiple forms shuddered and juddered the whole structure as if it were a giant jelly being jiggled from its inside. As the temperature and energy inside the chamber increased, the powder changed colour from cold blues to oranges and then fiery red, indicating that the moment of release was on its way.

Again another series of count-down numbers began on the underside of the ship. Some in the crowd joined in the count but many were just speechless at the sight. At the last moment, a balloon that was blocking the hole to the spiral tube at the back of the chamber was removed and out shot Uncle Jack. Through the spiral tube he went and then out, his swirling, twirling body spun across the sky and the firework wheel device on his back, remotely controlled by Uncle Jack's helpers on the ship, suddenly came to life. In those moments that followed Uncle Jack became the centre for the spray of a giant Catherine Wheel. The sight was spectacular. He spun through the air with sparks flying off in all directions, lighting up the sky as he went and pouring out the many colours of firework flames. A living, shining star, he shot across the heavens from one side to the other amidst the dancing display of flashing lights and exploding firework powder. The gasp and intake of breath from the crowd was almost as loud as a shout!

Most people would have thought that would have been the end of Uncle Jack. Surely he was going to be bounced from roof top to roof top across the city and finally land in some back alley where someday someone might find him, broken and cold from his injuries. But Uncle Jack knew how to keep himself safe. Months of practice on the moors at the back of his mansion had allowed him to perfect the technology of firing an elastic cable at a propelled object whereby tracking devices on both the cable and on the flying object homed in on each other and locked themselves together.

As Uncle Jack flew across the sky, his ship's crew, manning what looked like a giant crossbow, shot a cable at him. Moments later the tracker around his waist and the ship's cable locked. The cable, one end secured firmly onto Uncle Jack and the other anchored to the ship's central mast, stretched and stretched as Uncle Jack's spinning body pulled against it. The mast bent and twisted under the strain. Then, twang! Uncle Jack was jerked back in an orbital rotation. Round and round and round the ship he went, above the heads of the crowd, the cable wrapping itself about the ship's mast, pulling him in with each turn.

Cheers, whoops and applause arose from the crowd as this final part of the stunt was pulled off with excellence and great precision. His giant Catherine Wheel drew the picture of a white halo in the sky. Then, slowly, the rotations lost their momentum and the disc on Uncle Jack's back ran out of powder to fuel the firework. The central mast on the ship pulled Uncle Jack in and eventually he was left just swaying to and fro on the night air a little underneath the ship, suspended between the boat's underside and the people below.

He didn't wave or move about too much. Catching his breath was probably the most important thing for him to do. After being hauled on-board, his crew quickly gathered round him to make sure that he was alright and a big 'thumbs up' was delivered on the ship's underside screen. Everyone cheered and clapped. What a sight it had been.

"Well, another bet lost," sighed Erepsin, "but that was awesome!"

Within just a few minutes Uncle Jack was on his feet, held up by his crew members and waving to the crowd. He was guided by his helpers along the edge of the ship so that he could wave to everyone in the city square. That was it, the event was over, everyone was amazed, and Uncle Jack had once again proved that, when it came to entertainment, he still ruled as the great king. After all of the waving was done, Uncle Jack began to unbutton the front of his suit whilst the crowds chattered to each other about what they'd just seen. It was that time when everyone knew the spectacle was over, but no-one wanted to go home just yet.

"Well I'm glad that's finished," Lord Stephen said, with a tone of relief. "If he keeps that up, one day he really is going to kill himself!"

As the crowd chatted and laughed about all that they'd just witnessed, and as money was exchanged by those who had made bets on whether Uncle Jack would survive his latest event, several city dignitaries unexpectedly boarded Uncle Jack's boat, each shaking him by the hand. They were so overawed by his work, and so pushy to spend just a few moments with him, that Uncle Jack didn't have time to get out of his suit. Handshake after handshake came his way and in-between each shake he attempted to get another button undone. One of those people pushing for attention and impatiently anticipating a moment with the great man was the city mayor. He initially stood behind Uncle Jack and, after taking an opportunity to quickly photobomb someone else's picture, rather than waiting his turn to say his personal congratulations with a face-to-face greeting, he gave Uncle Jack a hearty slap on the back. This was unfortunate. Not because Uncle Jack had much strength left within him to protest about the unwelcome slap that he'd received, but because the remains of his Catherine Wheel was still attached to him. The mayor's slap went squarely onto the Catherine Wheel's disc, giving the wheel a judder which accidentally jolted the insides of the firework and, if you know anything about fireworks, you'll know that sometimes, even when a firework has spent itself, there's often some powder left inside that's hot and volatile. Something inside the Catherine Wheel ignited. Without warning a segment of it fizzed and the disc on Uncle Jack's back began to jolt around. Then, within moments (and to the mayor's absolute horror), the rest of the firework blazed into life again, roaring itself into a high-speed spin.

Uncle Jack, completely caught off guard, jumped forward in surprise, knocking over everyone in front of him. Without his helmet on he could feel the heat of the firework on his back and each rotation of the disc brought a more than uncomfortable moment of blistering heat onto his neck and then his bottom. Large sparks flew everywhere and people scattered in all directions. Uncle Jack could do nothing but run up and down his ship, trying to get away from the Catherine Wheel that was still firmly strapped to him. This way and that, he went, waggling his legs and leaping up into the air as sparks flew under his feet. At the same time he shook his arms from side to side, trying to loosen the firework from his back. The combination of hops and waggling arms made it look as if he was trying to fly. Then, BANG, BANG, BANG, BANG, went the Catherine Wheel, as the last bits of powder blew themselves out of the disc's sides. One final BANG! and Uncle Jack found himself launched several feet off the ground before landing squarely on his bottom. Then, it was all over. To everyone's relief this signalled the end of the unfortunate episode. Their relief, however, was short lived. This final blast from the Catherine Wheel ejected a small, dormant rocket, perhaps a firework that shouldn't have been in the Catherine Wheel at all – packed in by an overenthusiastic factory worker who wanted to give this particular whiz-banger that extra bit of punch! High into the air this rocket went, up, up, and up; it's shriek catching everyone's attention. It arced its way across the sky, away from the boat and towards the palace grounds. Finally the firework came down and, to Lord Stephen's horror, straight into the mouth of the funnel and into the balloon chamber.

As soon as the rocket entered the chamber it began to ferociously bounce from side to side, trying to get out with an ever-increasing intensity. Whizzing here and there, the flashing, sparkling lights of the trapped firework burst into a fizzing frenzy with such a concentrated force that it caused the powdery substances within the balloons to quickly turn red hot.

"Carriage!" shouted Lord Stephen. He firmly guided Lady Melanie and the rest of his group towards a quick exit. Within moments the carriage was there, and Lord Stephen was literally pushing each person into it.

"Is this really necessary?" asked Georgiana, still wanting to see what the firework would do.

"Better not argue sis," said Richard, whilst helping Emma onto her seat next to his sister.

Even before Erepsin, as the last person to enter the carriage, had closed the door (leaving his school chums stranded in the square), a quick sound of the whip was heard and off they all went. From the carriage's back and side windows they could see the giant balloons wobbling and shuddering as the enraged firework bolted its way between them, trying to get out and at the same time energised by the unusual properties of the methanthiol gas.

Then 'poof' it all popped as the firework finally exploded. A mushroom cloud of red and orange powder filled the air and from within the heat an odorous stink, like a leakage of rotten eggs mixed in with decomposing cabbage, was released into the atmosphere. As the colourful, smoky haze advanced, so did the stink! People began running everywhere, hands or hankies over their noses.

"Better make your investment in clothes pegs now if I were you," said Richard.

Erepsin finally pulled himself into the carriage and then kept his face pressed against the window to take in every moment of the catastrophe as it unravelled before his eyes.

"That would be a very wise thing to do," he replied, with a wry smile.

"Full speed ahead," shouted Lord Stephen.

There was another crack of the whip and the speeding carriage jerked into a full bolt down the street. Despite their increase in speed, however, Lord Stephen knew that by the time they reached their mansion, the smell would have most probably have caught up with them. Getting into their home would require a deep breath and a dash to avoid inhaling the foul, stinking air!

Chapter 9 – The Governor's Ball

After the disastrous event that ended the annual celebration of the city's freedom, Clearwash City found itself in turmoil over the following weeks. Firstly because it took around ten days for the desert winds to blow the foul air out and away from the city streets; for some reason, the rotten egg and decomposing cabbage smell seemed to linger longer than expected. Perhaps it was the peculiar properties of the methanthiol. It seemed to have the ability to seep into not only cloth fibres but leather and other materials too, even wood. Secondly, many of the betting shops had arguments with their annual punters as to whether they had won their bets against Uncle Jack. The punters said they had a claim as the last entertainment event went awry. The betting organisations insisted that Uncle Jack *had* fulfilled his role perfectly and that the accident at the end was the mayor's fault. These arguments led to some nasty scenes until the law courts found in favour of the interpretation that Uncle Jack had indeed *not* failed in his entertainment role. After this judgement, everyone tried to sue the mayor for damages to property and clothes that still stank of rotting eggs. The mayor in turn simply blamed the firework manufacturer, a foreign company from a distant country that couldn't be held to account, so the political wrangling in court finally ran out of steam.

Once life in the city had settled down, the last few days of late winter gave way to early spring and the next date on the social calendar was the Governor's Ball. It wasn't an event for everyone. Traditionally nobility, the rich, the famous (and infamous), the intellectually astute and the political elite were the only people guaranteed on the guest list. Its exclusivity was notorious. Not everyone approved of the pompous parade that so many put on when arriving to display themselves at the event; flaunting and trumpeting their wealth and social status. In some circles it turned their stomachs to see such a peacock pageant. The majority of the city populace, however, loved the occasion. The growing social frenzy would explode six weeks before the ball took place when twelve random wild card invitations were picked from a lottery and announced to allow anyone from any background to gain entry to the ball. The 'Cinderella few', as they were called, were treated like spoilt millionaires. Each person was given a new wardrobe of clothes to wear, a complete head-to-toe makeover along with dancing lessons so that they could join in the ball as gracefully as they knew how. A daily newspaper diary, along with a weekly magazine, were produced to sensationalise their progress. Here all of the 'in-talk' and chatter was published on the subject. The general hysteria surrounding the build up to the ball was also boosted by local businesses who tried to advertise their products by giving each of the wild-card winners an assortment of 'freebies' (normally clothes, perfume or fashion accessories) - each gift given on the basis that it had to be used or worn in the run up to the ball or on the night itself. These businesses and the Cinderella few quickly became overnight 'best buddies' as the lottery winners talked about their excitement about the event and how much the 'gifts' they had received meant to them. Not many people actually believed the chatter but sometimes the fantasy world is so attractive that submerging oneself in it, believing it because you wanted to, wasn't so difficult a thing to do. The average person's hair styles, clothes and general attire, therefore, changed from week to week during this preparation time as the pace of change in the fashion world accelerated into a full sprint. One thing became 'in' for the moment and others were then 'out' – even if they'd only just been 'in' a couple of days ago, and then the next 'in' would be in until it was out again! "The Hokey Cokey fashion parade of in, out, in, out, shake it all about,' would be the motto slapped onto the event by the critical few!

As well as following each of these wild-card participants, the weekly Governor's Ball magazine also published interviews with the city's 'B' class celebrity social lights (who attended the event every year) getting their views on not just *what* was 'in' but also *who* was 'in' or 'out' and speculating on what the final guest list might look like. 'A' class stars were rarely seen during this preparation period and it was always a deeply guarded secret as to what they would be wearing and with whom they would be arriving. The fashion world in the city held its breath and looked to them to set the trend for the rest of the spring and summer season. Fortunes could be won or lost on this evening and sometimes whole wardrobes of clothing were created overnight as soon as the stars set foot from their carriages.

On the day of the ball, crowds lined the streets from early morning and throughout the day to catch just a glimpse of each arrival. Smaller warmup events whetted the appetite from street artists to airship flyovers. Then, around mid-morning, the full guest list for the evening ball was released. Copies of it zoomed around the city at rocket speed as it quickly became the focus of everyone's conversation.

As evening approached, lights on the city palace grounds lit up the marquees that had been erected especially for the evening. This particular night was a little chilly for the time of year. A cold sharp breeze had found its way into the city in the late afternoon and those guests who had arrived earlier in the day, who had thought that dressing in a more scantily fashion was the 'in' thing for that year, found themselves wishing they'd put a little more on. The inner palace rooms or the outside marquees quickly became their refuge from the crisp, sunset air.

Cheers from the crowds in the streets made it clear that the more well-known guests were starting to arrive. Carriage after carriage pulled up at the palace gates and each person, who had been given their time slot, arrived, disembarked, waved to the crowd and entered the palace grounds. All of this happened to orchestral music and live background commentary – provided by loud speakers attached to the palace clock tower.

Georgiana held the thrill of the coming evening tightly in her gut so that outwardly no-one could see how delighted she was to be attending the ball. Sat in the family carriage next to her brother and sister-in-law, she gently waved to the crowds as they passed through the streets of Clearwash City. Elegance was the word to describe the family. Georgiana remembered a conversation she'd had when she was much younger, the night she'd attended her first Governor's ball.

"Where are our big outfits Daddy?" the young Georgiana had asked.

"We're nobility with an excellent family name," whispered her father in her ear. "We don't need to put on an act to be special."

"But I would like to dress up," she gently protested.

"Then dress up on the inside," replied her father. "Dress up with honour and having a noble heart. Dress up with honesty, modesty and good deeds. Let your conduct be your cloak and your countenance the crown upon your head. A noble heart, my dear, is a garment beyond the skill of any weaver or seamstress. It is fashion that never goes out of style."

The young Georgiana didn't know what some of those words meant but they sounded marvellously mysterious. Still, she would have liked to dress up a little more than she did.

Now, however, dressed in a dark green, off-the-shoulder, sleeveless, floor-length satin ball gown, Georgiana knew how to carry herself on the inside as well as appearing highly in vogue. Lord Stephen had given up trying to dissuade her from being too fashionable and so he and Lady Melanie just sat opposite, dressed fairly modestly, and chatted about everything and nothing. They paid particular attention to Emma, whose whirlwind romance and marriage to Richard, meant that this was only her second Governor's ball. She clearly was still feeling nervous about the event and being pregnant didn't help her to feel relaxed about the evening.

The carriage drew up to the palace gates and out they all stepped to the background cheers of the crowds. It felt so good to have the pleasure of the people. The Pluggat-Lynette family had done so much over the years for the city and this event facilitated the moment when the crowd's affections could be openly displayed. A wave and a gentle nod was all they needed from Lord Stephen and then the family was gone with the next carriage drawing up to deliver more guests.

The guests continued to arrive until everyone on the list had been signed off by the Governor's ball organisation team. Uncle Jack had appeared in one of his steam-driven horseless carriages – a marvellous contraption that was shaped like a large overgrown pumpkin and had multiple legs. After disembarking, he sent his carriage off to park itself whilst the big man strode into the palace.

His wife was rarely seen at this event, much to the relief of the Governor's ball organisers. She preferred her own alternative ladies night at the other side of the city. So Uncle Jack made his way, as usual, to the gentleman's lounge. There he would spend most of the night surrounded by cigar smoke and talking to his friends. That is, until the annual 'Jacob versus Jacob' event got underway, where Jacob Ville would challenge Jacob McArnold Crispus Ken-Worthington-Brown to a game of Barrac, a cross between backgammon, chess and gin rummy . Each man was joined by a team of supporting thinkers and then the evening was set with intellect battling intellect, until the ball was over in the early hours of the morning.

Speaking of the Ville family, one of the shocks of the evening was the arrival of the Ville family carriage. Out stepped Jacob Ville followed by his son, Erepsin, with no-one else to accompany them. Jacob walked straight through the iron gates without any recognition of the crowd whilst Erepsin made much of the moment, giving bows and waves that were exceedingly, overly exaggerated. Rumours spread quickly, however, that they were alone and many tongues began wagging as to why this might be the case. Front page newspaper headlines were drawn up to report on this being one of the shock events of the evening, even before the night was properly underway.

Another event that caught everyone's attention was the late arrival of an airship that hovered over the palace towards the back of the building. A landing stair was let down and some people disembarked onto the palace roof. The ship was too far away for the crowd to see what was happening and soon it was forgotten when the large screens that hung on the palace walls lit up to show the event that was taking place inside. Multiple camera angles and commentary followed the guests as the crowds in the great market square looked on at the ball's events.

Inside the palace, Georgiana quickly made her way round her regular acquaintances, enjoying the varied social interactions that the event facilitated. She was careful, however, not to become tied down to one group of people. For her, this event was about being seen and growing her personal connections. Like her father, she was becoming a political animal, but this occasion gave her the freedom to pursue her own place and identity in the city on her terms, not standing in his shadow. Many years before she'd discovered that her family name and her outgoing personality was pleasing to other people and that, by them, she was strong enough to quickly establish her own relationships; a mere introduction and a smile opened the door to almost instant friendships that she could build upon over time. The Governor's ball was the ideal place to fulfil her ambition. To her politics was all work *and pleasure* and she loved the romance of an evening well executed. By the end of the night she'd have talked to over a hundred people, only danced a handful of waltzes, and made many new friends.

On this particular night she hadn't been long into her schedule when her flow was interrupted by her mother, who signalled to her to come and join her party. Reluctantly she went over to see why her company was needed. Lord Stephen was already in conversation and Lady Melanie was with the other women of her social group. Emma, however, had been briefly left alone when Erepsin had asked Richard to *momentarily* join him and some other friends at the back of the palace grounds to help make up the numbers for a skittles team – an activity that was discouraged by the ball organisers but which seemed to still take place each year (along with the exchange of money where bets were made on skittle game outcomes). Richard hadn't returned as quickly as he'd promised and Emma found herself left with her mother-in-law and without anyone of her age to converse with.

"Georgiana dear," Lady Melanie whispered in her ear. "Emma needs to be shown to the lady's rest room. Her delicate condition and nerves seem to be getting the better of her. Do show her the way and keep her company until Richard gets back."

With a smile, Georgiana took Emma by the hand and together they wove their way between the various groups of people towards the palace main stair. Up they went and along the first-floor corridor that ran around the edge of the room; where they could still look down on all that was happening below. Finally into the rest room they went and the buzz of the crowded hall was dulled.

"Oh I'm still all nerves," said Emma a few minutes later when they were preparing to go back to the ball. "I don't know how you do it. Everyone seems to know just when to talk and what to say. I don't know how to fit in with it all."

"Spend the evening with me," Georgiana replied, "...or until Richard gets back. If you get tired then tell me and we'll take some time out together for a sit and quiet chat."

"You're so kind," Emma replied. "I know how much this evening means to you."

"I shall be glad of your company," Georgiana smiled in response. "Having a sister with me will be quite refreshing - and I'll be more easily able to refuse some of those overly keen young gentlemen who want to dance with me each year, and at the same time to tread on my toes. Now I shall be able to say that I have a companion and am socially engaged at the moment. What an escape you'll be!"

"Well I'm glad that I'll be of some use to you."

"You'll be more than that," Georgiana asserted. "You and I will be the social lights of the ball and, by the time we've finished the evening, everyone will be talking about us."

"Oh I do hope not," said Emma. "I'm still not used to that kind of thing. Remember, you're the one with the big name and reputation."

"Well I don't know about that," replied Georgiana.

The two young women laughed together and went arm in arm back onto the first-floor landing where they could see the ball below. As they appeared in the corridor, a sudden hush descended on the crowd. Georgiana and Emma peered over the banister to see what had caused the unexpected silence. All the guests had stopped and turned to face the main stairway, which wound its way from the upper floor palace library down to the marbled, great hall where many of the guests were. Near the top of the stair stood the one person that everyone thought hadn't arrived that evening. All cameras tuned in on her and, as each monitor on the palace walls displayed her picture, the crowds outside in the great market square took in a great gasp of breath.

Chapter 10 – A Grand Entrance

Maltrisia Ville stood approximately six steps down from the top of the stair, gazing out at everyone below and waiting until all eyes were looking in her direction. Effortlessly dressed in a sleeveless, off-the-shoulder, haute couture bodice dress, she wore twisted black silk from top to bottom; except for a lime green taffeta drape that wound itself upwards from the base of her dress, like a coiled, constricting snake, until it finally found its home at the base of her neck – where its snake-like head pointed back out at the crowd, mouth open wide with fangs on display. Atop her perfectly coiffured hair, gathered and braided into a low chignon bun, sat a jet-black pillbox hat with a meshed half veil to shadow her face. Most startling, however, were eight semi-transparent dragonfly wings that protruded from the centre of her back. They were so wide, they spanned the entire width of the staircase. Each wing shimmered as the tiny jewels which were woven into its fabric caught the light, scattering glistening rays of illumination in every direction.

Once she was sure that every eye was on her, Maltrisia paused for a few more moments and then, with one hand on her hip, began her slow and purposeful descent; as if the palace were her home and she was welcoming everyone to her most illustrious party. Her black cape followed, rippling its way down each step and matching the pace of her walk, spreading its influence right across the stair. Behind the cape, her daughter Seleucia Ville paraded herself down the stairs, as if a supporting act in a great play. She clearly enjoyed walking in her mother's shadow and proudly held her head high to enjoy the moment. Once Maltrisia reached the last step, a supporting group of servants came to attend her. In one swift movement, two young gentleman unclipped the wings and cape from Maltrisia's back and carried them back up the stairs. Seleucia and the servants quickly gathered themselves into a huddle behind Maltrisia as she began to move through the crowd, engaging in lively conversations as she went.

"What was that all about?" asked Emma, once Maltrisia had disappeared into the crowd.

Georgiana relaxed the frown that was etched across her face as she gazed down on the party from their vantage point.

"A bit over the top, don't you think?" continued Emma.

"Quite," remarked Georgiana with a sigh. "But then again nothing's potentially over the top for Maltrisia. You can see where Erepsin gets his overt personality from!"

"You really don't like him, do you," said Emma.

Georgiana hesitated for a second. She'd momentarily forgotten that Erepsin was Richard's best friend and that Emma was still getting used to life within the Pluggat-Linette family circle. Georgiana's dislike of Erepsin ran deep, over many years in fact, but Emma mainly saw him through the eyes of her husband.

"He and I don't seem to see eye to eye on many things," Georgiana quickly added – though Emma had already seen the attitude behind her speedy reply.

"Come on," she said to Emma with a smile. "Let's go and mingle. There's plenty of walking, talking and champaign sipping to do."

The two ladies moved on together towards the stair.

"I am pregnant," Emma reminded Georgiana. "I can't walk too far and I won't be sipping champaign."

"Yes of course," replied Georgiana. She paused for a moment to think through their approach to the evening and then added, "Well, you do the talking and I'll do the sipping."

With a laugh they joined the ball again and were soon surrounded by smiling faces and lively conversation. Emma quickly forgot Richard's absence and was introduced to the world of Georgiana's light chatter, verbal banter and friend making. She was amazed at how well Georgiana stepped into friendship groups and then, after a quick chat, left them feeling all the better for their time together. With every social huddle they encountered, a new friend was made and Emma noticed how Georgiana took a mental note of her new acquaintants; making them at ease and treating them as if they were a 'treasure discovered', then leaving with a promise of deeper friendship the next time they met.

Finally they found themselves in the vicinity of Lord Stephen and Lady Melanie and Emma felt as if her adventure for the evening was over. She was sure Georgiana would leave her, especially when Richard came back to join them, apologising most profusely for the extra time he'd spent away from his wife and at the same time avoiding his mother's corrective eyes. The family group stayed together, however, and seemed to be a magnet for all kinds of people who just wanted to be seen with the Pluggat-Lynette family circle.

"Time for some refreshments," Lord Stephen eventually declared. That was the signal for all conversations to be drawn to a close and they were off to the open dining area. Offering his wife his arm, Lord Stephen led the way; showing by his body language that he was not going to stop for anyone to chat. He took the family into one of the dining lounges where there were spreads of cold meats, pastries, sandwiches, salad bars and a whole variety of puddings made from sugary syrups with lashings of cream. After pointing out to the waiters the types of food they desired, to ensure each person had a plentiful supply of what they preferred, there was of course the need to sit and eat whilst still enjoying the ball. So out to the terrace they went to view the entertainments in the palace gardens whilst sitting under the stars.

The cool evening breeze made the outside air so pleasant compared with the stuffy atmosphere of the great hall. Drinks were served by the outside waiters and the conversation flowed as the family ate, laughed and enjoyed each other's company. As their spoons plunged the depths of custard-soaked puddings, a group of boisterous young men walked up the main pathway that led from the palace gardens. Among them was Erepsin who, quickly seeing the Pluggat-Lynette family, left his friends. Sending a waiter to obtain some food, Erepsin sat on the edge of their company and tagged on to the general conversation. Ignoring him, Georgiana looked out at the various marquees and stalls that were dotted across the palace grounds and gardens. No expense had been spared. Floral bouquets were displayed on posts at the head of every pathway and at every turn there was either a fun performance to watch (perhaps an acrobat or drama scene from a play) or a place of tranquil rest where you could sit on a decorated bench and take in the night air.

As usual the Governor's Ball tent was set up in the middle of the palace lawn, from which the city governor and a specially selected guest would deliver a final speech, just before the ball was due to end. It was normally someone who had recently distinguished themselves in some way, often an inventor providing a product or a service that had enriched city life. Sometimes the talk was interesting and useful. Often, however, it was quite boring or unnecessarily focused on the intricate inner workings of some new gadget where the inventor went into great detail about how their contraption worked.

Over the years the invention list had grown to quite a substantial length. They had listened to speeches about automated facial hair trimmers – for busy men who needed to keep their beards neat and trim but didn't have the time to visit the barber, or nose and nostril warmers – for those taking night-time walks when the city had to endure the desert evening chill, or even explosive hips – an invention for anyone who tended to fall over a lot whereby your padded hips ballooned outwards as you fell, to bounce you back up again. Then there was long, long talk about the tele-ear communicators – whereby to receive a wireless Morse coded message you wore a tall top hat to turn yourself into a personal signal mast. To make the connection for any incoming calls you simply stuck a finger in your ear, or up your left nostril, whilst a friend turned a handle on your back that wound up the clockwork receiver mechanism. Probably the worst speech ever, however, was the one that focused on what was called the 'Jelly Belly' product, an invention at the heart of the campaign against 'tubby tummies', as they were called. To promote general health within the city, a contraption had been made whereby a false squidgy tummy was strapped around the waist of a person who wanted to lose weight. This contraption was designed to stop the individual from sitting for a long period of time at a table to eat. The longer they sat, the more the jelly belly filled with air and the false tummy protruded so much that it became impossible for them to reach their knife and fork and so partake in the meal; so sitting down to eat food of any kind was made impossible. Wearing the device made you dependent on other people feeding you and so your ability to choose what and when to eat was taken away. "Tubby or not tubby," was the motto that accompanied the sales pitch. This, however, started a long court case against the advert by a local playwright who felt that he'd had one of his most famous stage lines perverted for the sake of cheap financial gain!

The identity of this annual speech making guest was meant to be a secret – but most years you could figure out who it was going to be by examining the guest list. This year, however, there had been a good amount of unresolved speculation on the subject. No one particular person stood out, especially from the 'one off' guests who were new ball attendees; in recent months nothing of interest had been achieved by any of them.

"Do we have any idea who's delivering the speech this year?" Georgiana asked, when a brief moment of opportunity presented itself.

"Not at all," replied Lord Stephen. "This year it's a mystery."

"You know it's always a secret," Lady Melanie added.

"Sometimes a name leaks out," Georgiana replied.

"Don't wish the night away sis," Richard added.

"I'm not," she replied. "I'm just asking the question, that's all."

"I hear," interrupted Erepsin between mouthfuls of sandwich, "that it's not someone from the arts and sciences this year. I hear that we may have a more political speech."

"Really?" said Richard.

"That's not possible," replied Lord Stephen. "The rules of the ball are very clear. No-one has ever used the speech for political gain and the governor's oath prevents him from taking a political stance."

"Well I'm just saying…" said Erepsin, but didn't finish his sentence due to swallowing down the remainder of his sandwich and picking up his drink to wash it all down.

Lord Stephen didn't take much notice of Erepsin's remarks but just smiled at his wife and moved the conversation on in a different direction.

"Time to go back inside," he eventually said.

With that remark he and Lady Melanie got up to leave.

"Are you alright for going back inside?" Georgiana asked Emma.

"I am feeling a little tired," she replied, "but I'm also a little too cool out here."

"Perhaps one of the smaller lounges will be best for us then," suggested Lady Melanie.

"The billiards room?" proposed Erepsin.

"Too much smoke," retorted Georgiana. "Not the place for a pregnant woman."

"The games room," said Lady Melanie, in a gentler tone. "Plenty of space to sit, rest and be entertained."

"We'll join you after we've had a couple of dances in the main ballroom," Lord Stephen added, offering his arm to his wife. "So far we've not had that pleasure and this event isn't going by without some time in the ball room."

"Are you up for a gentle dance too?" Richard enquired of Emma.

"Well perhaps if we don't move too fast," she replied. "I'd love a little time in the ballroom hall with you."

With that in mind, the family moved back into the palace and into the great hall. Lord Stephen and Lady Melanie glided in and amongst the crowd of other dancers, moving together with great elegance and style. Richard took Emma to one side of the dance floor and gently swayed and moved with her so that they had their moment together without having to think about any other dancers around them.

"Might I..." Erepsin ventured.

"I have appointments to keep," Georgiana bluntly stated and off she went to talk to a nearby friendship group.

Finding himself alone, Erepsin dealt with his embarrassment by quickly inviting another young woman to dance and, being eagerly accepted, entered onto the dance floor with the rest of the crowd.

After a time of dancing the family decided to take a break. They had just gathered, and were waiting for Georgiana to join them to leave for the games lounge, when Jacob Ville entered the ball room.

"Jacob," said Lord Stephen. "I thought the gentleman's lounge was the place where you spent this night?"

"It is," he replied, in his usual surly tone.

He manoeuvred his eyes around the ballroom as if it were something foreign to his conscience.

"I was having an interesting card game with the McArnold Crispus," he added (meaning Uncle Jack). "And to be honest I'm only here for the obligatory dance with my wife. Just need to get this job done and then I can get back to the real business of making some money this evening."

"I thought Maltrisia's entrance to the ball this year a rather interesting one," Lady Melanie commented, trying to keep the conversation away from the subject of gambling.

Jacob sighed. "I never know what she's going to come up with next. Mind my own business I do these days, can't keep up with her to be honest."

"Well she certainly turned everyone's gaze," Richard chipped in. Then, without thinking too much about what he was saying, added, "Plenty of mouths dropped open when she first appeared on the stairway."

"That I don't doubt," Jacob replied. "She's never shied away from being the centre of attention. Ah, here she is now."

Maltrisia entered the room with an entourage following in her wake. Seeing that her husband was waiting, she glided in his direction to find his arm extended for her to relax upon.

"Lord Stephen and Lady Melanie," she said. "How delightful to see you both again." The tone of her voice was warm and yet quite devoid of emotion.

"Always a pleasure to see you both," Lord Stephen responded, glancing at both her and her husband. "I hope that you are fully recovered from your illness, it's been a while since we've seen you."

"Oh that," said Maltrisia. "Came and went in a few nights," she added. "It's so wonderful to be out and about again."

"You certainly made an entrance tonight," Emma said, finding the confidence to speak for the first time.

Maltrisia looked at Emma as if she were a child learning to talk.

"One does one's best," she replied in a condescending manner.

"I was under the impression that all guests were instructed to arrive in carriages," Georgiana pointed out, as she joined her family.

"Oh carriages are so yesterday," replied Maltrisia.

"So we'll never see you in a carriage again?" enquired Georgiana.

Maltrisia paused for the briefest of moments and then, with a dismissive half-smile at Georgiana and a nod at Lord Stephen, moved her husband onto the dance floor.

"Well done sis," whispered Richard, with a slight giggle.

The family left for the games room and a little peace and quiet.

Erepsin finished his dance and, after leaving his dance partner with her social group, was about to follow the Lynette-Pluggat family when his sister, Seleucia, stepped into his path.

"Where were you when mother arrived?" she demanded.

"Out the back of course. Where else would I be?"

"Typical," she snapped.

"Needs must," he added, trying to walk past her.

She was having none of it, however, and blocked his way with her arms on her hips.

"As usual your excuses are pathetic," she commented.

66

"Pathetic they might be, my dearest sister, but at least I don't pamper to mother's every whim. Unlike you, I have a mind of my own."

"Unlike you, I have a future," she countered.

"Well, enjoy your life on a leash," he replied, pushing his way past her. Walking away he paused for a moment to comment over his shoulder.

"I'm sure she'll lengthen the tether enough at some point as a reward for your undivided loyalty and mindless obedience."

As evening turned into night, the different events that took place in the many rooms of the grand palace came to an end. Many of the guests went outside to stand in the gardens for the final official occasion, the Governor's Ball speech. This was not the most treasured part of the evening. Those guests in love with dancing or card playing would rather skip the experience but all music stopped and monitors in every palace room would turn on and focus on the speech marquee to ensure that it wasn't ignored.

The speech marquee itself was only a small tent, erected in the middle of the palace lawn. It was, however, highly decorated with flora and ribbon accessories to give it a distinguished look. As usual the governor started by giving a small speech to compliment the organisers; those providing the food and drink, those delivering waiter and waitressing services, the cooks, musicians, entertainers and of course the guests who had completed the evening by turning up to enjoy themselves. The ball had once again been a great success and it was a night to be remembered.

"Many of you have been wondering over the last few weeks about the identity of our guest speaker," the governor said. "I know, of course, that every year this is kept secret until the very last moment; most years it is possible to work out who it might be from the guest list. It's normally a person who has recently distinguished themselves within the life of the city and has provided a product or a service that has enriched our lives and made living in this most excellent place all the more pleasurable. This year, however, we are going to slightly deviate from tradition and give the honour of this speech to a woman who has captured the hearts of so many people. She has pushed through recent personal adversity, overcoming ill health, and provided us with an ideology that will serve our city for decades to come, the notion of a 'People's Republic'. Sometimes it is the intellectual gifts that are not only the most precious but also the gifts that deliver the greatest dividends. So I want you to warmly welcome a woman of great style, great standing and intellectual vision. I give the honour of the Governor's Ball speech to the lady of the hour, Maltrisia Ville."

A great intake of breath across the gardens and palace rooms showed just how controversial this decision was. Maltrisia, however, stepped out from the crowd that had gathered on the palace lawn to listen to the governor. To the background sound of cheers from her gathered supporters (who for some reason knew she was about to speak) she effortlessly glided up the path and into the marquee. The din of her cheering followers drowned out the murmurings and verbal complaints of her political opponents who stood stunned and amazed at what was taking place in front of their eyes. Political ideology was banned from the ball and nothing like this had happened before.

After ascending three steps, Maltrisia stood on the small platform inside the marquee and leaned into the microphone stand. With arms open wide to welcome everyone she said,

"Ladies, gentleman, citizens of Clearwash City, my friends. It is with the greatest pleasure that I have accepted this kind offer to deliver the Governor's Ball speech this year. Unlike other speakers from the past, I shan't keep you waiting for too long; I know that you'll want to finish off those most excellent pies and sweet pastries that are still left in the food halls before retiring for the night after such an excellent evening of social interaction and communion. Sweet talk and chatter must, I believe, be complemented by sweet taste; often the calls of the tummy are even more pleasurable than the calls of the heart – and I can see from the size of some of the waistlines that belong to a fair number of gentlemen tonight, that this truly is the case."

Many in the crowd laughed at her joke, but quickly hushed for her next words.

"We are a city that has achieved so much and we have come such a long way in order to finally grow up and leave behind those ancient scripts that once outlined our daily lives when our culture was formed in the time of its innocent naivety. To grow, change, evolve and metamorphosise is the call of any moral people who seek to enter into a more mature way of living. This call to maturity is not something to be ignored. Our consciences being clear, we need to press on into the unknown, knowing that we follow a certain path that calls us all to higher ground. This opportunity will not go away, and it should not be ignored. Everyone should embrace the prospect of embracing moral elevated living: surely that's a given for all of us.

In a people's republic everyone has something to say. In our current climate no-one is truly listening to each other and this needs to change. We need to live in an environment where we all listen and value the treasured opinions that belong to the community's corporate life. Only together can we find the truth. That truth belongs to everyone, not to tradition or the few. We all have a right to speak and a right to carve out our future together, to go on a journey of discovery so that we can all be that which we choose to be. So I encourage you to free yourself, be yourself, honour yourself, empower yourself, choose your liberty, each and everyone. How will we do this? Well the politics is quite simple:

infinitus imperium - libertatem personalem
infinite government - personal freedom

This is the motto of a people's republic. The new challenges that face us are there to be overcome, not shied away from. Life is not for the timid. I would say, though I'm sure that there are some who disagree – (but I do indeed still listen to them) I would still say that King's Law prevents us from becoming who we truly are. We need to provide a political framework where we can spend more time listening rather than being entrenched within our own traditional, intellectual boundaries."

As Maltrisia spoke her supporters were heartily clapping and shouting out enthusiastic affirmations at every opportunity. They could not, however, stop the increasing number of descending voices from across the palace gardens as they called out their disdain at the fraudulent usage of this event.

"This is the vision we are setting before you," Maltrisia added. "A vision that will deliver what it promises. Hope, freedom, new opportunities and equality for all. Surely that really is a given for all of us. As we look to begin the political new year, we will hopefully, this time, allow ourselves the space and liberty to choose wisely and take the opportunity for the freedom that is set before us. History is here for the making and it is the bold, the brave and the fearless who pave the way to take a hold of that which is waiting to take a hold of us. Let us not be afraid of letting go of the past and let us trust one another enough to deliver a future that is grounded in mutual trust and affection.

infinitus imperium - libertatem personalem
infinite government - personal freedom
The prospect and the choice is yours."

With those last words Maltrisia waved to the crowd, shook hands with the governor, stepped down from the platform and walked up the path towards the palace. She was quickly surrounded by her supporters who cocooned her from any dissenting voices.

Once inside the palace she swiftly made her way through various rooms until she entered the main entrance hall. A couple of drinks were thrown in her direction as she passed from room to room but she was only slightly splashed by their impact. At the main stair she found Seleucia and other supporting staff waiting for her. Together they ascended and finally exited the building the same way they'd first entered, by way of the palace roof. There they were picked up by a luxury airship and, once on board, were away. Those who remained at the ball were left speechless, wondering how what had happened had been allowed to happen and just what was going to happen next.

Chapter 11 – A So Called Noble Trait

The political fallout that arose from Maltrisia's speech gathered in strength over the following week. More and more voices of dissent were added to the running condemnatory commentary that surrounded the event. Posters, pamphlets and leaflets were created and handed out by those loyal to the King's Law political stance. The momentum within the lobby group seemed unstoppable. One of the movement's chief critics was Lord Stephen. Normally a reserved man on the public stage, now he was very outspoken about the breaking of the rules and the subject matter that Maltrisia had expressed. Georgiana could not have been prouder of him. She knew he was a capable man, but seeing him in action like this caused her admiration for him to swell to new heights. Every day he was in the city hall debating chamber, airing his thoughts on the subject and verbally running circles around his intellectual opponents. He was quoted and requoted by newspapers and many a political analyst who took great delight in his daily discourses; being so fresh, forthright and engaging in his approach. Soon he became the voice of the people and so he grew daily in influence and power. Pressure was also mounting on the city governor to resign his post and it seemed impossible for him to escape his political pending doom. From the time that the governor's ball ended, he was hardly seen in public; making the excuse that he had much planning work to do, but everyone knew that his time was up and it was only a matter of days before he would have to step down.

The other strange positive that came out of this pressured time was Erepsin's absence from public life. The Pluggat-Lynette family hardly saw anything of him for at least a couple of weeks, much to the relief of Georgiana who found the social space most refreshing. She thought the reason for his absence could have been because he was ashamed of what his mother had done, and saw how firmly Georgiana's father was in standing up to her in public. Still it could have been that he'd seen an opportunity to make some quick money amidst the current chaos and was excessively busy, pursuing one of his 'make me rich quick' schemes.

"Chaos," he once said, "is the hunting ground of the wise entrepreneur. Whilst everyone is running for the hills, you can sell transportation at five times the normal price and no-one will blink an eye."

Whatever it was that kept him away, she was grateful for it. She began to truly relax for the first time in years and at the same time enjoyed the exhilaration of a political debate that was going her family's way.

Maltrisia was also strangely absent from public life. She normally faced head on any opposition to her influence within the city. Rumours spread that she was ill again and could not cope with her constitutional adversaries. Lord Stephen, however, found this hard to believe and, though he understood that the political momentum was with him, he still felt uneasy about the silence on her part.

"She's not a woman who does things without planning," he once remarked.

Georgiana, however, saw her silence as weakness and a sign that she was regretting the overstepping of her political reach.

It wasn't until the third week after the Governor's Ball that Maltrisia re-entered the city's social life. Her come-back campaign was very well organised with her followers knowing exactly where she would be and how to gather themselves at her events in order to give the impression of large crowd support. She opened up her full rhetoric of inclusive care and a joint vision for everyone, but the impact of her remarks on city life was clearly limited. If persistence was the only thing needed, then she put in more than her due. She followed a schedule that few politicians could attain or maintain, appearing in debates, newspaper columns, magazines and in her own rallies where she talked and talked until she'd covered every possible angle of her vision for the future.

Still the political tide didn't seem to be turning in her direction. Her 'openness' and 'oneness' speeches that would lead to so called new political freedoms seemed to be falling on deaf ears. As the weeks went by her influence waned and her popularity was clearly in decline. Lord Stephan was too much of a match for her and his quick wit, down-to-earth composure and common sense prevailed. The death blow to Maltrisia's political career was finally delivered in a person-to-person debate where she at last stood opposite Lord Stephen. Newspaper reporters filled the room, taking notes on every word that was uttered. Their talk would fill both the front page and the central pull-out pages of the city news the next morning. Maltrisia had launched into her usual anti-King's Law rhetoric.

"Ancient scripts are not the way forward for a progressive society," she said.

"Just because something is old and labelled as a 'script' (whatever that means) doesn't mean that it is automatically wrong," Lord Stephen countered. "Labelling laws and arguments in that way does nothing for true political debate. Ancient ways have kept societies safe for millennia; whilst there's many a modern ideology that has worked havoc in cultures over recent times. 'Modern' does not mean right and 'ancient' does not mean incorrect. This argument is quite flawed and without substance. You'll have to do better than that if you want to say anything of relevance in today's modern world."

"You and your King's Law followers disrespect the natural order of the ever-evolving political process," she countered. "You keep us entrenched in ideology rather than freeing our minds to follow more open ways."

"If to disagree means to disrespect, then every time political debate takes place, we all enter into disrespect," replied Lord Stephen. "We, however, don't manipulate our culture's language to enforce a political stance, as you do. Disagreement is healthy and wholesome. Without it we cannot wrestle our way through life's troubles and challenges. Disagreement, debate and consultation bring to the forefront of our corporate thinking the arguments that are necessary for us to tackle life; it is only by them that we clearly see the way forward. Making certain political ideologies 'untouchable' by calling them 'natural' or 'ever evolving' (and so giving them a high moral status that puts them above the right to be disagreed with) that is a road to disaster. There is nothing better for a culture than to be able to openly disagree. A healthy opposition makes a healthy society. Any culture which takes opposition away, by calling its opponents 'disrespectful' or by labelling arguments against itself as expressing 'hatred speech', is on a one-way trip to ideological lockdown and dictatorship."

"King's Law keeps us from enjoying the diversity of human opinion," Maltrisia cried out.

"King's Law facilitates opinion," Lord Stephen countered, "and when you talk about diversity, all you mean is variant expressions within your own closed political ideology. You're not diverse at all, simply expressing the same anti-King's Law stance from different perspectives within your own political framework and calling that 'diverse'. There is no such thing as diversity in politics," he added. "All political stances are exclusive and to say otherwise is to live in an ideological, delusional pretence."

Before Lord Stephen could say anything else, she then launched into a long justification for her political stance. She advocated her latest version of what was called 'Min/Max theory' – how to minimise your losses and maximise your gains. Then she flowed into 'gain theory', as she called it (the mathematics of cooperation and conflict) and declared that this failsafe ideology was now her underpinning political strategy which ran her new political system. This, she assured everyone, gave the average person a strong say in the running of the city. She then gave the example of the city's food production, energy and water supplies.

"We currently have just a few farming communities in charge of all our food resources," she said. "Along with this, much of our energy needs are still provided by a single reservoir turbine system and our complete water supply is delivered by a waterworks that no-one knows how to operate. It just sits amongst us, doing its thing, put together by the ancients who are now long forgotten in our culture. We're dependant on that which we do not understand and vulnerable whilst we do not publicly own all these areas of our culture. This is just one example as to why a

People's Republic will enable us all to have a say in how we operate and work together."

"People do have their own water storage units, kept topped up by our wonderful waterworks," replied Lord Stephen. "And on the matter of land ownership, you've been purchasing quite a lot of farming land over the last few years. Are you going to give it all up when your new political system comes into place?"

"Of course," she said. "I will happily give up my farming land and machinery for the good of this city."

"As long as you're in charge of the city at the same time," commented Lord Stephen.

"We will all be in charge, together," she added. "Only then can things run properly in this city without personal gain and selfish intent being at its heart. When we all have our say, everyone's needs can be met."

Lord Stephen pointed out that King's Law already provided all of those very things and that there was no need to restructure a society that already worked perfectly well. Then he turned on her, calling her political system closed, tilting power towards the few and how she would build a culture that would enforce change rather than accept opposition.

Maltrisia then took the debate onto a broader base where she vaguely outlined why her vision for a new political system would get the best deal for society. She talked about our current 'no-win conflicts' which King's Law permits and actively facilitates, whereby political stalemates can happen and all parties lose out. She said that her political model would turn general life impossibilities, classed as 'lose/lose' situations, into to 'win/win' for all."

"What happens to those people who will not agree with you?" Lord Stephen countered. "What happens if some will never agree with you and the changes you want to make, if they block what you want to do in the political arena."

"To gain the best in life for the many in the midst of small minority unwanted conflict, there is often a need for 'subservient cooperation'," she admitted."

"So you would enforce your political will if you found it necessary?" Lord Stephen enquired.

"For the good of all it may sometimes be necessary to force cooperation," she conceded.

"*Sometimes* necessary?" enquired Lord Stephen.

"Yes, sometimes," she replied.

"And who decides when those 'sometimes' occasions happen and how often they occur?"

"They occur when needed due to troublesome minorities," she curtly replied.

"I think the word 'dictatorship' and 'sometimes' do not mix," Lord Stephen added.

"I didn't use that word," Maltrisia said, her eyes almost flashing in irritated anger.

"You didn't need to," he flatly replied.

She quickly countered by stating that everyone in her political system would have a voice and, at the same time, we all needed to recognise the necessity to minimise the state's losses and maximise the state's gains. King's Law prevented such a thing. When challenged about how she would proceed with those who wanted to maintain King's Law she replied,

"We need to be continually evaluating the outcomes of those who do not want to comply with the will of the people and the will of the state; those who will not see the true options that are available to them. In the midst of those ideological no-win conflicts that King's Law causes us to continually face (where people will not bow to the will of the state and so create those lose/lose situations that naturally follow on from such stubborn attitudes) in such instances we would need to develop momentary suppressive political strategies to force cooperation. This would only be done for a short season, recognising the impact of the tragedy of commons that these small groups of dissenting voices are having on the rest of society who are toeing the line."

"So you would take away human rights," Lord Stephen stated. "You would lock us down to enforce your political model."

"Taking away the short-term individual interests of personal freedoms in order to ensure the long-term gain of the culture," she replied, "is the only moral option available to us. The state momentarily acting selfishly and against other people's rights in order to win for society is appropriate – because those who rebel, like little children, don't know what's good for them."

"You would take away freedom of speech, freedom of movement?" Lord Stephen enquired. "That doesn't seem fair," he pointedly added.

"We don't always have to play fair when in the end everyone, on some level, finally wins; society is better off without those troublesome King's Law voices within it."

"And what would you do with those troublesome voices?" enquired Lord Stephen.

"Well that's very simple," she replied.

"Tell us," said Lord Stephen. "We're all listening. How would your political model deal with them?"

"Those who oppose sensible change and the development of our culture into a better place of equality and diversity would need temporarily isolating and re-educating," she said.

"Where would that be done?" enquired Lord Stephen.

"In a safe place where they could learn," she replied.

"What if they didn't want to learn?"

"Well, they'd be encouraged to do so."

"And if they still refused to learn?"

"Then, due to their unwillingness to go along with the culture, they'd lose their general freedoms until they did learn," she said. "Co-operation always brings about freedoms," she added. "This is why we have prisons, to confine those who do wrong."

"Since when has political disagreement been a crime?" countered Lord Stephen.

"Oh we can all disagree to a certain extent," Maltrisia added. "We just need to deal with those people who oppose those central core values that run our culture.

Those who will not go along with the corporate voice of common consent, who oppose equality and are intolerant of our values."

"Putting *your* values above *their* values," commented Lord Stephen.

"Our joint values are there for everyone to share in," she replied.

"And you'd deal with these 'small minorities' as you choose to label them (though they might not be small at all) by putting them in a place of confinement?" asked Lord Stephen.

"Exactly, "she quickly replied. "A temporary place to relearn what is good and right and true. Education is such a wonderful thing and we all need the opportunities to embrace a more varied, broad and diverse curriculum."

"What do you mean by confinement?" asked Lord Stephen, ignoring her attempt at moving the conversation towards the topic of education. He sensed he was about to hit the core of Maltrisia's control mechanism. Pressing the point further he asked, "Where would they be confined?"

"In education centres," she flatly stated.

"To concentrate the mind?" he asked.

"That's right," she replied.

"Education centres to *concentrate* the mind," Lord Stephen echoed her words, as if thinking out loud. "What you actually mean is concentration camps," he added.

A gasp went up from the press when Maltrisia failed to answer this statement but immediately launched into a dialogue about greatness and the need to move away from being timid. She talked about the changing world that was on our doorstep, locally, nationally, and internationally and the political bigotry that kept them from moving forward in this way in order for everyone to be in a final, better place. Lord Stephen pointed out that the city had already gained a name for itself and that our trade deals with our current international partners were firmly in place.

"Branding people as being politically bigoted just because they disagree with you is not helpful," he added. "In fact it's quite irrational. Not only that, philosophically it's immoral and does nothing but spread political hatred amongst those who hypocritically call themselves morally superior. Your arguments are quite illogical and irrational," he added.

"Being what seems to be irrational in the face of reason can, at times, be the best way forward to teach people to behave in a different way," she replied.

"Not if it takes away the rights of the people groups who want to oppose you," said Lord Stephen. "You'll destroy the lives of anyone who opposes your vision," he added.

"A little political damage happens whenever there is great vision which initiates great change," countered Maltrisia.

"Damage!" replied Lord Stephen, he was clearly getting angry. "Damage! I don't call people who have lost the right to their lives, *political damage!*"

At the end of the debate, with great verbal skill, Lord Stephen summarised his opponent's words; showing them to be nothing more than control covered over by flowery, vague promises.

"It's the ability to say everything and nothing at the same time. To sound open, welcoming, full of hope and to present well-meaning promises whilst giving nothing away to anyone except options that will relieve them of their freedoms; all done in the name of personal liberty. Shouting freedom on the one hand and then sucking the life out of the political system to give power to the few to enforce change is nothing short of an insult to the intelligence of the hard-working families that make this city great! We're great because of where we've come from, governed by King's Law, not for where some ideological fantasy-chasing misfits want to take us in the future."

"You say that just to protect your wealth and privilege," Maltrisia countered. "You think that by birthright alone you have the right to rule over us all. It's easy to say the things you do when you've been born with a silver spoon in your mouth!"

"You're very wealthy too," he replied. "Not nearly as wealthy as I am," he continued, "yet I can guarantee that I invest more money in the people of this city than you do, along with so many of my friends and political colleagues. You're full of ideological superiority. It's very easy to spend other people's money and pretend to be moral; history has proved that to be the case time and time again. Such a system does not allow a culture to grow up but keeps itself bound over to centralised control that takes away people's choices to give. I'm a practical man who makes sure that solutions for our people's wellbeing are effectively put into place on a daily basis. Open ended and vague ideology never helped anyone. The enforcement of so-called equalities from a centralised state always leads to the loss of human rights. King's Law facilitates the strong helping and protecting the weak."

"In my political model there's no such thing as weak," she retorted.

"In your political model everyone becomes weak who wants to oppose state rule," replied Lord Stephen.

A momentary handshake at the end of the debate ended it all, but Maltrisia's face was as sharp as iron as she exited the stage. Off she went home and the thunder of her temper let itself be heard as soon as she entered her house. Domestic servants either made themselves completely scarce or rushed quickly to her every whim. She threw items around the room and bellowed at anyone who even breathed out of place. Finally her husband came down from his reading room to find out what all the commotion was about. Seleucia also had timidly walked in to offer some support to her mother, but only from the safe distance of a chair close to the stairway that facilitated a quick exit from the room if it was needed.

"Sit down my dear," Jacob said.

"I will not!" she yelled back. "I will have no rest until that Pluggat traitor is dealt with!"

"Lord Stephen may be a narrow minded, old fashioned, snooty traditionalist," said her husband, "but he's not a traitor."

"If I say he's a traitor then he's a traitor!" she shouted back at him, throwing a small porcelain cup in his direction.

Jacob ducked the object, which smashed on the floor behind him. With a quick sideways swish of his hand, he signalled to his daughter to keep her distance and slowly he approached his manically strung wife.

"I hate him," she yelled. "I hate him, I hate him, I hate him!"

"He's a very gifted man and a difficult political opponent," said Jacob.

"I want him gone," she said.

"Well you can't just make a man disappear," replied Jacob.

Maltrisia glared at her husband, but there wasn't anything at hand to throw.

"If you want to remove his influence from this city you'll have to think again," said Jacob. "Like you, he has a science background but, unlike you, he's also a seasoned politician."

Maltrisia sat in a heap on her chaise sofa. She kicked off her shoes, curled up her legs and put her head on the sofa's arm. Jacob approached his wife now that she'd adopted a more subdued, almost foetal position, in which to rest. Leaning in towards her, Jacob spoke with a very calm but forthright tone.

"You'll have to come up with something else if you want to win this fight."

"Go away," she replied. Her mood had swung from hyper hysterical to deeply depressed.

"Every man has his weaknesses," Jacob replied. "You're just looking in the wrong place. Find his weak points and then go to work on them. It's as simple as that."

Jacob left the room whilst Maltrisia lay there with her eyes closed, her knees now tucked up to her waist and one hand on her forehead, as if trying to stop some all-consuming headache from troubling her mind. Finally she sighed and repeated her husband's last words, "weak points," she said. "Weak points, weak points, weak points. What do you do with a man who has no weak points."

"Everyone has weak points," Seleucia chipped in.

"Not this one!" retorted her mother. "Oh how I hate him and his whole snooty family."

"They are quite annoying," said Seleucia, with a snort. "They'll be even more annoying when the peasant girl that Richard married gives birth. One more family member to be annoyed with."

Maltrisia pondered her daughter's words.

"Weak points," she said again, but this time sitting up as if she'd had some kind of revelation.

"What is it?" Seleucia asked, seeing that her mother's attitude and mood had suddenly changed.

"Everyone has weak points," she said, thinking out loud. "And his weaknesses are nothing to do with his politics."

"What then?" asked Seleucia.

Maltrisia called in her butler and told him to bring her a drink and a writing desk from the other room.

"What are you doing, mother?" asked Seleucia.

"Evening up the odds," she replied.

"What?" Seleucia enquired. "What do you mean?"

"Oh do be quiet," said Maltrisia, still working through her idea.

Once her drink was in her hand, she began to scrawl down instructions on letters, all to be sent out to influential people within the city.

"He feels deeply for people and this so-called noble trait can be used in our favour I think. Grief will stop a man in his tracks," she added.

"Do we change our tactics?" asked Seleucia.

"No," her mother replied. "We hold our course. We do everything that we've been doing. Let him think that he's won. Let him think that we're just die-hard losers who won't give up."

Maltrisia sipped her drink and stared off into the distance.

"Let's see how much strength he really has," she finally said, almost in a whisper.

After scrawling some more instructions into the letters on her desk, she sealed them and, without even looking up at her daughter, held them aloft for her to take out of her hand. Seleucia quickly took the letters and waited for her orders.

"Don't give these letters to anyone except the person they are addressed to," she said. "Hand them out yourself, in person," she added.

"What are they about?" enquired Seleucia. "How are you going to bring Lord Stephen down?"

Maltrisia relaxed back on her couch, sipped her drink and closed her eyes.

"I want to know about his son, Richard," she said. "I want to know what he does, where he goes, if he has any habitual behaviours. If there is anything to be known about him, I want to know it."

"That sounds very promising," Seleucia replied, a slight giggle in her voice.

Maltrisia put her feet up and rested the ice-cold drink against the side of her face. Enjoying its frosty touch, she felt the heaviness of the day melting away.

"I shall weave a web that no mere man can survive," she finally said. "Conquer from within," she added. "There's no better way to destroy a man, than through his very self. Perhaps today is not such a loss after all."

Chapter 12 – The Turning of the Tide

A couple of weeks went by with Maltrisia continuing her public speaking schedule. Her die-hard fans stuck with her, despite her public humiliation by Lord Stephen.

"There's a certain level of support that some politicians can always expect to be loyal to them," Lord Stephen had once commented. This seemed to be the case. A slight change of tack on Maltrisia's part, however, meant that she was now appearing in smaller venues which were more personal to her audiences. This also gave the impression that the room was always packed out with people wanting to hear her speak, though if you attended her rallies you could be sure to see the same faces again and again. Her latest venture was in an old school house for girls. There she had invited many of the school's young teenagers to attend her meeting and also many of the younger members of the city's social groups who, once she had delivered her talk, would be invited to debate with her the many things that she had said. The school saw it as a great opportunity to further their young people's educational experiences, as well as to heighten the school's profile within the city.

So on this day, when Maltrisia delivered her speech, the upper room where the debate was taking place was packed not only with school pupils but also with young people from across the city, along with the general public. On this same day Richard had been attending his weekly young gentleman's club. Many of his school friends were there and, as usual, they'd been having a boisterous time talking, laughing and eating. After his weekly social chat was over, Richard made his way back down the streets of Clearwash City. On this occasion Erepsin wasn't with him. He'd been called away, or taken away, by some messengers from his mother who said she needed his help on some urgent family matter. So Richard walked alone, following his normal route down familiar streets. It was a hot afternoon and he hung his jacket over his shoulder to help what breeze there was to cool him a little. Life was good and he looked forward to getting back home to be with his wife and family.

His route took him initially down the central road that ran through the city and then through several back alleys. Finally he rounded the corner of a building and found himself in the vicinity of Maltrisia's political rally, where Maltrisia was in the process of delivering one of her speeches. As Richard cornered the back of the building, he was surprised to see Seleucia, standing alone, outside the school room's back door.

I'm just taking a break from one of my mother's speeches," she said, as he passed by.

"I can understand that," he replied, and continued to walk down the road, not wanting to engage in any obligatory social pleasantries that were required from him.

"At least we libertarians know what's good for the people," she added.

"I'm sure you think that you do," he replied, without turning his head.

Richard continued to walk on, quite contemptuous of Seleucia's attempts to engage him in conversation.

"How's that servant girl wife of yours?" asked Seleucia, half shouting her words down the street so that they could be clearly heard by anyone in the locality.

Richard stopped.

"What!" he said, half turning towards Seleucia.

"Just asking and enquiring about your growing family," she said.

Richard very purposefully put his jacket back on. He was about to walk away when Seleucia added,

"I was just wondering how that lowly wife of yours was," she continued. "You know that girl you married to prop up the family servant numbers."

Richard turned to face Seleucia. He walked over to her with a reddened neck that showed the offense within him.

"Just be glad you're not a man," he said. "If you were a guy you'd get what you deserve."

"Go ahead," she said.

Richard stared at her mocking face.

"It's not right to hit a woman," he finally said. "Not even someone like you."

"I'm not afraid of you," she said, keeping up her mocking stare.

"You're not worth it," he eventually replied, and turned to go.

He hadn't walked more than ten paces when Seleucia shouted out again.

"You'll have another servant too I presume when that baby of yours is born. You'll be teaching him how to scrub the floor by the time he's two. You Pluggats really know how to get underlings into your self-serving family."

That was it, Richard snapped. Seleucia made her escape by quickly nipping through the door she was standing against. Richard ran through it to grab her, not quite knowing what he was going to do after he'd laid hands on her. The room he entered, however, was darker inside than he'd expected. To his right was a stone staircase which wound its way up to the lecture hall where Maltrisia was speaking and to his left an open archway that led into the shadows of a room filled with various junk. A sniggering giggle came from somewhere behind the large boxes and discarded furniture. Richard moved a little closer, determined to get his hands on Seleucia. He made his way round several containers and assorted junk till he could see a shadowy figure standing against the far wall. Walking over he recognised the outline of Seleucia's facial features.

"Well," she said. "What are you going to do?"

Richard hesitated. The agitation within him had calmed just enough for him to get control of himself again.

"I," he said, but no more words came out.

"A little something for you," she replied.

At that moment something, or someone, hit Richard from behind on the back of his head. He dropped to his knees and then flopped to the floor. Turning the dial on a small device that lay in and amongst the junk, Seleucia and her accomplices quickly exited the room. Seconds later, BOOM! The back part of the building blew apart, demolishing it completely and burying Richard in the rubble.

When the blast happened Maltrisia was still in full flow, spewing out verbal challenges to King's Law. The room almost instantly filled with smoke and all was chaos. People in the street outside looked on in terror as part of the building collapsed and, once the debris had settled, they began to frantically dig through the rubble to reach the victims inside.

Two young people had died in the stampede to get out and numerous others were injured. Maltrisia's supporters whisked her off and rumours abounded as to her condition. It was only later that evening that the report came back that she was alive and had suffered only minor injuries and facial scarring. The newspapers, however, were not front paging Maltrisia's troubles. They were filled with the fateful news that Richard was dead. His body had been found in the late afternoon and pulled from the rubble. Lord Stephen had been to the scene to collect him and accompanied the carriage in which his son was taken to be temporarily laid to rest before burial. Shock waves were sent throughout the city.

In the middle of this trouble the city governor came out of hiding. He quickly found himself a prominent role in investigating the cause of the explosion. It was determined that it was a deliberate act of sabotage. Later that same day an anonymous letter was delivered to Maltrisia's home whereby a King's Law organisation, calling itself 'The King's Liberty Group' took responsibility for the explosion and threatened Maltrisia with death if she continued her political activities. In a public speech the city governor read out the letter and then said,

"It is my opinion, based on the evidence found and upon the receiving of this letter, that this dreadful event was not an accident! I have to share the sad news with you that there are those in this city who are not content with mere words to express their opinions on how we should live. They have moved from endorsement to enforcement. This explosion was nothing short of an assassination attempt upon the life of our most excellent Maltrisia Ville. Whether you agree or disagree with her stance is not important. The main thing to note is that all have the right to speak and all have the right to take part in common debate. The young lives that have been lost today and the others that have been forever damaged have paid too high a price. This violence must stop and it must stop now!"

Late that night Maltrisia stood on the front steps of her town house and condemned the attack. She vowed that she would continue her work in order to bring stability to the city. She said that the political process would not submit to such deadly tactics and that all such intimidation would be overcome by the brave souls within the city who, like her, would not bow their knees to aggression. When questioned about the death of Richard she said,

"Obviously our hearts and prayers go out to the Pluggat-Lynette family who are suffering so severely at this time."

The next day another anonymous letter was sent to the governor, saying it was from the King's Law Liberty Group. The message stated that Richard's death was an accident, a mistake, and that they regretted his death. On the same day, however, two more devices were detonated and then another three days later but thankfully no-one was hurt. Letters from King's Law separatists continued to claim responsibility for these explosions justifying their actions by claiming a divine right for King's Law to remain in place.

"This is the final straw," the governor reported. "We will not let our new freedoms and political debates be forcibly snuffed out by those who cannot or will not embrace them. In the light of this intolerant aggression we are initiating a temporary junta."

A 'Director of Public Affairs' political position was suddenly presented to the city populace as a solution to the problem. This political position would allow that individual to have sweeping powers in order to keep the city safe in a time of crisis. Before anyone knew it, the position was filled by the mayor himself. Using his new level of authority all public meetings were temporarily banned and a restriction on people's movements put in place. The once mayor and now Director of Public Affairs, however, had overestimated his influence. The city was not prepared for this level of lockdown and he lacked the resources and political personality to enforce it. In the end he employed groups of so call law enforcers, who turned out to be nothing more than gangs of overzealous, unruly young people, and these he sent out to roam the streets in order to keep them clear of people. In reality, however, they just added to the chaos that was already there. Street brawling broke out in response to their presence and the safe streets of Clearwash soon became a battle ground for rowdy behaviour. Another week went by with this partially enforced lockdown in place and then all eyes were turned towards the Pluggat-Lynette family as Richard's burial took place.

A grey and dull morning. The raindrops fell like pellets of lead onto the coffin. Bouncing off the polished charcoal-black exterior, each drop echoed as a constant reminder that Richard was gone. Emma buried her head into Georgiana's shoulder and wrapped her hands around her sister-in-law's elbow. The two of them huddled together for comfort and strength. The sound of the minister's voice was somehow dulled in the midst of the dream they were all living through.

The night before the family had gathered at the city cathedral where Richard's coffin had been placed for a final overnight vigil. There they had stood, shoulder to shoulder, seeking some comfort from each other amidst their corporate grief. Unbeknown to them, Erepsin had walked in and stood a little back from the group, looking on and sharing their pain. Then after standing in absolute silence for what seemed like a never-ending moment, the family turned back and went home. Erepsin stayed behind, however. He walked up to the coffin and placed his hand on it.

"Goodbye Mr R," he said. "Goodbye my brother," he added.

Once home, Emma went to bed, emotionally exhausted from the day. Being now very heavily pregnant, she needed to sleep. The little strength she had was gone and Georgiana sat next to her for a good time before she fell into her unsettled and anxious dreams. Later Georgiana came back downstairs to the family lounge to be with her mother and father. Lady Melanie sat at one of the small coffee tables which were scattered around the room and ran her finger around the rim of her coffee cup. Lord Stephan sat in an armchair, his head resting back and his eyes tightly closed; clearly his distressed mind was tormented with the loss he felt. Georgiana initially sat on the sofa with a book but couldn't concentrate. She got up and walked about the room, touching objects as she went, not knowing what to do with herself. Numbness clung to her and there seemed no way of escaping it. Life was surreal and the lack of Richard's noise in the house was deafening.

The front door bell went and the butler walked down the corridor to open it.

"Not more visitors," said Georgiana with a sigh, whilst running her fingers for the second time over a decorative silver mantelpiece clock.

"Probably more flowers being delivered," replied Lord Stephen.

Footsteps were heard down the corridor and then into the room came Erepsin. He walked over to a nearby chair and sat down in a lump. Georgiana scowled at him.

"What are you doing here?" she said, in an accusational tone.

Erepsin found himself put on the spot. "Well, I thought, I thought that…" He mentally fumbled for a few moments. "He was my brother too," he quickly answered.

"You're not family!" Georgiana bellowed at him. "You're not family! Not family!"

Momentarily there was a stark silence in the room with everyone caught off guard by Georgiana's sudden ferocity.

Georgiana, surprised even by her own outburst, walked over to the nearest sofa, buried her head in a cushion, and wept.

Lord Stephen sprang out of his chair.

"Thank you, Erepsin, for coming to see us," Lord Stephen said. He briefly took Erepsin's hand and shook it as if to say goodbye and then in the same moment guided him to the door.

"I'm sorry," Erepsin almost whispered to Lord Stephen. "I thought…"

"I know you are, and I appreciate your coming here today," Lord Stephen replied in a tone that acknowledged the comment but at the same time closed the conversation.

Erepsin glanced back at the sobbing Georgiana and, with tears in his eyes, tipped his hat and left.

Lord Stephen moved back into the room and went over to his daughter.

"Don't lecture me…" she began to say, expecting her father to tell her that she'd been out of line in the way in which she had spoken to Erepsin. He just put his arms around her, however, and hugged her whilst she wept and let out her flood of tears. There the three of them sat, on the sofa at the end of a long day, inconsolable in grief and with nothing else to do but cry.

Erepsin made his way down the street, his heart pounding, mind racing and a dagger through his already wounded soul. His hasty walk quickly turned into a run. Knocking into person upon person, he pushed and shoved anyone and everyone out of the way. Finally he was home. Running up the steps of his parent's luxurious town house, he ignored the welcome of the family butler and headed straight for his room. Maltrisia saw him speed past her and followed her son to find out what was wrong. When she entered the room, he was sitting on the edge of his bed with his face in his hands. His mother came to sit near him.

"What's wrong?" she asked, in a cold tone.

"I hate that Pluggat family," he eventually replied.

"Finally something that we agree on," replied his mother. "The less time you spend with them the better in my opinion."

Her words, however, didn't reach the spot in Erepsin's soul that needed to be touched.

"I don't mean I hate them like you do," he said.

"Whatever it is that's causing you pain, you'll get over it," she said. "Get some new social chums," she added. "There are plenty of school pals you can associate with from your past."

"Not like Richard," he said. He cried for a while longer and eventually wiped his eyes.

Maltrisia picked some tissues out of a box and began to wipe her face. She had had a long day and her son's bawling wasn't helping her to relax. Taking off her makeup to reveal that there wasn't a scar on her face after all, she sat down again next to her son.

"You're not hurt," Erepsin said, seeing that the scarring on her face was only makeup.

"That's right," she replied, a little awkwardly. She'd forgotten that her son was not part of her scheming and Erepsin's distress had distracted her from that fact.

Maltrisia eyed her son. She picked up his hat and toyed with it, running its rim through her fingers.

"Why are you not hurt?" he asked.

His mother didn't reply.

"Why is that scar on your face fake?" he persisted.

"Many things aren't real my son," she replied. "That's something you're still yet to learn."

"What else isn't real?"

"That's for you to find out," replied his mother. "Time for you to grow up, my little boy," she added. "Life is never what it seems."

Reflecting on his mother's words and the fact that no part of her was hurt, Erepsin asked, "Was the assassination attempt not real?"

His mother paused for a moment, wondering how to continue the conversation.

"I was never in any danger," she finally conceded.

"You knew it was going to happen?"

"It was planned," she replied.

"What was planned and by whom?"

His mother sighed. "Everything," she said. "Everything that's happened over these last few weeks has been planned," she finally admitted.

"Planned!" he said again.

"Yes, that's right."

"Was Richard planned?" he asked.

Maltrisia said nothing.

"You had him killed?!" Erepsin enquired.

"You really do need to know how to play the game of life," she replied.

"He was my friend!" A yelp of pain wailed out of Erepsin, petering out into a whimper as the last word left his lips.

"Friend!" his mother remarked. "My dear, pathetic little boy. Are you still living in that imaginary world where you have friends? We take what we need. We dispose of the rest," she added, dropping the hat onto the floor.

Maltrisia examined her fingernails for any signs of imperfection, more interested in the quality of her last manicure than her son's distress.

"If you are to succeed in this life you will have to learn to be tough," she said. "The strong rule the weak," she added. "Right now you're acting like a baby. Your snivelling and whimpering attitudes show you still to be a mere boy. A child without personality, without meaning, without value; a pathetic, blubbering wimp who has no hope and no prospects. Grow up my boy and face life for what it is."

Erepsin began to hyperventilate as the reality of the situation dawned on him. His thoughts danced around his mind. The loss of his friend, his rejection by Georgiana to be a part of a family that he'd always seen himself as being a member of and now the news that his mother was responsible for all their grief. He glanced about the room and saw a glass of water nearby. His mind entertained notions of throwing the liquid over her. In those seconds Maltrisia read her son's facial expressions.

"Don't even think about it!" she shouted.

Standing up, she poked him in the chest.

"Don't think for a single moment that I won't have you cut down and disposed of before you can blink, be you my son or not. You toe the line like everyone else," she added.

With those words she left the room. Calling a household servant to her she said, within Erepsin's hearing, "Watch him! My son does not leave his room tonight!"

The following day the funeral took place. The streets were packed with sympathisers. The Pluggat-Lynette family had touched the lives of so many people that this corporate show of compassion and grief was quite overwhelming. The cathedral was packed with mourners, not only with local dignitaries and political allies of Lord Stephen, but also friends of the family such as Uncle Jack. The solemn occasion flowed seamlessly as person upon person paid their tributes to Richard.

Erepsin was greatly pained not to be able to take part. He wanted to stand up and talk about his friend. He was forced, however, to watch the funeral from a safe distance. It wasn't that he was deliberately giving Georgiana a wide berth for fear that she might add more to his pain. He found himself shut out from everything and everyone because Maltrisia had assigned some of her household servants and political supporters to keep Erepsin out of trouble; which meant to stay with him throughout the day, to physically surround him and make sure he didn't speak to anyone. So he watched everything unfold from amongst the crowds as if he was a 'nobody' to the Pluggat-Lynette family; at the same time continually feeling the encroachment of his mother's supporters. It sickened him to see his mother attend the funeral along with all the other hypocrites who faked their distress; their false tears and solemn faces turned his stomach and filled him with a rage that he could hardly contain.

By the end of the day he just wanted to be away from it all. As he moved through the dispersing crowds, he made a sudden bolt for freedom, quickly shaking off his so-called bodyguard by giving them the slip through the maze of back alleys that were common in Clearwash City. Then he made for the hills. He ended up near the local reservoir. There he sat, looking down onto the city with the evening breeze caressing his face. The gentle touches of the wind was the only comfort he'd received that day.

"I'm all alone," he said to himself. "Erepsin, you're the only person you can rely on." In those moments he took an oath, an inner vow. "I will never trust anyone ever again," he said. "You live for yourself now. You make what you want of life. Be loyal to no-one Erepsin, only to yourself."

Chapter 13 – Watch the Fire Burn

It only took one day to pass after the funeral for protest groups to reappear on the streets of Clearwash City. Their banners were filled with anti-violence and anti-King's Law slogans. Maltrisia began her speeches again, despite the so-called political lockdown that was in place.

"King's Law has prevented us from becoming who we truly are, who we truly want to be. It is those traditionalists who keep us locked in the past," she said.

The new Director of Public Affairs also added to the political conversation.

"Time to start arresting those who will not enable our culture to develop and grow," he said. "Time to stop those who are responsible for this violent restraint, who take away our freedom to choose our own destiny."

Then he added, "In the light of current aggression from King's Law supporters, I have been left with no alternative but to ban King's Law rallies in the city. All movements of King's Law supporters are now restricted."

This did not go down well. There were many politicians who claimed that the King's Law Liberty Group, whoever they were, did not represent them. Despite the ban, other political rallies began in support of King's Law and clashes began to take place between the warring political parties. As the weeks went by the scenes grew ugly as the militancy on both sides of the political divide deepened. The rhetoric grew sharper as both sides claimed the high moral ground.

"It's time to clean out the house," Maltrisia preached. "Time to wipe away the grime and the scum. We need a deep cleansing of our culture. Just as the kidneys filter out the contaminants, so too we need to rid our culture of the toxins that pollute its purity."

Georgiana read the city newspapers at the breakfast table as the political story unfolded.

"'Ancient scripts,' that's what they're calling the old King's Law," she said. "Anyone disagreeing with the new political ideology is being branded a 'loyalist bigot' who is opposed to the new 'freedoms' as they call them."

"I don't want to hear it," replied Lady Melanie.

"Just because something is old doesn't automatically make it untrue, but that's the push of the new political order. They've taken the idea of kingship and made it mean tyranny; very clever piece of spin really."

"Georgiana, I don't want to hear it!" replied her mother.

"Untouchables they are," she continued. "Dad will have to get involved again soon," she said. "Otherwise it's all going to be over."

Her mother, however, didn't answer.

The weeks went by and things went from bad to worse. As the unrest continued to grow, the streets became tense and fraught with emotional support for both sides of the political debate. Out of frustration, riots had begun and there seemed to be no stopping them. Fuelled by the 'traitor' and 'scum' rhetoric of Maltrisia, her anti-King's Law movement saw buildings trashed, shops looted and, at times, roads barricaded. The city military had on one occasion been called in to clear the streets and it was very possible that their presence might be needed again. It became clear that their main targets were King's Law strongholds. The city slipped into complete turmoil and seemed on the brink of civil war.

It took a visit from Uncle Jack to stir Lord Stephen back to life. Perhaps he just needed a friend to talk to. Whilst the city streets were in turmoil, the pair of them went off for a long walk, from early morning to the time when the evening shadows had begun to form. Across the hills on the outskirts of the city they went, stopping and talking as and when Lord Stephen felt he had the need. Uncle Jack had packed a good amount of food in his rucksack and there were plenty of springs on the hillside from which they could drink.

As the evening breeze rolled in from the desert, taking its chill across the city, both men stood on a hilltop next to the city reservoir.

"I don't know if I can do it," Lord Stephen finally said.

"We're not left with many options," replied Uncle Jack. "You do have the resources to get yourself and your family out of the city if you want. No-one would blame you for doing that."

Lord Stephen didn't answer. He gazed at the setting sun and wished the serenity of the horizon would somehow invade his shattered world.

"I will not be driven from my own home," he finally said. "But I don't know what I can do now. It all seems out of control and hopeless."

"Maltrisia certainly has stuck her knife in the political process whilst you've been away," said Uncle Jack. "Under the circumstances you're bleeding like any other man would. But a broken man in my view is always the best man for any great task. He's not there for his own glory and he'll make decisions based on what's right rather than what's convenient. She thinks that she's done enough to politically kill you. Personally I think she's primed you to be the very thing that saves this city from disaster."

"It might not end well, Crispus," said Lord Stephen. "We could all end up dead."

"Better a dead lion than a chained and caged animal, put on display for other people's contempt," came Uncle Jack's reply. "We don't have a choice," he added. "This whole mess wreaks of Maltrisia. She's woven a web of deceit and is riding a populrist tide of emotional triumphalism."

"And what does Jacob, her husband have to say about it all?" asked Lord Stephen.

"From what I hear, I think he's a prisoner in his own home," replied Uncle Jack.

Lord Stephen let out a long sigh as he gazed across the city.

"You're the only one in this city that can turn the political tide now," continued Uncle Jack. "I hate to put it on you, but the future wellbeing of Clearwash is now in your hands."

"That's too much for any man to bear," commented Lord Stephen.

"You're not alone," Uncle Jack pointed out.

"What if I fail?" Lord Stephen asked. "What if my actions lead to war?"

Uncle Jack shuffled on his feet.

"No-one is in favour of war. Only a madman wants military prestige at the expense of others. But if other people's freedom requires it, then military options may be the only moral choices open to us."

"I'm not a warring person," replied Lord Stephen. "I'm a man of peace."

"There are always alternatives to war," said Uncle Jack.

Lord Stephen cast a glance as his friend. "Such as?" he asked.

Uncle Jack paused for a moment. "The removal of essential resources," he finally said.

Lord Stephen pondered the idea.

"We are in the middle of a desert," Uncle Jack pointed out.

"True," replied Lord Stephen. "So true."

As they spoke the floodgates to the reservoir opened and the water poured through them, turning the turbines that generated power for the city. The sound of the rushing, gushing water filled the air and somehow it began to wash away the cares and troubles of yesterday.

"Let righteousness flow on like a never-ending stream," said Uncle Jack, quoting an old proverb.

"And if I can't turn the political tide?" asked Lord Stephen.

"Then yes, we'll have to resort to more forthright means," came the reply. "This political beast has shown itself up for what it really is," he added. "If it won't give way to sensible debate and continues to destroy all that we hold dear, then it will need caging and killing," he said.

"I'm not a soldier, I'm a talker, a debater, an arguer, a person who reasons things through. I can't start a military fight."

"If it comes to a time of military intervention, then I'll take the lead," replied Uncle Jack. "Until then, you have to take charge."

"And you'll be with me all the way?" asked Lord Stephen.

"All the way," replied Uncle Jack. "I've lived out most of my years now and to be honest, I've not had much purpose for decades. Entertaining the city once a year doesn't cut it for me. My time in the military, as a mercenary, gave me a real sense of making a difference. It's something that I've sorely missed. I've been itching for a cause, a fight. I don't want to slowly decay into old age and finish life with a whimper. I'd rather die in the arena than fade into nothingness. You have my support right to the end, no matter what that end might be."

"Does your good wife think the same?" asked Lord Stephen.

"She's no friend of Maltrisia," replied Uncle Jack. "She'll never live in a place where we lose our freedoms; especially to a self-styled, self-egoed dictator. Anyway, she'll be glad that I've a cause to fight for, even if that fight is a literal war. When it comes to principles, she's just as forthright as me. You know what she's like."

Lord Stephen stood and watched the night sky gather its strength as the sun dropped behind the hills. Just as night time was unavoidable, so now he perceived the inevitable encroachment of the current political darkness upon his beloved city. There was nothing to do but embrace the change. The sun would soon set over Clearwash, but it would rise again and who knows what sort of day it would bring with it. Unless you live through the night, you don't get to decide the sort of day that unfolds before your eyes. Sleeping and hiding away only gives permission for your enemies to choose their day over yours. There were no other options for him, except to run the race set before him.

"I'll do it," he finally said.

"And I'll be with you," replied Uncle Jack.

With that the men gave each other a nod, a mental handshake if you like, and both felt a new sense of life and purpose within. Together they came down from the hills with a resolve, an all or nothing attitude. In those few hours their friendship had grown to a new level of trust and, as they parted, they were more like brothers than friends.

"Shall we meet next week?" asked Uncle Jack.

"No," replied Lord Stephen. "We'll meet tomorrow."

"That's more like it," Uncle Jack muttered under his breath.

The next day Lord Stephen was up with the sunrise. The night before he'd spent hours in his study, sending out messages to his political friends and allies, requesting their presence at his home. Now, the following morning, his mansion was abuzz with people all wondering what was about to happen. After shaking hands with each person they sat around the family dining table. Uncle Jack lit his pipe whilst Lord Stephen outlined his plans.

"After a long talk with Crispus," began Lord Stephen, "I've called you here to tell you that I'm willing to come back into city life."

The comment was met with much relief and enthusiasm.

"I'm not promising I can solve the problems we now face," he continued, "but with your support, I may be able to turn the tide in our favour."

"Of course you can," came one loud voice from the other end of the table.

"We know you can," said another.

For the next few moments, comments rang out from the group until Lord Stephen signalled with his hand that it was time for the compliments to stop.

"I see that you have more confidence in me than I do," he said. "Well, we'll see what reality really is, once time has gone by and we've initiated our plans. Until then we need to keep clear in our heads that nothing is certain."

"Very true," said a ginger-bearded, balding man - sitting on Lord Stephen's right. "Let's not put an unnecessary burden on our friend. We are all here to work towards a common cause and no single person has the answer to our current troubles."

"Thank you, Tristram," said Lord Stephen. "Now," he continued. "I want succinct feedback from all of you about your experiences over the last couple of months. I don't want elongated stories, I just want the basic facts. Tell me what freedoms have been lost, what speeches have been made, who made them and how they've affected things. I want to know where and how the troubles have broken out; whose been arrested and where they're being held. Give me a detailed overview. By the end of this morning I hope to be fully up to speed with all that's happened. Then, this afternoon, we'll consider our options."

So the morning went on. Apart from a short break for refreshments and an opportunity to stretch their legs, they all talked and shared their experiences and perspectives until lunch time. Lord Stephen provided a buffet lunch and told everyone to take a break for an hour. During that time he conversed with Uncle Jack to clear his head, whilst walking around his rose garden on the outskirts of his grounds.

"Lady Melanie insists that you eat something m'lord," said the butler, who stood on the gravel path with a tray of sandwiches and a drink.

After taking a few bites to eat and a quick swig of his iced juice, he signalled to his butler that he'd had enough and wanted to be left alone. Uncle Jack decided to go back to the house to chat with the guests, to get a sense of how the morning had gone, and to also remove the tray of unfinished sandwiches from the butler's arms.

"I'll leave the tray in the lounge for you to pick up once I've finished," said Uncle Jack.

"Very good sir," replied the steward. "Shall I bring a bottle of port to accompany them?" he asked.

"Most certainly!" replied the big man.

Lord Stephen slowly walked the full length of his walled garden, often letting his gaze settle on the path at his feet or staring up at the sky. Finally he sat on a bench and closed his eyes. His mind was saturated with the stories and reports he'd heard throughout the morning. Contemplating his options, he reasoned through possibilities, problems and strategies; pouring his intellect into the creation of a way forward. Time slipped by, as the afternoon sky rolled its clouds in a continuous show of parading, cotton-wool structures.

"We're ready for you," interrupted Uncle Jack's voice. "Do you need more time?"

"No," he replied.

The two men walked back to the house and together took their seats. Georgiana had now joined the group, looking quite annoyed with her father. Their exchanged glances showed their mutual disapproval of each other's agendas; his disapproval that she had joined without asking his permission and hers, that he'd begun such an event without telling her and inviting her to be a part of it.

"Well," he began, "after listening to you all this morning, I think that the time for tactfulness has already come and gone. Maltrisia clearly has a set plan that she is executing with great effect. The local authorities are already full of political bias and this keeps the momentum with her. It seems, however, that much of the city populace are not content with her movement and how things are progressing. She's not riding a wave of complete popularity. Our message needs to be about losing our current freedoms to a people's republic. We need to create slogans that encapsulate that loss. We need pamphlets that carry a single message, reminding them of our great past, disassociating ourselves from this violent King's Law Liberty group and calling people back to their senses. We need to hit those intellectual targets and our movements need to be quick and hard. It must happen out of the blue to catch everyone off guard. The one thing we still have up our sleeve is the element of surprise."

"How do we get that message out?" someone asked.

"I'll write our message this evening, said Lord Stephen. "If we work the printing presses all night, we could have thousands of them available by the day after tomorrow. Can we do that?"

A couple of Lord Stephen's friends exchanged glances with each other and nodded.

"We can," they answered.

"Good," he replied. "And by the end of the week we'll flood the city with them. I'll pay the expenses of the printing press," he added.

"What about the ban on our movements as King's Law supporters?" asked Tristram.

"We'll create what looks like spontaneous speeches that take place on easily assembled platforms. Faceless people who can't be recognised and arrested but who all speak the same message."

"And what about you, Lord Stephen?" asked a man, sitting just to the right of Georgiana. "What part are you going to play? Surely you're not going to keep a low profile? We need your name, your personality, your moral character to help fight this war of words."

"You're quite right," said Lord Stephen. "I'm not going to live in the shadows, I'll be right there in and amongst it all."

"But if you deliver speeches you'll be recognised and arrested," Georgiana interrupted. "These make-shift, quick to setup and quick to leave speech platforms may work very well, but you won't escape if you try and speak from them yourself."

"Oh I won't be using those particular devices," replied Lord Stephen, trying to keep his attention fixed on his team rather than on his daughter. "I can't be seen to be involved in any activities that are illegal at this point in time."

"So how to do you intend to gain a high profile?" asked another. "The only way to get involved is to speak and if you're not going to be part of the quick speech programme, then how are you going to gain a space for your voice?"

"I shall speak at events that are completely legal," he replied.

"But the only legal political events that are taking place in the city right now are Maltrisia's rallies," came the reply from another member of the team.

"Then I will just have to gate-crash her party," replied Lord Stephen, with a wry smile.

Everyone laughed.

Lord Stephen lit a match and hid it's burning glow between his fingers. Using a magician's trick he let the flames dance in front of him, as if they belonged to the palms of his hands.

"She has lit a fire," he said. "Now let's see whether or not she's prepared to watch it burn."

Chapter 14 – The Brink of War

"You shouldn't have been there!" said Lord Stephen, once his guests were gone.

"Why not?!" came his daughter's sharp reply.

"I was in the middle of a confidential meeting and you suddenly decide, by your own whim, to gate-crash it and interfere."

"I wasn't interfering," she replied. "I was giving a valuable contribution to the discussion. Anyway, you should have invited me in the first place," she added. "You need all the help you can get."

"You have nothing to bring to that kind of meeting," he coldly replied.

Georgiana was galled by his statement.

"You think so little of me to say such a thing!"

Lord Stephen said nothing in reply.

Georgiana's mind whirled in the silence, trying to make sense of it.

"You think I'm naïve and inept!" she finally concluded. "You think that my connections, my efforts to become someone influential, a person who can make a difference in this city, you think it all nothing but personal playtime; a child's imaginary game that I play and that you entertain until your *little girl* grows up!"

"No I don't," said Lord Stephen, a tone of regret in his voice. "I don't think any of those things."

"Then what do you think? Because if you think otherwise, I don't see why I shouldn't be involved."

"I think you're a very capable young woman who has a great career ahead of her," replied her father. "But right now, in this situation, when we're on the brink of war, you're out of your depth."

"On the brink of war?" Georgiana echoed, a tremor in her voice.

In that moment, Lord Stephen saw that he'd let slip more of his thoughts than he intended.

"Yes," he finally admitted. "I think we're on the brink of civil war. I don't want you involved. Not because you're not talented, anyone can see that. Not because you can't contribute, you can - and did in the meeting today. I don't want you involved because I've already lost one child and I don't want to lose another."

A noisy hush lingered in the air whilst Lord Stephen's words were soaked up by the atmosphere.

"I would hardly describe myself or Richard as a *child*," she quietly replied.

"You don't understand," he said, and got out of his chair to leave.

"If war comes, it will affect us all," she said.

"If war comes, I'll make sure that all of you are out of here," he flatly answered. "You'll not see any of it! You, your mother, Emma, none of you will even be in the city if it gets that far."

"I'm old enough to make my own choices," she said.

"And I'm too old to take any more losses and still be of use to anyone. If I lose you, I can't do anything for this city!" he replied.

Lord Stephen turned to face his daughter. Right in front of her, Georgiana watched her father's countenance change. Momentarily his features withered and he seemed to her to be nothing more than a shrunken, wilted old man. She'd never seen him struggle like this before.

"I can't lose you too," he finally added, tears in his eyes. "What's left of me is so little of what I once was. If I lost you, I'd lose the will to live. I can only serve these people if I still have you, your mother, Emma and our grandchild," he said.

His last few words were spoken through gritted teeth. In that moment, Georgiana looked right into her father's soul and didn't have any reply.

"You're stronger than you think," she eventually said, but as soon as the words left her mouth, she immediately regretted them, dropping her eyes away from her father's gaze.

"You have no idea," he replied, and walked out of the room.

Later on that evening, Lord Stephen took himself away from everyone by retiring to his library. Lady Melanie, however, followed him there, wanting more of his company. They ended up sitting together on a high-backed leather chair, she on his lap, and his arms around her waist. For a while they just cuddled for comfort but eventually the subject of Georgiana found its way into their conversation.

"She takes after you," replied Lady Melanie.

"That's the problem," he replied. "I can't lose her," he added, in a distant tone.

Lady Melanie stroked her fingers through her husband's hair, kissed his forehead and then laid her cheek on the very same place, to put her head on his.

"I can't lose her," he repeated. "I can't. I just can't... I won't lose her. Not even for the sake of this city."

She continued to hold him tightly.

"Then you need to send us all away, even before it becomes clear what's going to happen," she eventually replied. "We need to leave and we need to leave soon."

Lord Stephen sighed. "You're right," he said, squeezing his wife's hand. The emotional scarring on his face showed his struggle at coming to terms with the letting go of his family. "She won't like it," he added.

"No she won't," replied Lady Melanie.

"I'll have to give her the job of looking after Emma and you. That way I can twist her arm and get her to do the right thing."

"And I shall play the part of a needy mother who can't cope without her," added Lady Melanie. "Then perhaps together we can move her in the right direction with some good old fashioned 'family obligation' and 'call of duty' responsibility talk."

"That may work," he replied, with an attempt at a half-smile.

A stilled, agreeable hush sat with them until Lady Melanie said, "When do you begin to stand up to all of this mess?"

"We begin the day after tomorrow," her husband replied. "I have a clear way forward for us to deal with Maltrisia, she's an easy political target to hit, but we still have to plan what to do if it all goes wrong, how we cope if war does break out. We begin that planning tomorrow."

"Then tomorrow, we also begin to pack and get ready to leave," she decided.

"How long will it take you to pack?" Lord Stephen asked, wondering how much time they had left before they would be separated.

"If we're going to leave properly we'll need to join one of the long-distance trade caravans," she said. "We'll need to use those dreadful horseless carriages to get across the desert and I'll have to pack a good amount of food and other goods to barter with once we're on the other side. I can't do all of that in less than four days," she added.

"Four days," he echoed.

She slid down her husband's lap to rest her head on his chest. Tears welled up within them both.

"What's going to become of us?" she asked.

"I don't know," he replied. "I really don't know."

The next day went by with Lord Stephen spending much of it away from the family home. He went off in the early hours with Uncle Jack. Together the two men travelled across the city in an unmarked, hired carriage; often stopping in a back alley or side street where both men would quickly disembark and hastily enter a nearby house, so as to not be recognised. Behind closed doors, meeting upon meeting took place as ideas were shared and strategies talked through; how to tackle the current situation and the tactics that they could employ if they had to face war.

Their meetings were just as much about asking questions as it was about trying to provide answers.

"Talk to the technicians," was one of Lord Stephen's mottos. "There are plenty of people in this world who make great sounding plans," he would say, "but if the people on the ground can't make it happen, then it won't work. Talk first to the people who you need to implement the job, rather than to the financial backers or political influencers."

Much of his time, therefore, in the early part of the day was spent talking about practical matters. It wasn't until towards the end of the day that he and Uncle Jack sat down with the political forces he was allied with. There he outlined the possible ways forward.

"The small armed force that we employ to defend our city is not large enough to enforce a political coup d'état," Lord Stephen pointed out. "Maltrisia doesn't have their loyalty either. However, there's enough ruffians on the streets and too many intellectually imbalanced and emotionally highly strung people for us to think that some kind of enforced political change could not at any point take place. We have to have plans for not only bringing back our culture into a safe place with a war of words, but we have to look at practical solutions to prevent some kind of forced takeover too, if that were to be attempted in some way."

"What do you suggest?" asked one member of the group.

"After much consultation with our friends today, to find out what's practically possible, we've concluded that the best way forward, if it comes to trying to stop an enforced takeover, is to hit the water supplies," replied Uncle Jack.

"Hit them?" came the reply.

"Shut them down," continued Uncle Jack. "That way we paralyse any sustained armed force that might be put together."

"Which water supplies are we talking about?"

"The main ones that supply the city," replied Lord Stephen. "Both the reservoir supply, which generates power for the city, and the waterworks."

The stunned silence that sat with them around the table spoke clearly of the immensity of the problem.

"We could all die if we lose those two supplies," came the answer.

"Yes I know," replied Lord Stephen. "We'd only switch the waterworks off, however, shut it down that is. That way we'd not shoot ourselves in the foot."

"What would you do with the reservoir?"

"Blow it," replied Uncle Jack.

"Blow it!"

"Yes, blow it. Puncture a hole on its western edge. That way the main wall remains in place but there's no water left behind to drive the turbines. Clearwash City would lose much of its power in a matter of days. As long as we held the entrance to the waterworks, we'd be in a position to stop an armed takeover."

"King's Law has prevented anyone from meddling with the waterworks for many generations," said another gentleman from across the table. "It is a self-automated water filtration and delivery system. It was built by the ancients and set in place to run for a thousand years. So why do you think it's right to begin to break one of our own laws now, laws that we're standing up for and seeking to defend?"

"That law was put in place for a time of peace," replied Lord Stephen. "This is different. We're not breaking a moral rule, simply a health and safety guidance directive. It's currently illegal to fiddle with the waterworks due to the fact that a whole city's wellbeing is dependent on its supply. If, however, the city population is being systematically murdered, then that changes things."

"How would you turn the waterworks off?" came the next question. "That place is beyond us. It's off limits to the general public. Very few people have access and no-one knows how it actually works."

"We've met with two of the caretakers this morning," replied Uncle Jack. "They're no friends of Maltrisia and they'll get us inside."

"But what would caretakers know about running that place?"

"They don't know anything," replied Lord Stephen, "but we do."

He picked up a large wallet that sat next to the table leg and placed it on the table in front of him. Unzipping the edge, he gently pulled out several sheets of large, folded parchment. He opened each peace and placed them side by side to form a plan-view picture.

"Blueprint plans of the waterworks," said Lord Stephen.

Several deep intakes of breath came from the committee members.

"Where on earth did you get those?"

"They've been in my hands for just over a year now," replied Lord Stephen. "Maltrisia isn't the only person in this city who uses connections. About a year ago one of the caretakers informed me that we had traitors amongst the waterworks research team. I heard that some blueprints of the building had been found and that they were for sale on the unlicensed market. They were going to be secretly sold to a city outsider, but my money was instantly available and I offered more for the purchase. So I managed to intercept the sale and I've had them in my care ever since."

"Why didn't you tell anyone?"

"Simply because I needed to try and find out who initiated the sale and to date I've not been able to do that. Also, by that time, I'd seen how fragile the city's politics had become and so I've kept these as an insurance policy; in case we ever ended up in the situation that we find ourselves in now."

"What do they tell us?" asked Tristram.

"They show how the waterworks feeds itself from water within the mountain," replied Uncle Jack. "They give detailed outlines of where the machinery is and how it works."

"We may not understand completely how the engineering integrates but we can clearly make out which parts do the job of feeding the waterworks with its supply," added Lord Stephen. "The plans also show the shut down and start-up procedures for the waterworks itself. We can shut the waterworks down safely without harming it."

"What's to stop Maltrisia and her supporters from simply turning it all back on again if we were to lose this war?"

"We'll have to sabotage the pump mechanisms within the mountain so as to make it impossible to start again," replied Uncle Jack. "We'll set charges deep within the mountain and boobytrap the very place where the waterworks gets its water supply. If they try to restart it without removing the traps, the motion of the internal pumps will set off the charges and will bring the whole mechanism down."

"Which means we'll all die," a committee member pointed out.

"It does mean we'd all have to flee the city," replied Lord Stephen.

There were various murmurs from the group who didn't like what they were hearing.

"The question has to be asked," said Lord Stephen. "Do we do nothing, walk away and let a dictator arise and take over, or do we ensure that this whole territory becomes unworkable and everyone has to leave. If we're all leaving, then the dominant aggressors might stop their agendas and look to their own survival if the city is thrown into crisis. That way we might all get a chance to escape with our lives."

"Do you really think it might get that bad?" asked another.

"We have to seriously look at every angle," replied Uncle Jack. "The blowing of the water supplies is our last resort but it may be necessary if we're to escape and live to see another day."

"We must not underestimate Maltrisia," added Lord Stephen. "The dirty tricks that she's put together are far worse than even I'd imagined. If our political fight back does not go well, then we'll have to consider the very worst if we are to ensure our own survival."

"If you put it that way," said another committee member, "then I do see the logic in your thinking. And is this all really possible?"

"Lord Stephen and I have talked to everyone today who would need to be involved in the series of events that would bring it all about. We can do it," said Uncle Jack.

Lord Stephen folded the blueprint plans in half, running his nail along the line of the crease to ensure a sharp depression in the page. Then he tore each page in two.

"From today onwards I shall split up these plans. Half will reside in my house and half at Crispus' residence. This will stop anyone except our resistance movement from being able to turn the waterworks back on again and will create one extra safety barrier to someone unwittingly blowing the charges in the mountain."

"And what if it comes to all-out war?" came the next question.

"If it comes to war from which we cannot escape, then at least one of us should be able to burn his part of the plans. That way no-one will ever have the full picture, showing how to safely restore our water supply. It will force everyone to flee the city and may open a door for us to safely get our families out."

"However," said Uncle Jack. "If we can both flee the city without destroying them, then we can meet up on the other side of the desert and, at some point, prepare a return when we know the city is empty. That way we can come back without any of our political opponents knowing and turn the water back on again. Then we'd secure the front gates and restart life with just King's Law supporters occupying our home."

This final message was greeted with general comments of cautious approval and so the meeting eventually came to an end.

It was late by the time Lord Stephen got home and his exhaustion was clear to see. The following day his political plan was executed like a professional military machine. Out of the blue, spontaneous speeches began to be made all over the city by highly organised King's Law supporters. They happened quickly and effectively. Before the authorities could be informed, a group would stand on a quickly erected platform, deliver its message, and then were gone; leaving behind leaflets in the hands of any who heard them. Fifty-two speech groups were simultaneously at work, supported by a legion of volunteers – quickly assembling their make-shift platforms to facilitate the speech. After the speech was delivered, the platform was ripped apart and each person responsible for its assembly bolted off into the side streets whilst the speaker fled.

City newspaper reporters, those who were sympathetic to King's Law, had been primed by Lord Stephen to photograph the events as they happened. They also had a full copy of the script that was delivered. The following day the newspapers were full of images of the speakers, their faces blurred out, along with a full copy of their corporate message. The headlines ranged from, 'City Flooded with King's Law Speeches' to 'Freedom of Speech Comes Back to Clearwash' or 'City Population Defy Illegal Intellectual Lockdown' and 'Over 250 King's Law Speeches made in a Single Day!' As impressive as this was, however, the front-page headlines were all about Lord Stephen. His gate-crash entry on one of Maltrisia's events was perfectly timed.

Maltrisia was holding a political rally in one of the parks, delivering her speech from a community pavilion. As she was discoursing, a whole set of banners were suddenly raised in and amongst the crowd. They had a variety of pro-King's Law slogans on them, along with pictures of Lord Stephen. Initially Maltrisia found their attempts at interfering with her speech a little amusing.

"Well," she said, in a mocking tone. "I can see that we've got an infiltration of King's Law supporters here today. Look at all those banners of Lord Stephen."

A jeer came out from much of the crowd in support of Maltrisia's words but that soon turned to annoyance when a chant began amongst the King's Law supporters. "Let him speak, let him speak," they said.

"Yes, well, I would love to talk to the poor man, but he's not been in public now for months and I don't think we're going to see him at any time in the near future," Maltrisia responded in a condescending voice.

Whilst she was talking, however, as if from out of no-where, Lord Stephen appeared from the back of the pavilion.

"It's amazing what a generous gift does," he later commented, when asked about how he got past the security guards.

He walked up to stand right behind Maltrisia and stood for a few moments whilst she talked about how much she missed Lord Stephen, hearing his voice and his opinions on life. It was only then that she sensed someone behind her. Turning round, she literally jumped with surprise.

"What!" she exclaimed.

In that moment, the space in front of the stand-alone microphone that Maltrisia was using became free and Lord Stephen stepped up to it.

"I'm so glad to hear," he said, "that I've been so badly missed these last few months. It gives me such pleasure to hear that one of my political opponents has so desired not only to see me, not only to hear my voice, but also for me to express the convictions that I have. So, in response to your invitation, I'd just like to say that there's nothing like King's Law for calling us to grow up as a culture and take responsibility for our own lives. The last thing we want is a nanny state, imposed by a People's Republic that would take away your right to own your property, your businesses and your hard-earned profits. King's Law preserves freedom of speech, freedom of self-governance, freedom of commerce and freedom of conscience. Life may be messy at times, as difficult issues sometimes need a lot of effort to resolve. At the end of the day, however, your life is your own. You're not owned by the state and you owe nothing to the state, except your taxes that benefit everyone. The ideological allegiance within you is yours and you're free to disagree openly with anyone you want to without fear of intimidation or arrest. Stay with King's Law and keep this city free from the tyranny of political dictatorship."

Then Lord Stephen paused, "Oh, and by the way," he added. "I don't know who these terrorists are, the ones who killed my son and caused so much havoc in our city. However, I must say that there's no proof that any of those letters which claimed responsibility for the terrorism actually came from real King's Law supporters. I've spoken to all of my political allies and all of them are full of disdain for those terrorist activities. Those actions could just as easily have come from People's Republic supporters, who just want to throw mud onto our political campaign. Real or not, however, true King's Law supporters are gentle, generous and always in favour of debate, not terrorism. We debate, we do not dictate!" he added.

Then Lord Stephen tipped his hat at the crowd and then at Maltrisia. To cheers from his supporters he waved and walked to the back of the stage and was gone.

Those few words sent political shock waves around the city. He was on the front page of every newspaper, "We debate, we do not dictate!" – was the main title that ran the story.

His hat tipping motion was the iconic picture in everyone's hands. The accompanying photographs in the newspaper showed a furious faced Maltrisia, yelling at the crowd and spitting poison as she vehemently condemned King's Law to the crowd. Her rage continued to burn as the King's Law supporters laughed at her attempts to gain back the momentum of her speech. So on the one hand you had Lord Stephen, tipping his hat, and on the other, Maltrisia yelling with a red face. It was clear to see who the seasoned politician was.

"You've done it Dad," said Georgiana, reading the newspaper the following morning. "You've stopped her in her tracks."

Lord Stephen did look very pleased with himself.

"It's gone far better than I'd ever hoped," he replied. "Must keep up the momentum," he added.

With that he was off to the debating chamber once more, to take his seat and pick up where he'd left off before all the troubles started. He'd arranged for the press to be there and again he delivered an excellent speech on the city's freedoms and why political change wasn't necessary.

From that day on, he was swept along on a tide of popularity. A broken man, one who'd suffered great loss, was back and more celebrated than ever. The rest of the week went by with newspaper upon newspaper backing Lord Stephen. His message, his dialogue, his character and his manner of speaking all came together to deliver blow upon blow to the new People's Republic movement. Riots stopped, slowly order returned and each day there came a sense of greater relief that the city had been saved from the brink of war.

Chapter 15 – An Unlikely Friendship

It was the very early hours of the morning. Hazy sunlight streamed in through the many windows that ran around the walls of an old, dusty reading room, one which had seen better days. The room was situated on the top floor of an old school house that belonged to the Pluggat family's country estate. There Georgiana sat with her face buried in a book. She'd gone there to get some personal space from the grief from which they all still suffered and because her father had banned her from accompanying him into the city.

"The worst might be over," he said, "but it's still not safe."

Lady Melanie had postponed her family's departure when her husband's success had quickly turned the tide in their favour. As the weeks went by, life had begun to settle and Georgiana knew that she had to get used to the new restrictions; she could not cause her parents unnecessary stress, even by being sociable. The possibility of her coming to harm could not be contemplated, so she stayed at home to rest, to be a comfort to her mother and Emma, and for the sake of personal space. To be honest, she really wasn't interested in city life anymore. It's hustle and bustle had lost its lustre. Life without Richard was still something that felt foreign, cold and raw. The silence that surrounded her and the book in her hands were all that she felt she needed to escape the realities of a world that, for her, had fallen apart.

After spending several hours alone, her solace was disturbed when the downstairs front doors briefly opened and then closed. Assuming that her mother had sent one of the household staff to give her a morning drink and some breakfast, as had often happened in the past, she almost didn't listen to the footsteps as they walked up the stairs and entered the room behind her. She didn't look up from her book either.

"Thank you," she said, whilst turning the page. "Just set the tray down for me next to the windows," she added, as the footsteps drew nearer.

"I need to show you something," a voice said, over her shoulder.

The voice caused Georgiana to jump out of her literary contemplation.

"Erepsin," she said, half turning round to speak. Then, thinking the better of it, she kept her back turned on him, feeling quite awkward and not knowing what to do or say.

"Why are you here?" she finally said, fumbling through the pages of her book, as if to give the impression that she was busy and didn't want to be disturbed.

"I need to show you something," he said.

The embarrassed hush that followed as Erepsin waited for her to reply was intensely uncomfortable.

"I don't think that you and I would find each other's company very pleasant," she finally replied.

"I'm not asking for your company," said Erepsin, his voice was cold and devoid of emotion. "I *need* to show you something."

"Show me what?" she replied.

"Come and see," he said.

"I'm not in the mood to see things," she replied, and tried to get back into her book. "You can tell me another time all about your latest fantasy 'make me rich' scheme," she added.

At first Erepsin didn't reply. "So that's how you really see me," he eventually retorted, more to himself than to her.

"I'm sure you'll make it rich one day," she continued. "In the meantime go play with your mates in the local bar and leave me in peace."

"Drop the rhetoric!" snapped Erepsin. "I don't want to hear any more of your flippant comments."

Georgiana glanced over her shoulder again and was taken aback by the forthright manner of Erepsin's words and his serious face.

"Just come and see," he added again, in a gentler tone.

"What do you want me to see?" she asked.

"Outside," he said, walking back to the stairway.

She nervously closed her book and followed him down the stairs.

He opened the front door for her to go through and, after stepping outside, she lifted her gaze across the skyline. There she saw a dirty haze resting on the city's north-western horizon.

"What is it?" she asked.

"The beginning of the end," said Erepsin.

"What?" she enquired.

"It's about to start."

"What is?"

"War," said Erepsin.

"I don't understand." Georgiana, mentally rummaged through her confused thoughts. "We may be in a political stalemate, but not war."

"That's what you think," Erepsin replied. "I know now why my mother took all that time out of society last year. She wasn't ill at all. She's been plotting all this time."

"Plotting what?"

"A complete takeover," he replied.

Georgiana hesitated, again casting her gaze over the skyline and seeing right before her eyes the pollution that was steadily filling the atmosphere.

"It's a pollutant," said Erepsin. "Her military machine is now ready and what you can see are the engine fumes from her newly created weaponry. They're ready to strike. She'll kill you all if she can't get her own way, I know she will."

"I don't believe that," Georgiana responded, wishing her own words to be true. "You were always one for over exaggeration."

"If you don't believe me, then you need to see it with your own eyes," he said.

"Why are you telling me this?" Georgiana asked. "My father and your mother have been at loggerheads for the last few months and you're choosing to side with us?"

"I have my reasons," he answered, looking a little uneasy.

Georgiana didn't like his reply and it was clear that Erepsin knew more than he was letting on.

"I need to talk to my father," she said, turning to walk up the long drive that led up to the Pluggat-Lynette family mansion.

"He's not at home," Erepsin yelled after her. "I tried to get to your father a few hours ago. He's in the city debating hall, but I can't get in. There are crowds and crowds of people surrounding the building and only members are being allowed entrance. That's why I've come to you," he added in a weary voice. "You weren't my first choice but, if you see it for yourself, then Lord Stephen will at least believe you."

"My father has banned me from the city," she replied. "It would devastate him if I came to any harm."

"Everyone will come to harm if you don't come along," replied Erepsin. "You, your father, mother, sister-in-law, everyone."

Georgiana looked up the long driveway to the courtyard gates that belonged to her family's estate. She wavered, torn between keeping her promise to her father and wanting to keep everyone safe.

"Show me what I need to see," she eventually said.

They walked quickly to the very edge of the family estate. There Erepsin had left his small carriage which now stood waiting for them.

"After you," he said to Georgiana.

"Wait," she said, pausing for moment. "How do I know I can trust you?"

Erepsin's delayed response didn't give her much confidence, clearly he'd not been expecting the question and not knowing how to react he finally said,

"I swear it!"

"That's not good enough," she replied. She was about to turn back when Erepsin took hold of her arm.

"I swear on my friendship with your brother," he added, staring her squarely in the face.

That was enough. Within minutes they were speeding along the road, as quickly as the horse could take them.

"Where are you taking me?" she eventually asked. "Why do I have to see it for myself."

Erepsin fumbled in his jacket pockets for some paperwork before giving Georgiana his attention.

"We're going across the city," he replied. "Into the agricultural zone."

"The agricultural zone?"

"Yes," said Erepsin. "You have to see it with your own eyes because otherwise you won't believe what I have to say and…"

"And what?"

"And I've provided a way out for you," he added.

"What do you mean?" she asked.

"I need to get you and your family out of here," he said. "Before it's too late."

"My father will never give in," replied Georgiana.

"I know," replied Erepsin. "That's why you have to see it with your own eyes. Once you see it, you'll be able to persuade your father to leave, or at least I hope you will."

"What is it I need to see?" Georgiana persisted.

Erepsin handed her the piece of paper that he'd just taken from his jacket. On it was a blueprint of an agricultural harvesting insect. These small robotic creatures were used to harvest small crops such as grapes or olives.

"It's just a harvester," she said.

"It *was* a harvester," Erepsin replied.

The horse's gallop took them along the southern edge of the circular road that ran right round the city outer circle. Running parallel to them on their right was the city canal, used to transport heavy goods from the city's western industrial zone and north-western agricultural fields. It was busy with traffic, like a main artery pumping life into the city, delivering the city's wares. Erepsin's horse seemed to stumble a little with the pace.

"Keep him going," he shouted at the driver.

With a crack of the whip the horse surged forward. As they went the landscape on their left changed from hills to forest to grassland and marshes. Slowly, after passing Uncle Jack's great mansion, the western industrial zone came into view.

"Whoa," shouted Erepsin. "Stop the coach!"

The carriage driver pulled tightly on the reins and brought the carriage to a stop. Erepsin jumped out to look over the canal. There he could see people on their boats talking, shouting and pointing to the water. Georgiana joined him to see what was happening.

"What is it?" she asked.

"There," said Erepsin, pointing at the water.

In and amongst the boats, a black liquid floated on the water's surface. Like a sticky pollutant, it clung to the sides of the boats that sailed their way through it.

"Looks like some kind of oil," said Georgiana.

"It must be mother's doing," he replied. "She's getting ready to strike. Come on," he added, "we've no time to waste."

Back in the carriage they sped down the road until there was nothing but marsh land on their left. Erepsin's driver guided them off the highway and onto the grass where the carriage came to a halt. Out Erepsin jumped, giving his hand for Georgiana to follow. Six horses, all saddled and ready to go, stood waiting for them alongside some of Erepsin's old school chums.

"The horses are rather large," he said. "I was expecting to be escorting your father when I set this up."

"I can manage," she replied.

"We'll have to travel quickly with no time to rest the horses on the way," he added. "Are you alright for riding at a good pace?"

"Of course," she said.

Georgiana soon found herself racing with horses on either side of her, all following Erepsin on her left. The pounding of the horse's hooves tore open the heavy turf, leaving behind a line of dark soil that was wet with torrential rainfall. The snorting of the horses' breath and the steady gallop with which they charged across the marsh brought the distant panoramic view ever nearer.

Eventually they slowed to a trot as the small company of riders approached the city's industrial landscape. The unofficial grand entranceway to what was commonly called the 'dirty district' was marked by the presence of two vast, red-bricked mills. With revolving, creaky waterwheels they stood opposite a group of grey factory buildings, smoke billowing out of their blackened chimneys. Together they made the corporate statement, "Welcome to the Gates of Grime!" This was the neighbourhood watch; the heavy guardians of the western wall. Clearly preferring their own company and, having created their own mini micro-culture, they stood aloof from the rest of the city. Like unruly, defiant adolescents, they insubordinately puffed and smoked their dirty fuel into the atmosphere, coughing it out in protest of Clearwash City's sparkling example of good health and tidiness.

Georgiana hadn't been in this part of the capital before. It wasn't a place she had actively chosen to avoid, she'd just not had the occasion to visit. The environment was quite alien and foreign to what she knew of her home. The drifting, grubby smoke and grey, thick smog, produced by the many manufacturing activities around her, tasted like a bland pâté; unfamiliar to her palate and quite indigestible. She would be very pleased once this part of the journey was over; brushing the smog to one side with a swish of her fingers had no effect whatsoever. She wished she'd had a good-sized handkerchief to tie across her face, but the only material at hand was a delicate piece of fabric for touching up makeup. Placing that over her mouth and nose gave a little relief but keeping it in place, whilst at the same time directing her horse and coping with it's up and down trotting movement, was something she struggled to do.

After passing into the industrial zone, Erepsin kept their route very tight, moving in-between and around grey, quarried stone structures, tall towers that belonged to smelting workshops and many elongated wooden sheds filled with tools, general stock and, I might add, the usual families of rodents who found those places the most splendid and hospitable hotels. In the distance, on their left, were the tin mines – set into the hills that sat just inside the great wall which defined the city's boundary. In front of them, on the horizon, were the woods and city parks that spanned the area between the industrial zone and the agricultural fields.

Through layer upon layer of industry they progressed. Erepsin took every opportunity not to be seen, quite the opposite to his normal behaviour. As they went, he would half wave at workers or briefly tip his hat in a friendly manner, as if they were on a jolly outing. He was clearly known here, which initially surprised Georgiana, but then again, she reasoned, he was a man to chase any economic opportunity. So why wouldn't he end up here, at times, with one or more of his many hairbrained money making schemes?

In time they left the industrial area behind and entered one of the city parks. Keeping to its very edge, they hurriedly galloped it's perimeter and finally passed between a tightly bunched cluster of elm trees. Whilst under the cover of this natural canopy, they followed an unmarked but clearly familiar trail. On and on they continued, pounding through bushes, weaving around brambles and hedges, leaping ditches. They scrambled up and down steep earthen banks, covered with a mantle of thick moss and through networks of small-interconnected wild flower meadows, laden with hardy shrubbery. After briefly dismounting and walking their horses down the side of a steep earthen bank, they remounted again and rode between the columns of one of the city's derelict aqueducts. A few hundred yards away were the iron gates that led to a woodland garden. This they circumvented, however, preferring to pass around the back of the woodland, close to the city wall.

At last the first fields that belonged to the agricultural zone came into view. Riding along the edge of a small section of woodland, they finally dismounted, left the horses with one of Erepsin's friends, and followed on foot the contours of land, keeping low in a ditch so as to not be seen.

"There," said Erepsin, pointing towards a large silver-grey building that sat just behind a set of glass houses. "In the engineering industrial unit," he added. "That's what I need to show you."

Gingerly, they made their way to the glass houses and, once inside, Erepsin seemed to relax a little.

"There's so many people involved in her scheme," he said, "she can't keep track of who's meant to be here and who isn't. Just act as if you know what you're doing and we should get away with it."

The glass houses were full of vegetable produce. Rows and rows of elevated tubs, full of plants, ran in long lines right down to the end of the building. From the ceiling other shrubbery hung from suspended bars, fed on liquid feeds that were delivered through rubber tubes, ensuring a perfect dose of their daily nourishment. It was like walking into a jungle, a 'hanging gardens' – full of vegetable delights. Here, much of the basic produce was created for the city to feed itself. Amongst the shrubbery, small, metallic insects buzzed. They were about the size of a man's hand and moved at great speed. Delicately they visited flowering plants to pollinate them, or picked fruits that were just ripe and transported them to a collection zone.

"These have not been altered," said Erepsin. She's kept some unchanged so that they can look after the city's food."

"What has she done to the others?" asked Georgiana.

"You'll see in a few moments," replied Erepsin, brushing aside an insect with the flick of his wrist.

He led them to the end of the row and then out of the glass house. Walking in-between groups of busy people, Erepsin smiled and continued to tip his hat as he passed them by. Moments later the group were at the foot of a metal stairway, leading up to the silver-grey building's backdoor. At the top of the steps an armed guard sat on a chair, legs crossed and clearly bored with his job but still ready to prevent any unauthorised entry. Erepsin, however, jogged up the stairs as if he owned the place, his feet clanging on the metal frame with every step. His friends followed on too, not leaving Georgiana any choice but to go along with the group who surrounded her. Without any hesitation the guard let them pass and closed the door behind them.

"Just one of my network 'school chums'," Erepsin said to Georgiana. "They're handier than you think."

Georgiana thought his statement a rebuke. She could see now that his network of friends were more than just a social group for a boy who didn't want to grow up. There was a measure of political weight in his connections, even if those connections seemed a little immature or unrefined.

Inside the unit was a corridor with doors set in the walls on both sides. Through the second door on the right they went and then down another short corridor to where a spiral staircase wound its way towards the ground floor.

"Guard the door," said Erepsin, to his three remaining friends.

He beckoned to Georgiana and cautiously began to descend the stair. Round they went for a couple of turns until the building's ground floor came into view. Erepsin knelt on the steps and poked his head over the railing. Georgiana crouched down beside him. From their vantage point they could see the room below. There were rows and rows of box-like machines, each of which contained molten metal at its core. Above the boxes were long chains, dangling from a central bar. Suspended at the end of each chain were what looked like circuit boards with cables and wires attached to them; some of which were live, every now and again sending out electrical sparks which shot across the room.

On each circuit board were metallic insects, the same as those which Georgiana had seen in the greenhouse. They were quite common in the agricultural industry, helping maintain the health of crops and harvesting the produce when the grains or fruits were ripe. These insects, however, were being modified. Every now and then a factory worker would use a pair of tongs to reach up, take an insect from its board and place it onto a mould that was pushed into the cuboid box. Buttons were then pressed and an automated process initiated by which the cubed machine would use its molten metal to add a new body part to the creature. It was a continuous process. Once the body part was made, up would go the insect, back onto the circuit board to receive updated programming on what to do with its new abilities.

"Why are they doing this?" whispered Georgiana.

"They're turning the insects into weapons," replied Erepsin.

Georgiana just stared at him.

"Each insect now has a sting," he said. "Look," he pointed as one insect was lifted from its mould and put back onto its circuit board. "It's just like the sting of a scorpion," he added. "One jab from that and you're done for. Three days ago one of my team observed some final tests from the venom that they're putting into those creatures. He watched them inject it into a pack of wild dogs that they'd trapped on the moors. Four out of five dropped to the ground within eight seconds. All of them were dead with a minute. Can you imagine what a swarm of those things would do in a war?"

"An army of hymenopteran," whispered Georgiana.

"Of what?" asked Erepsin.

"Insects!" said Georgiana.

"Oh," said Erepsin.

"How many does your mother have?"

"I'll show you," he replied, signalling that they should return back up the stair.

Once in the corridor, Erepsin hastily led Georgiana to the windows at the front of the building, all looking out onto the agricultural zone. There Erepsin pointed out a domed hanger, originally built as a grain store.

"That one is now an insect chamber," he said. "We estimate it can sensibly house over ten thousand of them," he added.

"Ten thousand!" echoed Georgiana.

"The chamber has been rewired and connected to the city's power grid to become a charging station where the insects are re-powered for action. We don't know how long they can operate before having to come back for more fuel. We just assume they can function for a good amount of time, perhaps hours on end."

"How many charging stations does your mother have?"

111

"So far, we know of around fifty other chambers which could be used for the same purpose."

"Fifty!" echoed Georgiana. "But that's..."

"Over half a million insects," said Erepsin, finishing off her sentence. "And those are the ones we know about."

"And she's going to use them to take over the city?" asked Georgiana.

"They're a swarm that will guarantee the outcome of the war," he replied. "Once she releases them, there will be no escape for anyone. Some of my team watched them being relocated in huge boxes first thing this morning. They've been positioned right across the fields. I'm sure they're about to be released. You have to get your father and family out, otherwise I know they'll be done for."

It only took Georgiana a few moments to process what she'd seen.

"We have to go," she said.

Erepsin nodded and signalled to his friends to open the door at the bottom of the corridor. Within less than a minute they were out of the building and back at the front entranceway to the glass houses.

"I have to leave you now," Erepsin said.

"Leave! Why?" asked Georgiana.

"I've got unfinished business to attend to," he replied. "My friends will escort you safely back."

With that Erepsin tipped his hat.

"Erepsin," Georgiana called, as he was about to leave.

Erepsin stopped in his tracks.

"Thank you," she said. "And, do be careful."

He briefly and affectionately took her hand.

"Don't mention it," he replied. "You watch out for yourself too. I know what you're like. If there's trouble about, you're normally in the thick of it. If we can survive the next few days, then I'll see you on the other side."

With those words he turned and quickly disappeared into the crowd.

Chapter 16 – A Mad Dash to Nowhere

Spurred on by the mission to rescue her family, Georgiana quickly retraced the route they'd taken that morning. Erepsin's friends took good care of her but, despite their kindness, the anticipation of war chased her across the countryside; anxiety growing within until she thought she was going to be physically sick. She wanted to stop to take a breather, to regather herself, but the danger that her loved ones were in kept her on the move.

As they left the industrial zone behind and the inner-city circle buildings came into view, she had her first decision to make; whether to go home and inform her mother and sister-in-law of the impending war or to seek out her father. It only took her a short time to make up her mind. Those in the greatest danger were in the heart of the city. Going home would delay getting the message out to them and she was quite sure that, once informed, her mother would not let her return to the city. So her first job was to locate her father, tell him her news and then return home.

The last report she had of Lord Stephen's whereabouts was that he was spending the day in the city's debating chamber. This ancient house of dispute sat on the edge of the main market square, opposite the presidential palace. The quickest route to this building was to cross a bridge spanning the canal near Uncle Jack's residence. From there she'd have to go on foot as the roads in that part of the city became too narrow in places for carriages and there were too many people in the streets for anyone to sensibly travel on horseback. She'd also have to make her way through the open market district, a maze of stalls, bargain booths, side alley boutiques and bustling shoppers, all on the lookout for a good bargain.

She kicked her heels into her horse and on they all galloped, racing across the marsh lands until they met the main road that ran alongside the city's inner circle canal. With Uncle Jack's residence coming into sight, the group stopped next to what was called Market Bridge. Dismounting, Georgiana tried to say goodbye to Erepsin's friends but they were having none of it.

"We've promised to keep you safe," they said, "and we've promised to stay with you until you're home."

Georgiana was quite surprised by their loyalty to Erepsin, so she gave way to their wishes. Two of them stayed with the horses next to the main road whilst the remaining two accompanied her.

"What's that?" one of them asked, peering over the side of the bridge at the water.

"Oil," replied Georgiana. "Erepsin thinks that Maltrisia's dumping oil into the canal."

Hurriedly the three of them crossed over and into the nearest street. Ahead of them was a narrow-cobbled lane and at the end of that, the first market square where lines and lines of market stalls stood, row upon row to welcome them with promises of unmissable, rock-bottom deals.

"The oil in the canal," said one of Erepsin's friends. "Why would she do that? Why would she..." but before he could finish his sentence, the reason became obvious. The first mortar shells of the war were suddenly fired from the agricultural zone. Together they whirred across the sky like a screech of yowling death. Landing haphazardly in and amongst the city buildings, it wasn't long before fire-burning debris found its way into the canal and set it ablaze. The flames quickly spread across the water as channel upon channel of the waterway began to burn. Soon there was a circular ring of fire burning right around the city inner circle, surrounding the city populace. As the flames on the canal licked up and around Market Bridge, Georgiana and her companions knew there was no way back to safety.

Down the cobbled alley they sped, but the market square had already become a place of chaotic mad-dash mayhem. Then there was the sound, a buzzing, humming, whirring noise that seemed to be echoing across the rooftops. Looking upwards, Georgiana could see hundreds of insects, whizzing through the air. It wasn't a huge swarm of hymenopteran, but enough to panic the already confused and unsuspecting public. The insects buzzed their way around the square, quickly scanning people's faces and clearly on the prowl for pre-programmed facially recognisable targets. Undoubtedly this wasn't the main horde of Maltrisia's insects, just scouts or maybe assassination hunters who were there to ensure a good first strike. Georgiana and her two companions quickly ducked under the canopy of the nearest market stall and then onto their hands and knees, shuffling and crouching to take refuge beneath the stall's metal framework. Together they peeked out from between the cloth sheets that draped down from the table they were under and waited to see what was going to happen.

Quickly unscrewing one of the market stall's metal legs and pulling it free from the rest of the table, Georgiana found her hands trembling with the anticipation of seeing an insect face to face. She tightened her fingers around the metal bar and slowly breathed in to steady herself. The small company of insects swarmed together for a few moments, as if sharing information with each other. Then up they all went, off into another street to carry on their searching. At the same time, the sound of shelling continued to fill the air as their part of the city was repeatedly bombarded.

Georgiana hand-signalled to Erepsin's friends and crawled under the tables to make her way to the end of the row. From there she scrambled to the edge of the shopping court, escaping into a side alley. The three of them ran towards the nearest door, the rear entrance of a restaurant. Up some steps they clamoured and tried to get in. It was locked but they could see through the door's window that the key was in the lock on the other side.

Insects buzzed overhead and the cries of random individuals from adjacent streets told the tale of their encounters. Then they came, the alleyway quickly filled with the sound of the whizzing, whirring, darting creatures. Smashing the glass with her metal bar, Georgiana's fingers scrambled with the key to turn the lock. It took a few moments to rotate but, with a shove of her shoulder, the door gave way and through she went. Turning around she saw the first of Erepsin's friends stumble in after her. The other moved forward only a step or two.

"Ahh" he cried, as insects dropped and clung to him.

Staggering back down the steps, twirling round and round, he wafted his arms from side to side, trying to brush them off and get away. It was no use, however. Within moments he was covered with the creatures. One scanned his face and immediately it sounded a recognition alarm. Other insects flew in to answer the call. A quick sting on the back of his neck and, after dropping to his knees and then flopping onto the floor, he was lifted up into the air and carried off.

The remaining hymenopteran buzzed in through the open doorway, searching, scanning for Georgiana and her companion. They were nowhere in sight. They'd run through the food preparation area and entered the main restaurant, now empty of people, who had all rushed outside when the shelling first started, then off to their homes. The entrance to the restaurant from the kitchen, however, was an open archway and so the small group of insects buzzed through and soon caught up with those they were pursuing. Blocking the restaurant's front entranceway to prevent any escape, in group formation they eased their way back into the room. Georgiana's remaining guardian picked up a chair and wafted it from side to side, pushing its legs at the creatures to keep them at bay. Seeing a gap in his defence, an insect sped in to deliver a sting but soon found itself flopping on the floor, beaten down by Georgiana's metal pole. Three insects remained, hovering, waiting, watching, twitching; poised for a moment of opportunity to deliver a stinging kill.

Georgiana and her companion slowly backed away towards the front windows as the insects pressed in on them. Slowly the buzzing creatures moved apart, seeking to encircle their captives. Three against two, their hostages stood no chance. Standing side by side, now with their backs to the windows, Georgiana and her friend fended off their attacks from every side. The insects swooped, darted and dived. Again and again they pushed in and each time they were beaten back. Georgiana knocked one sideways but moments later another dropped from above, passing right across her face. It scanned her facial features and Immediately it seemed to sense who she was. The other two insects stopped their attacks and flew alongside it, exchanging the scanned information.

Seeing an opportunity for escape, Erepsin's friend lowered the chair that he held in front of him, to rest his arm. Placing his other hand behind his back, he flipped the latch on the window.

Taking one step forward, he whispered to Georgiana, "Get behind me."

"What?" she asked.

"I said, get behind me," he replied, from the corner of his mouth.

He gently stepped forward again to give her more space.

"The window," he said.

As the three insects were finishing their information exchange and turning to face them again, the young man lunged forward with his chair, waving it madly in the air and thrashing it's four legs in all directions.

"Go!" he shouted.

Georgiana pushed the window open and dropped outside. Turning to help her friend she saw him wildly swinging the chair in circles about his head and finally throwing it across the room. He lunged for the window and, scrambling through, Georgiana gave him her hand and pulled. He dropped through onto the floor and she closed the window behind him with insects flapping at the window pane on the other side.

"Come on," she said, moving across the street.

He didn't get up, however. Not a limb moved, just a heap of a person lying in a crumpled state.

"Are you alright?" asked Georgiana, running over.

In that moment, from the back of his neck, an insect flew up into the air, its sting twitching and preparing itself for another attack. It hovered at head height, a short distance from Georgiana's face. Her heart dropped, knowing her companion was dead.

An alarm sounded from the insect's head, a 'come and join me' signal to any other insects that were in the area.

"Ahh," she screamed, waving her iron bar at it. It dodged her first few blows but then she struck the creature firmly on its skull, knocking it back towards the windows. Its alarm faded to a whine before it dropped to the floor. The insects on the other side of the window withdrew, no doubt to exit via the restaurant's back door. Georgiana knew she had to get away.

Down to the end of the street she ran, her heart pounding almost as much as her feet on the walkway's stone slabs. Round the corner she pelted, dodging a couple of people running in the opposite direction and seeking to put as much space between her and the insects as she could. The sound of military guns firing out their shells continued to fill the air. There seemed to be nowhere to go to escape danger, except that is, towards her original goal, the great debating chamber at the heart of the city; to find her father, to see if he was still in the area, to see if he was still alive.

Along the road she went, dodging people and hoping that every screeching shell that was fired across the sky would not find its target nearby. She was almost at the end of this street, ready to turn its corner, when she heard the familiar cries of someone ahead of her, scrambling to get away from insects. Hurriedly ducking into the alcove of a doorway, Georgiana shrank her body into its shadow. Within

116

moments the buzzing noise of a swarm of maddened creatures sped past, their mission to do nothing but fulfil their malicious programming.

Georgiana held her breath until the sound of their buzzing was gone. Then, stepping carefully from her hiding place, she continued to the end of the road. The street sign above her head read, 'Nowhere Avenue.' It was a city joke. 'Nowhere' was the converging of several popular streets in the city, all of which ran from somewhere, that is places with restaurants, shops, theatres, communal gardens, open air cafés and cosy enclosed tea rooms. Where the roads met, however, like the converging spokes on a bicycle wheel, there was nothing but small manufacturing works, storage containers and factory waste disposal units. 'Nowhere' was the temporary dumping ground for everywhere around. Most people avoided Nowhere, choosing instead to squeeze through small side streets to get to their destinations, but sometimes you had to go through 'Nowhere' to get to somewhere, but no-one stayed for long in 'Nowhere' – simply because there was nothing to do.

Slipping onto Nowhere Avenue, she began to walk and then trot along the edge of the factory buildings. She felt very exposed, there was little cover. Quickening her pace, she began to run, to push on past this 'nowhere land'. Then she slowed a little, so as not to lose her stamina. On her left was a high bricked wall, the perimeter boundary which contained within its enclosure a coco factory facility. To her right, on the opposite side of the street, a series of smaller factory outlets, each producing an assortment of unconnected items, from high society fashion goods to common knick-knacks; some outlets had recently begun a modest output of gourmet delights. She stopped to consider the route she was on, whether to keep on the road or to enter a factory. Moments later the ground shook as a shell landed squarely on the coco plant. The building blew apart and only the perimeter wall kept Georgiana safe; to the ground she went, the shock of the impact leaving her temporarily disorientated.

Scrambling to her feet, she picked up her iron bar and decided to walk on. Suddenly, from behind, came the sound of gasping and pounding feet. Momentarily turning, she saw a young man pelting towards her, then past her, panic written all over his face. Within moments he was away, far down the street and not stopping for anything. Looking down from where the young man had run, there it was, a gathering of flying hymenopteran accompanied by a buzzing sound that chilled Georgiana's blood. She was about to turn and run when she heard ahead of her the same young man cry out as other insects dropped onto him. He was quickly stung and fell to the floor. Georgiana looked forwards and then back down the road. There were swarms in both places. Nowhere Avenue had become a trap.

Next to her was a brick wall, tall and unscalable. On the opposite side of the street was a small factory unit. There was nowhere else to go. Running across the road, she plunged through the outlet's entrance, slamming the door behind her. She found herself in a small workshop; manikins dotted across the floor, standing to attention and displaying a variety of fashionable clothes. A variety of richly coloured fabrics hung from the walls and towards the back of the room were tables, chairs and sewing machines. Georgiana didn't have time to tarry. She had to move on and somehow get out through a rear exit. Within moments, however, the sound of buzzing could be heard all around. At the factory outlet's main window, hundreds of insects had gathered, all bumping, thudding and scratching their bodies against the glass pane and seeking to get in. It was a terrifying sight. Together their corporate forms so thickly filled the air, they were like a silver curtain of death, blocking out much of the late morning sunlight.

"Stay calm," Georgiana said, out loud to herself. "They can't get in."

She searched about the room, looking for an exit to another part of the building or for ideas for self-defence. There seemed to be no way out.

"This is ridiculous," she exclaimed.

Running her hands across the drapes that hung on the far wall, she felt the shape of a door handle behind one of them. Dragging the drape to one side, she pulled on the handle and opened the door. Behind it, a small kitchen unit with another open door to a water closet. In she went, closing the door after her. A small sink, worktop with kettle, toaster, mugs and assorted biscuit tins, the room was tidy and windowless. Her heart sank, no way out. Into the water closet she went, her eyes immediately fixing on a small window above the toilet cistern. Closing the toilet seat lid, she stood on it and poked her iron bar at the small window's latch, trying to lift it. It was tricky. The latch had clearly been left in place for years and the grime and rust had formed a glue-like grip that would not easily let go.

Georgiana positioned her iron bar underneath the latch, ready to give it a shove. She was about the push it upwards when she stopped. To her left, a pipe ran down the wall to feed the bathroom and kitchen with water. A sound, however, came from high up in the pipe and slowly made its way downwards. As it came parallel to her, she placed her hand on the pipe and felt the juddering of something metallic inside. Then another followed down the tube.

"They're in the pipes!" she cried.

To her right, a sudden buzzing noise. It came from the wash basin, to be exact, the sink's plughole. Between the gaps in the plughole's metal grid, small metallic arms poked through, trying to get out, accompanied by a buzzing noise that filled the air. Moments later more noise seemed to be coming from under Georgiana's feet. Something had come through the toilet main waste pipe and was now fluttering around in the main bowl. She could feel it ramming its body up towards the seat she was standing on, each knock shaking the soles of her feet. Looking up at the small window, more insects appeared on its outside, tapping on the glass and making escape impossible.

What to do, she didn't know.

"Help me!" she yelled out, but there wasn't anyone to hear.

Other sounds appeared in the toilet's main bowl as more insects arrived through the waste pipe. Georgiana flushed the toilet to be rid of them. Within moments, however, one remaining insect sought to squeeze through the gap between the toilet seat and the lid. Pushing its head through the space, the rest of its body buzzed frantically to manoeuvre itself into room. Taking the end of her iron pole, Georgiana crushed its head. She leapt off the toilet seat and ran through the kitchen; back through the doorway, into the workshop and shut the door.

Even though only a handful of hymenopteran remained outside the large window, her relief was momentary. It soon became clear their method of attack had changed. From all across the wooden floor, she could hear sounds of scratching, splitting and tearing. After glancing about the room, she gingerly got on her knees and put her ear to the floor. More scraping sounds and pulling met her ears, as thin layers of the floorboards were being methodically ripped away. Then a buzz. The insects were under the floor and eating their way through. She could feel the tremors of their activity under her hands and feet. It would only be a matter of time.

Her lip quivered in anticipation of their arrival. Looking about the room she wondered what could be done. Grabbing some fabric from a manakin, flicking her wrist several times to wrap the cloth around her left hand, she left enough material dangling down from her fingers to flick outwards as a weapon. Now each hand was armed, a pole in one and some cloth in the other. Still she felt so vulnerable, her defences were terribly lacking. Minutes ticked by as Georgianna slowly turned on her heals, constantly glancing this way and that, watching and waiting as her ears tuned into the buzzing, scratching and scraping sounds which echoed from all corners of the room. The expectation of their entrance was appalling.

From behind one of the wall drapes, two bulks caught her eye, silently moving beneath the fabric. Her heart pounded with fear. Quickly stepping over to the wall she brought down her pole on each shape. Both dropped to the ground and fizzed to their deaths. She let out a sigh of relief, leaning on the wall for support, but her victory was short lived. On the other side of the room, two more hymenopteran flopped onto the floor from out of a mahogany air vent, having eaten through the decorative wooden panel. They quickly soared into the air, scanning their environment and seeking out their target. Georgiana ducked in-between the manikins, holding her breath whilst peering out into the room. She watched as the insects made their preliminary movements, up, down and then in circular arcs, assessing their surroundings. They began to move forward, searching along the room's perimeter and then across the central floor space.

From her crouched position, Georgiana watched their progress. She could hardly breathe. Sometimes she lost sight of them, only their buzz told her of their general location. Every now and again, however, the insects would land and walk, silently making their way across the floor. This was terrifying. In those moments she had no idea where they were. Up they flew again, to continue their search. One hovered over the sewing tables whilst the other flew down the room's centre and towards the manikins. As it drew level with Georgiana it twitched its head from side to side, sensing that someone was close by. Slowly it rotated its body to move in-between the manikins. Somehow it knew she was there.

In that same moment, Georgiana flicked out the cloth that was attached to her left hand, dropping it over the metallic creature. Under the weight of the material it fell to the floor and immediately received a battering from Georgiana's rod. The other insect buzzed over to where she was. Georgiana swished at it with her pole and flicked at it with her cloth but it kept dodging her attempts at destroying it. Circling the room opposite each other, their gaze became fixed on each other's positions. Sensing that attack was the best means of defence, Georgiana lunged at the creature. She swished her rod here and there and flicked and re-flicked the cloth that draped over her fingers. Whizzing around in twirling movements, the insect ducked and dodged the assaults. Seeing its moment of opportunity, it dipped under her pole, buzzed forward and landed on the back of Georgiana's left hand, locking its legs about her wrist. Franticly shaking her arm, Georgiana sought to shake it to the floor. Despite its body flopping up and down, the creature stayed locked on, clinging to the jerking hand it was attached to. It plunged its tail into the cloth. Immediately a stabbing pain shot through her wrist.

"Ahhh," Georgiana cried out.

A couple of seconds more of frantic hand shaking and the creature lost its grip but, before it flopped to the floor, its sting managed a glancing scratch along Georgiana's arm. Bouncing along the wood floorboards, the insect fluttered its wings to regather itself. Down on its head came Georgiana's metal bar. Again and again she struck it until it stopped moving. Hastily unwrapping the cloth she looked at the back of her hand. There was a long scratch across it, and then another which ran right up her arm. Both looked bad but the scratch on her hand was quickly turning into an open wound. Next to the gash was an oily yellow liquid which Georgiana assumed was the insect's venom. She was about to wipe it off with the cloth around her wrist when she saw that it too was also dripping with poison. Dropping the material to the floor, she staggered over to the nearest manikin and wiped the back of her hand and arm on a shirt sleeve.

The deep scratch throbbed with pain and steadily grew worse. How much poison had entered her system, she couldn't tell. Clogs of white, foggy haze came across her vision along with silvery streaks that cut through her line of sight. Her head thumped with a sickening migraine and delusions began to invade her perceptions of reality. The buzzing noises of the insects grew louder and their scratching echoed in her ears. Were they again in the room? Were they around her? She couldn't tell. She thrashed out into the open air, thinking she was once more under attack. Backing away into and amongst the manikins she thought she could see insects hemming her in from every direction. Thrusting her metal bar here and there, she struck nothing but air. Then, in a delirious maddening rage, she threw her metal bar at the vision of hymenopteran that filled her mind. The bar went sailing through the air and struck the factory outlet's front window. It cracked with the impact and the insects outside immediately began to work on the weakness of the glass, tugging with their front jaws and pulling the splintered shards apart to make a hole big enough to get through.

Georgiana stumbled backwards and bumped into the wall. She turned round and, feverishly reaching up, grasped the drapes that hung there, pulling on them to steady herself. Away from the wall the drapes came and on top of her they fell. She stumbled under their weight and, after grasping at some rolls of stacked fabric, fell backwards; bringing everything on top of her, including several manikins that tumbled together under her impact.

The factory's front window pane finally gave way and in came the insects. Their corporate hum was an echoing sound of swarming victory. They buzzed around the room, seeking, scanning and communicating with each other. Georgiana closed her eyes under her fabric covers. Amidst all the humming from the hymenopteran, the continuous long whines of mortar shells screeched their way across the city. Into Nowhere Avenue they fell, pounding down the buildings and exploding along the road. Together they filled the room with a deafening, booming, shaking resonance that echoed all around. Georgiana knew she was dead. Then, all went dark.

Chapter 17 – Goodbye my Sweetheart

Sometime later Georgiana awoke from what she thought had been a deep slumber. Her head spun, her breathing was erratic and she felt as if she was suffocating. Chewing on what tasted like an assortment of gravel and bland paste, she coughed and spat out her mouth's contents. Bewildered and disorientated, she peered into the late afternoon sunlight. Hours must have gone by, it was mid to late morning when she'd initially blanked out. A drape and three manikins still covered much of her along with a thick layer of dust and debris; she wondered why they were so difficult to push away from her trapped arms and legs. Wriggling seemed to be the only method that would work to get her free. She pulled and twisted her frame, but by doing so felt a surge of pain through her legs. Something was wrong and she didn't know what.

After dragging herself out from beneath the drapes, fabrics and assorted factory furniture, she was surprised to find herself outside. The walls of the room she had been in were gone. In front of the factory outlet, where the main road used to be, there was now a gaping hole from where a mortar shell had landed. It's blast had blown through the small factory, knocking over its walls and destroying everything in its path. This was the closest brush with death that she'd had, but its kiss to kill her had been her salvation. Not only had she been half buried in plaster, brick and glass (the wall hangings, drapes, fabric rolls and manikins cocooning her to keep her safe) but scattered across the debris were bits of metal legs, heads, abdomens and wings, the remains of the hymenopteran swarm that had entered the room. Clearly they had not survived.

Now it seemed that, for a season, for a time, the shelling had stopped. The eerie calm that had fallen on the city showed an environment discovering its wounds. Much of Nowhere Avenue had been demolished, along with adjoining streets; pounded to the ground and turned into a smoking haze. As the dust settled, the smoke from many fires showed where much of the city was damaged. With so many buildings demolished Georgiana could now see, in the distance, the debating chamber; deserted and partly destroyed from direct hits, its far end burning away like a hot oven. She had no idea if her father was dead or alive. If he was still alive, he certainly wouldn't be in this part of the city. Now the only thing to do was to get away from the city centre in anticipation of the shelling restarting and to try and find a safe place to rest.

Before she could move, another explosion rocked the city. To the south of the metropolis was the great reservoir, the turbine driving powerhouse that delivered electricity to the homes, businesses, factories and public buildings. Georgiana watched in horror as the western edge of the reservoir wall blew and the water came gushing down the hillside to flood the lower grass and marshland plains.

"She will kill everyone," Georgiana thought.

It wasn't Maltrisia's doing, however. When the shelling first began Lord Stephen had been ending his main speech of the morning. Crowds of people had turned out to see him in action and today the rhetoric was flowing better than ever. During the mid-morning break, Lord Stephen and Uncle Jack sat and talked about their progress.

"Well Crispus, I think we've finally got her on the run," Lord Stephen commented. "She's not turned up again and, from what I hear, she hasn't any rallies organised in any part of the city today or tomorrow."

Lord Stephen sipped his coffee and relaxed in his 'members only' leather armchair that belonged to the debating chamber's communal lounge.

"Better to keep going and drive the nails right into her political coffin," replied Uncle Jack. "We don't want this serpent's crushed head recovering; in my experience so called mortal wounds have a nasty habit of resurrecting themselves. Keep bashing away until you know it's truly dead," he added.

After their morning break, the two men took to the chamber again. There had been only a handful of supporters for Maltrisia still left in the building during the first session of the day and many of them had maintained a low profile. During the break, however, they all seemed to have disappeared. Now all who were left to observe the day's debate was a large King's Law supporting crowd who sat in the debating room's public gallery; poised and ready to listen to what would probably be Lord Stephen's final speech on the subject.

"I hope you will allow me to spend a few more minutes giving you some final conclusions on these matters," he began. "Signing off on a subject isn't always easily done, especially when the lives of so many people are influenced by its outcome. Yet today I feel confident that we've achieved a level of success that will secure our city's future and keep her safe from ideological tyranny. Deception is a terrible thing, especially when emotionally motivated by a misplaced sense of moral outrage or false obligation. As a result, reason is often thrown out of the window, along with common sense, and all that's left is to rummage around in the ideological garbage in order to sample that which is philosophically and politically indigestible; impossible promises and half eaten assurances that rot in their own putrid decay."

The crowd laughed and applauded Lord Stephen's comments.

"Now it seems we're finally in a safer place. We've worked through the deception, seen through the ruse, the duplicity and trickery and now we've survived the treachery and betrayal that almost took over our home. We just need to guard that which we've won. We just need to hold our ground and firmly take a stand whenever any new attempts are made at resurrecting those same old lies; lies that promise liberty but in the end take away freedom of thought, freedom of speech, freedom of conscience and freedom to object. Oh how good it is to disagree without fear of a tribunal," he said.

More cheers, whistles and whoops came from the crowd.

"Arguments have never been so attractive!" he added. "Argue, argue, argue, argue, and argue some more. You're now quite free to do so. Whenever you like and wherever you like."

Many people laughed and applauded.

"Argue in the streets, argue in the malls, argue in the cafés, restaurants, tea rooms or next to the hot-dog stalls. Argue in the parks or along the dusty country lanes, argue anywhere you'll want, you're free to argue again and again. Argue as loud as you like or even with quiet, soothing, soft tones, even argue, if you dare, in your own homes... not that my wife agrees with me on this last particular point," he added. "She likes a more harmonious house where matters are talked through on a more sensible level, and I totally agree with her. As a husband I know my place, which is primarily to nod and agree with whatever decisions she makes about the household!"

"You'll be in trouble when you get back home," someone shouted from the crowd, amongst the general laughter.

Lord Stephen smiled and nodded.

"But at least in *this* place of serious politics we're now able to once again, disagree without disdain, oppose without fear of prosecution and engage in dispute without being accused of disrespect or moral hatred. Oh how nice it is to be able to breathe!"

Everyone applauded.

Lord Stephen stood for a few moments in the silence. Then, in a very serious tone he said,

"As a city we've had a very close escape. This city could have lost its life. In and amongst the chaos, however, my son didn't keep his."

The crowd went very quiet when Lord Stephen brought up the subject of his great loss.

"We must never forget that. When politics spills over into overt hatred, one side casting disdain on the other in order to gain a so-called unshakable moral ground that can't be disagreed with, then we know that militancy is knocking at the door. Let my son's death not be in vain. I still don't know who killed him and now that this present crisis has come to an end, I shall take it upon myself to find out. As for our political stability, it's up to you now. It is your calling and your place to carry on this battle. If you will not yield to tyranny, then tyranny will be kept outside the door."

Everyone applauded.

"Now," he said. "We have to corporately build on this solid foundation so that it becomes something unshakable. We must understand the foundations of our culture rather than simply adhere to them out of a traditional obligation. Relying on tradition as a reason to do something never won any argument. We must be educated, clear, concise and able to stand our ground. That way we will close the door to ideological fraud and our city will be made safe for generation after generation."

The applause that met his ears was loud and seemed to be the perfect closure to his work. Lord Stephen lifted his hand as a thank you gesture and applauded back at their approval. It was a job completed and now he could move on. Then, in the midst of the rowdy applause, the shriek of a mortar shell screeched through the air and landed a few streets away. The explosion rocked the building, sending the crowd into a temporary bewilderment, quickly followed by a stampeding panic. Then another shell fell, slamming its explosive presence into another building nearby. This was followed by another and another. Soon the drumbeat of war found its momentum as explosion upon explosion dropped all round them.

Uncle Jack leapt out of his seat, ran across the room and up a spiral stair to get to the top balcony windows. Lord Stephen followed him. Standing side-by-side, they watched the city being pounded from incendiary projectiles; shot from the agricultural zone, then raining down and scattering their explosive packages on anyone and everything.

"We've been fools," said Lord Stephen.

"She's insane," replied Uncle Jack.

Lord Stephen hesitated, not believing all that was taking place in front of his eyes. Uncle Jack shook his arm.

"You're to the waterworks and I'm to the reservoir," he said.

He turned to go but immediately sensed Lord Stephen wasn't following.

"I didn't actually think we'd have to do it," replied Lord Stephen.

"We have no choice," said Uncle Jack.

He looked at his friend and knew he was right.

"Alright," he said. "I'll shut down the waterworks, you blow the dam."

Down the stairs they went, across the deserted chamber floor and out onto the building's front steps. Already waiting for them were some of their team members who'd gathered as soon as the first shells were fired.

Down the street they ran, ducking and dodging groups or individuals who sped past them in a blind panic, racing for their lives. Finally assembling next to a small converted pumphouse, now used to distribute wine, they waited less than a minute for the rest of their group to join them.

When their horses and carriages arrived, Lord Stephen took one of his crew members to one side.

"Marcus," he said. "Get word to my family to leave the city. Tell them I'll follow as soon as I can. Get the waterworks blueprints and my notebook from my study, my wife will show you where they are, and then come and join us at the waterworks."

Marcus nodded and rode off.

Turning to Uncle Jack, Lord Stephen shook him by the hand and said, "Well Crispus, this is farewell."

"It is indeed," replied Uncle Jack. "Keep your head down and I'll see you in a few hours."

"I hope so," said Lord Stephen.

The two men parted company.

Lord Stephen and his company of twelve set out in three carriages. Driving their horses through the streets of Clearwash City, they eventually left behind the burning buildings and the shells that randomly fell from the sky; clearly Maltrisia's weaponry had a limited range. Following a north easterly course, they kept to the city's backstreets and alleyways, the main roads being full of people running here, there and everywhere in their panic, not knowing where to go or what to do to keep themselves safe. Finally they came to one of the more affluent parts of the city where there were some open park spaces, playgrounds, general recreation areas and sports pitches. Full pelt, the carriages sped across the land, churning up manicured grass lawns and destroying pristine flowerbeds. Plunging through a series of shallow ponds, they eventually wove in and amongst the last set of trees on the edge of the park before finally going back out onto the streets again.

Within minutes they were at the border of the north eastern canal which created the city's inner circle parameter. There they could see fire, spreading its way across the water from both directions as clumps of oil caught light. Over the bridge they went and onto the raised ground of grassy meadows that led up to the mountains, in front of which was the waterworks.

"Take it steady," Lord Stephen called out to the driver. "We need enough strength left in these horses to get us back to the city circle again."

A sturdy gallop took them up and across the grassy incline of the terraced fields.; their ridged markings on the landscape showed where tiered generational farming had once dominated the terrain. Past a set of red bricked buildings they went, across a court yard and there, in front of them, was the waterworks. Stepping out of their carriages, the group stood gazing back across the city. Smoke drifted across the sky and fire upon fire leapt into life as more mortar shells continued to land; exploding their presence amongst the quivering buildings which stood, huddling together and wondering who would be next to die in the great metropolis.

Lord Stephen and his team headed off towards the back of the waterworks. With explosives and detonators in their backpacks, they used pre-set cams and nuts, put into the rockface a few weeks before, to scale the wall. Climbing up and up to where the pipes entered the mountain, they squeezed through the gap between the pipe and the rockface and disappeared from sight. Once inside the mountain they walked on top of the great pipes for about a quarter of a mile, its steady incline meant that much of the walking was done on their toes. At the pipe's end were a series of pistons, pumps and large cogs which controlled the water flow from a great hidden lake. Setting up explosive devices and detonators, two members of the team were left behind with instructions to wait until the pistons and pumps stopped moving.

"Wait here until we've shut the waterworks down," said Lord Stephen. "Then booby trap the stationary pumps so that, if they start moving again, they'll set the detonators off."

Lord Stephen led the remainder of his team back into the open air and finally approached the waterworks' front door. Scaffolding was fixed right across the front of the building where cleaners had laboured that morning. They'd abandoned their work as soon as the shelling began and now the door to the building was left ajar. In the three of them went, into a place that was normally off limits to the general public. They were surprised at the internal décor. Stretching across the foyer was a multi patterned marbled floor, beautiful in shape and form with swirling colours that overlapped each other like tongues of fire. Arches opened up exits in each wall and through the opposite portico was a short ornate corridor – at the end of which was a large, spacious aisle with two lines of pure white marble pillars standing to attention on either side. Like ever watching, aged sentries these ancient stone custodians towered above them, stretching up from the ground to the roof where they became soaring branches that met each other on the high ceiling in remarkable swirling patterns. In appearance they looked as if they were the tangled mass of a glorious tree canopy. Their heavy beauty made the central walkway feel airy and spacious. The three companions thought themselves as small as insects as they gazed about them, feeling that they were looking into some kind of religious, sacred space.

"We're not going this way," Lord Stephen said to his companions, "but we'll go no further in the waterworks until Marcus arrives with my blueprints and notebook."

They stood for about twenty minutes, gazing at the corridor until they heard the sound of Marcus' footsteps in the foyer behind them.

"I'll have to ride back with you in the carriages," he said. "My horse is spent."

Lord Stephen nodded.

"My wife and family are out of the city?" he enquired.

"Lady Melanie asked for you to join her as soon as you could," he replied.

"But she is leaving the city?" Lord Stephen asked.

"I assume so," replied Marcus. "I did give her your message."

Lord Stephen looked worried. Taking the blueprints and notebook from Marcus, he followed their directions, leading the group through an archway to their right, along a short corridor and then left onto a grand stairway. Up, up they went, taking great strides on the velvet carpeted floor. It was like entering a royal mansion or sacred cathedral. The air felt thick with anticipation, everyone on the stair felt it. It was as if the space inside the waterworks was continually expecting something to happen, perhaps an answer to your dreams or it wanted you to dream a dream you hadn't realised needed dreaming. (Over the years, some members of the waterworks research team had deliberately resigned from their work because of this phenomenon. They had become unsettled and unnerved by it, finding that they couldn't cope with the 'dream carrying' as it became known).

At the top of the stair they went through another archway and straight onto a spiral staircase. Up they ascended, step upon step, until their legs were tired and heaven seemed just a few paces away. Finally down another corridor, through two rooms and one final door which opened up onto a metal platform that seemed to be built over a high open space. Running along the very edge of the platform was a waist high metal railing, to prevent anyone from falling over and into the abyss below. Directly in front of them, dividing the railing in two, was a narrow walkway, a bridge, which went straight ahead and across the room to another platform on the other side.

Immediately above them, three clusters of suspended spotlights shone a dazzling and illuminating radiance, flooding the area with a brilliance so intense it was close to daylight. Shielding their eyes from the glare, they could see these lights were hung from a vast, high domed, metal ceiling, but they couldn't make out much beyond that due to the astonishing brightness. On the wall around the great circular chamber, smaller lights shone, giving illumination right down to the engine room basement.

Tentatively, they stepped onto the metal platform. Each footstep clanked its presence on the steel structure and the hollow sound beneath their feet was more than an unsettling reminder of the large drop that was directly below. Walking to the platform's edge, they peered over the side of the railings and gazed down to where the colossal machines were dotted across the great expanse of the engine room floor. Driven by pistons, pumps and running wheels, this engineering facility was the heart of the waterworks; the machinery that steered its powerful mechanisms and pumped water throughout the city. It was astonishing to look at, a marvel of mechanical engineering. Their fluid, motorised movements cast an almost hypnotic spell over the group who stood absolutely still, mesmerised by what they could see. All that could be heard was the humming of the main engines and the clunking of the pistons and wheels. It was a musical song; the chimes, clicks, clanks and clunks of a vibrant tune.

Moving onto the bridge, they walked the line and, after a short time of wavering, arrived at the bridge's end. Striding onto another metal platform, they saw opposite them a tall, broad door, above which were the words, "Main Control Room." Turning the handle, the door creaked open to reveal a musty smelling chamber. In the middle of the room was a control desk with buttons, dials and other measuring instruments on it. On the opposite wall, at the far end of the room, were the pictures of four wheels - one large, two medium and one small.

Above the central control desk, suspended just above head height, were around twenty monitors. These displayed images of rooms within the waterworks. They could see luxurious offices, hallways, different parts of the engine room below, a great pipe chamber, storerooms, other rooms that looked like water purification chambers and many stairways and corridors. All the rooms looked stylish and grand with leather bound chairs, silver framed windows and doorframes made of gold, like that which would be made for the residence of a wealthy king or queen.

Lord Stephen spread his blueprints onto the control desk whilst his team sat down in front of the desk's control panel. Together the three of them worked from his notepad and the blueprints to begin the shutdown process.

"Welcome to the waterworks control system," said a computer voice from the control desk. "Please enter pass code to continue."

Marcus, typed in a code and waited.

"Code accepted," said the computer voice. "Enter secondary pass code."

His colleague turned more pages in the book and found amongst the vast number of scrawling letters another code, which she pointed at for Marcus to type in. After waiting a few moments, "Secondary pass code accepted," came the computer voice again.

"What would you like us to do?" she asked.

"Bring up each of the pumps that push water through the waterworks system and shut them down," said Lord Stephen.

"Which ones?" she replied.

"All of them," said Lord Stephen. "I want every one of them turned off."

"We'll have no water," she replied.

"That's the idea," Lord Stephen said. "It's only temporary. We cannot allow the enemies of our city to have the power to rule over us."

It took another twenty minutes for this process to work. One by one the pumps and pistons on the waterworks engine room floor began to halt and their fluid motions juddered and came to a standstill. Their song faded away and something beautiful came to an end.

As silence descended, so too the lights in the waterworks began to dim. The different monitors above the control desk switched off and retracted into a recess in the ceiling.

"This wasn't expected," said Lord Stephen.

"We may have closed too many systems down," replied Marcus. "It's difficult to know exactly what does what."

"Well we'd better get out of here before this place becomes completely dark," and with that Lord Stephen led the group out of the main control room, over the bridge, through the upper rooms and corridor, down the spiral staircase, down the main stair, through the archways and back into the foyer. The atmosphere was already changing and the promise of something new that had lingered in the air was now beginning to be replaced with a yearning and empty hunger.

"Time to make a quick exit I think," said Lord Stephen, not liking what he felt.

Once they were finally outside, their eyes were met by a terrible scene of mindless destruction as the city continued to burn. Soon the team from within the mountain joined them and they waited for their next orders.

"Marcus," said Lord Stephen. "I'm going back into the city to help the people. I want you and the team to help my family get out of the city."

"Yes, of course," he replied.

"Thank you," said Lord Stephen, a look of desperate gratitude on his face.

"Look," said Marcus, pointing towards the south western part of the capital.

In that direction, over the rooftops, he thought he could see small silver dots, darting here and there.

"What on earth..." he said. "Are they birds?"

"Possibly," replied Lord Stephen.

They both watched as streams of people continued to flow from the city centre towards its outer edges, away from its inner circle.

"I'm still needed on the streets," he said. "Tell my wife, I'll follow on as soon as I know Crispus has the upper hand in this war. She'll know what I mean by that."

Marcus nodded.

Taking his carriage back the way it came, Lord Stephen went straight into the heart of the troubles. It was clear that Maltrisia's motor shells had a limited range, (some of her airships, however, managed to drop random combustible projectiles onto the eastern edge of the city before being shot down). Lord Stephen secured three buildings, one bunker and several underground pods as makeshift hospitals. Working with a team of people to collect the wounded, his face was the most welcome sight for so many people who fled from the relentless pounding and the terror of war.

After several hours of work, he was almost at the end of himself; seeing first-hand the terrible sufferings of his people. Without warning, an explosion rocked and shuddered the whole landscape as the reservoir wall blew.

Lord Stephen lifted up his head from his work to see the sight.

"Well done Crispus," he said. "She will wake tomorrow morning to a city without water and power, he added."

- -

Georgiana saw the dam blow. Feeling that their lives were lost forever, she stumbled forward, one step at a time, just to get away from the mess that lay behind her. It must have been about an hour, perhaps more, that she found herself leaving behind much of the devastation. Every now and then people ran past her, hurrying away from the terrors that surrounded them. Eventually she just wandered, not knowing exactly what she was doing or where she was going. She just kept hobbling down street upon street, seeking to come to the end of the city's inner circle. She rounded the corner of what looked like an old court house, windows smashed in and glass shards scattered across her path. The crunching of the splintered fragments and gravel under her feet shouted out the story of lawlessness that had settled on the city.

Briefly stopping to gain some strength, Georgiana leant against the wall and let her head rest on the brickwork. She lifted up her left hand and held it in front of her face. The scarring where she'd been scratched and partially stung was still inflamed and it made her stomach sick just to see it. Wondering if she still might die from the wound, she decided to press on, trying to find some medical help. Ahead of her she could see an earthen bank and beyond that a crater, recently created by an exploded shell. Nearby soldiers were positioned in groups, on the lookout for any movement of Maltrisia's forces. A short distance from them, a group of medics and general helpers – the very people Georgiana had been looking for. She walked step upon step and finally found herself standing next to the earthen bank. There was a gentleman close by, sitting with his back to her. She wanted to call out to him, but her strength was gone. Down she flopped onto her knees and then onto her face; for a few moments, she was completely out.

Georgiana came round to water being poured onto her forehead. Glancing upwards, her vision was blurred and her mind a haze of confusion. She felt the water dripping down her cheeks and a gentle hand rubbing and washing off the dirt. There was something familiar and most loving about the touches she was receiving. Flickering her eyes, she finally focused on who was attending her.

"Oh Dad!" she said, once she could see who was leaning over her. Despite the pain, her joy at seeing him was immeasurable. Here he was, alive and well and they were together again.

"Steady," came his reply, his voice was quiet and almost breathless.

"Oh Dad!" she blurted again, but her body and mind was so dulled with exhaustion and pain, she was unable to speak.

"Stay calm," came her father's reply. She felt him give her a quick peck-of-a-kiss on her forehead. "You must stay calm," he whispered in her ear.

Georgiana felt the desperate need to share her news that her father was in great danger but the delirious exhaustion within her was totally consuming.

"I'm going to give you something to take away the pain and it may briefly put you out," she heard her father say. "This will hurt only for a few moments. Then you'll see me again when you come round."

Georgiana shook her head, the panic now growing inside of her. She tried to sit up so she could speak more easily. She had to tell him about the hymenopteran.

"Must listen," she said, trying to get her words out. "You don't know…" she continued, but she was already out of breath.

"Stay still," came her father's voice again. She felt his hand behind the back of her head, supporting her and the gentle touch of his other hand under her chin. Together both hands guided her head back onto the grassy earth. Breathing in for a few moments, Georgiana felt her chest tighten and then cough to clear her lungs. The pain this released almost caused her to pass out. All she could hear was her own heart beat as she went in and out of consciousness. Eventually she came round to see her father preparing an injection.

"No," she whispered through trembling lips, her throat still sounded hoarse and dry.

Her father ignored her and continued to finish preparing the injection. Seeing she didn't have much time, she shook her head from side to side, trying to overcome the pain that shot through her body. Her efforts finally brought forth a burst of tears, but crying was so painful.

"Stay still," her father said, taking hold of her arm.

Georgiana panicked, if he put her out, how could she tell him about the danger he was in?

"You don't know what's coming," she finally said, in great anguish; just getting the words out brought another overflow of tears.

"Georgiana," came her father's rebuke. "You must stay still."

"I have seen it," she blurted out. "Dad, I have seen it with my own eyes."
More tears streamed down her cheeks.

"You must get away from here, right now," she said. "There's no time…"

Briefly, all went blank. The injection she'd received took away the pain and Georgiana immediately dipped into a state of semiconsciousness. She could feel herself being lifted onto a stretcher and then the stretcher being lifted up. Unable to move, she just lay there, a sense of wellbeing going through her body along with a call to deep sleep. Moments later, there was her father's face, close to hers.

"Goodbye my sweetheart," she heard him say.

She felt his kiss on her forehead. Then he whispered in her ear,

"I will love you forever."

She sensed his fingers run through her hair and then the movement of the stretcher from side to side as she was carried away. Slowly, her mind dulled and the darkness of sleep consumed everything.

131

Chapter 18 – On the Move

Back in her attic, Lady Georgiana continued to write the account of her city's fall.

"That moment was the last time I saw my father's face," she wrote. "So it was that I woke up the following day in Basil's pod; a broken young woman, not knowing who was dead and who was alive. The rest of the events of that period of time were hidden from me. It was only much later that I discovered a measure of the truth. Having only seen the reservoir blow from a distance, I initially thought it was Maltrisia's work, not understanding it was actually Uncle Jack's doing. Nor did I know that at the same time my father had purposefully shut down the waterworks or that his team had also set explosives within the mountain that would be triggered if anyone attempted to turn the supply back on again. All of this had been kept from me, my father's desire to keep me out of a potential war. It was only years and years later, when we tried to restart the waterworks, that we came face to face with the reality of what those explosive deterrents could do."

Lady Georgiana sat back in her chair and rested for a few moments, rubbing and massaging her wrist between her fingers. Her hand ached from the writing process. Casting a glance at her left arm, the faint scarring that ran along the back of her hand and up towards her elbow caught her eye. She ran her finger along its lines to remember what now seemed a wound from a distant yesterday.

"Another push," she said to herself, "and we'll be half way there."

The writing had taken more out of her than she'd imagined, perhaps she wouldn't be able to finish this task today.

"But I have to finish today," she said to herself.

She panicked for a second, seeing that her account so far may have been too detailed. Time was running out and there was still so much more ground to cover. Getting out of her chair, she walked the length of the room; glancing through the attic's front and then its rear windows to make sure all was clear before sitting down again. Dipping her pen to fill its nib with ink, she breathed in, breathed out and started to write.

"So here's the rest of the story, how our city fell. Walking in the dark is always a difficult thing, whether physically or mentally. Both require careful steps. It only takes one false move, one trip, and everything comes crashing down.

- -

It had only been just over a day since Georgiana had awoken in Basil's pod. Now she leaned on his arm as they picked their way through the charred debris. The safety of the horticultural shell was now behind them and tentatively they inched forward, keeping an eye out for airships and other places that might house Maltrisia's troops. Despite the shroud of smoke and dust that blew in the breeze, they felt very exposed in the open air and so decided to enter the nearest building that looked somewhat safe.

From the outside it seemed structurally sound, most of the windows and doorframes were intact and none of its walls seemed to lean. Originally a busy office block for financial services, now it was an empty lifeless shell; confirmed as such as they made their way down its abandoned corridors. Georgiana's heart felt heavy from the lack of life around them. After taking the lift, she stared out of one of the top floor broken windows, trying to see past the haze of misty dirt that filled the air. She still couldn't see too well and so instead listened to the breeze bouncing its way down empty streets. It seemed as though no-mans-land had laid claim its rights to the very heart of the city.

"I don't think that anyone has survived this war," she said.

"I can't hide the hard facts," said Basil, "that terrible things have happened whilst you were asleep and I don't expect there to be much left of this city or of the people who were in it."

Georgiana was still a little unsteady on her feet and, after searching through two more buildings, was quickly growing tired.

"We can come out again for longer tomorrow," said Basil. "All I need is some extra water for my tanks in the pod, just to top them up, and then we're set for the next few days."

For once, Georgiana agreed with him. She had little hope of seeing anyone ever again and she knew that searching for a longer time today would not help her recovery. She sat in an empty office café, waiting for Basil to come back with his bottles filled with water. Within minutes, however, a grumpy faced Basil returned from the kitchens.

"No water here either," he said, in an exasperated tone. "It's as if the city has run dry!"

"Well we're not out of water yet," she replied. "Perhaps this part of the city has damaged waterpipes."

"Perhaps everyone has fled the city and, apart from Maltrisia's troops, we're the only ones left," replied Basil.

The idea had not occurred to her. Perhaps her family were alive after all, they'd just left the city. The idea briefly gave her a measure of hope until it dawned on her, "My father would never leave me behind," she thought. With the devastation that she'd witnessed today from the top floor window, along with everyone else in this locality, he must be dead.

After putting his water bottles into his rucksack and slinging it onto his back, Basil gave her his arm and they returned to the pod. Georgiana was both depressed and relieved to be back. The pod had been a place of comfort but returning empty handed and none-the-wiser about the city's state and fate meant they'd failed to achieve their goals; back to square one almost and another night of rest before they would venture out again. Settling down for the evening, Basil noticed that the lights in the pod were dimming.

"We're losing power," he said. "Not sure how long this electric supply will last. I've gas to cook on, and some old gas lamps if we need them, but that won't do for staying here for more than a few weeks."

Georgiana had no intention of staying for a few weeks. She would be off as soon as she was healed, hopefully within a few days.

"Let's just get some rest," she said. "We can talk about what to do in the morning."

"Do you mind sleeping in the pitch-dark tonight?" asked Basil. "We need to save the gas and the lamps should be a last resort."

"I don't mind," she replied. "It gets light pretty quickly in the morning."

That evening, therefore, Basil settled Georgiana onto his settee with cushions and blankets and made his own bed at the other end of the room. Before turning off the lamp, he lit a slow burning coil, made from fire resistant fabric, put it on a metal tray and placed the tray on a coffee table.

"That way we can at least see where something is in the room and keep our bearings," he said.

With night time approaching they both settled down and, after a short talk about Basil's plants and herbs hobby, they fell asleep.

"Wake up, wake up," came Basil's hushed voice.

Georgiana felt his hand on her shoulder. He held a dimly lit lamp next to his face as he bent over her.

"What's the matter?" she asked, alarm in her tired voice.

"People in my pod," he whispered.

"People?" she echoed.

"Up, up, up," said Basil, motioning for her to get off the settee.

Georgiana rolled her legs off the sofa and put her feet straight into her boots. She pulled them tight, but had no time to tie the laces.

"With me," said Basil, as he moved towards the back of the room.

Together they went into the small kitchen area where Basil opened up a pantry door. Behind it was a set of stone steps going down into a lower part of the pod. Motioning for her to follow him, they descended the stairs and into a stone chamber. Mushrooms grew on long tables along with the long stalks of maturing rhubarb plants. Basil led the way down to the end of the room and then through an open archway into another chamber. He took Georgiana to the far end wall and blew out his lamp. It all went completely dark.

Above them, they could hear the sound of footsteps, voices and furniture being moved.

"Who are they?" asked Georgiana.

"I didn't get a chance to look," said Basil. "I just heard them in the corridor and thought only of you."

Touched by his friendship, Georgiana gave his hand a squeeze and waited with him as the people above continued their searching activities. The noises continued for some time, the people must have been searching through every room in the pod's network of growing chambers. Then the sound of footsteps coming down the stairs. Lantern lights danced their way through the open archway and voices spoke about the plants they could see. Round the corner they finally came. Basil and Georgiana stood motionless, the lights from the lanterns leaping about the room. Here and there they jumped till they settled on the pair of them. The dazzling brightness was painful to the eyes, but whoever was pointing them didn't drop the beam from their faces.

134

"Shall I arrest them sir?" a voice asked.

Silence.

"Shall I arrest them sir?" came the question again.

Still there was silence.

Then, "You're alive," came a whispered tone.

Georgiana took a few moments to recognise who was speaking to her. Her emotions rushed about her heart. Normally this voice brought a shiver of distrust through her veins but now its familiarity was surprisingly comforting.

"Erepsin?" she enquired, her hand still held across her eyes.

The lamplight dropped a little and then a figure stepped out from the group and walked towards them.

"Georgiana," he said, and put his arms around her to give her a hug.

Georgiana was a little taken aback to find herself in this friendly squeeze but allowed him to do so, even patting him a couple of times on his back as a brief recognition of the embrace.

"Where have you been? How did you get here?" were Erepsin's first two questions, relief etched all over his face; but before there was any chance of reply, Erepsin seemed to remember who was with him.

"These are friends," he said over his shoulder in an official tone. "Go about your work."

With that, all but one of the group dispersed, shining their lights off into other rooms that made up the maze of Basil's underground herbal pantry.

"Can't talk here," Erepsin whispered softly into Georgiana's ear.

She gave him a brief nod. Erepsin looked at Basil standing nearby.

"With you?" he asked Georgiana.

She nodded.

"Ok," he said. "Come with me."

135

"Georgie can't walk far," said Basil to Erepsin. "She's been injured," he added.

Erepsin's face was etched with lines of concern as he flashed his lamp's beam up and down her.

"I'm on the mend," she replied.

"We'll use my carriage," said Erepsin. "It's not far from here. Do you want to be carried?"

"I can manage," she said.

"Georgie needs rest tonight," said Basil. "She should stay and rest and move in the morning."

Erepsin lowered his voice to a whisper, "You can't stay here any longer," he said. "It's too dangerous. You're fortunate I found you first. You have to come with me. It's the only way to keep you safe."

Together they made their way back up and into the pod's upper room. Basil was most unhappy that his things had been disturbed, turned over and rummaged through, but Georgiana calmed him down whilst Erepsin sent for transportation.

"There'll be a little walk before we get to the road," he said. "Too much rubble to bring the carriage right outside the door."

Basil had to carry Georgiana the last part of their walk but eventually she found herself in a comfortable carriage. After a short journey through various back alleys and a short open space signposted Moorepark, Erepsin called the driver to halt. He jumped down and held out his hand for Georgiana to follow. Basil assisted her exit from the carriage and both looked at their surroundings. They were in a small plaza, known as Govan Square, in what must have been one of the more overlooked parts of the city. Surprisingly, hardly a building was damaged and all seemed quite normal.

"I thought the city was completely destroyed," she commented.

"No," replied Erepsin. "Just parts of it. My mother wants something left to rule over it seems."

In front of them was a large court house. Next to it was a police building called 'La Petite Bastille'. Erepsin led Georgiana and Basil into the Bastille, where there was much hustle and bustle. Person upon person gave him a nod of recognition as they passed by. Erepsin had certainly gained for himself quite a following among the many associations that were with him. Finally, after descending a few flights of stairs, he entered a reception area where Basil had to sit down to catch his breath. Supporting Georgiana's walking throughout the day had begun to take its toll.

"Give this man some refreshments," Erepsin ordered. Then he took Georgiana gently by the arm into a back office. There he helped her to take a seat and then sat behind his desk. Erepsin's friend closed the door and, as soon as they were alone, the conversation flowed.

"What are you doing?" said Georgiana, leaning across the desk.

"Working for my mother, officially," came his quiet reply.

"And unofficially?"

"Trying to sort out the mess," he replied. "Probably doing something similar to you."

"I've been out of it for a few days. Don't even know who's alive or dead."

Erepsin seemed a little taken aback at her lack of information. She was normally at the heart of city matters.

"You don't know what's been going on? Where have you been?"

"Unconscious," came her reply. "One of your mother's mortar shells landed next to a building in which I was hiding from her insects," she flatly added.

"I'm very sorry," he said, in a subdued tone.

Erepsin glanced down at his hands, his fingers fidgeted with each other.

"I really didn't know this was going to happen in the way it did," he added.

"Well it has," Georgiana replied. "Now your mother's caused a chaos that will never go away."

"I thought you were dead," he finally said, tears in his eyes. "When the shells started falling, I knew you'd be in the city centre. I watched the first wave of her insects go off to capture and carry back so many of her targets, but you weren't amongst them. I thought you must be dead."

"I almost was," she said.

They sat silently for a few moments, wondering what to say next.

"So you're trying to *fix things*," she said, a slight tone of accusation in her voice. She struggled to control her contempt for Erepsin's mother, which she found rising within her, and the fact that her son now sat on the opposite side of the table wasn't helping.

"As much as I can, in the current confusion and madness," he replied.

"I'm sure right now that there's plenty of people out there who'll be doing what you are, trying to *fix things*," she sarcastically replied. "Now's the ideal environment for any two-bit opportunist to jump at to gain power and influence," she added.

"You're right," replied Erepsin, his tone of voice matching her sarcasm. "This manic killing has indeed provided an environment that can be used to one's advantage; if you're brave enough to take a hold of the messed-up life that's left behind. Lots of prospect for anyone who wants to capitalise on the opportunities provided by the chaos and other people's pain. A really great place for me and my schoolboy chums to run and play in, don't you think?"

Georgiana looked embarrassed at Erepsin's statement. He clearly meant it as a rebuke to her.

"I'm not actually like that you know," he said.

"I'm seeing that you're not," she finally replied.

"And I know that you're not like that either," Erepsin replied. "You're too good for that kind of thing."

Georgiana just stared back at him, wondering where the comment might be going.

"We could work together," he said. "You and me. This city needs us. With your abilities and my connections, we could turn this place around. You'd be surprised to know how many people are still alive, not everyone is dead."

"I've already had enough of death," she said. "The dead are dead. Let the living do what they want, I'm not for bothering with them."

"Not even with your father?" replied Erepsin.

Georgiana took in a deep breath, gasping at Erepsin's words.

Seeing that she needed some assurance that his words were true, he leant across the desk and purposefully gave her his gaze. "He's alive!" he reiterated. "Your father is still with us."

The stare between them lasted for a good few seconds before Erepsin repeated himself again.

"He is still alive," he said, reassuringly placing his hand on hers.

Tears welled up in Georgiana's eyes and she continued to stare at him, making sure he was telling the truth.

"Does that change things for you?" he asked. "Ready to fight for his freedom now?" he enquired.

"Where is he?" she demanded.

Erepsin sat back in his chair and picked up a piece of paper from his desk, as if to read it.

"In the lower cell block that lies beneath the main detention centre," he said. "Alive, well and waiting for his public trial I do believe."

"Detention centre? What detention centre?" she said.

"My mother has taken over one of the old tin mines and turned it into a prison," he replied.

"And how do I get in?" she asked, a tone of urgency in her voice.

"Whoa, slow down," said Erepsin. "I'm not going to let you just charge in there and get yourself arrested. You are on my mother's hit list too you know."

"Hit list," she echoed.

"Seems like you've upset her on one too many occasions with your wit," he replied. "She's not a very forgiving woman."

Georgiana felt her heart sink.

"I should turn you in you know," he added. "I'm under strict orders to find anyone whose name is written on any of my many lists and turn them in for public trial."

Erepsin stared and sat in silence for a few moments, watching Georgiana shrink in her chair. Then he laughed out loud.

"Oh come on!" he said. "You really think I would actually do that!"

Georgiana put on an 'almost smile' to go along with Erepsin's comment, but inside there was nothing to laugh about.

"However, you are on her hit list," he said. "So I'll have to get you out of this part of the city. Not all of Clearwash is in my mother's hands, not yet anyway. She's still not been able to take up residence in your family home, for example."

"I beg your pardon?" she replied. "What did you say?"

"Oh, she's had her eye on your mansion for years," said Erepsin. "Didn't you know?"

Georgiana felt revulsion at the idea of Maltrisia living in her family's residence.

"I'll blow it up before she gets her hands on my home," she curtly replied.

Erepsin smiled, "I'm quite sure that won't be necessary," he said. "In fact, I can assure you that won't happen – don't blow up your home for nothing," he added, with a smile.

"I don't understand," said Georgiana.

"She won't get that far," said Erepsin.

"She won't?" echoed Georgiana.

"No," replied Erepsin.

"And how is that?" asked Georgiana.

"There are certain things I can guarantee," he said. "One of those things is that my mother will never own your house."

"I take it you're up to something," said Georgiana.

"Correct," replied Erepsin. "Just remember that we do have some things in common."

"And what's that?"

"I want what you want," he replied.

"Which is...?"

"Freedom for the city of course. Freedom from my mother."

Georgiana looked at him again, trying to read his face and to get at the meaning behind his rhetoric.

"I can get rid of them, all of them," he added. "Her and every single one of her followers. One fell swoop and they're gone!"

"Get rid?" she said, in a tone that posed a question about the method and the final result.

"Yes, get rid," he replied.

Georgiana wasn't sure she liked the sound of this, but she was so out of it, it was hard for her to weigh up what was being said.

"Hasn't there been enough killing?" she asked.

"Not quite," he replied. "There's still a little more to be done; got to get rid of the bad people you know."

Not knowing how to respond, Georgiana simply said, "Revenge isn't really my family's thing, We prefer to talk about justice being done."

"Depends how you see it," replied Erepsin. "Sometimes you have to work justice for yourself – which other people may or may not call revenge."

"Whatever you do is your business," she finally responded. "I just need to rescue my father."

"Well I can't help him right now," said Erepsin. "That's several moves away on my chess board. First I have to overthrow my mother," he added. "If you want to attempt a rescue I suggest you find what remains of the resistance movement, which still has control of the eastern side of the city. Personally I think they're all going to die. So, if you want to stay with me, then we can talk about the options that are available and perhaps at some point look at rescuing your father."

"There's a resistance movement?" said Georgiana.

"Yes," Erepsin eventually replied, mentally kicking himself for letting out the information.

"People are still fighting her?" she asked.

"Of course."

"But I thought she'd have killed everyone by now."

"Well she hasn't."

"What about her harvester insects? I thought they were the end of everyone."

"They are," replied Erepsin. "But it seems that your father's speeches got the better of my mother. As far as I can tell, she was so enraged by his success that she went to war too early, just to shut him up, make an example of him."

"Too early?" echoed Georgiana.

"Seems that most of the insects, hymenopteran as you call them, were not fully fuelled when they were first released. For many of them, their initial attack could only last a little over twenty minutes, then they had to return to be recharged. However, the reservoir had been blown and that took the city mains supply out, so she's struggling to recharge them. At the moment she can only send them out in small bouts. Beyond that, she's stuck with limited resources."

"Well she's shot herself in the foot, destroying the reservoir like that."

"She didn't destroy it," replied Erepsin.

"Who did?"

"That I don't know," he replied. "But, whoever it was, put a stop to her plans. The city is in crisis. We're almost out of power, the waterworks has stopped delivering water and no-one has won. Shortly it will be a battle to the end and who knows how it's going to turn out. So you'll have to make up your mind pretty quickly which side you're on if you want to stay alive."

"I'm still a little out of it," she finally responded. "I'll have to find my feet before I make any commitments."

"That's perfectly understandable," Erepsin remarked, sensing that the conversation between them wasn't going any further. "Don't wait too long to decide," he added. "There are a limited number of wind turbines available to my mother and she is using them to generate power to refuel her insect army. It won't be too long before she can launch them again."

He was about to get out of his chair when the door to his office suddenly burst open.

"We have another one sir," said one of Erepsin's workers, who only then noticed that Erepsin had a guest.

Erepsin looked a little irritated by the information being shared in front of Georgiana.

"Well done," he said, trying to look matter of fact in his manner.

"Another what?" enquired Georgiana, staring in Erepsin's direction and then at the young man.

"Another…" he began.

"Just go about your duties," interrupted Erepsin.

Off the man went and Erepsin got out of his chair, indicating that it was time for Georgiana to be leaving as well. Before seeing her out, he held out his hand and, out of politeness, Georgiana half-heartedly took it.

"I would really like to think that at some point we could help each other," he said.

"I'm sure we can," she replied. It was a half promise.

Erepsin looked disappointed that he hadn't managed to persuade her to stay.

"I know that your father means everything to you," he said. "So I'll make inquiries about his exact location and safety. At the same time I'll make sure that you're safely on your way and going in the right direction to connect with people who may be able to help. You need to move out of here. Everybody straying around in this part of the city is considered a traitor."

Basil looked quite irritated when he saw them return from Erepsin's back office. He obviously thought their private meeting had gone on far too long.

"I'll have an escort take you in the direction of your home, but you'll have to make the last part of the journey yourself. My people can't be seen going over into resistance territory."

"Thank you," said Georgiana.

Without warning Erepsin gave her a hug.

"I'll see you again, I'm quite sure." Erepsin whispered in her ear.

After finishing the hug, they parted company.

Chapter 19 – Divided we Stand

"Don't trust him," whispered Basil, on their way out of the building.

"I already don't," she replied. "However, he's not what he seems."

"I already see what he is," replied Basil. "You can't trust him."

During the next few hours of darkness, two of Erepsin's staff floated Basil and Georgiana down one of the many canal veins that ran through the city. Their boat was small, only large enough for four people, and without lights – it felt like a continuous journey into ever thickening darkness. The smoke from burning fires and the dirt from blown up rubble filled the air with a smog that was both smothering and disorienting. There were several bumps along the way and both Basil and Georgiana were told to keep their fingers inside the boat. Finally they pulled alongside the canal wall and were told to disembark. One of the crew pointed at a brick building that was but a stone's throw away.

"In there," she said. "Spend the night in there and in the morning you'll be able to cross over without being shot."

"What do you mean, without being shot?" asked Basil.

"If you try and cross in the dark, you'll be shot for being part of Maltrisia's armed force," she said. "If you wait till early morning, in the light the resistance forces will be easily able to see that you're not armed and not a threat."

She smiled, gave a nod to say 'goodbye' and was gone.

"I don't see what there is to smile about," Basil commented. "Come on," he said to Georgiana. "Let's get you inside."

The room was dusty, dirty, draughty and dull – as depressing as any could be; three windows blown in and the table, chairs, carpets and curtains thick with debris. There was nowhere to rest, to lie down and sleep, so Basil put a chair in the corner of the room, away from the windows. Georgiana sat on it and rested her legs on another chair which Basil had placed under her feet.

"Not very comfy, I know, but it will have to do for a few hours," he said.

The night eventually passed and the chill from the desert wind rapidly gave way to the heat of the morning. Sensing that the longer they delayed, the more dangerous it would be, they decided to make their move as soon as the sun began to shine its first rays over the hills that marked the boundary of the city's eastern wall. Tentatively they stepped outside, squinting about them in the low-level sunlight. After glancing over their shoulders at the building in which they'd spent the night (quickly concluding they wouldn't have slept there if they'd known of its fragile state) they began to find their bearings. A small park lay ahead, one of the many open spaces which used to offer the city a break from the continuous row upon row of brick buildings that made up the living spaces of the aged metropolis – but today there was no invitation to play in this open arena. The carefully planted beds of shrubbery, manicured grass lawns, trimmed hedges and matured trees were all dusted over, just like the scatterings of finely sieved icing sugar across the surface of a grand cake. In this case, however, there was nothing sugary to look upon as the element added to this particular dirt-based recipe was a delicate layer of powdery grit. With this depressing ingredient evenly deposited across the whole neighbourhood, the park looked nothing but bleak. Everything was grey, looking now more like a multi-teared sponge that was well past its sell-by date.

Through the park they moved, very much aware that they were probably being watched. Georgiana's hobbling way of walking made it clear that they weren't a threat, yet at the same time it increased their vulnerability; no ducking or diving if someone began to use them as early morning target practice. Like refugees, they walked the familiar ground as if in a foreign land, on the one hand seeking out a friendly face and, on the other, not knowing if they'd soon encounter a hostile reception. Onwards they travelled until they reached the edge of the park's perimeter, unchallenged and unhindered. The silence that surrounded them was sinister, keeping them on a knife's edge. It was as if death itself was doing the stalking and would pounce just at the moment when they thought themselves to be safe.

Nothing happened, however. At the park's edge was a ditch and on the other side a fresh bank of earth; piled high to stop the advancement of troops. Here was the boundary they'd been looking for. How to approach it, they didn't quite know.

"If we take them by surprise, we might come under fire," said Basil. "Calling out, however, might be an open invitation for someone to take a pot shot at us."

They stood for a few moments, wondering what to do.

"We'll call out," said Georgiana. "We'll stand in the trees on the edge of the park, and shout from the cover they provide."

This seemed the most sensible way forward. Together they stood next to an old oak and called out a hearty 'hello'. Nothing happened. They called again, still nothing.

"One more time," said Basil. "Then we'll know if there's someone there or if…" but there wasn't time to finish his words.

From out of nowhere volleys of bullets scattered about them. Basil and Georgiana found themselves on the floor, scrambling to get behind the tree. Shielded by the great oak, bits of wood splintered in all directions as the bullets continued to pummel the area.

"We're unarmed," shouted Georgiana, slumped on the floor with her back to the tree as the bullets whizzed on either side.

The shooting slowed a little.

"We're unarmed," she shouted again.

All went quiet.

"So much for your friend Erepsin's advice that we'd be safe," Basil remarked.

A few moments later, from within the park from which they'd just come, soldiers appeared, rifles aimed at the recoiling pair. Holding up their hands, Basil and Georgiana slowly stood to their feet, helpless whilst watching them approach.

"We're unarmed," shouted Basil.

"We don't mean any harm," Georgiana called. "We're civilians, on our way home."

The group of soldiers approached and dropped their aim as they got closer. One of them walked up to Georgiana and smiled.

"Good job you've got a recognisable face," he said. "Otherwise you might be dead by now."

143

Standing next to the tree, he waved at whoever had been shooting to confirm the ceasefire.

"I suppose you'll be wanting a ride home," he added.

"Yes, yes I would," replied Georgiana.

"Well miss," he replied. "I think we can do that for the daughter of Lord Stephen."

Never had a family name been so valuable to Georgiana as in that moment. Within minutes the soldiers had escorted her and Basil over and around their defences and finally they were in a carriage which wound its way in-between craters and around debris, towards her family residence. Georgiana felt an immense sense of relief that home was just a short ride away. In times of war, however, nothing turns out as you think it should. As they approached the main archway at the top of the drive, Georgiana could see that her family mansion was a busy place, lots of comings and goings from a variety of people she'd never met before. The intrusion of these 'unknowns' into her home felt quite unsettling. After the carriage stopped at the front entranceway, she climbed the steps to her home and, with Basil's help, walked through into the main hall. A variety of people were there, mostly talking in groups or walking from place to place. Georgiana stared for a few moments, trying to make sense of their presence in her private property but then made her way towards the main lounge, to sit and rest. As the strangers in her home caught sight of her, however, they stopped and stared. Not liking the attention, she continued to walk on, hobbling a little as she made her way towards the large oak door that led into the family living room. Pushing it open, she stepped inside and finally, there in front of her, a face that she could recognise.

Standing around a table with a group of people about him was Uncle Jack. She hobbled forward and he turned to see her.

"Uncle Jack, oh Uncle Jack!" cried Georgiana, hugging the big man as if he were family.

"What on earth are you still doing here?" asked the big man, whilst wrapping his hefty arms around her. His bear-hug grasp was the most comforting thing that she'd had in a while and their embrace lasted till she felt ready to let go.

"Where are my mother and Emma?" she asked.

"Your father made sure they were on their way out of the city," he replied. "Marcus here helped them out." Uncle Jack gestured to a young man on his right.

"Thank you Marcus," she said.

"We were all looking for you," replied Marcus. "Your mother was distraught. She didn't know where you'd got to."

"I was invited by Erepsin to see what his mother was about to do," she replied. "Before I could get back and warn everyone, the shelling started."

"That young meddler," said Uncle Jack. "He never could leave things alone."

Before Georgiana could defend Erepsin's actions, however, Uncle Jack shouted, "Fetch me some refreshments for the lady of the house."

They were strange words to hear, 'the lady of the house' but it dawned on her that, with her mother gone from the city and her father in captivity, she was now the rightful owner of the property.

144

"And also some refreshments for…" Uncle Jack paused, looking at Basil who clearly was accompanying Georgiana.

"This is Basil," she said. "He's been looking after me since the day the war started."

"For Basil," shouted Uncle Jack down the corridor.

The sound of rushing feet and the clattering of trays confirmed the order was being put into place.

"You're very welcome here," said Uncle Jack, turning to Basil.

Basil nodded, but said nothing in reply, clearly a little intimidated by Uncle Jack's presence and all the hustle and bustle that was going on around him.

As soon as they'd sat down, Georgiana launched into her questions.

"How did my father get captured?" she asked.

Uncle Jack hesitated, not sure how to break the news.

"I know he's still alive," said Georgiana, giving a good reason for Uncle Jack to share what he knew with her.

"He's still alive?" echoed Uncle Jack in a cautious tone. "How do you know?"

"Erepsin told me a few hours ago when we were escaping from the city inner circle," she replied.

Uncle Jack just looked at her.

"He was emphatic about it," she continued. "He knows exactly where he is."

Uncle Jacks face briefly welled with tears.

"You thought he was dead?" asked Georgiana.

"We all did," he replied. "When we saw him captured by the harvester insects, we thought that was the end of him."

"They caught him?" asked Georgiana.

"All over him," replied Uncle Jack. "Took him off into the air and carried him across the city."

Georgiana's heart sank, it must have been a terrible thing for her father to experience.

"But this news that he's alive changes everything," said Uncle Jack, sitting back and stroking his beard, thinking through the new information.

"He got carried off…" echoed Georgiana again. She was finding it difficult to come to terms with.

Basil sat next to her and put his hand on hers.

"Did Erepsin give any more information about where he is?" asked Uncle Jack.

"He told me that Dad's being held in one of the tin mines," she replied, swallowing the lump in her throat.

"Is that so," said Uncle Jack, looking a little more positive.

"Can we get him out?" she quickly asked.

"That is something we'll have to figure out as we go along," Uncle Jack replied. "Within the hour we'll be having another meeting with what remains of the city's political groups and they're not a bunch of people that I easily get on with," he added. "We're going to attempt to form a single, united resistance to Maltrisia, or that's the theory anyway. I shall inform them that your father is still alive."

He patted her on the arm and stood up. Signalling to Marcus and the rest of his team, they gathered around him.

145

"Prepare the room for the meeting," he said. "I shall need everything we've got at my fingertips. Can't be outwitted or outtalked by any of those blundering idiots again."

His team nodded and left the room. Calling Marcus to one side, Uncle Jack added, "Make sure that no-one has access to any of the family rooms upstairs. Lady Georgiana is back in residence and has the right to her family privacy."

"Of course," replied Marcus, and off he went to make sure that all the upstairs rooms were clear.

"We've had to use your home as a base from which to plan our work," said Uncle Jack. "It's beyond the reach of Maltrisia's weaponry and there's enough resources here for us to organise ourselves properly."

"I understand," replied Georgiana. "My father would be using our house in the same way if he were here."

The refreshments arrived and were placed in front of Georgiana and Basil.

"Eat up and then get some rest," said Uncle Jack. "I shall have need of you from now on."

After being refreshed with some food, Georgiana decided that a bath, a change of clothes and some rest was in order. Basil was given a guest room to stay in and was able to source some fresh clothes from the wardrobes that were in that part of the house – clothes that the family had put aside for visiting guests who, due to unforeseen circumstances, needed a change of attire but who hadn't come prepared for spillages or party life.

Georgiana woke a few hours after taking what she'd hoped was going to be a mid-morning nap. The bath and change of clothes had been most welcome and she'd just rested her head on her pillow, intending to snooze. Her exhaustion, however, had got the better of her and it was early afternoon by the time she came round. Deeply annoyed with herself, she remembered that Uncle Jack and his team were having a meeting with the other political people of influence who together formed what was commonly called the 'resistance movement'. She hurriedly pulled on her boots, draped a shawl around her shoulders, and walked as well as she was able down the hall and to the stairs. Moving as gently as she could, with one hand firmly on the banister, she made her way down each step. At the bottom she glanced here and there to see if she could locate Uncle Jack. A quick question to someone passing by informed her of his whereabouts and within a minute or so she'd found him, Tristram, Marcus and Basil in the main dining room.

"I'm so sorry," she said. "I didn't expect to sleep as long as I did."

"You obviously needed it," replied Uncle Jack. "From what Basil here tells us of your adventures, you're fortunate to be alive."

Basil pulled up a chair for Georgiana.

"Here you are Georgie," he said.

Ignoring the slight embarrassment of his nickname for her coming into the open, she smiled and sat down.

"How did your meeting go?" she asked.

"Not as well as we had hoped," replied Tristram.

"They need their heads banging together," said Marcus.

146

"Perhaps the phrase, 'They need to wake up to reality' is a better way of expressing it," suggested Tristram, thinking that Marcus wasn't striking the right tone.

"Marcus got it right the first time," commented Uncle Jack. "Now," he continued, "we're struggling to get a united military push against our enemy. Some of those blockheads aren't willing to help us push back through the city and to take the fight to her. Therefore we don't have all the military capabilities that we would otherwise have if our allies were being sensible. So, for the moment, we're stuck holding our ground."

"Why are they not willing to fight?" asked Georgiana.

"They think that time is on our side and time is all we need to sort out this mess." added Marcus. "They reason that Maltrisia will be willing to talk about a truce once the city's water supplies are totally run dry,"

"And by that time, we'll all be dead," Uncle Jack retorted.

"What about her war crimes?" asked Georgiana. "What about all the suffering and death that she's brought to us? How is she going to be brought to account for all of that. Are they going to talk her into the dock?"

"I know, I know," said Uncle Jack, looking extremely exasperated with the whole situation. "As we've just said, the meeting didn't go well and we've not been able to persuade them to do anything sensible towards winning this war."

"And what about my father?" she asked. "How is he to be rescued?"

"He isn't," replied Tristram. "The committee could not see any reason why, at this stage, resources to win the war should be redirected to seek to save Lord Stephen's life."

"This can't be true," said Georgiana. "My father gave everything for this city. He could have got out, but he chose to stay, chose to risk his life for everyone. Now you're telling me that his life isn't worth saving?"

"That's not what the committee is saying," Tristram replied.

"I'm sorry Georgiana," said Uncle Jack, "but on this issue the committee is right. Wars are not won by saving individuals."

"I thought you said you'd stand with him to the very end," she retorted.

"That I did," replied Uncle Jack. "And I'll not stop fighting for his or our freedom until we're free or we're all dead. When your father and I made the decision to rescue this city, we both knew that we could possibly die as a result. We both possibly will. No-one is safe in this environment. As fond as I am of your father, our focus has to be on rescuing the city and taking out our enemy. Individual and personal agendas come second. If I can in any way or at any time save your father, I will, but with diminished resources under my command, saving any one person is a secondary aim now. We must take Maltrisia out and all of those associated with her. Then we can look at personal rescues."

"So on the one hand they're not going to use any of our resources to win the war, they're just going to sit it out. Then, whilst we're just sitting it out with our soldiers doing nothing, I'm told that we don't have the resources to get my father out. That doesn't make much sense."

"I think we needed you with us in the meeting," remarked Basil.

Tristram sighed. Giving the lenses in his glasses a clean, he added "They still wouldn't have shifted their stance, they're quite set in their ways."

"Much of the military is not under my command," said Uncle Jack. "I can't simply take over. There are people in this city with a strong enough will to take me out if I rock the boat too much. If I tried a military coup at this point, I might find myself arrested."

"We'll get your father out at the earliest possible opportunity," Marcus assured her.

Georgiana, however, wasn't convinced that anyone could offer her any solid promises about the future.

Uncle Jack reached across the table and briefly tapped her hand. "We have another meeting in about an hour," he said. "I want you to be there. You may be able to turn some of their thinking in our favour. A fresh face and a fresh brain might be just what we need at this time."

The next hour rolled by and the meeting started again with little ceremony. Marcus, Tristram, Uncle Jack, Basil and Georgiana all stood together and watched as the city dignitaries came into the room and seated themselves at the table.

Once everyone was settled, a young clerk opened up a wallet and pulled a paper from it.

"We have something to say," he began, even before any introductory talk had started.

Reading from the paper he continued.

"After serious consideration, the authorities of Clearwash City have concluded that military action against our current aggressor will only result in our total annihilation. Such is the level of stalemate between the two sides, it is impossible for anyone to win. Therefore, for the good of the city and the long-term future of our

148

culture, we propose that a group of peacemakers be forthwith elected and sent into the heart of the agricultural zone to discuss an initial ceasefire with our opponent and then to propose talks that will put us on a road to lasting peace."

Uncle Jack grunted his response to what had just been said, but remained silent. Georgiana could see his face redden with anger.

"This is our final decision on the matter and the military committee is not willing to entertain any more thoughts of aggressive strategy until we have exhausted all peaceful possibilities."

With that the clerk folded the piece of paper, put it back into his folder and zipped up the wallet. Silence surrounded them as each group waited for the other to say something.

"So here we stand, divided and already defeated," Uncle Jack finally said.

"We prefer not to see it that way," the clerk replied.

"Well, you've made your decision," he said.

"Shall we vote on it now?" the clerk answered.

"Vote?" said Uncle Jack, in a breathless tone. "Vote!" he suddenly yelled. "Do you really think that I'm going to vote my freedom away? What do you think this is?"

"This is a place where we negotiate and find our way forward," the clerk replied. "That's what King's Law is all about."

"Since when is handing our freedom over to a dictator an act of King's Law?" Georgiana replied.

Uncle Jack nodded his approval at her comment.

"We're in a time of aggressive war," she continued. "Voting about agreeing to a dictator's demands isn't even on the agenda."

"It's not an aggressive war if we don't choose to be aggressive ourselves," the clerk replied.

"What!" exclaimed Marcus.

"Good heavens" added Tristram.

Georgiana waded into the conversation, curtly pointing out the error of their thinking.

"When a dictatorial administration goes to war," she said, "the opponents of the regime don't bring about peace by putting down their weapons. That kind of behaviour doesn't bring about a cessation of hostilities, it just allows the dictator to walk all over you; to slaughter as many innocent people as they wish whilst leaving the weak and vulnerable completely helpless and at the mercy and whim of a people who are heartless, without pity or compassion. How could you suggest such a thing?"

"We don't see her as a dictator, just a misunderstood woman," said the clerk. "We feel that talking and working our way through these things is the only real way forward."

"You're living in a dream world," said Uncle Jack.

"We're having a conversation you don't understand," he replied.

"My father understood very well what was going on," Georgiana said. "He saw through her rhetoric and her agenda. She doesn't want discussions or negotiations. She wants to rule."

"Some would say your father has added to this calamity by his strong stance against Maltrisia," came his reply. "If he'd been more lenient and tolerant in his behaviour towards her, then perhaps this mess might not have happened in the first place."

Georgiana balked at the statement. It's twist on reality was offensive in every way. Before she could open her mouth and articulate the anger that instantly welled up within her, Basil put his hand on her arm to steady her. Tristram chipped in.

"I think most people would not adhere to your way of seeing things," he said. "You forget just how forthright Maltrisia was from the start."

"You also forget," added Marcus, "that this city was on the verge of social collapse before Lord Stephen stepped in to rescue us. There were riots in the streets. We were about to turn in on ourselves and Maltrisia was the chief culprit; saying that she had to wipe the house clean, scrub away the grime and the scum! Her rhetoric was very violent and aggressive."

"Well, we see and understand things rather differently," replied the clerk. "Maltrisia could have destroyed us all by now, but she hasn't. She's withheld the full might of her military force. There's something to be said about that. Seeing things from that perspective changes things and we want to capitalise upon it. We see a door of opportunity for peace. So, in the light of our decision, we have to declare that if we see any violent action being taken on your part towards our current opponent, then we'll consider that activity as a direct attack on our attempt at peace. Any military aggression from any of you or your co-workers will be seen by us as illegal and needing our attention."

"You don't speak for us and you've no right to dictate anything!" shouted Marcus.

"We are still the city authorities," the clerk firmly responded. "Society has not fallen apart yet and we intend to be proactively good in resolving our current problems. The evils of war are not for everyone and therefore we seek to use reason, rational argument and goodness to bring a resolution to our current situation. We will not tolerate any interference with this process. You are to stand down from any acts of aggression until we have fully entered into our discussions with our current rival."

"Our *current* rival?" echoed Uncle Jack.

"Yes," replied the clerk. "We do not see her as a long-term foe."

Uncle Jack sat back in his chair, scratched his beard and sighed deeply with frustration.

"You said 'fully entered into'," Georgiana pointed out. "You said until you have 'fully entered into' your discussions with Maltrisia. You sound as if you've already started them."

"We've received a message from Maltrisia that she's willing to entertain the possibility of a ceasefire whilst talks get underway."

Georgiana was indignant. "You've already contacted her!" she exclaimed. "The people here have had all these talks with you about the way forward and all of the time you've withheld the information from them that you're already talking with Maltrisia!"

"It was necessary for us to talk to all sides in complete confidence before we made our decision," replied the clerk.

"So you're not on our side," Tristram pointed out.

The clerk shifted in his seat for a moment and then stared at them all.

"We see our role as positively neutral," he said.

"That's ridiculous," exclaimed Marcus. "You're here to represent the people, not to stand aloof as if their troubles are not your own."

"If or when your talks get underway, how will you know whether or not you've had success?" asked Tristram, his tone of voice, as usual, quite monotone and matter of fact; unmoved by the emotions of the group around him. "How will you ever know if the person you're dealing with isn't lying to you? And, will you at any point go back to military action if you sense you're being lied to?"

"To some extent, that all depends," replied the clerk.

"Depends on what?" asked Marcus.

"Depends on the extent to which the talks have developed and grown in their scope," they replied.

"Unbelievable," remarked Marcus.

"Verbal mumbo jumbo," said Basil.

Uncle Jack leant across the table and eyeballed the political elite in front of him. He could see their disdain for him and his group; obviously having made the decision to speak to them only through the clerk and not to utter a word themselves.

"You betray us," he said, "and I'll personally hunt each of you down."

That statement didn't go down too well. Georgiana could see that Uncle Jack's method of negotiating was very different from that of her father's. He was clearly a military man, not a diplomat and his method of resolving conflict was quite forthright. Not surprisingly, with that, the meeting was over.

After most of the people had left, Uncle Jack took a break in the entranceway to the Pluggat's old coal house where he smoked his pipe. Georgiana stood nearby, resting her back on the outside wall.

"That went well," she sarcastically remarked.

Uncle Jack nodded his agreement but made no reply.

"I don't know what planet they live on," she added, "but clearly their high notions of negotiation and discussion fly in the face of common sense. How can people even begin to think as they do? Anyone with even a grain of rational thought would have the presence of mind to see Maltrisia for what she is. It seems that prudence is out of fashion these days."

"I won't lie to you," interrupted Uncle Jack. "The chances of us getting your father out alive before this war is over are almost zero."

"I see," she replied.

"I don't think that we're going to win this war," he added. "My advice to you, once you're physically able to do so, is to get out of this city as soon as you can; join your mother and sister-in-law. We're about to enter into a time of total chaos and I've no idea who will survive or what life will be like after it's all over."

Georgiana dropped her head.

"I thought you could save him," she said.

151

"So did I," replied Uncle Jack, "but not with the outcome of this last meeting. They've derailed us and I don't know how we can succeed now."

The big man saw his young friend begin to crumple. He put his arms around her and gently gave her a hug whilst she cried.

"I just want him back," she said. "And these people are fools, they don't deserve to be saved!"

"Indeed they don't," he replied. "But they have the resources that we need, so try and save them we must, or we all die."

Chapter 20 – The Master Plan

Around the dining room table sat a group of dishevelled people.

"So," said Uncle Jack, in a tone of resignation, "we're a diminished group but here we are. We need to find a way forward to turn back this tide." Glancing over towards Georgiana, he leant back in his chair and lit his pipe.

"I hope you don't mind," he added.

She smiled, tobacco wasn't something that she liked but her father didn't have any rules about pipe smoking indoors.

"Without any war machine behind us we're not going to get very far," replied Marcus.

"Perhaps we don't need a war machine," said Tristram.

"I don't see what can be done without one," replied Basil. "Force is the only thing Maltrisia knows. She's not going to stop until she gets her way. Talking only puts off the inevitable."

"The question still has to be asked," said Uncle Jack, "as to why she hasn't released the full force of her insect army on us."

"What do you mean?" replied Georgiana. "I thought you said that my father got carried off in the insect storm that she launched on you all."

"He did," replied Uncle Jack. "At that time we thought it was all over, but within about half an hour of them dominating the city, most of them withdrew and we've only seen them in small numbers ever since."

"We need to figure out why she's showing restraint," Marcus added.

The rest of the group all agreed, but Georgiana sat quietly for a few moments, wondering why they were asking the question at all.

"But she's not showing restraint," Georgiana eventually replied.

"What do you mean?" asked Tristram.

"She can't release the insects," replied Georgiana. "They're not fully fuelled."

The rest of the group just stared at her.

"How do you know that?" asked Uncle Jack.

"Do you *not* know?" she asked.

"Obviously we don't" replied Tristram.

Georgiana paused, a little surprised at their lack of knowledge.

"Erepsin told me," she said. "Erepsin told me that my father so provoked Maltrisia by his speeches that she went to war too early. She released her insect army before they were fully ready. They were recalled due to needing an energy boost. However, the dam was suddenly breached and, with the turbines out of action, the city's power supply quickly became diminished. Since then she's struggled to get them fuelled up again. The reason why we've not seen them is because they've been out of action."

The group sat for a few moments, soaking up the information that Georgiana had shared.

"I wish we'd known this before," said Uncle Jack. "This would have changed everything."

"I was more than a little out of it," replied Georgiana, a little defensive about her being asleep during their first meeting that day.

"Not your fault," replied Uncle Jack, assuring her that there wasn't any blame being sent in her direction. "This information is most welcome, however."

"They'll still not change their minds," said Tristram, referring to the politicians who'd just left. "They'll still go for an attempt at peace."

"When all the while she's the one on the back foot and in a place of weakness," replied Marcus.

"Do you know if she's going to be able to get them back into action?" asked Tristram.

"Erepsin said that she was using the limited resources of a few wind turbines to get them ready again. It takes much longer than using the city's power grid, but at some point they'll be fully fuelled and ready to go."

"So she *is* going to be able release them against us once more," commented Uncle Jack.

Georgiana nodded her reply.

"If the wind turbines are the only source of power she now has, then the longer we delay, the more she is able to prepare for a final strike," said Basil.

"So going to war really is the only option for us to defeat her," added Marcus. "Can we persuade the military commanders to ignore our stupid politicians?"

"Maybe, maybe not," replied Uncle Jack. "Clearwash City hasn't been at war for nearly one hundred years, so our current military leaders are just as ideological as our politicians. They're inexperienced and naïve, convincing them to go to war might be impossible and put us at a disadvantage if we want to take Maltrisia by surprise.

"Perhaps we don't need to convince them, or even involve them," commented Tristram. "There may be another way."

All eyes in the room settled on the ginger bearded man.

"What are you proposing?" asked Georgiana, sensing that Tristram had something up his sleeve. "Do we take out the wind turbines and stop her that way?"

"Many years ago," Tristram replied, "I was a student in the city's science and horticultural centre. "These insect harvesters, these hymenopteran, were originally designed and produced at our university for the application of food care and harvesting. During the time of their development I worked on a beta version of the coding that currently runs them."

"You know how they work?" asked Uncle Jack.

"It's quite a simple control method," he replied. "Each insect has basic programming about what it thinks are its duties. That programming is quite easily changed, as we've seen; now, rather than performing the role of harvesters and pest killers for fruit trees, they're reprogrammed to be human collectors and assassins."

"You think we can reprogramme them?" asked Marcus.

"That's not the point I'm trying to make," replied Tristram. "Despite their abilities, these insects are not as intelligent as they seem. They need telling what to do and how to go about their assigned work, they can't think very well for themselves. Each hymenopteran can work individually or be tuned in together to perform their duties in clusters, within a numbered group. For an insect or group of insects to go about their work there's a 'send out' command and a 'recall' command to bring them back to base. A shut down command also puts them to sleep in order to recharge their fuel resource tanks. This enables us to micromanage what each cluster is doing. However, there's always an overruling 'send' or 'return' command that all of them have to obey. This enables corporate return and shutdown. Get that command and that changes everything."

There was a silent pause in the room whilst everyone processed Tristram's words.

"So you're telling me that we can shut them down with just one command," remarked Uncle Jack.

"In theory, yes. To do that, we need to have what's called a base unit," replied Tristram. "It's a surprisingly small device, about the size and shape of a shoe box. They were originally kept within the greenhouses where the insects worked, but I assume that Maltrisia has moved them to where she keeps her creatures for refuelling purposes."

"The containers from which they were released on the first day of the war," said Marcus.

"Most probably," replied Tristram. "It wouldn't surprise me if each of those containers has its own base unit. That way each cluster knows where to return when it's time to recharge."

"And how would we get one of these base units, base stations?" asked Uncle Jack.

"We either steal one from her," replied Tristram, "or we create one ourselves."
Which is easier," asked Uncle Jack.

"Not sure," replied Tristram, in his open and honest way. "I've no idea which would be the easier option."

"But can you do it?" asked Basil. "Create one or steal one, I mean."

"Possibly," replied Tristram. "The stealing would have to be down to you, if we chose to go down that route. Once we had a base unit, then it would simply be a matter of re-programming it."

Everyone shuffled in their seats, getting used to this new information.

"The programming we wrote for the insects didn't have any military application written into it," Tristram continued. "As there were no war implications in our thinking, we just created them with the harvesting of fruit crops in mind along with the driving off of pests such as bugs, rodents, etc. I'm hoping that the programming is still basically the same."

"Why? What does that mean for us?" asked Basil.

"No high-grade encryption to stop them from being hacked," replied Tristram. "In theory the programming that runs them is quite unprotected."

"So all we have to do is to create a base that calls them home and sends them to sleep?" asked Georgiana.

Tristram nodded, "Exactly!"

"And what stops Maltrisia from waking them up again?" asked Marcus.

Tristram scratched his nose., "We could add a simple update to their code, once they were asleep, that will prevent any wakeup command being initiated without a password code first being delivered. That way we could keep them asleep for as long as we needed them to be in that state."

155

"How do we know that Maltrisia hasn't thought of that already?" asked Georgiana.

"We don't," he replied. "That's where the risk lies. But, to be honest, being the person that she is, driven by her desire to rule, and from what you say about her going to war too early due to being enraged by your father's speeches, I think it's highly likely that in her passion to get what she wants, she's most likely to have overlooked this detail."

Everyone sat quietly for a moment or too, thinking through the new plan.

"It's quite a gamble to make a strategy based on something you can't be sure of," commented Basil.

"War is never a sure thing," replied Uncle Jack. "How long would it take to make one?"

"With the right equipment, just a matter of hours," responded Tristram. "We'll need to send some foragers into the city academy campus to raid the labs for components. I would need to visit my home and get a copy of the code from one of my archive storage disks."

"That won't be easy to achieve without our activities being observed in some way," replied Uncle Jack. "It'll have to be a night mission."

"And how would we deploy this base unit?" asked Georgiana. "What range would it have? Could we guarantee that all of the hymenopteran would be disabled?"

"These are all answers that we would find out with time," replied Tristram. "Until I get the parts to make a base unit or until we steal one, it's hard to know. However, I assume that if Maltrisia has kept the foundational coding unchanged and, if she launches all her insects at the same time, that just one base unit, placed at the heart of the city, would be enough to bring them down. If not, then we could make some booster boxes to raise the signal, and so put them all to sleep that way."

"There's still a lot of 'ifs' and assumptions there," replied Basil. He wasn't happy with the plan.

"It's a slim chance," admitted Uncle Jack.

"It will take a miracle to pull it off," added Marcus.

"Then we will all have to get very religious," replied Tristram.

Everyone gave a brief half-smile at the comment.

Georgiana still needed to rest. Most of the conversation was now about who would do what. Marcus began planning his night-time raid of the city's academy whilst Uncle Jack prepared for a brief visit to some of his military connections to sound-out the depth of their loyalty to the city authorities.

"If they'll break with their immediate allegiances to the current political elite, then we may have a chance to implement our plans with a measure of force," he said.

"What can I do?" asked Georgiana.

"In your physical state," replied Uncle Jack, "just get better as soon as you can and give your support from here."

That didn't sound too good, but Georgiana knew Uncle Jack was right. There was no way that she could be of any sustained help to anyone until she healed from her injuries, though she also suspected that he was trying to keep her out of trouble for the sake of her father. So a rest was needed whilst the others planned their next moves. Basil promised to fil her in on what had been said. She had in mind, however, to also ask Uncle Jack or Marcus for the same information. Basil had proved himself to be a wonderful friend, but she still doubted his ability to be thorough in delivering information. Up the stairs she went, her hobble was far less pronounced than it had been. She could feel her movement coming back, but it would be a good few weeks before she'd be feeling normal again.

Finding herself on the other side of drowsy, she decided that a lie down was probably the best thing, however, not wanting to lose the final part of the day, she relaxed in an arm chair instead. Within moments, she was asleep. The next thing she knew, it was dark outside. More time gone and yet another occasion when she felt that life was slipping by and she had nothing to show for it. After making her way downstairs, Georgiana sought to catch up with the discussions that had taken place. To her dismay, she found that most of the group were gone. The house butler told her that Uncle Jack had been away for a time, had returned, then disappeared again. No-one quite knew where or why. Marcus was probably in the heart of the city fetching the components from the university campus from which Tristram would build a base unit whilst Basil had been given the job of seeking out extra helpers for their plan, whatever that plan was. Tristram had visited his home, then returned and now was no-where to be seen. It was as if he'd simply vanished in the night. This was all that she managed to find out from the people who were left in the house. Uncle Jack's and Tristram's disappearances were a bit of a let-down. It didn't seem like a very well-run rebellion.

Feeling a little dejected, she asked for some food and went into the main lounge to relax. Within a few minutes a tray of very plain sandwiches were in front of her and she tucked in, not realising how hungry she was until she began to eat. Eventually she heard the front door to her home open and in came another troop of unknown people; Georgiana felt that her home would never be hers again. Amongst them was Basil. He seemed very busy, getting everyone ready to be debriefed in some way. Georgiana waited for him to finish his task, getting everyone out of the foyer and settled into one of the back reception rooms to await what would probably be their orders from Uncle Jack. Eventually Basil found his way into the lounge and sat down opposite Georgiana. He looked very pleased with himself.

"What have you been up to?" she asked.

"I was given the task of finding more volunteers who would be prepared to work with us," he replied. "People who had no liking for our political elite but at the same time would be loyal to a good cause."

"I hope you were discrete," Georgiana responded. "You all came in together as if you were on some kind of community walk."

Basil hadn't quite thought about it and looked a little embarrassed by her statement.

"Well," he said, "we did our best to keep a low profile."

Not wanting to dampen her friends success, she asked, "And who are these people that you've recruited?"

"A stroke of luck really," replied Basil. "Many of them are members of the horticultural and rambling society that I've belonged to for many a year. I thought that most of them would have fled the city by now, but with rare flora in many of their pods, this group had decided to stay and salvage as much as they could. I came across them when I visited some pods near the foot of the reservoir."

Georgiana felt her heart grow weary, Basil clearly didn't have much of a mentality for war.

"And you think that these people will be useful to us?" she asked.

"Of course," he replied. "Not as agile or as young as many, but I'll vouch for them that they're as faithful and reliable as any soldier."

Georgiana smiled the best smile she could, one that would hide her disappointment and not discourage her friend.

"I'll introduce you," said Basil, and got up to go and prepare his new recruits to meet her.

Georgiana sighed and forced herself onto her feet. This wasn't what she wanted but she felt obliged to go along with Basil's enthusiasm. After hobbling through the foyer she found herself greeted by a group of very enthusiastic individuals; people eager to shake her hand and tell her how much they appreciated being asked to be part of something that would make a difference in the city. Georgiana was as polite as she could be and chose to smile with each handshake.

"Oh I recognise you," said one of them. "With your family still here we're all going to be fine."

"Is your father around?" asked another.

"He's, he's not available at the moment," Georgiana replied, quite taken-a-back at not only their minimal knowledge on the progress of the war but also their failure to grasp the fundamentals of what they were all going through.

"I'm sure he's a busy man," said another.

"So what's the plan?" came the next question.

"Yes, what is it that you want us to do?" asked another.

Basil struggled to provide a coherent answer the question and it became clear to Georgiana that he'd given an invitation to these people without telling them much about what was required of them.

"We can't tell you the details just yet," replied Georgiana, trying to be as discrete as possible. "You'll receive some specific orders very soon from our leader, Jacob Crispus Ken-Worthington-Brown."

"Ah, Uncle Jack" said one of the group.

This comment was met with much enthusiasm.

"At some point, he'll tell you the final goal," replied Georgiana. "First, however, we need to take some very careful steps into what we're asking you to do." She hoped this type of talk would keep them in the dark and halt the flow of questions.

"So it's a bit of a coddiwomple," one of them replied.

Basil smiled.

"A coddiwomple!" said Georgiana, in a bewildered tone.

"Yes, a coddiwomple. You know, when you're travelling in a purposeful manner towards a vague destination – a coddiwomple."

Georgiana's patience was beginning to run out. These friends of Basil were obviously gentle folk; a well-meaning and upright people who were not acquainted with the matters of war. Her trust in any military aptitude or strategic abilities that

158

they might have was wearing thin. Leaving them with Basil, she gave instructions to the house staff to provide them with refreshments and went back upstairs.

"Get a good night's sleep, Georgiana," she said to herself. "You'll need to be refreshed and clear-headed in the morning."

So to bed she went.

Georgiana awoke to streaming sunshine. She'd not thought to close her curtains the previous evening, simply because she'd been so focused on getting a good night's sleep. Despite the bright light doing a good job to awaken her, it was much later in the morning than she'd wanted. After a brief wash, she made her way downstairs to a busy household. Tristram, Uncle Jack and Marcus were all working in a garden conservatory with a team of people to assemble a base station. Box upon box of equipment was scattered about the floor. Clearly Marcus and his team had found it difficult to follow Tristram's orders and they'd brought back a hoard of items, hoping that amongst them all was that which Tristram needed. It seemed, however, that the gamble had paid off and everyone around the table was in a positive mood.

Georgiana couldn't get close to the frenzied activity as there were too many 'helpers' in the room, so she watched from a distance for a while as they continued to cannibalise parts from other machines and reassemble them within a small box which sat in front of Tristram. Seeing that she wasn't going to be of any use to the group, she eventually left and walked about her home, trying to get her leg movement back. After some food, she went back to the garden conservatory to check on progress and was surprised to find it empty. Casting her gaze across the variety of small gardens that formed the first perimeter of her mansion's property, she could see a little crowd of people, standing in a line next to the garden maze; all facing away from the house with their backs to her. Together, their corporate standing made a human wall which concealed the event that was taking place on the opposite side of them.

Making her way over, she could hear Tristram's voice explaining how his devise worked.

"So, let me activate it again," said Tristram, from somewhere behind the wall of observers. "And this time, don't scatter like a pack of spooked chickens!"

Everyone laughed, but it was clear from their stance that they still weren't too confident about Tristram's actions. Many of them wavered on their feet, displaying feelings of anxiety and obviously thinking through their options if something went wrong. What Tristram was doing, Georgiana couldn't quite tell. Standing next to the group was the Pluggat-Lynette family head butler, clearly waiting for the right moment to interrupt the event.

"So the wakeup password code is what?" called out Tristram.

"Ninety-nine, twenty-two, nine, two, nine, two," came the crowd's response, they wrote the numbers in the air with their fingers as they spoke, obviously being taught to do so as a visual aid to help them remember.

"And the kill code is?"

"One, one, one four," the crowd replied, also drawing the numbers in the air as they spoke.

As Georgiana continued to approach the group she heard a metallic rotating sound, as if something was being started up. A small engine purred for a moment and then stopped. It started again and then stopped. Then once again, it started and stopped.

"Seems like this one doesn't want to wake up," came Tristram's voice.

The crowd mumbled a moment of muted laughter.

"Come on Basil," said Tristram, "put the passcode in again."

Basil was out of sight, obviously doing something behind the wall of people. His bumbling activities, however, were a source of amusement to his onlookers.

"That's it," said Tristram. "Now press to activate."

Moments later there was another rotating sound that purred, hummed, whirred, whined, whizzed, vibrated and finally buzzed itself into life. Corporately the wall of onlookers shrank backwards from the sound, wanting once again to run away.

"Hold your line," shouted Tristram, over the hum of the buzzing sound. "It won't hurt you! It's just scanning for identification."

Georgiana felt her insides churn and her heart almost fail as the buzzing sound roared into life. She recognised the noise straightaway. Stopping in her tracks, about ten paces from the gathered crowd, she automatically found herself stepping backwards, to move away. Then, she started to hobble, as quickly as she could, back towards the house. There, buzzing in front of the heads of the people was a harvester insect. One by one It worked its way along the line of onlookers, scanning their faces.

"You see," said Tristram, "it's not going to recognise any of you. It has a predefined hit list which none of you match. It doesn't, therefore, see you as a threat."

The gathered party seemed to relax a little more as the harvester buzzed its way amongst them, clearly not interested in their gathering.

"Now who wants to input the shutdown code this time?"

"I think it knows it's about to be shut down," said a member of the group. "It looked as if it was going to sting the last person who inputted the code."

"Nonsense," replied Tristram.

The small base station was passed from person to person but none seemed interested in holding on to it. It was like watching a child's party game, passing the parcel down the line whilst waiting for the music to stop, with each person not sure that they wanted to be the one to do the job of unwrapping the present. As they were fumbling around, without warning the buzzing creature caught a glimpse of Georgiana, making her way back to the house. She cast a quick glance over her shoulder, to see if she was safe, and instantly it seemed to recognise her. In one swift movement the metallic killer sped between the crowd and buzzed its way across the lawn. Hearing its sudden acceleration, Georgiana changed direction, hobbling into the conservatory on her right and slamming the door behind her.

A loud 'thud' resounded throughout the hothouse's framework as the hymenopteran's accelerated body impacted one of the glass panes that stood directly in front of Georgiana. She watched in horror as a large crack appeared across the window. On the other side of the glass, the creature's jaws and sting continually bit at and thudded against the already brittle barrier in a frenzied killing motion; its

160

claws constantly scratching and scraping at the splintering shards to try to find a way through. Georgiana looked about her for something with which to defend herself. There was nothing but bits of cannibalised machinery which the team had ripped apart to make the base station. In those following moments, all she could do was grab a nearby stool, not a good item to fend off an attack.

Realizing that it couldn't get through the glass, the hymenopteran sped away from the conservatory, across the lawn and over to the far side of courtyard. It then turned on itself and zoomed back again, gaining speed to impact the same window to force its way through.

"Shut it down!" yelled Basil, when he saw the crowd of onlookers simply standing there, dumb struck by what was happening in front of their eyes.

The first job was finding out who was holding the base station. Once that was done it was a matter of putting it on the ground to enter the number.

"Ninety-nine, twenty-two, nine, two, nine, two," shouted some from within the crowd.

"No!" cried Marcus. "That's the passcode! Shutdown is one, one, one four!" he cried.

The sound of breaking glass echoed across the gardens as the hymenopteran, on its second attempt, managed to smash a hole in the pane. The gap was big enough for its head to get through. Wiggling its abdomen, the insect frantically jerked its body to squeeze itself between the narrow gap. Georgiana hobbled forward, pushing the stool's seat against the creature's head, trying to stop its entry. Through the vibrations in the stool's wooden frame, she could feel the strength of its jaws, vigorously scraping and pushing with a single-minded intent. She felt it coming through and knew it was only moments away. Pulling back the stool, she thrust it forward again, trying to crush the creature before it could enter. It was too late, the glass shattered and in it came.

Georgiana swished her stool at the creature, missed, stumbled backwards and fell over some discarded equipment. The impact sent pain through her back and down her leg. Lifting her head, she saw the harvester hover for a second, raise its sting, and with a high screeching buzz, it surged forward for the kill.

"I'm dead," she thought.

Georgiana felt the force of its impact on her stomach.

"Ahh!" she cried, but couldn't say more, winded by the force from the creature's metallic body.

Then nothing. No sound at all. Lying prostrate and still, she was unable to move. She tried to breathe in, but found no strength to do so. Eventually she let out a groan, her head dropped back onto the floor with the expectation of her life to ebb away. Moments later there came the clatter of feet along with a rushing about her. The limp insect was removed from her side and then appeared the faces of the head butler, Marcus, Basil and others leaning over, concern etched across their brows.

"Are you hurt?" came the first question.

Georgiana had no idea who was speaking to her.

"Depends on what you mean by hurt," she replied.

"I mean, did it sting you?"

Georgiana felt her stomach but found no wound.

"I don't think so," she replied, beginning to breathe again.

Amazed by her own answer, she felt across her stomach again.

"No," she said. "It hasn't stung me."

Tristram walked in through the door, the base unit tucked under his arm. "It must have shut down in mid-flight," he commented.

"What on earth was it doing here?" asked Georgiana, finally able to breathe.

"Marcus and his team captured a couple of them whilst in the city last night," replied Tristram.

"There's more than one?" asked Georgiana.

"We captured two of them," replied Marcus, looking rather embarrassed.

"Why on earth did you do that?" she asked.

"We needed some to test our base unit on," said Tristram. "Without live hymenopteran, how could we have known if the station works?"

"We didn't think it would be dangerous," said Marcus. "None of us here are significant people in the city's political life. In theory, the insects would leave us alone."

"In theory?" echoed Georgiana.

"We didn't see the danger," added Tristram. "You must be high up on Maltrisia's hit list. I am deeply sorry."

"Well I'm still here, and that's all that matters," she eventually replied. Georgiana thought, however, that Tristram's tone of voice was still too aloof to carry any strong sentiment. Men of logic, she reasoned, were an emotionless bunch!

Basil stood up to address the crowd of onlookers and raised his voice in a way that Georgiana hadn't heard before.

"It's one, one, one, four, for shut-down!" he said, indignantly. "Ninety-nine, twenty-two, nine, two, nine, two is entered after the shutdown code, to enable the encryption code to stop someone hacking the machines and turning them back on again."

The rambling society group stood awkwardly, looking on and feeling duly rebuked for their lack of clarity.

"Then to restart the insects, we do the same but in reverse order," he commented.

"Sit up and rest," said Marcus, squatting next to Georgiana. "That must have been a terrible ordeal."

"I shall be fine!" she insisted. "I just need to catch my breath."

"We should help her ladyship back to the house," said the head butler, in a tone that meant he was to be obeyed.

"Are you ready to be moved?" asked Basil.

"Yes, just get me to the house," replied Georgiana, not wanting to be the centre of attention.

Once Georgiana was inside her home, the butler turned to address the crowd of people.

"The Primor, Lord Jacob McArnold Crispus Ken-Worthington-Brown asks for your company in the lounge," he said, giving Uncle Jack his full title.

162

En masse, everyone made their way back to the lounge whilst the butler and Basil helped Georgiana to a nearby chair. A few moments later they could hear the explosion of Uncle Jack's temper when he was told what had just happened.

"I think we need to go into the lounge to rescue them from Uncle Jack," said Georgiana.

"You need to rest," replied Basil, perhaps not wanting to venture into the lounge himself.

"Basil's right," added the butler, "You must rest."

"I'm fed up with continually being out of the loop," replied Georgiana. "I want to be part of the meeting."

As they entered the room they could hear Uncle Jack saying, "When you do any more testing of those devices, you'll do it in a closed, locked room until each of those creatures is shut down and put into a secure box!"

Muted nods were given across the room as everyone felt the force of his displeasure. Georgiana smiled a 'thank you' to him and sat down to listen in on the rest of the meeting. Uncle Jack then sat at the table, picked up a note that he'd just been given, and frowned.

"What is it?" asked Marcus.

"Peace talks begin tomorrow," he replied, with a sigh. "They've actually agreed to having peace talks with that venomous woman," he added, disdain written across his face. "And it seems that my presence is also required as a sign of general solidarity. I am invited to attend as, 'a witness to the day's proceedings in anticipation of a historic deal' – which they expect to be brokered."

"They've invited you there in order to keep an eye on you," remarked Tristram. "To make sure you're not up to something and so disrupt their plans."

"It will also put you directly within Maltrisia's grasp," said Marcus.

"It's absolute folly," added Basil.

"She'll have everyone in place for her takeover," said Marcus. "She'll make her strike as soon as the talks are over, or as soon as they're underway, releasing her insects for the kill."

"Can't you just not turn up?" asked Georgiana.

"It may not be a sensible place to be," said Tristram, "but if we want our plan to go ahead, I assume you'll have to attend."

Uncle Jack scratched his beard and thought for a few more moments.

"I'm to be *escorted* there first thing in the morning along with the other invited guests," he eventually replied. "Not turning up, as Tristram says, would cause an unnecessary focus on our activities and I'll most likely be arrested for non-compliance. We'll have to reassign the responsibilities within our group."

"In what way?" asked Georgiana.

Uncle Jack thought for a few more moments.

"Marcus, you'll have to take my job," he said, "and Basil, you'll have to cover for Marcus."

"I don't know what that means," replied Georgiana, feeling quite fed up with not knowing exactly what was going on.

"It means that I shall go to the ceremony to keep up the appearance that we're complying with their wishes. Basil, you and your team put the bases in place and

Marcus, you set out with your team to deal with Maltrisia at the nearest opportunity. Then, once our enemies are taken care of, whoever is the first to be able to rescue Lord Stephen from the tin mine, that's their job too."

At the end of this long day Georgiana felt more out of step with events than ever before, even Basil seemed to have a clearer role than she. Finding some space in her father's private study, she relaxed back into her father's arm chair, rested her eyes and dozed. Her exhaustion was still getting the better of her, but she felt a measure of strength coming back into her limbs. Sleep came upon her once more but, when she came round again, she was grateful that, this time, not much of the evening had been lost. She'd slept for an hour, perhaps a little longer, and now felt for the first time in days as if she was ready for some purposeful activity. Before she could make any decisions, however, a small white object on the left side of her chair caught her attention. Once she could focus her eyes properly, she picked it up. It was a neatly sealed envelope. Had the paper been there before she rested in the chair or had someone walked into her father's study whilst she had been asleep? The thought quite unnerved her. Using her nail to scrape up the envelope's flap, she flipped it open. Inside was a note. It read,

> To the sister of my friend Mr R,
> Having understood that there is a temporary ceasefire in place and that a delegation from your side intend to make a peace treaty with Maltrisia, there are developments here that I think you ought to know about. I'd like to meet up with you, so I've come over to your side for a talk. This evening I'll be in Eastbridge, third house along Poplars Street, adjacent to the main road.
> Yours,
> Mr E.

The note's authenticity was clear to see, knowing how her brother and Erepsin used to refer to each other as 'Mr R' and 'Mr E'.

"Very clever," Georgiana thought.

The Eastbridge community was, strangely enough, on the eastern side of the city, located near the easterly bridge that spanned the canal; a route which led onto the main road which ran right up to the city front gates. This Eastbridge community was a small and exclusive collection of buildings, together forming an almost closed community for the rich and wealthy. It was due north of the Pluggat-Lynette mansion and got much of its status from being located near to the family estate. It was too far for Georgiana to walk, but an easy enough journey on horseback.

She read the letter again. How Erepsin had managed to get the note to her was still a puzzle. His reach was far wider than she had expected. Perhaps she'd severely underestimated his influence in the city. Perhaps he was far more at the heart of things than anyone had imagined. She wavered for a moment, mentally limping between two opinions.

"Do I trust him, or do I not?" she thought. It seemed an impossible question to answer. Seconds later she called down the corridor. Finally a young gentleman ran up the stairs to answer her call.

"Saddle my horse," she told him. "I'm going out for an evening ride."

Chapter 21 – You Still Don't Know

"I didn't expect to see you so soon," said Georgiana, casting her gaze about her. She was standing in a room with blown out windows and charred walls. She reasoned Uncle Jack had been wrong when he said that Maltrisia's guns did not reach this part of the city. Eastbridge had been hit several times and the building she was in had suffered extensive damage. Perhaps it was Maltrisia's desire to own the Pluggat-Lynette family home that had kept it safe.

"Things have changed," replied Erepsin. "I hear that your people are going to try and reason with my mother."

"They're not *my people*," said Georgiana.

"Well they certainly claim to represent everyone on your side of the divide," he replied.

"They don't represent me or Uncle Jack or anyone else associated with us" said Georgiana.

"So, Uncle Jack is still alive," said Erepsin, out loud to himself.

Georgiana could already see that she was unintentionally spilling information and bit her lip as a reminder to be more careful.

"Well good for the old codger," added Erepsin. "Glad the old chappie is still breathing. Would be a pity if the city lost such a character. No doubt he has enough kick in him to cause my mother plenty of worry."

"You talk as if he was just an object of amusement," she replied.

"Well I find him so," said Erepsin, "but he won't be able to help you, even if your foolish politicians wake up to the futility of their plans. They're walking into a trap and, once she has sprung it, it'll be game over for everyone."

"We're not involved with them," she replied.

"Oh but you are," interrupted Erepsin. "From what I hear, those political nincompoops still hold sway over your military. Once they are lost, the rest of the city is open to my mother. You, whether you like it or not, are caught up in their plans."

"We already have our own plans," she replied.

"I'm sure you do," countered Erepsin. "I'm sure there are all kinds of small splinter groups who think that they can make their own plans and save this city, despite the fact that the main resources that should be used against my mother are all but paralysed. But whatever those plans are, no matter how clever, they won't be robust enough to bring this city to its knees. This rebellion, on both sides, has to be crushed. My mother and those political, ideological idiots on your side have to be crushed and completely removed for our freedom to come back."

"On both sides?" she echoed.

"Yes," replied Erepsin. "Both sides, if we're to have any lasting peace."

"What do you mean by 'crushed' and 'removed'?" she enquired.

"Removed means removed and crushed means crushed," said Erepsin, a tone of irritability in his voice. "Dealt with, gotten rid of. Don't you understand?"

Georgiana hesitated for a moment, mulling over his words.

"I understand very well," she finally replied, "that you're not just about fixing things for the wellbeing of the city. You're motivated by more than just a desire to put things right. You want to play the judge. You're out to get at anyone whom you deem to be incompetent and anyone who has crossed you."

"Perhaps," he openly admitted, not shying away from the comment. "The weak need someone to stand up for them. Sometimes strong decisions need to be made on behalf of others who can't make them."

"Some would call that an excuse for revenge," commented Georgiana.

"What's so wrong with that?" he replied. "In the midst of all this trouble, I want revenge and I want to avenge. Who wouldn't? We have an opportunity not only to put things right, but to deal with all of those pompous individuals who have placed themselves in positions of power within the city and betrayed us with their so-called high notion ideals. Once they're out of the way, we can finally live in peace and put life back together again."

"You're not the authority on justice over everything that's gone wrong in this city and there are better ways of establishing peace than crushing everyone and anyone who's made a wrong decision about which side to be on," she replied.

"That's a very noble way of thinking," replied Erepsin, "but it doesn't deal with the reality of the problems that we face. My people don't play like yours do," he added. "You're too nice and naïve to take them on."

Georgiana just stared at him.

"You don't know how my mother thinks," he continued. "None of you do. She, and the people with her, are going to destroy you all and there's nothing any of you can do about it. I am the only person who can stop her. She's already outmanoeuvred you once," Erepsin insisted. "You have no idea what's in her head."

Georgiana gave no reply.

"You still don't know, do you?" he finally added.

"Know what?" she replied.

Erepsin turned his back on her to stare at himself in the cracked mirror on the wall opposite.

Within its reflection he could still see Georgiana's gaze, solidly fixed on him and waiting for his reply.

"Who put your brother to death," he finally said.

Moments of silence passed between them as Georgiana mentally processed Erepsin's words.

"It was an accident," she whispered, holding her breath as she sensed she was about to be corrected.

"That bomb was as much an accident as it was a real attempt on my mother's life," replied Erepsin. "She was never in any danger. The scarring on her face is fake. None of it was real, except Richard's death. It was all planned, right down to the last detail. She was never in danger. She just wanted Richard gone, that's all. Destroying Richard would paralyse your father."

"How do you know this?" Georgiana demanded.

"I know, because I live in the same house as my mother," he replied.

"You knew it was going to happen!" Georgiana exclaimed.

166

"Of course not!" snapped Erepsin, spinning round to face her. "Do you think I would let anyone murder my best friend?"

"Of course not," Georgiana hastily replied, stepping backwards to put a bit of space between her and Erepsin's aggression.

The hostile features on Erepsin's face calmed and his demeanour relaxed into a more controlled manner.

"I'm sorry," he said. "But you should have known better than to say that."

Georgiana nodded, but her head was still reeling from this new information.

"I found out the day before the funeral," he added, turning his back on her again. "Then I was placed under what was as good as house arrest and, when I did go outside, I was surrounded by her guards."

Erepsin picked up a sample of stony debris from the floor and, walking over to the window, threw it out onto the street.

"I was a prisoner in my own home," he added. "There was nothing I could do. I briefly escaped, but they caught up with me. It was only when war was just days away that my so-called mother properly took her eyes off me. So I took the opportunity to find out what she was up to. Then, after the war had started, and she failed to get her full and complete victory, I decided, as you know, to enrol in her ranks and so was given the delightful job of clearing up this mess; clearing up her mess and, at the same time, planning a revolt against her right under her nose. So I'm preparing my 'personal justice' as you would call it; this most noble thing called 'payback' or as I call it, making sure that justice is done even if you have to do it yourself."

A stilled hush lingered in the room for some time. Erepsin stared out of the window whilst Georgiana leant on the wall, seeking to desperately make sense of the evening.

"I still don't trust you," she finally replied."

"You're quite wise not to trust me, but you don't have a choice if you want to see your father again."

"What do you mean?" asked Georgiana, bracing herself for yet more information."

"The peace deal," he replied.

"What has my father got to do with the peace deal?"

Erepsin continued to stare out of the window, not wanting to look at Georgiana's face. He seemed embarrassed by what he had to say next.

"The public destruction of your father will be part of the peace deal," he flatly stated.

"What!" exclaimed Georgiana.

"My mother plans to put your father on public trial as part of the peace deal," replied Erepsin, in a tone of voice that showed he was disgusted by the information he had to share. He felt the shame of it as the words left his mouth. "She plans to make a spectacle of him, to humiliate him. It has to go ahead as part of her 'terms for peace' and from what I hear, those so-called political rulers of yours are going to go along with it, even though they know it will end in your father's condemnation."

"I'm sure there will be plenty of voices tomorrow who will try and stop her from pushing forward that agenda," she replied.

Erepsin dropped his head and almost leaned out of the window, trying to get away from what he was about to tell. The flow of his speech was broken as if he was forcing the words out of his mouth.

"They're not going to talk *about* him going on trial at the peace talks," he said. "His trial will be *part of* the peace talks. They're going to take him out of the tin mine, put him at the centre of the city, and let my mother try him, face to face, on the same day!"

The weight of this information caused Georgiana to sit in the nearest seat. She trembled with fear.

"They've already decided to sacrifice him. Did they not tell you that?"

"No," she replied.

"Such is the loyalty of your political leaders," he added. "That's why I need to not only get rid of my mother, but I also need to get rid of them as well."

Georgiana didn't know what to say. She could feel herself beginning to hyperventilate. Unaware of her distress, Erepsin continued to gaze out of the window.

"They've already betrayed you," he said. "They're as much betrayers of the state as my mother is. It is just that they parade themselves as being legitimate custodians of the city's authority. They're nothing of the sort, just a bunch of self-honouring, self-seeking political hypocrites who want nothing more than to pat themselves on their backs and shower each other with mutual affirmations, pretending to be defenders of the peace but at a cost to everyone except themselves."

Georgiana's head spun with this new information and it was hard to come to terms with what was happening.

"During the trial, whilst everyone is focused on your father, she's going to unleash the whole of her insect army and there'll be nothing you can do about it," he continued.

More silence went by. Sensing something was wrong, Erepsin glanced over his shoulder and saw Georgiana's crumpled state. He rushed over to her.

"I'm so sorry," he said. "I didn't see…"

"I'm alright, I'm alright," interrupted Georgiana, trying to regain her composure and at the same time to keep Erepsin at arm's length. "I shall be alright."

"Just breathe," he said.

"I am breathing," came her reply.

"I know, I know, but breathe deeply."

"I am breathing deeply, just give me some space to do so!"

Erepsin stepped back, not knowing how to comfort his friend. As usual, she kept his attentions at bay.

After briefly leaning over the side of the chair, heaving and retching with nerves, she sat back and rested her head.

"I'm alright now," she finally said.

"Sure?"

"Yes, I'm sure."

"I didn't mean to distress you," he replied.

"You haven't," she responded, still breathing in a little more deeply than normal. "I had to hear the truth."

Erepsin went back to staring out of the window. It was the only place where he felt comfortable with the conversation.

"So you can see why I need to win this war for everyone," he added. "No-one is seeing what's really happening. No-one has the resources to stop my mother and deal with every other self-styled, self-serving politician who loves their own pompous position of power rather than the wellbeing of the people. I have to do it, otherwise everyone's going to die, my mother will win and it will be over before you know it."

"We're well prepared enough," Georgiana insisted, trying to regain some ground in the discussion.

"In what way?" he asked, turning to face her again.

Georgiana kept quiet, not wanting to give away any information that she already had. She was so distressed, however, that she was right on the verge of divulging their plan, but knew in her heart she had to keep that secret at all costs.

"Is there something I need to know?" Erepsin asked, sensing that he might be on the brink of a breakthrough. "I need all the help I can get in order to win this city back," he added. "Just the smallest bit of information could change everything for us. It could rescue you, rescue this city and rescue your father."

Time stood still as Georgiana pondered his words. She'd never heard Erepsin talk like this before. His earnestness for other people's wellbeing was such a surprise. Could it be that he'd actually grown up over the last week or so? She closed her eyes to shut out Erepsin's gaze and fumbled with her thoughts, not caring that he could see her struggle.

"What you do is your business," she finally replied. "I still don't trust you."

"I see," he replied.

Erepsin sighed and paced the room a couple of times, thinking things through. Georgiana began to feel that she may not be quite safe. Finally he stopped, having come to some kind of decision.

"Do you want to see your father?" he asked.

Georgiana didn't know how to reply.

"I know you want to see him," he continued. "The last time we met, you were ready to single-handedly storm the tin mine where he is being held. I assume your desire is unchanged? I can finally take you to him, without us being caught that is. You could then ask his advice as to what you ought to do."

"How is that?" she asked.

"My mother has moved her troops in preparation for a final assault," he replied. "Her insects are nearly ready and with the ceasefire in place, she's pretty confident that she's won. The tin mine where you father is, is virtually unguarded. There's a small security group there and, even though there's still a good number of troops on the outskirts of the industrial zone, they're not close enough to see what's going on. I can't break your father out of prison, but I can get you to him."

"How?" said Georgiana. "How on earth can you get me across this city without being seen or shot? I can't ride for very long. It took much of my energy just getting here tonight."

"You forget," he replied. "I have resources at my fingertips. How do you think I got here without your side shooting me?"

Georgiana again hesitated.

"Do you trust me?" Erepsin asked again.

"No," she replied.

She sat for a few moments and thought.

"But," she finally said, "I'll go with you anyway, if I get the chance to see my father again."

Chapter 22 – You Only Live Once

Under the cover of darkness, Erepsin and his group of followers helped Georgiana back onto her horse.

"We're going east towards the city's outer wall," he said.

"East?" she enquired. "Shouldn't we be going west?"

Erepsin shook his head.

"We're going to the city's front gates?" Georgiana asked.

"No," replied Erepsin, "just to the wall."

It was quite a puzzle, but Georgiana knew there wasn't any point in asking any more questions. Erepsin had always relished having 'one up' on his friends and associates. For him it wasn't just an ego boost, however, strangely enough it was a sign of friendship. He'd done it on many an occasion to her brother and now he was doing it to her. He seemed to gain some kind of delight, when helping others, to catch them out with surprise information. She didn't press him, therefore, just let him get on with it.

Leaving Eastbridge behind, they moved across some open fields. The cloud cover made the grassy banks difficult to make out. No pounding of the horses hooves in this limited light. A gentle trot was all that they could manage, and Georgiana was relieved that it was so. After crossing over a rolling embankment they moved through a small woodland, trees well-spaced apart and easy to navigate. Once through the coppice they could see ahead the great wall that surrounded the city. Tall and immoveable, it was the steady guardian of the ages that constantly kept the city safe; a reminder of their ring-fenced lives, keeping the desert at bay, and to which they were continually in debt.

At the base of the wall was an object that initially Georgiana couldn't make out. As they drew closer she could see that, whatever it was, it was large enough to be some kind of transport device. Dismounting, Erepsin's team pulled away the tarred cloth sheets which covered the object to reveal a wicker basket, ropes and canvas. Within moments the basket was on its side, ropes in place and a hot air discharge began to fill the inflatable fabric.

"You came across the city by balloon!" Georgiana exclaimed.

"It's a cloudy evening," Erepsin replied. "Some of my friends are expert balloon flyers and there are wind channels that you can use to take you so high over the city that you're undetectable. At this time of night, it's a clear westerly wind all the way."

Within minutes the small balloon was ready to go. Erepsin ascended some wooden steps that were put by the basket's side and climbed in. Georgiana followed, finding it difficult to get herself over the last wicker barrier. With a gentle pull from Erepsin and a push from behind, she found herself inside.

Three more of Erepsin's friends entered, leaving two behind with the horses.

"They'll take them back to your stables," he said.

"They're *my* horses?" she enquired. In the semi dark, she hadn't looked too closely at the steeds Erepsin and his friends were riding.

"Of course," replied Erepsin. "You don't think we brought ours over in a balloon did you?" He laughed at the idea.

Pulling the ropes clear, the balloon began to ascend into the sky. Georgiana looked nervously about her. Their ascent was quicker than she expected. The height of the city wall soon lost its grand status as visually it became smaller and smaller. As they continued to rise, Georgiana thought she could see some people gathered outside the city gates and wondered what they would be doing there. Whoever they were, they might well be disappointed if they wanted entry into the city at this time of night. The gates were normally shut and it would take a very illustrious or persuasive person to get them open again.

"It's quite safe," Erepsin exclaimed, seeing Georgiana's slight distress at her surroundings. His smile, however, didn't put her at ease.

"All you need is that extra bit of courage when coming down at a good speed when we get to the other side of the city."

"Why do you have to come down at a good speed?" she asked.

"So you don't shoot over the wall and end up in the middle of the desert," he replied.

That didn't sound very comforting, but it was too late to turn back now. Georgiana felt as if she was on a 'schoolboy run' where some kind of dare had been issued and it was the 'honour of the stupid' that kept the people involved, committed to fulfilling the challenge that had been delivered.

Up, up, up they went, ascending very rapidly and so high that the city was quickly hidden beneath the clouds. The wind picked up the balloon and took it across the sky. Georgiana felt the push of its strength and immediately sensed she was now in the hands of a tempestuous power, raw, relentless, untameable and friend to no-one; carried along by the hand of the divine, she had never felt so small. One of Erepsin's friends leaned over the basket, trying to catch a glimpse of the earth below, getting his bearings for where the city was. Erepsin himself stood with his hand on a rope, eyes closed and enjoying the wind blowing in his face. Clearly this was something that he'd done many times before and he knew how to take in the moment.

The balloon continued to swish its way through the swirling clouds. They were like curtains of vapour that briefly engulfed them, leaving a watery kiss behind on all that it touched. As wonderful and marvellous as the experience was, Georgiana felt as if she'd been swallowed each time they disappeared into the white shroud and was relieved when they exited its moist and hazy grasp. She shivered from the cold, so one of Erepsin's friends gave her a hooded cloak to wear and then also put a blanket about her shoulders.

"Thank you," she said.

It wasn't long before one of the crew called out a signal to get ready to return to the ground.

"City wall sighted," was the cry.

Within moments Georgiana found herself presented with two cushions, one placed behind her back and one on her tummy.

"Sit here," was the firm command given to her.

Sitting down, she found a belt passed around her waist, over the cushion, and fastened to the wall of the basket. Firmly locked in place, she knew that the cushions were there to break a difficult landing. All of the other crew members did the same with one of Erepsin's crew peering through a slat in the wicker basket's floor, gazing to see the moment when he pulled on a rope above his head.

"What are you going to do?" shouted Georgiana.

Moments later, however, she found out. A pull on the rope released a small round hatch at the top of the balloon and out began to shoot the balloon's hot air. Georgiana felt the basket begin to fall out of the sky but her cry for help was smothered by the schoolboy whoops of Erepsin and his friends.

"You're all mad," she shouted at them, once their initial whooping was over.

"Mad and crazy," said one of the crew.

"You only live once," said another.

They all laughed, except Georgiana.

Down, down, down the balloon plummeted, leaving the clouds behind. Once again the young man pulled the chord to close the balloon's lid, but with the lack of hot air, the balloon still continued to plunge towards the ground.

Erepsin leaned across to briefly put his hand on Georgiana's arm.

"Don't worry," he shouted, "we've only hit the wall on one occasion."

Hitting the wall, however, was the least of Georgiana's worries. It was hitting the ground that concerned her.

The balloon began to swish and sway from side to side as it fell, pushed here and there by a wind that could no longer get a proper hold of its captive. Like fingers fumbling not to drop a prized item, so the gusty breeze fumbled with its trophy, not willing to give up its newly acquired treasured possession. Its fumblings, however, just made things worse and the basket began to spin out of control. This was the end, the air rushing about her, the basket being tossed from side to side and the ground rushing towards them, she was dead and all because she'd trusted some overgrown schoolboys who hadn't learnt restraint.

"Now!" shouted Erepsin.

His friend didn't respond.

"Now!" he shouted again.

His friend just laughed.

"A little longer," he called back.

"No, you stupid idiot," shouted Erepsin. "Now!"

Moments later the young man pulled a chord again to release hot air back into the canopy. A long, long blast of fire and air filled the atmosphere above them and the balloons falling descent changed into a swoop. Another blast of hot air and then another. The balloon's deceleration jerked the belt around Georgiana's waist. This was followed by a hefty thud as the basket impacted the ground. Georgiana felt her insides bounce as the force and shock of the crash left her wheezing whilst the basket was dragged along the ground. Finally it stopped, with one of Erepsin's friends still whooping to himself. Erepsin quickly untied his belt, went over to his whooping friend, and gave him a thump.

"I said now!" he shouted. "Now means now! Not when you feel like it."

"We were perfectly safe," he replied.

Erepsin turned and helped Georgiana out of her belt.

"Are you alright," he asked.

"Don't ever do that to me again!" she said, trying to regain her breath.

173

Another thump and Erepsin's friend was duly admonished.

The basket had landed on an area of marshy wasteland, just beyond the industrial zone's outer border.

A little way ahead of them was an old brick building, one of the city tin mines. "That's where your father is," said Erepsin.

"We'll need to approach it cautiously, but getting you inside the mine should be quite easy. I know the guards. They're a bunch of lazy layabouts who like nothing more than a bit of light entertainment and gambling. We'll walk in through the front door, make ourselves at home, and once the party is in full swing, you open the door on the right. You'll see a makeshift stairway going down into the mine. Your father's kept in a locked metal chamber several floors down. There's only one room like it, so you'll find him easily enough."

Georgiana nodded in reply. Her heart was full of churning emotion at the thought of seeing her father.

"One of us will come outside again in about half an hour, to see if you've finished your time with your father," he added. "If we see you, then we'll make our excuses to leave."

Once again Georgiana nodded her reply. Erepsin could see she was already struggling.

"Do you want one of us to come with you?" he asked.

"No," she replied. "I want to be alone."

"Don't stay with your father too long," he added. "We can't keep this group of slackers entertained all evening."

Georgiana nodded that she understood. Going ahead of her, Erepsin and his crew entered the building with plenty of loud cheers, whoops and laughter. The noise of the boys having fun showed a plan well executed. Georgiana followed on once Erepsin was briefly seen closing the main front door; the dulled sound of laughter told the tale of a good time taking place inside. After cautiously approaching the tin mine, Georgiana took hold of the door handle and slowly pushed it down. The door was heavy, so putting her weight on it helped move it ajar. Slipping through the gap, she pushed the door behind her back to where it had been and released the handle. There was an immediate sense of relief that she had made it inside. Looking around, it took a few moments for her eyes to adjust. Before her was a wooden stair winding down into what looked like a bottomless pit. The damp, dirty walls were illuminated by the odd gas lamp dotted here and there along the way. The place was dismal and her heart immediately broke when she thought of her father in the belly of this dark, humid place.

Seeking to somehow keep out the chill from the moist atmosphere, she pulled her cloak more closely about her. Then, with her hand on the wooden rail and always putting her good leg first, she began to tentatively move forward, making her step-by-step, descent of the stair. Her progress was slow. The steps were uneven and sometimes the lip of the tread was rounded and slippery, warn away with years of usage.

"How far down did Erepsin mean by 'several floors'?" she wondered. It made her sick to think of her father in this deserted hole. How had he survived and what condition would he be in when she found him? These thoughts plagued her, almost paralysing her with heartbreak and anguish. She wanted to call out her father's name, to make the quickest connection to him that she could, to tell him that she was on her way and she'd be with him any moment now, but she also knew that risked her being overheard, which would ruin everything. So, restraining herself and forcing out of her head these sudden and terrifying ideas, she continued to move on. Just finding him was the task at hand.

Down, down, down she continued, it seemed an unending task. How would she get up again? That didn't seem to matter. Her love for her father drew her on. Every now and again she'd pass a wooden door, from behind which she could hear coughing and perhaps some talking or arguing. Surely these were the other prisoners captured during the war. Whatever conditions there were behind those doors, the people were obviously in distress. Not wanting anyone to be aware of her presence, however, she made each step down the stairway as quiet as possible. She may have compassion for anyone caught in this dreadful place, but it was her father she was here to see.

Eventually, after descending around eight flights of stairs, she came across what looked like a metal container, built into the wall. Originally it must have served as a staff room, a place of rest for a weary workforce who needed to eat and talk over a lunchtime break, or a place where resources were held for the mining work that was undertaken here. She remembered Erepsin's words, "Your father's kept in a locked metal chamber several floors down. There's only one room like it."

The door had a bolt and a lock attached. No way in, no way out. Scanning her eyes over the structure she saw a metal grill above her head. She lifted up her fingers and tapped on the metal framework.

"Who's there," came a man's voice from inside the cell.

"Dad," whispered Georgiana, her voice trembled with concern. She cleared her throat. "Dad, is that you?"

Chapter 23 – Reunited at Last

"My darling girl," came the shaky voice from behind the wall. "You're alive!" he exclaimed.

Within moments Lord Stephen's hand was on the other side of the metal grill and his fingers slipped through the bars to meet hers. The sheer delight and bliss Georgiana felt when her fingers touched her father's hand was something that she had not expected. Just to make even a fingertip connection after all of this time was enough to make them both cry. Here was her father in the flesh, his voice, his touch.

"Dad," she whispered through her tears.

"I'm here," came his reply, though his tone sounded a little hollow, as if much of his strength had been sucked out of him.

They spent a few moments just pressed against the metal wall, fingertips touching through the iron grate above their heads and moving over each other - hearts pressed against the solid boundary that separated them. Heart to heart, finger to finger, a connection at last.

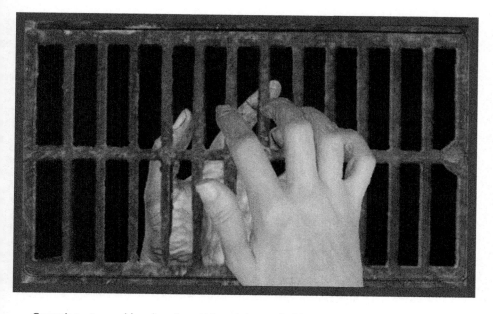

Georgiana turned her head and kissed the wall. "I've missed you," she said. Her dad couldn't reply except to give a muted sigh and a silent nod.

More moments went by and, when their fingertips had said their "hellos" a thousand times over, they seemed to be satisfied a little with their current joining and linking with each other.

"How are you here?" her father asked.

"I came to find you," she replied.

"Is the war over?" he enquired.

"Far from it," she replied.

"Then what are you doing here? Are you in danger?"

"I'm here alone."

"I don't understand. How did you get here?"

"It's a long story. I've come right across the city. Uncle Jack's heading up the rebellion. He's trying to save the city and you."

"Crispus let you travel over to me?"

"Uncle Jack doesn't know I'm here. No-one knows I'm here. Not my friends, nor our enemies."

"Oh my daughter," sighed her father, seeing that she'd overstepped herself and gone beyond what was sensible. "You need to get away," he said. "It's too dangerous."

"I'm going to get you out," Georgiana suddenly declared, though she had no idea how she was going to go about that task.

"No," her father replied to her great surprise.

"No?" she echoed.

"You must not try anything that will endanger yourself," he said. "If Crispus is working to end the war and get me out of here, you must trust him. Whatever your plans are, you may be captured."

"I don't think you understand what's happening," she replied.

"What do you mean?" he enquired

"They're not making it a top priority to save you," Georgiana said. "They've decided that they need to take out Maltrisia and her weaponry first."

Lord Stephen sat quietly for a few moments.

"That sounds quite logical," he finally said. "Crispus knows what he's doing. No one individual is more important than winning the war. He'll save me as soon as he can, I know that. He knows what he's doing."

"Uncle Jack doesn't know all that's going on," she replied. "That's why I'm here. He's underestimated some of our enemies."

There was a pause before Lord Stephen said,

"Tell me what you know."

"There are peace talks to take place tomorrow," she said.

"Peace talks?" echoed her father.

"Our pompous political elite have decided to enter into peace talks with Maltrisia. They've shut down our military response in favour of a peaceful solution, thinking that they can reason with her. Uncle Jack has been required to attend those talks as a witness, or he'll be arrested." she added. "He says he's going along just for the show of it, but he doesn't understand what's happening. Our politicians have betrayed you. They've promised Maltrisia that she can put you on public trial tomorrow as part of the peace process. Uncle Jack knows nothing of it and still thinks you're going to be held here until he can rescue you. Once you're moved and taken to the city centre, he might not be able to save you at all!"

"What plans does Crispus have?" asked her father.

"He's going to try and shut down Maltrisia's insects and then open up an attack on Maltrisia herself. But he doesn't have an armed force with him. I can't see how he can succeed. Getting at her and keeping you safe at the same time may not be possible."

"If he can save me, he will," replied Lord Stephen. "If he could swap places with me, he would," he added. "If my trial is a good enough distraction for the war to change, then so be it. I'll play the part as well as I can to keep all eyes off what Crispus is doing."

"He can't guarantee to save you," she said.

"No one can guarantee anything," he replied.

"I'm not letting you go," Georgiana declared.

"Based on what you've told me, they're still making the right decisions, even if they're working from slightly false assumptions. Crispus thinks well on his feet, he'll deal with the problems as they arise." replied her father.

"You're going to be put on trial! You might be killed even before Uncle Jack can make his move."

"If I go down in the process, then so be it."

"But I love you Dad, and I'm going to get you out of here."

"We must not put personal ambition before the good of the city," replied her father.

"I would hardly call you 'personal ambition'," replied Georgiana, more than a little affronted.

Her father signed. "Georgiana, you know what I mean," he said, in a tired voice. He took his hand away from the grill above his head and sat with his back to the wall that was between them. Rubbing his hand through his hair to stem the itching of a red sore, he rolled out the next few words as if his mind was dulled and a little sedated.

"I can't always get all of my words right all of the time," he said, something that he had often said to her over the years when she was in one of her particular moods for perfect discourse.

He paused for a moment to gather his thoughts. Then he spoke a little slower and more purposefully.

"What I mean is that you and I both know that our desires can't always come first. Out there, others too have fathers, mothers, brothers, – people from all kinds of families. All of them just as precious to each other as you are to me and I to you."

Georgiana slid her back down the wall and slumped heavily onto the floor to listen to another discourse from her father.

"Are you listening to me?" a tone of slight irritation in his voice.

"Yes," came her tired reply, "and no," she added a few seconds later, being truthful in a way that surprised even herself.

"Good, bad and rotten," her father started to add to the list.

"Dad, I don't' want to hear this," she bluntly interrupted.

"Why not?" he enquired.

Georgiana didn't reply. She felt as if there was something almost repulsive about the conversation.

"Why not?" he enquired again, but she didn't reply.

"I'm not where you think I am," she finally said, "and I don't want you to lecture my love for you with cold idealism," came her eventual reply, when she understood what was going on in her heart.

The physical, emotional and intellectual gap between them facilitated an awkward series of momentary thoughts, which strung themselves together like beads on a string of tension. Mentally running her mind across each bead, understanding what they were, she spoke from the depths of her spirit.

"Is my desire to have you back so low and undeserving that it just has to be swept aside for the greater good?" she flatly stated. "Is my love for you of such little consequence that you expect me to listen to a lecture on the greater good and then to just walk away and let you die?"

Her father didn't reply.

"Well is it?" she pressed her point.

"No," came her father's reply. "You know that's not true."

"It might as well be," she added. "I would rather lose this whole wretched city and have just one extra day with you."

No reply. Her father quickly saw that his daughter had grown up. It had been a matter of days since their last meeting but years had really passed.

"You have to love not only me but others too," he said. "Georgiana, without love we're nothing," her father spoke softly, sensing that he had lost his daughter's attention.

"That's pure idealism Dad," she replied. "I'm human, not some limitless divine being. I cannot love everyone, only a few people at a time."

More silence.

"Don't ask me to be more than I am," she added.

"I'm not," replied her father. "I'm asking you to do what many other people have done before you, to make the right choice."

"I'm sick of choices," she said. She turned her head to look up at the stairwell above from which she'd recently come.

Time sat still and nothing was said between them. It was Lord Stephen who eventually broke the silence.

"My darling girl. Crispus and I both understood what we were getting ourselves into when we decided to stand up to Maltrisia. We both knew we could end up in civil war and lose our lives. We both understood that difficult decisions would have to be made. I know that if Crispus could give more to get me free, then he would. You must trust him and his judgements."

Still no reply from Georgiana.

"Georgiana!" came her father's stronger tone. "Trust Crispus. Now I want you to get your mother, Emma and yourself out of this city. I want you all safe. That's the greatest thing you could do for me."

"Mother and Emma have already left," she replied. "Your friend Marcus says he escorted them out of the city on the day you were captured."

A loud sigh came from the other side of the wall and Georgiana thought she could hear her father sobbing with relief.

"You must follow them," he finally said, clearing his throat. "Please leave this city and follow them. I need to know that you're safe."

"I'm not leaving you," replied Georgiana, letting the back of her head rest on the wall behind her.

"You must!" came her father's forthright reply. "This war is no place for you."

180

"I'm not going to leave you to die," she said. "You're my dad and I won't give you up."

"You're my daughter and I won't give you up to this war either," her father was becoming angry. "You're to go and join your mother and Emma and that's that."

"I shan't" came Georgiana's quick reply.

Lord Stephen stood up and paced his cell in frustration.

"Why can't you listen to reason!" he finally said, in an exasperated tone.

"Perhaps because I'm as stubborn as you are," she replied.

"I would never do something so irresponsible as you're doing right now," he replied.

"Really?" she countered.

"Really," he replied. "You have no experience of war, no resources, no options and you want to stay and perform some kind of single-handed rescue! Well done Georgiana!" he added. "You'll just get yourself killed and add to mine and your mother's pain. Don't you think that we've suffered enough? I'll die all over again if I lose you!"

Georgiana didn't reply.

"Well?" said her father, in the hope that he'd finally broken through.

Silence.

"You don't know," Georgiana finally said.

"Don't know what?" asked her father.

"How Richard died," she eventually replied.

"What do you mean?" said Lord Stephen. "Of course I know."

More silence.

"What is it you're trying to tell me?" Lord Stephan eventually asked.

"I'm saying that you don't know how and why Richard died. It wasn't an accident, nor was it done by that fake King's Law group."

More silence.

"What is it that you know," he tentatively enquired.

"Erepsin has told me, he's told me that it was all planned. He said he knew nothing of it until it was all over. He found out that his mother planned the whole thing. She had Richard killed to get at you, to put you out of the picture. It was all her doing. She's the one who's behind all of our troubles."

Both sat for a time, saying nothing. The damp in the air clung to Georgiana's clothes, making her shudder with the chill; she wondered how her father could stay warm in such a place and knew he had to be rescued soon.

"If that's the case, then she's twice the sorceress that I thought her to be," he finally said.

"Well Erepsin's going to deal with her himself," replied Georgiana.

Suddenly it all began to become clear to Lord Stephen. Now he knew how his daughter had been able to visit him without Uncle Jack knowing about it. Now he understood how his daughter had received such insider information on what was about to happen. Realising for the first time that his daughter was working with Erepsin, he said,

"You cannot trust that young man! Whatever he's up to, you can't get involved!"

"Richard was his best friend," she replied. "He's doing everything for him and for us."

Georgiana paused for a moment.

"As far as he's concerned, we're his family now," she added.

"He isn't family!" replied Lord Stephen, "and he never will be – as you made clear to him. The boy is unreliable, unstable and full of wild imaginations."

"He wants to help us," Georgiana insisted.

"I'm sure he does, but I don't trust him," replied her father. "Georgiana, you must not get involved with Erepsin. He'll shipwreck the whole counterattack. Not only that, but you'll also put the lives of those still fighting this war at risk. You must make the right choice. Let Crispus do his job and, for my sake, get out of this city."

"Uncle Jack can't do what he wants," she replied. "He's got his hands tied, I've already told you that. He can't do as he pleases and there are plenty of people with him who are completely naïve about what's going on. They're incompetent!"

"If other people are involved, wanting to help, you have to put their lives first, before mine or that of anyone else for that matter," Lord Stephen replied. "You cannot risk them, or anyone else, for me."

"Really?" she replied.

"Really!" he countered.

"And what did you say, to mother, about me when you were both in the library together? What did you say about me? 'I won't lose her. Not even for the sake of this city.' That's what you said!"

"You were listening in on our conversation?" asked Lord Stephen.

"I was passing by and stopped at the door to see if it was appropriate for me to come in," she replied. "I heard what I heard and that's that."

"You weren't meant to hear any of it," replied her father.

"Well I did hear. If that's how you feel about me, then that's how I feel about you. I want you back and this wretched city can lose itself in war if it wants to. These stupid people have let Maltrisia get to where she is today and they'll have to live with it. They're the ones who have agreed to your trial. They're giving her the stage from which to publicly humiliate and then condemn you. I'm not putting up with it. I'm not playing their game. There are no rules to live by. No-one is in charge and there is no right way forward. It's everyone for their own interests now. So I'm getting you back and that's final!"

Georgiana stood up and dusted down her dress, perhaps to brush off the conversation too.

"Georgiana, please don't," came her father's voice. "Promise me. Promise me that you'll do as I say. Please leave this city and keep yourself alive."

Georgiana put her hand on the metal grating again and, with her face as close to the cell wall as she could. "I love you dad," she said. She kissed the dividing wall that was between them and began to walk away.

"Georgiana!" he called, but she had already quickened her hobbling pace and each step took her one more step away from her father's influence. He knew he was losing her, so raised his voice as she departed.

"Promise me," he called, but it was no good, her mind was made up.

"Family before friends," she said to herself, "even if he hates me for it."

Her heart was set. Her father was a possession she refused to give up, no matter what the cost.

"You're the only thing I have left," she added in the depths of her soul, but moments later her thoughts strayed to her mother and Emma and Emma's unborn child. Quickly putting this out of her mind, she pressed on.

Having climbed the stairs, she tentatively exited the mine and quickly was found by Erepsin's friend who had quietly left the party to wait for her. Together they made their way to some derelict buildings on the edge of the mining community.

"Stay here," he said. "Erepsin will be here shortly."

Georgiana felt very exposed in this dump of a place. How had she ended up here, once again isolated and alone? Amongst the debris was a chair and so she sat for a while, kicking the rubble with her good leg and wondering what to do next. She wasn't happy with the way in which her conversation with her father had ended, but there was nothing she could do about that now. It's bitter taste, however, still lingered in her mind.

Within about ten minutes she heard footsteps. Erepsin entered the room and immediately went over to her.

"How did it go?" he asked. "Is your father alright?"

"He's in a hole," she replied. "How can he be alright? If he's left down there much longer, he'll certainly die."

Erepsin sighed. "We'll have to see what we can do," he said.

I'm ready to make a deal," said Georgiana. "I'll do whatever is necessary, whatever you think best, I need to work towards getting him free."

Quite taken aback at this sudden turn around, Erepsin adjusted his hat and then looked at her.

"I thought you Pluggats didn't agree with revenge," he said. "You know what my intentions are."

"What's in your heart is your problem," she replied. "You do what you want to with your own family and so-called friends; I just want my father back."

"Alright," said Erepsin, "tell me what your plans are. What is Uncle Jack and his gang up to?"

Georgiana hesitated. Help was one thing, betrayal another.

"I've not come here to tell you our plans," she finally replied. "I'm here to offer my help, just as you asked a few days ago. I'll help you do whatever it is that you're up to and, at the same time, you make every effort to get my father back."

"In order for you to help me," replied Erepsin, "I need to know what other people are up to."

"Can't tell you," she quickly replied.

Erepsin sighed.

"Your team will fail," Erepsin finally said. "They will not succeed."

"You can't possibly know what we're up to. You've no idea if we'll succeed or fail," replied Georgiana.

"I actually know all about your plans," he said, in a matter-of-fact tone. "I know far more than I'm letting on. I just wanted to see if you would trust me," he added.

Erepsin paced the room a couple of times.

"I know that you're planning to take my mother's harvester insects out," he finally said.

"What!" exclaimed Georgiana. "How on earth do you…"

"And I know that your friend Marcus intends to take my mother out tomorrow (good luck to him) and that you've got a base station which you intend to deploy to put her insects to sleep and I know that your friend Basil has found a load of well-meaning souls to help you all out. What a great body of people they will be when they are deployed against my mother," he added sarcastically.

"They may well succeed," said Georgiana, feeling that all her options were being taken away from her. "I believe that they can do it."

"That they might," he replied. "But let me tell you what I believe. I believe that I think more of your Father than they do. I believe that I understand my mother more than they do. I believe that I can make the informed decisions that need to be made in order to get the job done and I believe that you trust me enough to know that I'll do what I need to do, no matter what the cost is to myself and those about me."

Erepsin leant with his back to the wall.

"First of all I'm here to take my mother out. Second, to rescue your father. Third, to set our city free and finally to deal with those idiots who have put us in this situation. The first three points on my list, we're in agreement on. The last one, well, you'll just have to turn your back whilst I do the dirty job of dealing with the bad people, that's all!"

Georgiana sat quietly, contemplating his words. Erepsin walked over to her and squatted down to her eye level.

"If your friends do succeed," he said, in a much quieter tone, "then as soon as those insects drop from the sky, the war begins again and the first military target will be the place where your father's on trial. He'll be dead before you can shout his name!"

Georgiana just stared at him.

"Now," said Erepsin, getting up to walk the room again. "What I need from you is the code. The wakeup code for those insects."

"What!" she replied.

"I said, I need the wake-up code for those insects," he repeated, knowing that she'd heard him perfectly well the first time.

"Why? What do you want that for?" she asked.

"I need to know the wakeup code so that I can shut them down again with a code of my own!" he replied.

"Shut them down again?" she questioned. "Why would you need to do that?"

"To make sure they don't fall into the wrong hands," he replied. "I need to shut them down for good, never to be used again. Shut down so that my people are safe to get on with the job of rescuing your father and the rest of the city. Without them being completely shut down, I can't guarantee my success."

"I can't do that," she said. "I can't betray Uncle Jack and his team."

"You'll not be betraying them," he replied. "You'll be helping them."

"I can't do it," she said again.

"That decision is not based on reality," said Erepsin. "You said to me just a few days ago that you couldn't decide what to do because you were, in your words, 'out of it'."

"Well I'm not out of it now!" she replied.

"You're quite certain about that?" asked Erepsin.

"Absolutely!" she countered.

"I'll give you one word that will change your mind," said Erepsin.

"Whatever it is that you want to say, I don't want to hear it," she replied, knowing that the conversation was out of her control and once again feeling completely manipulated by him.

"Really?" he answered. "You don't want to even hear one word from me? One word that would put you in the picture so that you could make the right decision and keep everyone safe from those insects being reawakened and used again. One word to stop the real turncoat in our midst from betraying you and all your friends, who has already set you up, set everyone up to fail tomorrow."

"There's a betrayer?" Georgiana cautiously asked.

"A traitor!" exclaimed Erepsin.

He walked over to her and bent down to put his face close to hers. Staring Georgiana squarely in the eyes, he cleared his throat.

"Tristram," he said.

Chapter 24 – A Day of Peace

It was very early morning, still dark, the day of the peace deal. The inhabitants of the Pluggat-Lynnette mansion erupted with the minor detail that Georgiana was missing. A single note was found by the side of her bed. It simply read, 'Following up a lead.' Uncle Jack thundered at everyone and anyone within shouting distance. Eventually an almost whimpering, jelly-legged young man was carried forward to confess that he'd saddled a horse for her the previous evening as she'd told him she was going on an twilight ride.

"And you let her go!" bellowed Uncle Jack.

After a quick search was made, all of the family horses were accounted for.

"Well that doesn't make sense," replied Marcus.

"I'll form a search party," said Basil.

"No," said Tristram. "You're all needed for todays' work. I'll delay my schedule and search for her myself."

"But you're meant to be with us," remarked Basil.

"You don't actually need me," he replied. "As long as you follow the instructions, all will go according to plan."

"Why can't someone else search for her?" asked Marcus.

"I have many connections within the resistance," replied Tristram. "I can use those to quickly find out her movements. She can't have gotten far. I can find her within a very short amount of time compared with the rest of you, without taking too many resources away from our mission."

All eyes in the room went to Uncle Jack whose outward demeanour showed that he didn't like this sudden change of strategy.

"Once I've searched and found her, I'll come across and support everyone from within the inner-city circle," Tristram added. "The rest of you must keep to your original arrangements. We must win this war at all costs. Individual needs are not more important than the welfare of the city."

Uncle Jack hesitated. He seemed torn between the task in hand and his obligation to keep his best friend's daughter safe.

"The sooner we all get on with the day, the sooner I can start looking for her," Tristram commented.

"Alright," said Uncle Jack, reluctantly giving way.

With that, each group went through their plans one last time before getting on with the day's business. Briefly pulling Marcus to one side, Uncle Jack discreetly whispered, "You and your team shadow Basil and the horticultural society," he said. "Make sure they're in place and their equipment set up properly before you get into position yourselves."

Marcus nodded. He understood that Basil's friends, though willing in every way, were not part of what was classed as political 'high culture'. Their simple approach to life was a pleasure to see, but not necessarily beneficial when dealing with matters of war.

"If they keep their heads and follow those simple rules, then we'll be fine," he added.

"Hmmm. It's the first of those two points that gives me the jitters," replied Uncle Jack.

Within the hour, the two teams departed, leaving Uncle Jack, Tristram and some house staff behind. Initially, Marcus and his company led Basil's band of rambling horticulturalists east, through the family vegetable gardens, through the orchard, down the gentle incline of the wild meadow and then traced the land's contours south; eventually fording the waterway that marked the southern boundary of the Pluggat-Lynette family estate. Under cover of darkness, they trekked across several fields which took them up, over, down and across undulating banks of earth (anyone with a child's imagination would say they looked like huge craters created, perhaps, by giants who had once walked that way and, with their heavy, muddy boots, left deep footprints in the ground). This uneven grassy terrain led to a small, dusty pathway – flanked on either side by tall, wild grasses; standing proudly to attention and which, as the movements of the early morning breeze rippled across them, gave brief, approving nods to all who passed by. At the end of the pathway were a series of small orchards, each bordered with newly planted hedgerow saplings. Stepping in-between the young shrubbery, they progressed through the trees and finally onto a small road which ran parallel to the city's main canal.

Casting their eyes across the canal's murky waters, all they could see was a mess. The petroleum pollutants which had been pumped into the waterway on the first day of the war, and the resulting blazing fire which had raged across it, together produced a mixture of rotting fish and charred materials – all of which floated in and amongst the oily waste. Collectively they delivered an offensive stink and many a handkerchief was placed over the nose by the horticulturalists. With the city still haemorrhaging its lifeblood and languishing from its wounds, it looked from the riverbank like a fallen hero who had lost his way and didn't know where to turn. Apparently there's no cure for desolation, except solemnity blended with dust and ashes. This finely mixed recipe, when baked in life's oven, produces a heavy loaf that's difficult to stomach. So it felt for the assorted band of onlookers who stood motionless, unable to move, feet fixed to the ground, as the first rays of the sun revealed a city that did not want to be seen.

Coming to their senses, Marcus led the teams in a south-westerly direction, following the canal's edge, until they reached several moored rowing boats; part of the tourist trade's 'fun day out' resources, normally used for enjoying the city's canal system. Quickly descending into them, they pushed out from the bank and let the flow of the water take them. The early morning mists, combined with the choking smoke from smouldering buildings, shrouded their progress, providing a stealth camouflage to cover their movements. Before long they passed under what was called 'Whey Bridge' and from there they steered north towards the other side of the waterway. Almost silently passing by an old watchtower, now used for producing dairy foods, they landed on the other side and hurriedly moved off the bank's edge, into the shrubbery that surrounded them. Finding themselves at the foot of a series of terraced almond groves, they began to carefully ascend its multiple levels. Up, up they went until half an hour or so later they stood at its summit, looking down and across the city's landscape, to the palace and the market square. Apart from Maltrisia's airships floating in the sky, the area was completely empty, not a sound except for the odd guard scraping his heals as he marched his tired legs alongside the palace walls.

"That's where it's all happening today," Marcus pointed out to Basil's team. "We'll set up the base station here and place booster stations along the slope towards the opposite side of ridge, next to the road that exits the market square. They will take the signals right into the city square."

After setting up the station, Basil and four of his friends were assigned to guard it, ready to turn it on at the right moment.

"Remember," said Marcus. "You must keep your heads. Don't turn on the base station until you think that her entire insect horde is in the air, otherwise she'll clock that we've got the better of her and not release the rest. We want to capture the whole lot in one go, which may mean waiting, even if you see some people dying from initial insect attacks. Whatever is happening to us in the square is irrelevant to your mission. You must wait! When they're ready, the insects will swarm. They'll gather themselves up into a great cloud, before soaring across the capital. Don't let your compassion for the few take away our main goal of rescuing the whole city!"

"We'll do our best," replied Basil, as confidently as he could. The rest of his team nodded their heads in sober agreement.

"Your best is not good enough!" replied Marcus, casting his eye over Basil's team. "You'll do it right!" he firmly added. "For the sake of the city, you'll do it right or we're all dead, Maltrisia wins this war and all of our efforts will have been for nothing. You're at the heart of this citywide rescue. Your mission is critical. You'll give your lives for the rest of us, just as we're giving our lives for yours, and you'll do it right."

His words sank in and the enormity of the 'coddiwomple' came home to his listeners.

"I never thought I'd be involved in such a thing," one of the horticulturalists whispered to his friend.

From there, Marcus took his group and the rest of Basil's team with him as he made his way towards the city square. At different locations along the route, he put into place the horticulturalists with their booster devices, giving each small group a brief verbal reminder of what they were to do when the events of the day got underway. When all was completed, Marcus and his team hid themselves in an old wash house, just off the main road that ran up to the market square. There they waited for the events of the day to begin.

- -

Tristram left the mansion not long after Marcus and Basil, taking two of the household's servants with him. They were to begin a general sweep of the area once more and then connect with different parts of the resistance movement to see if Georgiana had been seen. Hours later, the city authorities sent a carriage to collect Uncle Jack; being required to fulfil the role of an 'official witness' to the day's events. As his carriage wound its way down and through the streets of Clearwash, he not only scowled at all of the devastation that was around him but also at the other people with whom he shared the ride. Wearing a pair of baggy trousers along with a

188

heavy-duty duffle coat, he clearly wasn't giving the event any special attention or taking it seriously. Sitting opposite were two lawyers and a junior clerk, all dressed in stylish, upmarket suits, whilst next to him was a prominent politician. Very little was said on the journey and any conversations that were started, quickly petered out. Upon arrival they could hear from the loud speakers in the market square that the event had already begun – the city clerk was already addressing the crowd. A few moments later they were met by a slight framed man who wore a dark grey suit and jet-black bowler hat.

"Mr McArnold Crispus Ken-Worthington-Brown," he said, looking up from his clip board at the large man. "You're required to register your name first before entering."

Uncle Jack was already in a bad mood.

"*Mr!*" he thundered. "*Mr!*" he said again.

Uncle Jack wasn't just a citizen of Clearwash City, his line of descent was from both nobility and gentry. Normally he didn't use his titles but today he made an exception.

"It's *Lord McArnold* to you, if you know what's good for you, you irksome little fellow!"

"Oh I am so terribly, terribly sorry," replied the man, shying away, almost bowing and speaking most apologetically. "Good, err, Lord," he continued, "would you please, err, follow me to register your name as an official witness to the event."

"When was this arranged?" queried one of the lawyers. "We weren't told about this. Are we to come too?"

"No I don't think so," replied the man, checking his list.

"Then why is this gentleman required to sign?" he enquired.

"Oh, I presume it's just some last-minute tweaks to the technicalities of the day," came the reply. "Mine is not to question, just to go along with providing the answers."

"Perhaps it's because I'm an official witness to these ridiculous events," barked Uncle Jack, over his shoulder. "You're just part of the ideological riffraff to make up the numbers."

With that, the affronted lawyers, clerk and politician received their invitation tickets by which they were to gain entry into the palace grounds. Through the gates they went, into the great market square, to join the rest of the 'riffraff' whilst Uncle Jack was shown down a side street to the front doors of a local theatre.

"Straight inside, through the foyer, up the steps to the main auditorium and then you'll see a table in front of the stage with a paper to sign. Just add yours underneath the other names that are there. Next to the paper is your admission ticket. Once you have that, you can exit via the back stage door which returns you to the market square. Then make your way through the crowds to the palace."

Uncle Jack grunted his acknowledgement of instructions.

"Is there not going to be someone to witness my signature?" he called back down the street.

"I believe you'll find some people waiting for you inside," the little man called back.

Uncle Jack snorted his contempt and made his way up the theatre steps.

"Little varmint," he muttered.

- -

At the same time, across the city, Erepsin rode in one of his mother's carriages, which his team had recently acquired. Georgiana sat opposite, still contemplating the day. It was a high-risk game they were playing. She was unsettled by her choices and felt an unusual pull in her gut. Erepsin, however, seemed so relaxed and confident she couldn't help but feel that it all might work out. Imagining her father with her at the end of the day kept her mind in focus.

"You promise me you can get him out of danger before the shelling starts?" she asked, one last time.

"As I've said, my team will move in for his rescue as soon as those insects fall out of the sky."

Georgiana nodded her response to his assertion.

"This is all for you my beloved father," she said to herself.

The carriage wove its way through the western quarter of Clearwash City, its family crest ensuring that it continued unhindered by Maltrisia's troops. Every now and again Erepsin made sure that his face was seen, looking out of the window and giving nods to the armed forces and assorted people who were scattered across the war pummelled streets.

"As you can see," said Erepsin, "everything is in place for my mother to take over. Troops, war machinery and insects, all hidden away and perfectly kept out of sight. Nobody sees them, unless you're literally passing through the streets where they're located. One word from her and they'll rise up with a final push to take the city."

The unfolding story of the day fitted so well with all that Erepsin had previously stated the night before. Perhaps he did know what he was doing after all. Georgiana contemplated those thoughts.

"I have anticipated her every step," he added. "As soon as she moves, I'll strike at the very heart of everything she's planned. Not all of her troops are loyal to her."

Again, Georgiana nodded her acknowledgement of his observations. He certainly seemed to know exactly what was about to happen. Listening to him, it all seemed so inevitable. After travelling a little further, they approached a crossroads.

"You do understand why you can't stay with me?"

Georgiana nodded her head, but looked disappointed.

"I wish I could change my mind on this matter," he said. "But if you're seen in the middle of the city, even by one of my mother's community watch team, you'll be arrested as a prize catch, if you excuse my base mode of talking."

"I'll go along with your decision," she replied. "I need to help my friends. I can't let them be betrayed. You just get my father out alive, that's all I ask."

"He's my top priority," he assured her.

Erepsin thumped the wall behind him to get the attention of the carriage driver.

"Turn off to the right," he shouted.

Turning away from the main road, they followed a trail that led them back out towards the outer edge of the city's inner circle.

Erepsin handed Georgiana what seemed like a smooth rubber band.

"Place this on your wrist," he said.

"What is it?" she asked.

"An anti-insect device. It will help keep you safe from any stray 'hymenopteran', as you call them."

Georgiana examined the thin rubber wrist band, running her fingers over its outer frame. Inside she could feel a metal wire running its way all around the rim with square-like blocks upon it.

"Don't press on it too much," said Erepsin. "I don't want you to damage it. It could save your life before this day is over."

"How did you create such a thing that would..."

"Trust me," interrupted Erepsin. "I've got more experience with these little critters than you know."

Georgiana wasn't sure that she'd ever label Maltrisia's hymenopteran as 'little critters' – Erepsin clearly did not know what it was like to be on his mother's hit list. She put the band on her wrist, however, trusting that Erepsin, as usual, knew more than he was letting on.

Erepsin sat back in his seat and cast his gaze onto the streets they were passing through. He looked very pleased with himself. A few more minutes of travel and they approached a T-junction. Two more thumps by Erepsin on the carriage wall and with that the coach stopped. Erepsin hopped out onto the road and gave instructions to the coach driver.

"Go beyond Market Bridge and follow the old Crofter's trail. Let her ladyship out of the carriage when you are adjacent to the terraced almond groves. Then come back into the city to find me."

The coach driver gave a nod, jarred the reins in his hands, and with just a simple wave from Erepsin, they were off.

- -

The sun shone its presence over the majestic palace which sat on the edge of the city's great market square. Despite the fact that the environment still smelt of burnt buildings, there was a promise of something new in the air. Perhaps it was airships which floated above the same space, displaying messages of peace, hope and freedom. Many parts of the surrounding area had been almost completely destroyed but the palace itself was mainly untouched, except for the clock tower which had suffered a measure of burn damage to its front face and timer mechanism. The lack of ticks, tocks and chimes would be something to get used to. The 'Old Chimer' as it was affectionately called, now stood to silent attention, like a wounded soldier; a voiceless guardian, not only with a bruised face but also as an enforced silent onlooker who couldn't call out his duties due to having had his tonsils removed.

Loud speakers and large screens had been mounted across the palace walls and clock tower and from these a 'tune of hope' (as it was called) was being played, complemented by images of happy, positive faces. With an overt, optimistic invitation from their confident politicians, the remaining crowds began to assemble with the expectation that the day was indeed their moment of peace. The surrounding streets and market square were open places for mass assembly but the palace itself was an 'invitation only' ticketed occasion where the success of the day's events would be toasted with glasses of fine sparkling wine. Marcus and his team mingled in with the gathering crowds. They made the perfect hiding place.

The peace deal event itself was not going to take part in the city palace. Maltrisia had insisted that all negotiations be done in the debating chamber, the very location where Lord Stephen had stood up for King's Law and outlined his opposition to her vision of a new society. One end section of the building had collapsed but the rest of the structure seemed to be intact and, apparently, safe to enter. Every now and then the relay screens on the edge of the market square would change from displaying pictures of positivity and briefly display live footage of those rooms. In particular, one room looked plush and ready for a debate of some kind to take place.

From within the palace the celebrations had already begun. Buoyant and carefree, toasts to the future were already being made. As there was more wine than food, the people of influence in the city quickly fell under the influence of the occasion. The more they celebrated, the more the wine flowed. The more the wine flowed, the more they became engrossed in their happy success. When the live camera images finally flickered onto the events that were taking place within the palace walls, there was a harsh intake of breath by the crowds, seeing the drunken, extravagant lavishness that 'the few' were already indulging in.

The cameras changed their focus again and all were now looking inside the debating chamber. On the screen appeared the city clerk, along with other politicians of various influence. In amongst them was Maltrisia, clearly at ease in their presence and spreading her normal air of confidence and purposeful social interactions. Other witnesses, who were invited to oversee the historic event, most gladly joined her in the room.

"We have achieved our goals," said the clerk, looking directly into the eye of the camera and addressing the crowds. "A foundation has been laid for a clear and walkable pathway to a lasting peace. A framework of co-operation has been put in place and now we are nothing but expectant of the outworking of that peace loving process. In order for this peace to go ahead, however, events of the past have to be dealt with. No society or culture can move forward without dealing with its past. So we're allowing a public trial to go ahead, whereby some of the main accusations of the past can be openly explored and accounted for. It is to be conducted in an atmosphere of openness and fair play."

His comments were met with scholarly nods from the herd of the 'politically compliant' around him.

"The accusations will be initially made in public and the accused will be allowed to defend himself," continued the clerk. "We will remain present to ensure that there is no foul play. Afterwards a jury will decide the outcome. Bring in the accused!" the clerk called.

The door at the end of the room opened and in walked Lord Stephen, two guards flanking him on either side. He looked in a bad way, as if in a bad state of health and he'd been mistreated. A stunned silence descended on the crowds outside as soon they saw him. Almost stumbling as he walked, he was escorted over to a seating area. There he was made to sit, behind a waist high panelled screen, making him look as if he were somehow in a dock.

Back in the theatre, Uncle Jack exited the foyer at the top of the stairs that led through to the main auditorium. The room before him was darkened, as if in the middle of a theatrical event. The long stairs down towards the front seats were dimly lit and smaller pinhole sized lights were dotted across the walls of the room. The only other illumination came from a spotlight which fell onto the main stage; next to which was a single table that stood waiting for him and upon which was a piece of paper to sign. He didn't like it. No human beings present, as had been promised, and the air of the place felt most menacing. Hesitating, the military man stood very still whilst his fingers fumbled with an item is his pocket. He knew a trap when he saw one. About half a minute went by and, as his eyes began to adjust to the semi-light, he still saw no-one about him. Weighing up his options and the events of the day, knowing that causing a disturbance might endanger the lives of his friends who were about their work just a few hundred yards from his location, he decided to go along with the scenario before him.

"Sometimes you have to walk into a noose in order to find out who the hangman is," he reasoned.

Having made the decision to play along, he slowly walked down each of the auditorium's steps, passing row upon row of seats. At the bottom of the stairway, he felt very exposed – each step took him towards the spotlight where he would literally be the centre of attention.

"If they wanted to kill me, they'd have done it by now," he reasoned. "They must want something else."

Making his way over to the stage, there was the table. No chair, no message, just a piece of paper with a pen, but no ticket for the palace event. No-one else's name was on the paper. The list, that was meant to represent dignitaries, was clearly a fraud.

"Perhaps they just want to lock me in to keep me away from the day's events?" he reasoned.

It a moment of exasperation, Uncle Jack picked up the pen and made some swift strokes of his hand on the paper.

"Lord Nincompoop of Nincompoop City!" he wrote, displaying his contempt for the whole event.

He was about to walk away when every light in the room went off. Complete darkness dropped. Silence followed, not a sound. Then, from within the blackness, over the loud speaker system, a whispered voice spoke. "Hello Jack!" it said.

Chapter 25 – A Trap for Uncle Jack

"Jack!" came the voice again, it's sound was delivered through multiple speakers that were hung on the walls about the room.

Uncle Jack began to move, seeking to use the darkness as cover to escape. Immediately a spotlight lit him up, stopping him in his tracks.

"You're not thinking of leaving us?" came the voice again.

"Who are you?" Uncle Jack called back.

"Oh, just a friend," came the reply.

Uncle Jack thought the voice sounded familiar but he wasn't for playing games. He began to walk off until he was hit on the shoulder by what felt like a bullet.

"Ahh," he cried out, stumbling backwards and leaning on the edge of the stage.

"Now, now, now," came the voice again. "It's rude to leave without saying hello to your hosts. Why don't you stay awhile and we can get to know each other a little better?"

Uncle Jack continued to hold his shoulder, bent over with the pain, at the same time he peered out into the darkness, trying to see who was speaking to him.

"Dearest, dearest Uncle Jack," came the voice again, it's tone was soft and gentle but full of condescension and contempt. "We're so, so sorry to take up your time, but we do need something from you."

Uncle Jack once again fumbled with something in his pocket.

"What is it you want?" he finally replied, through gritted teeth.

"Information," came the reply.

"And what information might that be?"

There was silence in the room for a few moments.

"What information is it you want from me?" called Uncle Jack again.

"The blueprint plans to the waterworks," came the reply. "Lord Stephen gave you half of those plans, we simply wish to know where you've put them, that's all."

"Well that's an unfortunate thing for you," replied Uncle Jack, between heavy breaths. "Apparently I have something that you're in desperate need of, which puts you in a rather difficult position."

"A difficult position, most noble sir, is something I'd personally describe you as currently being in," came the reply. "It so saddens my heart to see you in this most dreadful state, but such is life, until you give us what we need."

"You obviously need me alive," said Uncle Jack, "or you'd have killed me by now. You're the one with the problem, not me, you pathetic, blundering blockhead."

"What a strange fellow you are," said the voice. "Such a mystery, such a character; a loveable, laughable friend to our great city. Let me show you how much I need you alive."

Searing pain ran through Uncle Jack's left knee as what felt like another bullet shot through it. He fumbled back against the stage again, letting the woodwork take his weight.

"That's how much I need you alive."

Uncle Jack let out another gasp of pain and took in a few deep breaths.

"There's no way out for you, my dear, dear fellow," said the voice. "You're at a dead end, if you forgive the pun... 'dead, end'. Oh dear, I am being funny today."

Uncle Jack didn't reply, the pain in his leg was excruciating.

"Give us what we want or you'll never leave this room, at least, you'll never leave this room in a state of being which others would classify as 'being alive'."

"You're a pompous windbag," muttered Uncle Jack, under his breath. "What exactly do you want to know," he yelled out, trying to keep the conversation going whilst he continued to fiddle with whatever item it was in his pocket.

"Oh most noble gentleman," came the playful reply. "Just the exact location as to where the plans are. Oh, and then there's the names of your contacts in the military who might be loyal to you, we will need to know about those lovely people too; we already have the names of the two teams of people you've been working with these last few days but your contacts within the military are currently strangers to our 'wanted' and 'need exterminating' lists. Once we have them, then our job here will be complete."

"So, you're nothing more than self-styled executioners are you?" bellowed Uncle Jack.

"No, good sir, we're part of the battalion of truth and honour; marching to the tune of a new order whilst stamping out the fires of injustice."

"Pompous idiot!" thought Uncle Jack.

Keeping his thoughts to himself and, wanting to delay the outcome of the conversation, he called out, "I've seen those types of military 'stamps' before. They're nothing to do with justice."

"That all depends on your perspective. Now, give us the information or we may have to slightly *stamp* on you."

"As soon as I share the information, you'll kill me," replied Uncle Jack. "What guarantees are you going to give me that I shall keep my life?"

"Oh my dear fellow, I give you my word that once the information is given, you'll be free to go, free to flee from this most terrible city. You'll be free to leave and to never come back, ever again."

"You expect me to live with myself after betraying my friends?"

"How you live isn't anything to me, my dearest Uncle Jack. It's the fact that you will be alive, that's all that matters."

"What if I can't tell you where the plans are?"

"Then that will be most troublesome for you."

"In what way would I be troubled?"

Uncle Jack was clearly trying the patience of his interrogator.

"I think you need to find more 'substance' to your words," the invisible inquisitor finally replied. "Your replies are leaving me wanting in my pursuit of information. So, let us start again - and this time I would ask that you not only answer the questions put before you but that you also are more forthcoming in the content of your responses. Words without substance, sir, leave my desire for information uncommonly hungry. Otherwise I may have to provide some more persuasive means by which I will loosen your tired tongue."

The sound of the voice fell to almost a whisper, its tone gentle, but menacing.

"What an ignorant, long-worded wind-bag you are," muttered Uncle Jack to himself. He wasn't for playing verbal games, but at the same time he needed to 'play along' with this self-promoting person to gain as much time as he could.

"Time is passing by," the voice continued. "It is slipping through our very fingers. Moment by moment it passes, but on this subject of time, you'll find, I have all the time in the world. You on the other hand, good sir, do not."

Something buzzed in Uncle Jack's pocket and he seemed pleased with the sound.

"I haven't got the blueprints," called Uncle Jack, a look of slight relief on his face. "They're lost to me."

"Lost? Lost? How can they be lost? I don't think that a man like you would lose such a precious set of items which, in themselves, hold the keys to the long-term survival of our most noble and great city."

"I said, 'they're lost to *me*'," replied Uncle Jack.

"And what, pray, does that mean?"

"It means that I no longer have them and I don't know where they've been put – it's a little thing called 'national security' where the weight of the nation is carried by the 'few', rather than just the 'one'. Giving away the plans made our culture that little bit safer."

Seconds ticked by as Uncle Jack waited for the next question.

"I assume you know the names of the people who now have the plans?" the voice from the loud speakers had become less playful and showed a measure of irritation.

"Some of them," replied Uncle Jack, "but not all. Perhaps you and your happy troop of marching, honourable soldiers had better be careful who you kill from now on, you might be taking the life of a person who has the keys to bringing back water to the city; signing your own death warrant, if you know what I mean."

"Well then, you'd better give me the names of those you do know who are now in ownership, otherwise, you're a dead man."

"Dead am I?" Uncle Jack muttered under his breath. "We'll see about that."

A final press on a device in Uncle Jack's pocket and the outer front doors of the theatre burst open. From within the foyer, crunching, thumping metallic noises could be heard which were quickly followed by the doors to the auditorium being flung open. There, at the top of the stairs, was Uncle Jack's pumpkin machine – his normal mode of travel for special occasions. Uncle Jack lifted his hand out of his pocket to reveal a homing instrument, about the size of a button. Flicking a small rotating wheel on its edge and pressing it once more, the machine responded by barging through the double doorway and rolling itself down the stairs towards Uncle Jack.

Shots were fired at the pumpkin as it rolled itself past row upon row of chairs, down to with a couple of feet from Uncle Jack and halted – swinging its door open, ready for its next passenger to enter. Bullets pinged off the machine as it was targeted again and again. Hobbling on one leg, Uncle Jack leapt to its side and got hit by another set of stinging bullets. Reeling from the pain, he fumbled his way onto his contraption's seat and the door automatically closed behind him. For the next few moments shot upon shot was fired till bits of the pumpkin were dropping off its sides.

A couple more room lights came on, taking away the immediate darkness that surrounded Uncle Jack. It was clear to see the pumpkin machine was surrounded by almost twenty soldiers, each standing with a rifle in their hands.

"Hold you fire," came the voice from the loud speakers, as Uncle Jack slipped off his chair inside his horseless carriage. He hardly had the strength to get himself back up again. He lay on his machine's floor, breathing heavily, his head spinning.

"Nice try," came the voice.

Steam rose from the pumpkin machine's inner engines. Its own mechanical motions gave off the noise of a wounded creature.

"Oh Uncle Jack, you do make life difficult."

One of the soldiers let off another round of bullets at the pumpkin machine.

"I said, hold your fire!" came the voice again.

Wiping his hand across his face, Uncle Jack moved his other hand down his chest and onto his leg. He gripped it to stem the pain as much as he could.

"There's nothing to be scared of," the voice continued, in a sudden change of tone. "All we want from you is the names of the people. Give us those, and you can go."

With a trembling hand the stocky, portly gentleman pulled himself up onto his seat inside his giant iron pumpkin. A pumpkin that had lost much of its padding from its sides; revealing a metal frame covered with a wire mesh of small iron strips that together made the shape of a battered rounded container. This thinly wired metal skin now gave the object, at some angles, an almost transparent effect. From its front, however, it still looked like a solid metal object, fully armour plated and ready for battle.

The pumpkin's dashboard steamed with the damage it had sustained. On it were the controls to operate the twelve long, spindly legs that were attached to the pumpkin's undersides. Seeing this mechanical creature move under the guidance of a master driver was normally a treat to the eye. It could travel in ways you wouldn't imagine. Right now, however, its movements were limited. The dials were broken, switches fused and a steady rise of steam and smoke erupted from the engine on the machine's underside.

The big man's injuries were quite clear. A left leg that ran red from the knee down and a wound in his side that obviously caused him great discomfort; bending him over and causing him to groan and wince each time he moved. From underneath his torn duffle coat, his bare right shoulder could be seen poking through. However, under that, you could perhaps catch a glimpse of what would normally be classed as a fully padded, armoured combat jacket - which itself was pummelled with holes. Perhaps the old man wasn't as mortally wounded as he appeared.

"Prepare yourself and stand up like a man!"

The voice echoed around the theatre walls and then was finally lost in the surrounding darkness.

"These light and momentary sufferings of yours, these slight grazes, are just a passing phase which will soon be gone upon your co-operation," the voice continued.

"I hardly think that my condition could be described as light, slight or momentary," mumbled the portly man through gritted teeth.

197

"The information!" came the voice again in a stronger manner. "The names of the people who hold the blueprint plans to the waterworks. Give me the details."

"I've told you all you're going to hear from me," replied the stout man, fumbling with the dials and switches to get his machine working again. "You've had all the words from me that you're going to get. If you're going to kill me, then just get on with it. I've no time for this impish, childish banter that you seem to need to engage in."

"The names," came the voice again.

Uncle Jack briefly lifted his head up and out of a hole at the top of his machine and looked into the dim and darkened theatre. "I have nothing more to say. So if it's death that we have to deal with next, be it mine or yours, then let's just get on with it!"

"Your words, good sir, are the things I am after," came the voice again, "not your life, pitiful as it may be. I would seek to have you command a better grasp of the situation you are in and to engage with us in the pursuit of our goals; the illumination of our minds as to the whereabouts of the people who hold the plans to the waterworks."

Uncle Jack just ignored him. Inside the theatre a figure moved out from the perimeter darkness and stood in the dimmer shadows. He began to pace to and fro, his walk confident and the frame of his body held in a manner of arrogance that showed a love of the power and influence that he held. He paused for a moment to think – or perhaps he was playing a waiting game.

Uncle Jack eyeballed him, trying to make out who had been speaking to him. He didn't have to wait long for his answer. Out of the shadows walked the city's governor and now self-proclaimed Director of Public Affairs.

"Dear Uncle Jack," he said. "All we want from you are the names that we've asked for."

"I'm glad you've put that microphone down," replied Uncle Jack. "Your voice sounds like its normal pathetic self, now that it's not being propped up by a speaker system. What a pitiful little man you really are. Your attempts at being intimidating are quite ridiculous you know."

"Do not think for one moment that anyone will be coming here to your rescue. Therefore I will give you good counsel, to co-operate completely with us, and to this counsel I would advise you to most carefully take heed!"

The large man groaned with the childish, playful, meaningless talk.

"Blabbering idiot," he mumbled under his prominent, protruding beard.

Pumping a pedal with his foot and pressing buttons on his dashboard, Uncle Jack continued to turn dials until the sound of the smoking motor underneath the pumpkin chugged and chugged and then stopped. He pulled on a series of rods that protruded from the pumpkin's floor and something clunked from underneath the machine, which seemed to please him.

Another man walked out of the darkness and stood a few feet away from Uncle Jack's horseless carriage.

"If you won't listen to him, then perhaps you will to me?" he enquired.

Uncle Jack stared at the man,

"Traitor!" he said.

Chapter 26 – A Trial and a Traitor

"Lord Stephen, here are a list of names, all bearing witness that you have betrayed this city by your subversive, rebellious actions."

Maltrisia looked directly into the camera, knowing that the people in the palace and the crowds outside were watching. Being once again the centre of attention, she smiled a confident beam of pleasure, her heart filled with the anticipation of the moment. Indeed, she could hardly breathe.

Lord Stephen sat, reading a scrappy piece of paper upon which numerous signatures were scrawled, some of which he recognised and others he did not.

"As you can see, you have no support left amongst the people. The politicians have seen through your duplicity and self-serving attitude."

Lord Stephen, however, could see through the façade that was before his eyes; both in the concern of Maltrisia in her attempt at showing genuine care for the wellbeing of the people and in the so-called integrity of the information she was presenting. He put the paper down and let it fall on the floor, as a show of contempt.

"There are questions for you to answer," she said. "You must be held accountable for stirring up the city to a point where there was no return. Your self-ego promoting campaign has brought us to the point of ruin. Your stubborn stance not to change with the times, to keep us locked in the past, to entrench those ideas that kept the many being ruled by the few, your promotion of inequalities, your protection of wealth from the masses, your unwillingness to let the privileged few be brought down to the level of the abused many (who lacked so much in life) these are just some of the things you must account for."

Maltrisia expected Lord Stephen to ready himself for a debate. Instead, he just looked at her with an emotionless gaze.

"Why did you kill my son?" he asked.

Maltrisia stopped in her tracks.

A gasp went up from the crowds in the market square.

"Why did you kill my son?" he repeated.

"Why Lord Stephen, what on earth gave you that ridiculous idea?" responded Maltrisia.

"My daughter told me," he replied, "and your son told her. I see the scar on your face has disappeared, just as Erepsin said it would. Make up comes off far more easily than real scars. You were never in any danger that day and the whole event whereby you claimed your life was threatened was a ploy, a deception in order for you to have my son killed. You killed my son in order to take me out of the political arena so you could pursue your own political gains."

An uncomfortable moment passed whereby Maltrisia didn't quite know what to say.

"Oh Erepsin, my silly boy, he will play his games," she finally replied, trying to shrug off the comments. "He has a wild imagination. I wouldn't pay any attention to his misapplied blabbering. Gossip really is a dreadful thing."

The damage was already done, however, and the crowd in the market square mumbled their displeasure at the news.

"But now down to the more serious business of the day," she countered, trying to move the conversation on.

"What more serious business could there be other than the life of my son?" asked Lord Stephen.

"The lives of the people!" Maltrisia flatly answered, a flash of anger in her eyes. "It is *their* lives that matter too! Look outside at the demolished buildings, the ruined lives! Look at the waterworks that's been shut down and the reservoir wall that's blown, by your influence. It's so typical, you Pluggats are always about your own needs and never the needs of others!"

"You started this war," responded Lord Stephen, "and once again your collective recollections of the past are highly filtered and misinterpreted. Even before you started firing on the city, and we lived in a time of sustained peace, I poured far more money into this city than you ever did."

"You were about keeping your wealth," she contradicted. "I was prepared to give it up, give it all away, just for the sake of the people."

"You did not once talk about giving up your wealth in any of your meetings," replied Lord Stephen. "It was all rhetoric about everyone being empowered but, as usual, no substance about how you would go about this. The only common factor in all of your speeches was you being at the centre of everything!"

"You are in no position to talk," she said. "You're here today to answer the accusations that are made against you, not to comment on me!"

"And you are in no position to dictate," replied Lord Stephen. "Seems to me that once again you're in a place of self-contradictions, in a world of juvenile fantasy, feigned promises and impossible dreams."

"You are a traitor of the state!" she shouted.

"There is no state to betray," he replied. "King's Law gave us everything we needed to survive, flourish and prosper. We didn't need or want anything else and your false moral high ground has done nothing but serve your need and desire to hold power."

"Shut up!" she yelled.

"Why should I?" he said. "You have no authority here. You're not a judge, you don't hold any official office in law. You have no legal status, no legal authority. You're just a self-proclaimed dictator, pretending to be acting in the interests of the people."

"Gag him!" Maltrisia shouted. "Gag him right now!"

Moments later Lord Stephen was held steady by two guards as a gag was tied across his face. An uproar began in the crowds outside as they saw the gag forcibly placed over and into Lord Stephen's mouth.

"I will have silence," shouted Maltrisia again. "And you will not be interrupting me anymore!"

The city clerk rushed forward to protest about the behaviour of Maltrisia's guards; the other politicians and witnesses to the event joining him.

"This is not what was planned," he cried. "Release this man!" he insisted. "This behaviour is completely out of order!"

Maltrisia's face darkened with rage at their interference.

"How dare you!" she demanded. "How dare you interfere!"

"This is not what we agreed!" replied clerk.

"Indeed," added one of the politicians. "We're here to witness a peace process, not the humiliation of an innocent man!"

"Innocent!" she screamed!

"Everyone is innocent until found guilty," replied another. "This has gone too far. Now let him go!"

Maltrisia's temper exploded.

"Arrest them!" she screamed to her guards. "Arrest them all!"

- -

Back in the theatre, Uncle Jack eyeballed the man who stood a few feet away from him.

"Traitor," he said again.

"I don't see it that way," replied Tristram. "I'm more of an opportunist really."

"How long have you been in her employ?" asked Uncle Jack. "Since when did you so lower yourself that you sided with her?"

"Oh I'm not working for Maltrisia," replied Tristram. "She's nothing to me. Since when would I want to serve someone like her? As soon as those insects of hers are disabled, our troops will move in. Maltrisia and everyone with her will be dead within minutes and we will emerge as the builders of the new order. No, I'm more of a self-service person, to be honest. The good Director and myself here, we sense a decent opportunity for a complete regime overthrow, which would obviously include you."

"You're not a man of influence," replied Uncle Jack.

201

"I have more friends in the military than you realise," Tristram answered.

"Not the men who are aligned with me," asserted Uncle Jack. "They'll never befriend or follow you! Even those misguided fools who support the politicians won't fall for following you."

"If you think those ideologically, highly-notioned idiots, who call themselves our political elite, command the respect of all our military, you're mistaken. I already have a good number interested in our new order and they'll open fire on our enemies the moment we give the signal."

"You'll get nowhere," replied Uncle Jack.

"And neither will you," replied Tristram. "All your team are dead. The hymenopteran we were testing the base stations on scanned the faces of all your team. They just thought it was an identification exercise. It was actually me programming them for a final kill, if there are any of them left to kill that is."

"What do you mean by that?"

"Simply, that as soon as those insects fall from the sky, the military leaders who are aligned with me will open fire upon your friends. They know their positions. At the same time, Maltrisia will be disposed of and we will enter the stage of life to take on the role of leading our city into its future."

"No-one will follow you!" exclaimed Uncle Jack.

"Oh but they will. Once we see who is loyal to us and who is not, we'll then resurrect the hymenopteran and they'll quickly do the rest of the job for us, starting off with your friends, Marcus, Basil and those delightful horticultural country walkers, happily going on their... what was the word they used? Happily going on their 'coddiwomple' way!"

"I'll get you if it's the last thing I do," replied Uncle Jack.

"You're in no position to do that," replied Tristram. "But perhaps I can persuade you to comply with another line of thinking that my good friend here hasn't thought of. In this new city that we're about to put together, I shall control much of who gets to live, who gets to die, who lives well and who takes on the life of obscurity. It's a burden that someone has to bear. Anyway, I'd like to bring to your attention the life of someone who is dear to you. A young woman you sent me out to find a few hours ago, if you recall?"

"Georgiana!" exclaimed Uncle Jack.

"The very person," replied Tristram. "My attempt at taking her life the other day obviously failed, much to my disappointment."

"Your attempt..." Uncle Jack paused.

Tristram waited for his words to sink in.

"So the insect *incident* wasn't an accident?" reasoned Uncle Jack.

"I knew she'd be on the hitlist," Tristram replied. "It was the perfect way of getting her out of the way. An 'accident' happened and how sorry we would be at her demise."

"You blaggard!" shouted Uncle Jack.

"But at least that failed attempt has brought about some positive fruits. You now fully understand that I have no moral inclinations holding me back that would prevent me from killing her. She means nothing to me. I like to see myself as a rather calculating person, aloof from the troublesome world of morality."

"You touch that young girl and...

"And you'll what?" interrupted Tristram. "You'll do what? I think you forget that this city's future has already changed forever. There's no going back now to where we were. Logic tells us your folk have lost and my folk hold the keys to the movers and shakers in the culture. You're half dead, I'm fully alive. Logic dictates that you listen to me or the girl dies, it's as simple as that."

"Where is she?!"

Tristram hesitated. "She's safe."

"Show her to me!"

"I shan't. Not until we have the names of the people who are the custodians to the waterworks blueprints."

Uncle Jack lowered his head and thought out what was being said.

"Show her to me," he said again.

"I shan't" replied Tristram. "You're in no position to bargain."

"You, don't have her!" Uncle Jack snapped back, both anger and relief etched across his face.

Tristram waited for a few moments before replying, not expecting Uncle Jack to have so quickly seen through his ploy.

"And you don't have any moves left," he blandly stated.

"You think this is some kind of strategy game!" barked Uncle Jack. "You'll get nothing from me!"

Tristram just stared back at the big man, wondering why the conversation he'd intended hadn't managed to trap or prise out of his opponent the information he'd wanted. Finally he said,

"You give me the names of those people who have the waterworks plans or, after we've dealt with Maltrisia, I'll wake up every single one of those hymenopteran and kill every person dear to you in this city."

"I have nothing more to say to you," replied Uncle Jack, and that was the end of the conversation.

The Director of Public Affairs moved across the room to stand next to the outer meshed frame of the pumpkin. In another pathetic attempt at intimidation, he glared at his opponent. Placing his hands flat onto the pumpkin's outer steel lattice he dropped, one by one, each of his fingers through the holes in the crisscrossed metallic grid. Taking a firm grip, he gave the wire frame a tug, then a shake, as if to lay claim to it.

"Who has the waterworks blueprints!" said the director in a low tone, staring at the big man with as much of an intense stare as he was able.

Uncle Jack continued to fiddle with the dashboard's control buttons and dials.

"No talk – no live," said the director.

"Why don't you just shut up, you irritating little weasel!" sighed Uncle Jack.

"Jack! Dear Uncle Jack, uncle to the city for so many years. Come now and be of good use to your new rulers. Give us the names. Then we can think about your future and that of your friends. We're not so fiendish as to be without any heart. Tell us who they are and we, being so full of generosity, we will let you and your friends go."

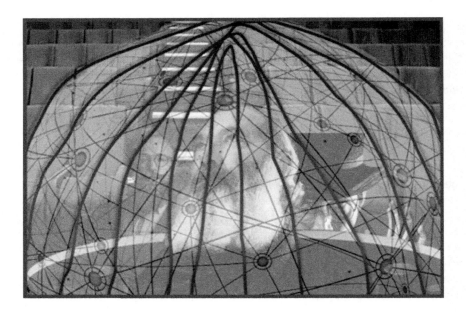

"Boy, you are so full of yourself," muttered Uncle Jack, quite underwhelmed with the city director's attempt at making this so-called interrogation sinister. Then he added, "There are many things, young man, that you're still yet to learn and one thing in particular that you'll discover today."

"What's that, dear Uncle Jack?" answered the director, in a mocking voice.

Uncle Jack turned to stare at him and moved his face just inches away from the wire mesh that separated them.

"Never let yourself get too close to a wounded hound."

With that Uncle Jack thumped his fist onto the side of the mesh structure where the Director's fingers were poking through, trapping them and crushing them onto the wire frame. A howl of pain yelped out from him as Uncle Jack, keeping his fist on the wire mesh, leaned on it with all his weight. At the same time he kicked at a pedal with his right foot. The pumpkin's engines burst into life, erupting out a torrent of smoke and juddering the machine from side to side. The shaking pumpkin sent the city mayor, with his fingers still trapped in its mesh, into a maddening high-pitched scream.

"I quite like the sound of your voice now," shouted Uncle Jack, teasingly through the wire mesh. "I had no idea you could hit such high notes. I should join a girls' choir if I were you, whilst you can. A man whose vocal sound is so close to that of a wee, shrieking lass like yours would be invaluable!"

The Director's face turned deathly pale as he continued to yelp out his shrieks and squeals.

"Let me go, let go, let go!" he cried.

"Why?" asked Uncle Jack. "When we were just beginning to get to know each other."

With those words Uncle Jack pushed on a pedal at his feet and the pumpkin rose onto its legs, squirting out a hot liquid in all directions, causing everyone in the vicinity to scatter. Finally letting go of the director's fingers, he took hold of the levers and instruments before him and guided his machine to walk across the room into the darkness.

"Lights," screamed the very wet Tristram, standing next to the Director who lay on the floor, clutching his fingers and rolling from side to side in hysterical agony.

As the lights in the room suddenly flickered and came on, Uncle Jack and his machine were already climbing the wall with the use of its many legs. Some of them were not working, making his progress a little hampered, but despite this he moved up the stone framework with considerable speed. Within moments he was on the balcony and making his way towards the upper exit. Shots were fired. Uncle Jack flicked a switch and the pumpkin's outer skins began to rotate and finally spin. With this spinning motion in place, the bullets just bounced off the machine's exterior. Finally, with a puff of smoke and combustion BANG from its exhaust, the pumpkin traveller passed through the open balcony archway and out of sight.

Down the corridor he went, some of the machine's legs moving the pumpkin forward and other legs knocking over the military personnel who were getting in the way of his escape.

"Don't mind me," cried Uncle Jack jovially to a bunch of soldiers, bowled over by a single swipe from his pumpkin machine. "Just on my way out to get some air you know. You should get some too by the looks of you!"

He navigated the bending corridor, before finding a large balcony that looked out onto Clearwash City. Through this viewing area Uncle Jack steered his machine and smashed through the great glass pane that enclosed it. With a leap, his pumpkin landed onto the roof of a nearby building and navigated its way over the next two roofs before briefly stopping. Uncle Jack popped his head through the hole in the upper lid of his horseless carriage and looked about him.

"Clearwash City," he shouted back at the city theatre from which he'd escaped, "will never fall into the hands of insolent barbarians," and with those words he popped his head back inside and set off in his chugging and almost broken-down pumpkin; over the rooftops and out towards the eastern city wall.

Chapter 27 – Stalemate!

The shouting and chanting in the great market square could be heard across the city. Maltrisia's troops had arrested the politicians who were opposing her, cleared the debating chamber of people, and these same military personnel now surrounded the building to keep any protestors at bay. As a riot began, Maltrisia could be seen on the big screens delivering her final words of condemnation over Lord Stephen. The gagged man looked on with utter contempt as his opponent pronounced her sentence upon him.

"Lord Stephen, amongst other felonies, you have been found guilty of cultural sabotage and plotting against the state. With all of these crimes committed, I have no option to but to sentence you with the immediate penalty of death."

A roar of disapproval went up from the people and only a volley of shots from the troops kept them at bay.

"Take him outside and shoot him!" ordered Maltrisia.

Stones, bricks, various objects were thrown towards the chamber building, some smashing the corridor windows through which Lord Stephen was being escorted. Then the missiles were turned upon the troops and they had to retreat into the building for their own safety. As a result, the execution squad couldn't immediately get outside to fulfil its duty.

As the crowds rioted, Marcus and his team quickly moved into the streets that surrounded the main square. After putting on a small breathing mask, each person reached into his/her jacket pocket and pulled out an object, about the size of a child's rubber ball. Rotating its core, the objects were rolled a few yards away down the pavement. Another of the same objects was also primed, this time being rolled in the opposite direction. Within seconds a chemical reaction within each ball began to pump out smoke. Soon, the streets that ran from the square were filled with smouldering fumes. Under this cover, the booster devices were set up at the very edge of each avenue, to send Basil's shut down code across the whole area. Once done, each pulled a roll of canvas from their coats and, squatting down next to the booster box, stretched the canvas out over the box and themselves.

From one of the debating chamber's top storey windows, Maltrisia looked on at the raging crowds. This wasn't what she'd expected. Still, it fitted in with her overall plans.

"Clear the streets of this rabble," she said. "Release the hymenopteran."

The guard standing next to her took out a flare pistol, put his hand through the open window, and fired a blue burst of flame into the sky.

- -

"Who's there!" shouted a voice from behind a row of trees.

Several of the rambling and horticultural society rushed out to grab whoever it was.

Georgiana, unable to move very well after her long ascent through the almond grove terraces, just held up her hand.

"It's me," she cried out, fearing they would wrestle her to the ground.

"Miss Georgiana!" they cried. "It's you!"

"It's me," she echoed back, a relieved smile on her face.

Basil got up from his position and ran over to her. Giving her a gentle bear hug, he almost wept with relief.

"We thought you were lost... or dead," he said.

"I'm fine, I'm fine," she replied, tapping her burley friend on the shoulder as if saying 'that's enough hugging, you're squashing me a little too much'.

Once Basil had let her go, Georgiana hobbled over to where they had all been sitting. There, in front of a tree she sat herself down, next to the base station. Casting her gaze out over the city, Georgiana could see and hear the riotous noise coming from the market square.

"What's happening?" she enquired.

"Looks like some kind of riot," replied Basil. "It's been going on for a good few minutes."

"And the smoke?"

"That will be Marcus," replied Basil. "It means the extra booster stations are now in place."

"Is it ready?" she asked, looking at the base station.

"Of course," replied Basil.

"Turned on?"

"Of course not," he replied.

"Why ever not?"

"We have to wait for all of the insects to swarm in the sky," said Basil. "Strict orders from Marcus."

"Oh I see," she replied.

At that moment a blue flare shot up into the sky.

"What does that mean?" asked Georgiana.

"No idea," replied Basil. "We'll have to wait and see."

Georgiana felt sick, knowing that her father was nearby, but still, so far out of reach.

"Have you seen my father?" she asked.

"He's in the debating chamber," replied Basil, but we're too far away to know what's happening. "Did Tristram tell you where we were?"

The name 'Tristram' hit Georgiana like a bullet in her gut.

"Tristram!" she said, suddenly remembering why she had made her trip to see her friends. "Tristram!" she said again.

"Whatever is the matter?" they asked.

"He's a traitor!" she replied.

- -

In response to the blue flare, hundreds of crates were opened within the western streets of Clearwash City and wake up codes initiated. Hordes of insects began to rise into the sky. Buzzing and darting down alleyways and avenues, the hymenopteran drove off anyone and everyone in their path. Maltrisia's troops held up their wrist bands for a brief security scan as the harvesters sped around and past them. The sound of their corporate buzzing was deafening, like listening to never ending echoes of low-pitched metallic vibrations, all playing the same tune on a continuous loop.

"What do you mean, *traitor*?" asked Basil.

Georgiana opened her mouth to reply.

"No time to talk," interrupted Basil. "Here they come!"

They watched as a river of metal flowed into the square, flooding the market place. The insects stung anything that moved and within seconds there were just piles of people, scattered across the floor whilst others fled through the many streets and finally into shops, malls or anywhere where they could close a door on their pursuers.

Basil flipped the switch to turn the base station on. It hummed itself into life, pulsing and droning out its booting up tune.

"Aren't you going to enter the drop code?" asked Georgiana.

"Not yet," Basil replied, keeping his hand over the base station's key pad so no-one could touch it.

"People are dying!" she cried.

"Not until they swarm!" asserted Basil. "I have orders!"

"Get ready to leave," Maltrisia told her troops, seeing that the way was being made clear for her to exit the building unhindered. "And someone find that execution squad and do their work for them; put a bullet in Lord Stephen before we go."

Into the space above the market square dropped a series of lightweight racing balloons, boosted not just by the wind but by noisy propeller turbine engines attached to each basket's sides. Their descent was accompanied by the 'whoops' and howls of young men on an adrenalin high; arms held high with white bands on both wrists whilst navigating their way through the rivers of hymenopteran. One balloon hit the ground just outside the palace, another landed in an adjacent street, but the other two landed squarely on their target, the debating chamber's roof.

"What was that?!" exclaimed Maltrisia, looking up at the ceiling.

The sound of masonry and tiles being churned up across the rooftop as the balloon baskets were dragged along, reverberated throughout the building.

"Go and find out," she shouted to some of her troops.

The baskets came to a standstill as iron hooks were dropped by the balloon riders and anchored themselves onto the building's bell tower or chimney stacks. Out of the basket stepped Erepsin and his men. Placing their wrists up in the air, they were quickly scanned by the local hymenopteran who immediately swarmed in and about them. Within moments they were left alone, their wrist bands giving off a signal that they were part of Maltrisia's armed forces.

Pulling a casket out of each balloon's travelling basket, they flipped open the lids. Inside each were a set of reprogrammed, dormant harvester insects that Erepsin and his team had been catching since the start of the war. Only a dab of blue paint on each insect's sides made it distinguishable from the rest of Maltrisia's hoard. Moments later, the wakeup code was delivered and they buzzed themselves to life. Moving along the rooftop with the blue dotted insects buzzing about their heads, Erepsin and his team approached the flaps that opened up from the debating chamber's attic. Before they could get to them, however, the roof space entranceways began to open and soldiers cautiously poked their heads through.

"Kill!" cried Erepsin, pointing towards the soldiers.

His insects flew on ahead of the group. As a simple reflex action, the soldiers lifted up their wrists, ready to be scanned, but even before they knew what was happening, the hymenopteran took them out. Climbing down into the chamber's loft space, Erepsin and his team made their way through the dusty beams to the spiral stair that ran down to the main building. Erepsin looked at his harvester insects which were buzzing about his head and around the room.

"Find and rescue Lord Stephen," he said.

In a moment of frenzied activity, down the stair they sped, systematically buzzing and zooming in and out of every room they came to. Erepsin and his companions waited a few moments for the insects the clear the way. After hearing shots and cries from defeated soldiers, they exited the upper floor and followed on behind the sounds of the buzzing horde.

Outside, Maltrisia's hymenopteran began to swarm. Up, up they went, clouding together to obscure the sky. Passing information to each other, they prepared for their next sweep across the city. The mass of swirling metallic objects split into two churning solid hives, ready to shift across the sky and drop into different parts of the city.

Hearing shots above her head, Maltrisia moved to the lower floor and out of the debating chamber's front door. There, in front of her, were her hymenopteran, storming together in their pre-kill frenzied activity. A beautiful sight that lifted her heart. Such a mighty army, all programmed for the purpose of her rule. She stepped further into the market square to get a better look and, to her delight, a measure of her creatures dropped down and spun about her person.

"Go!" she shouted. "Off you go!" she shouted again, lifting her arms into the air.

As each column of silver mushroomed upwards for the strike, more shots were heard from inside the debating chamber. Maltrisia briefly turned to look up at its first storey windows, seeing shadowy figures inside chased down the corridor by more buzzing insects. She laughed, thinking they were hers. Looking back at the two towers of humming, pulsating silver, she once again lifted her arms as if to be a part of their imminent departure.

"Now," cried Georgiana, standing to her feet!

"I know, I know," replied Basil.

Basil entered the code into the device, speaking out each number.

"One, one, one, four," he said.

It pulsed out its message and everyone held their breath. Had they done it as Tristram had advised they should or had Maltrisia protected her insects from being interfered with? Then there was that name again, 'Tristram'. It was like a sting in their minds. The swarms now looked like two twirling cyclones, spinning, twisting, whirling, spiralling; getting ready to jettison out from their inner cores in an explosion of metallic mass annihilation. The sound of their roar was deafening. It was a horror to even look upon.

Seeing the wave that was about to be unleashed, Basil stood up and turned to Georgiana, wondering why they hadn't dropped out of the sky.

"How, exactly, has Tristram betrayed us?" he asked.

Georgiana opened her mouth, but nothing came out. Turning back to look at the silver storm, there seemed nothing that anyone could do.

- -

Erepsin and his men pushed through the corridors of the debating chamber, stepping over Maltrisia's military personnel who lay scattered across the floor. Into every room they burst until they found Lord Stephen, his crouching figure at the end of a long room, a circle of blue dotted hymenopteran about him and a dead execution squad just a few feet away.

"Withdraw!" called Erepsin, and immediately his buzzing insects moved away from their target.

Going over to Lord Stephen, Erepsin held out his hand to offer him help to stand.

"I'm pleased to see you alive sir," he said.

Lord Stephen looked up, saw the hymenopteran had moved away and looked surprised to see the figure of Erepsin before him.

"Is my daughter safe?" he asked.

"I've made sure she's not in the heart of the city," he replied. "Now please Lord Stephen, we must leave this building. It will be targeted within the next few minutes. We haven't much time."

Taking the hand that had been offered him, Lord Stephen stood to his feet and followed Erepsin and his men out of the room. Going down the corridor he stopped at one of the windows to see the terror that was the hymenopteran storm.

"Come on sir," said Erepsin. "We must leave immediately!"

Moments later both insect cyclonic squalls opened their column's core to reveal the bulging, buzzing undulations of iron which violently flowed in continual multi-layered currents; the light from the sun catching the whitecap breakers as each bubble plume mushroomed towards insect release. Sprays of scattering silvery clusters gushed and frothed their presence about each fluid core, getting ready to spew out their mass of flowing bodies. With one final surge, each cyclone of hymenopteran pushed their volume of twirling metal frames upwards, like the tidal wave of a foaming, rippling, swell. The moment of release had come. Time to eat up the sky. Time for everyone to die.

Georgiana took hold of Basil's arm. It was difficult to stand in the face of such a foreboding body of aggressive power. The scene was beyond their ability to endure. Being past any hope of keeping their lives, despair coupled their hearts – they both felt within the unescapable sentence of death. No-one could deliver them from such a deadly peril.

A thunderclap of hot air resonated across the heavens as each core ejected its load. Up and out the insects went, surging high into the firmament; a plague of steel, a curse, a scourge, a pestilence, a living calamity ready to disperse. Together their bodies cast the shadow of a corporate veil; a mantle of despair, a prophetic baleful curtain. Communally blanketing out the sun and shrouding the city – their collective outline formed the drape by which this burial garment would be laid and those under its shadow put to rest.

In those suspended seconds of time, Maltrisia's heart soared. The terror of her supremacy was about to be felt by all and no-one was going to deny her the right to rule, to be that which she had always known she was called to be; a goddess – loved, worshipped and adored. The power and will to govern was now hers, given not by mere humanity or even by divine right, but by her right to be divine. The insect terror before her was nothing but heaven itself.

But, as quickly as her hymenopteran rose, so they toppled and fell back on themselves, both pillars of metallic creatures collapsing, tumbling and cascading to the ground. The buzzing stopped and their stilled bodies rained down a hail storm of clattering noise; their falling forms quickly accumulating, piling up on top of each other and then overflowing into a wave of rolling metal. The tidal ripples of silver swept across the square, knocking over Maltrisia and her team, who were quickly buried in two feet of flowing dead metal. Once all was still, the sound of quietness saturated the atmosphere.

"We've done it," whispered Basil, the sound of unbelief in his breath. "We've done it!" he cried, now jumping up and down with glee.

"Err hum!" said a voice.

Basil looked to his right to see one of his horticultural team with his finger on the 'activate' button.

"Don't forget to press activate," he said.

"Oh," replied Basil, looking very sheepish. "Silly me."

Moments later Basil and his rambling, horticulturalists were dancing their success in and amongst the almond trees.

"Get down!" Georgiana urged. "You'll give our location away! This war is not over!"

"Oh of course," they replied, more than a little embarrassed.

The group looked on to see how the events would unfold. Georgiana, watched intently, waiting to see any signs of her father's rescue.

On the outskirts of the market square, from beneath thinly stretched canvas that covered their bodies, Marcus' team got off the floor, rising up from keeping the booster boxes safe and also from playing dead; though two of his team failed to survive, hymenopteran having seen movement from beneath their canvas sheets in the first wave of their attack and relentlessly stung whatever it was that was there. The surviving few, however, quickly followed Marcus as he waded through and over the still and lifeless bodies of the floppy insects. As the soldiers began to pull themselves out of the sea of metal, trying to find their feet again, Marcus pulled out more smoke devices from his jacket. This time, however, he twirled their centre till a 'snap' was heard inside. Lobbing the spherical balls into the air, they landed around the group and exploded their contents. The stun grenades knocked over Maltrisia's armed guard, causing temporary bewilderment and disorientation. Into this chaos, Marcus and his team pounced, rushing to catch Maltrisia. She was quickly grabbed by the wrists and ankles, dragged across the metal bodies of her fallen insects and pulled away from her guards. Marcus lifted Maltrisia to her feet, but held her in his tight grip.

"Let me go!" she shouted at him.

"Not on your life!" he replied.

Shells began to be fired from the city's eastern quarter into the central zone.

"What the..." exclaimed Basil.

"That's Tristram!" said Georgiana, as the missiles continued to be fired.

"What's he up to?" exclaimed Basil.

"To gain the city for himself," she replied.

Casting her eyes back at the city square, gazing in the direction of the debating chamber, in her distress she muttered.

"Come on Erepsin! Where are you?"

Basil's eyes widened when he heard Erepsin's name mentioned. Obviously, there was more than one plan going on here. In those next moments, however, the sound of whirring shells dropped onto the almond tree groves.

"Take cover!" shouted Georgiana, and they all scattered as their location began to be ripped apart.

Erepsin stepped out of the debating chamber's back door, no sign of Lord Stephen with him. His hymenopteran hadn't been shut down by Basil's base unit. Instead, they swelled about his person and, with a quick command, lifted him up and carried him across the city towards Govan Square.

"Look," cried Basil, shielding himself behind a tree. "What was that?"

"Erepsin?" Georgiana whispered under her breath. "Where is my father?" She sensed that something had gone wrong.

Maltrisia's troops got to their feet again, only to see their leader in the hands of Marcus and his followers. Finding that their weapons had been taken from them, the soldiers tentatively waded their way forward through the insects towards their leader.

"That's far enough!" shouted Marcus. "Any more movement towards us and she dies."

Maltrisia laughed as more and more of her troops appeared at the head of each street, blocking off Marcus' means of escape.

"You can't win," she said. "You'll not get out of here alive."

"Who says we want to get out alive?" he replied. He was about to shoot her when, in that moment, one of the roof flaps on the debating chamber opened. Through it stepped figures from Erepsin's team and amongst them, the figure of Lord Stephen. He'd been rescued and was now free.

"No!" shouted Maltrisia!

"Oh, my father!" cried Georgiana. She was sitting with her back to one of the trees, using it as a shield to protect her from the incoming shells. Despite her current danger, seeing his small figure from a distance brought a rush of overwhelming joy.

"Shoot him!" shouted Maltrisia.

The few troops that had their weapons at hand began to take pot shots at Lord Stephen and Erepsin's team. All fell, spreadeagle, onto their faces, seeking to avoid the rifle discharges and at the same time trying to cling onto the sloping rooftop.

"No!" shrieked Georgiana, in despair.

"One more shot and she dies!" screamed Marcus.

He pulled Maltrisia to her knees and stood over her, a pistol at the back of her head. Maltrisia's troops fell silent, seeing the stalemate that everyone was caught in.

"Shield me," said Marcus, to his team.

His brave friends stood in a circle around him, forming a human shield so that Marcus himself could not be easily shot.

"Tell them to stop firing!" he ordered Maltrisia.

"Hold your fire!" she yelled.

Glancing down to see the mini ceasefire in place, Erepsin's men jumped up, helping Lord Stephen to his feet and assisting him as he entered a balloon's basket. Joined by his trembling rescuers, they helped each other fire up the motor engines at the basket's sides. Once ready, up the balloon sailed into the sky. Georgiana clapped her hands with joy, tears running down her face. A sudden jar, however, kept the balloon locked in place with the anchor rope still being firmly attached to the roof. In their panic, Erepsin's men had overlooked this minor detail.

"Cut the rope," shouted one.

"I haven't a knife," the other replied.

With shells still dropping out of the sky and into her locality, Georgiana continued to watch, holding her breath again, seeing that her father's escape wasn't yet complete.

More mortar fire fell from Tristram's military machine, scattering in the adjoining streets around the market square. The newly started fires and the smoke from Marcus' grenades filled the air with a choking haze, blurring the visual senses.

"Go down and unhook the anchor!" screamed one of Erepsin's men to another.

"No, you do it!" he yelled back – not wanting to risk being left behind.

So the first man went over the side of the basket and slid down the rope. Approaching the anchor, he tried to pull it away, but the pull from the balloon on the rope was so strong, it kept the anchor held fast. He didn't have the strength to pull it out or to slide it from its secured position.

"I can't unlock it!" he called.

"Get another balloon and sail over to us," came the reply. "We'll jump baskets on the way up!"

This the young man did, pulling out the other basket's anchor, running along the roof to catch up with the now moving basket, he leapt in - finally setting the direction of the turbine engines to move the balloon over towards the other.

From the direction of Govan Square, a small squad of insects buzzed across the city, over the palace grounds and into the great market square.

"We missed some!" cried Basil, pointing at the group of hymenopteran.

Maltrisia lifted her gaze and laughed at the sight of them, but Marcus made her very aware of her frailty by pushing her head further down and pressing his pistol barrel more firmly onto the back of her head.

The hymenopteran buzzed their way about the square, not seemingly interested in anyone or anything.

"What are they waiting for?" asked one of Marcus' team.

"Don't know," replied Marcus. "They seem to have a mind of their own."

The blue dotted insects continued to buzz, hovering over their fallen, metallic comrades, as if mourning their deceased state.

On the far side of the square, one of the legs of the sleeping harvesters twitched. It twitched again and then buzzed its fragile wings. The blue dotted insects immediately sensed the activity and zoomed over to it. As it came back to life, Erepsin's group zoomed in tight circular motions around and about it, as if invisibly passing over and enforcing their programming into the awakening creature. More hymenopteran began to stir and the same happened with their reawakening too. Soon, whole groups of insects buzzed and swooped together in exactly the same manner as the first group, zigzagging about the market, not interested in anyone or anything except the other sleeping insects.

Marcus cast his gaze up at the balloon rescue fiasco that was taking place on the roof, unsure what he should do. If he killed Maltrisia, Lord Stephen would be shot by her troops. Yet, before his very eyes, her insect horde was being reawakened, as if raised from the dead.

With the shelling on their position coming to a halt, Basil watched the same event in horror as the hymenopteran horde slowly stirred itself into an awakened state.

"What's happening?" he asked.

Georgiana stood to her feet but remained silent, sensing that Erepsin was going back on his word. Basil stared at her uncomfortable countenance.

"Is this Erepsin's doing?"

"I'm not sure," Georgiana replied. "He said he was going to keep them asleep, give them a new code to stop Tristram getting control of them!"

"You gave him the wakeup code?!" exclaimed Basil.

Georgiana briefly turned her back, looking ashamed of herself.

Within a short time, two clouds of insects began to emerge from the floor.

"What have you done?" asked Basil.

"I'm trying to save my father!" she retorted.

With a small, essential number of zigzagging insects keeping a watch over the remaining insects that needed to wake up, the rest of the harvesters began to scan their surroundings. The soldiers held up their wrists and Marcus and his team just froze as they passed by.

Having formed a central information exchange unit at the centre of the square, where a group of the insects served the purpose of receiving and passing on what was found by the others, the insects returned to hover in front of Marcus and his team, once again scanning them for identification. They seemed to hesitate, as if calculating or deciphering something within their programming. Perhaps there was some conflicting data?

"I don't think they're too interested in us," said Marcus, speaking from a position of logical hope. "I think they would have killed us by now. These insects have clearly been reprogrammed as they've woken up. Just don't do anything to agitate them. We don't want to teach them that we're their enemies."

Within moments the insects seemed to have processed their data blockage. Returning to their information exchange, they shared their data conclusions with other clusters of harvesters nearby.

"See," said a relieved Marcus. "We're fine."

Groups of fifty or more hymenopteran began to weave their way about the market place. This way, that way, now back to where they had come. Over and over they went, as if mapping out their route. Some went parallel to Maltrisia's troops whilst others followed the perimeter border, down to the bottom of the square and then made their way back up again. Passing Marcus and his team, they zoomed their way to the top and then made their way back, doubling back on their own route.

"Hold steady," called Marcus, as the insects passed them by. Within moments, however, Marcus and his squad were attacked from multiple directions. Stung, their limp bodies flopped one by one to the floor with loud thuds, dead before they hit the ground.

"No!" exclaimed Basil, when Marcus and his team fell.

Maltrisia stood to her feet and laughed.

"Kill the people on the roof!" she shouted.

But before her guards could respond, they too were set upon and, almost immediately, were dead.

All of the hymenopteran now rose into the air, their reawakened buzz once again deafening the city sky. Shells continued to be fired from Tristram's soldiers but they had no effect on the corporate shape of the gathered creatures. Forming two great clouds, they got ready to scatter across the city.

Maltrisia ran to the palace grounds, waving up at an airship to come and get her. At the same time, one of Erepsin's men guided his newly ascending balloon over to the stranded one, and gently bumped the baskets together. With all their might, they bundled Lord Stephen from one basket to the other, grabbing and hauling him across the narrow gap. As the wicker sides scraped along each other's edges, a tired Lord Stephen flopped onto the floor of the ascending balloon and just lay there, listening to the yelling of the other men, trying themselves to scramble in before the gap between the balloons became too wide.

Down rested the airship in the palace grounds, and Maltrisia climbed on board. Up the ship ascended, moving gracefully into the sky, keeping a distance from the hymenopteran storm. Away went Lord Stephen's balloon. Georgiana yelled her relief at the sight, but before it could fully get away, more shells fell into the market square from Tristram's military machine; scattering bombs across the whole area, hitting the debating chamber and the two floating balloons. The fuel tanks ignited and a huge explosion ripped through the air sending bursts of erupting fire in every direction and killing everyone in sight.

Georgiana fell forward onto her knees.

"Oh, my father!" she wailed, staring at the fireball and crumbling to the ground.

Chapter 28 – We Take What We Need

Maltrisia walked up to the airship's command deck to stand next to the ship's captain.

"Take us out of here," she said.

Looking back at the explosion happening in the market place, she laughed at Lord Stephen's demise.

As its engines roared, the airship turned on its axis, ready to speed out towards the western side of the city.

"As soon as we dock," she said, "put out the command to call the hymenopteran home."

A sudden pull on the ship jolted everyone.

"What's happening?!" she demanded.

Checking their instruments, the crew couldn't understand what was going on. The captain rushed from person to person, post to post, but couldn't make out why they had decelerated.

"We must have an engine fault," he concluded.

Another jolt, however, and the sudden rushing sound of the hymenopteran told a different story. Suddenly the open sky in front of them filled with the bodies of the buzzing creatures. Locking themselves onto every part of the airship, they buzzed in unison to pull the great vessel out of the sky.

"Full power to the engines!" yelled the ship's captain.

The roar of the turbines put the ship into a juddering, vibrating state that shook the slimly built metal structure right down its central frame. Despite all of its thrust being sent in a forward motion, the great ship simply tilted on its side and was dragged back and down towards the ground – several hymenopteran entered the ships turbines and allowed themselves to be diced up by the blades, at the same time disabling the engines.

Basil and his friends looked on as the airship collapsed back onto the market square. They'd never seen anything like it. The corporate strength of the 'minute many' overcoming and bringing down a mighty vessel. On its side, the great ship was disabled and never going to rise again. Its engines failed and gave way. Groups of insects pounded the windows till they smashed and in they rushed. Locating, stinging and capturing, they went about their work with great efficiency. About a minute later, a large group of them appeared carrying a screaming Maltrisia in their grasp. In one swift movement she was whisked up and taken off into the sky.

At the same time, a large band of insects broke away from the horde and headed out to where the mortar shelling had been delivered in the eastern part of the city. Whoever they were, they were dealt with in minutes and the mortar shelling ceased. Basil and his group got ready to go.

"Come on," he said to Georgiana. "It's not safe here. We have to flee the city."

Georgiana was in a crumpled mess, however, and didn't care what was happening about her.

"We have to go!" he urged, but it was too late.

A wave of hymenopteran flew across their area and they were spotted. Into the almond grove they sped, whizzing their clicking, clacking bodies through the trees. Basil's team scattered in all directions and one by one, they were picked off. Basil himself backed up to a nearby tree, watching his fleeing friends fall. A harvester identified him and flew over, hovering a few feet away and swaying its abdomen from side to side. Basil felt his insides churn; a suffocating, sickening feeling of his imminent demise. Closing his eyes, he could hear the creature buzz its moving presence to right in front of him. Wincing, waiting for the pain, he gasped for air, hyperventilating with stress. The pain didn't come.

As Basil opened his eyes he saw an arm had reached across his chest. There, just inches away, was the creature. It's approach had been stopped, however, by a hand, about the wrist of which was a white, rubber band. The person standing next to him pushed the white band towards insect. It backed off, as if not able to move in for the kill. As the space between Basil and the insect increased, it was filled by the presence of Georgiana, still with tears streaming down her face but nevertheless, waving her wrist band from side to side, keeping her friend safe.

Another insect moved towards Basil from the side and Georgiana had to step into that space too, warding off its advances. Other sides of Basil were filled with hymenopteran, each trying to get at him, even from above. Georgiana found herself swishing her arm, left, right, up, and down to block their path, but they continued their encroachment, determined to take him out. It was as if they knew he wasn't the owner of the wrist band.

"I think they want me," said Basil, seeing that his friend was in an impossible situation. "Get yourself out of here whilst you can," he added.

"I'm not leaving you," she replied.

"You've no choice," said Basil, tears streaming down his face. "That band only works for one person and they know it."

Georgiana continued to sway her arm from side to side, but the insects were determined, pressing in on her to get closer to her friend. Once again Basil closed his eyes. He prepared himself for the moment when he would wilfully step away from the tree, out of Georgiana's shadow and give himself to the insect's sting. Putting his hand onto his beating heart, he steadied himself for a moment before making his move. As he did so, Georgiana embraced him.

"I love you, my dear friend," she said.

Then she moved away and the insects followed her. Basil looked down at his arm. About his wrist was the white, rubber band.

"Oh my dear child…" he said.

He turned his head just in time to see Georgiana standing on the edge of the grove, more and more hymenopteran surrounding her. She lifted her arms, not in surrender, but in a welcome gesture, lifted her head and closed her eyes, giving herself up for her friend. The ever-increasing cloud of hymenopteran encircled her and then corporately fell on her. Under their weight, she fell to her knees, a cry of pain from the impact on her left leg. Up she went into the sky, she cried out again, expecting to die. Instead, the hymenopteran carried her off towards the market square.

- -

Maltrisia's screams could be heard across the capital as the swarm of hymenopteran swept her up and carried her throughout the cityscape. With their claws firmly locked onto every part of her, she found herself constantly swished from side to side as the insects ducked, dodged, darted and dived down in and amongst the buildings, gardens, back alleys and parks of Clearwash City – before leaving the inner circle behind. They flew over the canal and then lifted her to a great height, before dropping to the ground and (to Maltrisia's surprise) gently setting her down, unharmed and unscarred. With buzzing insects still flying in close proximity, she battered her arms to fend them off. Glancing this way and that, wondering what to do and where to go, she saw directly ahead the imposing presence of the waterworks, casting a deep shadow over her small frame. Scaffolding covered its front where the window cleaners had been busy before the war began. Having nowhere else to go, she ran up its three sets of steps and momentarily leaned on the front doors to catch her breath. Gasping for air, she couldn't linger, the sound of the metallic creatures hovering nearby drove her inside. Heaving on the great oak doors, she slipped through the gap, then pulled on them again until they closed with a loud 'clunk'.

Feeling a small measure of relief that her pursuers were outside, she staggered across the entrance foyer, her shoes clacking on the marble flooring, echoing off the pillars and walls. Through the open archway and down the corridor she stumbled, it was her first time in the waterworks and everything was strange and new. She was instantly enshrouded by a dreamlike, prophetic atmosphere along with a hunger to keep a dying promise alive; she felt nothing but hatred for it. Every part of Maltrisia was revulsed at the thought of not being in control of herself and her destiny. Pressing on, she continued to move deeper into the heart of the building.

On either side of the decorative corridor on which she walked, alcoves appeared – within which were small statues of historic figures, heroes of old, whose stories witnessed of great adventures that still speak today. Above her head, the ceiling was slightly domed and overlaid in gold whilst beneath her feet the floor was made up of one mosaic after another. Towards the end of the corridor was a wide-open aisle, tall pillars stood to attention on either side, each of which stretched up to a high and lofty ceiling. Before she could get to that area, however, she found her way blocked. In the middle of the corridor sat a strange, large machine. It appeared quite out of place. Fresh scratch marks etched their way across the floor, going right up to its base; making the machine look as if it had been recently dragged and dumped in the middle of the walkway. Beyond the machine, it looked as if the floor had been freshly dug up, but Maltrisia couldn't see much of that detail.

The bizarre, metallic contraption that sat at the centre of the walkway looked like an enormous, metal box with a polished, domed lid. Rising out of its top and sides were various pistons, pipes and rubber tubes sprouting in all directions like the hairdo of a mad professor. Across its front sat a large glass pane with frothy water inside, it looked as if it were something similar to a giant washing machine. At the foot of the machine were several large levers, pedals and switches. All around the machine's base were small interlocking wheels that looked as if they were ready to turn together in rhythmic unison. To the left of the machine stood a small room made from pure crystal glass; very expensive and obviously created by a master craftsman. It shone somehow, radiating an inner light that brightly illuminated its surroundings. Sticking out of the glass cubicle's top was another large pipe which bent back and re-joined itself onto the machine's lid.

Maltrisia walked up to it, to touch its frame, but before she made the connection, the machine itself seemed to sense her approach and churned its water inside. The sudden noise of moving water caused her to jump back with surprise.

"What is this thing?" she wondered.

Whilst this thought ran through her mind, it was interrupted by a buzzing noise ahead of her.

"No!" she whispered, through gritted teeth.

Dismay filled her heart. She still wasn't safe. She sought to hide behind the edge of the machine but her closeness to its proximity brought the machine to life once more. Instinctively the hymenopteran sped in her direction. Running from one side of the machine to the other, Maltrisia immediately found her way blocked by the creatures who quickly appeared at the machine's edges. Steadily, after cutting off her escape route down the corridor, they buzzed their way forward, pressing in until there was no-where to go. Retreating from what seemed to be every direction, Maltrisia found herself pressed against the cold, hard, crystal surface of the small glass room.

"I am in charge!" she shouted at them.

The insects just buzzed about her, hovering, swishing, swaying, twitching and ready for the strike. Still facing off her enemies, Maltrisia's fingers fumbled behind her back for the glass room's door handle. After finding it, she folded each finger tightly around to form a strong grip and, in one smooth motion, flipped it downwards. Twirling on her heels, she flung the door open, entered the room, and closed the door behind her.

There she stood, inside the small glass room with nothing except the see-through walls between her and the humming hymenopteran. Buzzing their displeasure at her, they rammed their heads into the glass cubical, making a firm 'thud' sound each time they impacted the chamber's walls. Each thud, each attack, caused Maltrisia to jump with fright, thinking that the glass would break any moment and that would be the end of her. Then, without warning, the flying insects left; each one suddenly turning on its tail to disappear from sight. Maltrisia wondered for a moment what had happened. Time went by and, understanding that they'd gone, she let out a sigh of relief. Leaning on the glass cubicle's walls, she waited a little longer to make sure they weren't coming back. Then, after peering around at all sides of the room for any signs of the creatures, she decided it was time to leave. Placing her hand on the glass door's inner handle, she got ready to make good her escape. Then, 'cluck' the glass door locked on her. She pushed down on the door handle, but it wouldn't budge. She hammered down on it with the flat of her hand and then with her fists, but still it would not move.

"What's happening?" she cried.

To her left, the machine which was attached to the glass room seemed to come to life. With a grinding, a hissing and a deep mechanical cough, cough, cough, its inner workings jolted together and finally formed a rhythmic tune. Whoop, whoop,

whoop, an alarm shrieked as water began to bubble up from beneath Maltrisia's feet. The room gradually started to fill with water.

"No!" she cried, not knowing what to do.

She took hold of the door handle again and jerked it from side to side, up and down to try and loosen its locked state, but nothing worked. She thumped with her fists on the door, but it would not budge. The water climbed higher and higher up the sides of the glass walls. Finally it reached the height of her waist and there, to Maltrisia's relief, it stopped. The icy cold water swirled around her; an ever-moving ripple that pinched its frosty grip and would not let go.

Maltrisia stood, trembling and quaking in the cold chill of the water's grasp, not knowing what would happen next. Just behind her the figure of Erepsin silently appeared . He stared at his mother's diminished frame. How weak and pitiful she looked. This once so flamboyant and elegant woman was now reduced to nothing more than shivering whimpers. In that same moment Maltrisia had the uncomfortable feeling by which she sensed she was being stared at, but before she could turn around...

"Beautiful isn't it," said Erepsin.

Maltrisia jumped in surprise. She turned her head to see the figure that belonged to the familiar voice.

"Erepsin!" she cried with relief on her face. "Erepsin, oh Erepsin. Help me," she said. "Get me out of here!"

Just then the hymenopteran came buzzing back into the room. They hummed their presence all around, checking out every nook and cranny before resting their gaze on the cubical in which Maltrisia stood.

"Erepsin, look out," Maltrisia cried, "seeing one of the metal insects hovering near her son."

Erepsin just ignored her words.

"I said, its beautiful isn't it," he replied.

"What?" Maltrisia enquired. "What are you talking about? Erepsin, look out there's a..."

"My machine," said Erepsin, ignoring both his mother's pleas for his safety and the metal insect that hovered at his side.

He placed his hands onto the glass as if to make a personal connection with the device; just the touch of it thrilled his sense of achievement.

"My Free Flowing Foamy Flusher Machine," he added, casting his gaze over the machine and the cubical in which his mother stood. "It's the first of its type you know."

"This is *your* machine?" she enquired, shivering with the cold.

"Some of my friends finished its adaptation yesterday and now it's ready for its first run."

"Erepsin, I don't understand," his mother replied. "I need you to get me out of here."

"You're going to be the first person to try it out," he added with a wink and a smirk.

"What do you mean?" she said. "What is this thing?!"

Erepsin ignored her words and once more cast his eyes again over the mechanical contraption.

"Beautiful," he said again to himself. "Absolutely beautiful."

"Erepsin! Erepsin!" Maltrisia yelled. "Let me out of here! Let me out!"

Erepsin stared back at his mother, not a single sign of emotion on his face.

She pounded on the glass, but he didn't respond.

"Please," she eventually said, through quivering lips.

Their gaze fixed on each other but all of Maltrisia's emotions went unanswered, knocking on a closed door that would not be opened. Erepsin wasn't for turning.

"Where is your heart?" she finally said.

Erepsin placed his face close to the glass and breathed onto its surface. Then, in the condensed vapour, he drew a heart.

"There it is Mummy," he said.

Then with one sweep of his hand, he wiped it away.

"Oops," he said. "It's gone. You obliterated it, remember? You killed my best friend and destroyed his family."

He moved around the outside of the cubical, never once letting his gaze fall from this mother's eyes.

"I have written a poem," he said, in a mocking tone. "I've written it just for this moment, my dearest mother,"

Maltrisia felt the cold chill of her son's hatred as he stared mercilessly at her.

"It goes like this,

Round and round and round we go,

Faster and faster the water does flow.

It gushes and froths with pure delight,

It swishes and sloshes till flushing is right!"

"Listen to me!" she pleaded, her voice hoarse from distress. "Listen to me, my boy."

"Your *boy*?" Erepsin echoed back at her.

"Yes, my boy," she cried. "Erepsin, *my* boy."

"My name is not Erepsin," he responded, "and I am no longer a mere 'boy'."

Maltrisia looked at him, not knowing how to respond.

"I don't have a name," he continued. "I have no identity, no personality, I am nothing but a letter," he added. "The letter 'E' to be exact. Mr E, and don't you forget it. Mr E, a man without character, without meaning, without value, a pathetic, blundering wimp! You remember, don't' you? A man without friends, family, hope, prospects and now, a man without a conscience..."

"I should not have said those things," Maltrisia said. "It was wrong of me."

"Said!" exclaimed Erepsin. "Said!" he shouted again. "I'm not talking about anything you said. I'm talking about what you've done! This," he said, "isn't for me! It's for Lord Stephen, for Lady Melanie, for my friend Richard and for all of those people who have gotten in your way."

"Erepsin!" Maltrisia yelped. "Have pity!".

"Pity?" he responded, with contempt. "Where was yours?"

Maltrisia had nothing to say.

"As the Pluggats would often say, 'Evil will slay the wicked.'" Then he added, "You are 'the wicked'. I can see that now, and you must be dealt with."

"I have my faults," she admitted.

He walked over to the flusher machine and placed his hand upon a dial.

"Don't you dare!" she shouted at him, pounding her fists onto the glass.

"Bye, bye mother," he said, placing his other hand on a lever attached to the flusher machine's front face.

"You wouldn't dare!" cried his mother, in a growling tone. "Erepsin, you are evil!"

"Quite right," he said. "Mr Erepsin Ville, or Mr E-Ville of Clearwash City. And E-Ville," he added, "will slay the wicked. You see, the Pluggats were right all along. Goodbye mother."

"Erepsin!" Maltrisia again banged her fists on the side of the glass room.

"We take what we need," he replied, impersonating his mother's voice. "We dispose of the rest."

With those words he twirled the dial between his fingers, pulled down the lever and the machine at once began to tremble and shake. Its inner engines stirring themselves into life. The lights across the machine's front beamed brightly. The small wheels on the outside of the machine whizzed around at a tremendous velocity. First one way they went and then the other, back and forth, until they all abruptly stopped. Then, from a speaker built into the side of the flusher machine, came a deep electronic voice.

"Flushing traveller, prepare for new destination. Direction downwards, lowest level and out," said the machine. "Have a nice trip."

"Erepsin!" she yelled again.

Erepsin walked over to stare his mother in the face for one last time.

"Goodbye," he whispered, with his lips against the side of the glass room.

223

He gave the glass window a quick kiss and then started to chant,

"Round and round and round and round and round and round and round we go," he said, throwing his hands up into the air as if performing a part in a theatrical play.

The clanking of the cogs and the grinding, clunking mechanical melody of the machine caused the small glass room to slowly turn round and round and round and round. Erepsin initially jumped onto the glass room, its rotation took him round with it for a few turns as he continued to stare at Maltrisia. Then he dropped off the cubical and turned his back on her.

"Erepsin!" yelled Maltrisia.

Clunk went another cog, clunk, clank and then clunk again, taking the room into a spin. Faster and faster it went, speeding up with every turn. From the glass room's ceiling the large pipe poured down bubbling soapsuds and from holes in the floor the water now gushed and spouted upwards, causing Maltrisia to lose her footing. Soon the small room was spinning and humming at high speed with a whirlpool of water inside. Faster and faster it went, gathering speed with every turn. Somewhere between the splashing water and the soapsuds, parts of Maltrisia could still be seen; every now and then an arm or leg would briefly appear against the glass walls before vanishing amongst the frothy bubbles.

Taking an imaginary ballroom partner in his arms, Erepsin danced around the glass cubical until his extended hand finally clasped the chain that dangled from the flusher machine's main water pipe. Down went the chain. There was a heavy clunk followed by a great gurgling noise which echoed around the room, just like a giant plug being pulled from a bath. Then a swilling, a swirling and a great sluuuuuuurrrrrp; the descending water gurgled and the glass cubicle emptied itself, flushing everything inside away. The glass room decelerated and then just sat there, very clean and very empty.

"And off she goes!" Erepsin cried. "Goodbye mother," he added, with a whisper.

For a brief moment, a pang of conscience hit him and his face dropped.

"What have I done?" he asked himself.

Then, shaking off the feeling, he bowed a gracious bow at the flusher machine, as if to say thank you for its services. Opening the door to the glass chamber he could see his mother's jet-black pillbox hat sitting on the edge of the hole that she had been flushed down. He picked it up and was about to toss it down the hole after her when he hesitated.

"Something to remember you by," he called down after her. He tucked the hat under one of his braces, locked the door and turned the flusher machine off.

"And that, ladies and gentlemen," shouted Erepsin, "that is what I call entertainment!"

With those words, he took a bow to an imaginary audience and walked off down the corridor.

224

Chapter 29 – A New Order & Identity

Within a few hours, the busy hymenopteran had cleared the city square of all 'unnecessary materials', as they would be labelled under the new regime. Now the market place was clean and ready for use as a location of public gathering. The people assembled in it, however, were not there by their own will. They had been rounded up, herded even, by the flying, buzzing creatures and kept in their place by the swarm still blocking off all exits.

"Ladies and gentlemen," cried a megaphoned voice through the city loud speakers, "I give you Mr E!"

From across the city, and out of a storm cloud of insects, the figure of Erepsin floated in, carried by his new insect servants. They gently dropped him onto the pavement just inside the palace grounds.

Walking up to a free-standing microphone, set up at the palace gates, Erepsin address the crowd.

"My most noble subjects," he said. "Welcome to the new order of things."

He gave a most gracious bow, taking his hat right off his head and then placing it firmly back again.

"I'm here as your new self-appointed, self-proclaimed ruler; supported by my excellent team of soldiers and, of course, my friendly insects – delivered into my hands by the loveliest Georgiana Pluggat-Lynette.

There was a sharp intake of breath when Georgiana's name was mentioned.

"As you may well know," Erepsin continued, "we've had a mighty bit of trouble over the last few weeks and months. But I'm glad to inform you that all of that is now over. My mother has been dealt with, I left her a few minutes ago feeling ever so slightly flushed, and she'll be bothering us no more."

The crowd murmured as to what that might mean.

"But there is the matter that there's still quite a few people who need to be called to account for their behaviour; not just the people who propped up my most woeful mummy, but also those nincompoops who tried to do a deal with her at everyone else's expense. Before we go there, however, I've another little family matter to deal with. To let you know that I'm not biased in any way, shape or form, I'm going to bring to your attention someone who has behaved rather badly.

The main door was opened to the palace and out was walked Seleucia, escorted by a guard on either side of her.

"This, ladies and gentlemen, is the personification of trouble. From what I've heard in these last hours, this young woman here has been selling our citizens to the Veles!"

The crowd grumbled at his words, many of them not knowing exactly what Erepsin was talking about but they certainly knew who the Veles were, a neighbouring country which specialised in the slave trade.

"So, dear sister," he said. "You've been a naughty girl! Do you have anything to say for yourself?"

Erepsin placed the microphone under Seleucia's chin and she opened her mouth to speak, but found the very same microphone immediately withdrawn.

"I thought so," commented Erepsin. "Nothing useful to say, as normal."

A prisoner's horseless carriage was brought into the square. Erepsin continued his talk.

"And you, my most dear sister, as punishment for your war crimes, I will banish you forever from this city. You will be paraded through its streets for everyone to see and then you will be sent out into the desert. Two days of provisions will be packed for you, to take you on your eight-day journey! Don't forget to tuck your belt in, now that you're on a weight-loss crash diet and don't forget that once the water has gone, you can always suck on a button or two, your own saliva will keep you going until about day five, I should think!"

With that Seleucia was forcibly pushed into the carriage and off it went, parading her yelling and screaming person through the streets of Clearwash City before taking its preprogramed route out into the wide expanse of the great desert.

Erepsin carried on his happy chatter and banter.

"Next its nincompoop time! Time for all of you nincompoops to face up to your nincompoopish ways! On this matter, I've got quite a list of you. It's all of the politicians who supported my mother or who tried to do a deal with her. Boy you've been stupid! If it wasn't for you nincompoopiness, we wouldn't be in this mess! So it's time for you to pay the price for our disaster. Off you go my friends and find them."

At that, about a thousand insects flew off into the city to locate them. It didn't leave anything to the imagination as to what would happen when they met their pre-assigned insect assassin.

"Now from nincompoops to traitors," said Erepsin. "In my opinion, the only good thing to do with a traitor, is to betray them back, to do to them what they've done to us. So, I've decided that we're going to capture them and then betray them back by selling them off to the Veles – so that they too can live as slaves for the rest of their lives! There, how's that for a good punishment? So the people who fall into this category are such people as the city clerk, the city governor, the governor's immediate administrative staff and, of course, the most noble turncoat and greasy, slippery toad, Tristram! We've already caught the city clerk and governor, in fact we sold them about an hour ago. As for Tristram, well, we're yet to find him, seems like he's gone into hiding but, once we have him, we'll be selling him off too."

Erepsin went through several more groups of people on his long list that he needed to get even with or people who needed dealing with for the sake of the city. Then he added, "but as a sign of my compassion and good sense of fair play, later on today I shall release from my care, forty prisoners who I know will cherish their freedom and seek once more to become proper citizens of this great city."

Some in crowd gave a nod of approval, it seemed that Erepsin was already winning some of them over.

"We will now put this war behind us and once again we shall soon have everything back to normal," he added. "Public services will be revived within the next month and we will rebuild all that we have lost. This city will be great and it is we who will make it so!"

Some in the crowd even gave a cheer and, with that endorsement, Erepsin lifted up his hands. Seeing his flying insects hovering in every direction he gave them one last command.

"Go!" he cried, and off they all buzzed to carry out their next assignment. The sky droned with their activity as they continued to search every part of the city. Erepsin gave a wave, exited the gateway and went back into the palace. Up the main stairs he went with a leap and a spring in his step. Straight into the west wing he trotted where the main palace bedrooms were. There he found Georgiana in the suite where his mother had briefly taken up residence when she thought she'd won the war. She was sitting on a chair in the corner of the room, guarded by two soldiers, who Erepsin quickly dismissed.

"There, I've done it," he said, when they were finally alone.

227

"Done what?" Georgiana replied, in a voice that showed complete disinterest.

"As promised, I've set the prisoners free," he said. "You see, I can be reasonable."

Georgiana sat in silence without looking up.

"What about all the dead people. Are you going to bring them back to life?" she asked.

"I didn't create this mess," he retorted. "I've just tidied it up. It was either let Tristram have the insects or me," replied Erepsin. "You decided to let me have them."

"I decided that no-one should have them!" yelled Georgiana. "You betrayed me! You lied. You betrayed us all!"

"I did what I said I would do all along, to avenge those who are weak and get rid of the pollutants in our city!"

"You've capitalised on other people's misfortune," she countered.

"Depends how you see things," he blandly stated.

"I don't want to have this conversation again," replied Georgiana. "If you had any regard for this city, you'd drop your so called 'right to rule' and give the people back their freedom."

Erepsin went to stare out of the window with his back to Georgiana, he hadn't expected this response from her.

"You're free to go too," he added rather coldly, glancing over his shoulder as he spoke.

She didn't move.

"I said you're free to go," he said.

"I heard you," she replied. "Free to go where?" she finally retorted.

"Home, I suppose," replied Erepsin. "Go home where you belong."

"Belong!" she replied. "Who belongs anywhere after all of this."

"Home is home," said Erepsin. "Yours, I believe, is still intact. That part of the city hasn't had that much damage so I assume you've still got your house, your gardens and your property. That is more than enough for anyone after a war. Go home." Erepsin's tone of voice grew tired and matter of fact.

"Really?" she said, in a bitter manner. "My father is dead. My mother and sister-in-law gone and you tell me to go home. My father is dead!" she repeated. "He's dead! You were meant to rescue him!"

"I did my best," he replied.

"If you hadn't been so concerned with getting your hands on your mother's insects, you could have helped him escape!"

"I had to send out the wakeup code and take control before Tristram did," he argued back. "Anyway," he continued, "my father's dead too."

Georgiana looked up.

"Seems like my mother had him disposed of on the same day the war started, something to do with him telling her she was crazy."

"I'm sorry for you loss," Georgiana eventually replied.

"We've all lost," he said.

"Some more than others," commented Georgiana. "Some like Marcus and his team and Basil's friends too. Your reprogramming of the insects didn't help them!"

"I don't know what went wrong there," he replied. "All I can think is that somehow Tristram must have already programmed their faces into their database for the kill, when the time was right. I can't be held responsible for every spinoff of every action that I or anyone else takes."

"Is that what you call them, spinoffs?"

There was no response from Erepsin. He just continued to stare out of the window.

"Do you know where Uncle Jack is?" asked Georgiana.

"No," he replied.

"Well he's probably dead too," she said. "Another one of your 'spinoffs'."

Erepsin breathed in deeply and let out a sigh.

"Go home," he said again.

"Why?" she curtly answered. "As if there's anything there for me now!"

Erepsin awakened to his moment of opportunity. He turned to face her.

"You could stay with me," he said.

She didn't look up or even register what he'd said. Erepsin cleared his throat.

"I would actually like you to stay with me," he said, in a gentler voice.

He shuffled on his feet.

"I, I mean, I really would like it if you would consider, if you would be able to think about, well perhaps, spending your time with me from now on. Not as someone to obey orders, but rather, as a friend."

Georgiana continued to stare at the floor.

"I've always been fond of your family," he continued, fidgeting with his fingers as he spoke. "Richard really was like a brother to me you know." Erepsin paused for a moment. Then, rather coldly, he said, "Even if you don't think that I qualify as family."

Life was put on pause for a few moments. Something had slipped out of Erepsin's soul and Georgiana sensed that there were still things to say. She looked across at Erepsin's face and saw the reality of a hurt, broken and lonely man.

"I did not mean to cause you pain," she finally said.

Erepsin took in another deep breath but gave no reply.

"You have always been a friend to us," she eventually conceded.

"A friend," he echoed, as if he didn't like the word. Erepsin shook his head. "I've never wanted to be your friend," he gently added.

Georgiana didn't quite know what to say in response. His statement was more than a little confusing.

"Well, even if your friendship was just with my brother, you did manage to be friendly towards the rest of us and you did try to save our lives, I'll give you that. So yes, in your own way, you have sought to be a friend."

"You misunderstand me," he responded, looking very uncomfortable with himself.

Georgiana just looked at him, not comprehending his meaning. His mannerisms were beyond her grasp.

"You misunderstand me," he said again, in a more definite tone.

He looked as if he were wrestling with some emotion inside but didn't want to let it out. Georgiana began to get unsettled, thinking that she had unearthed some hidden hatred within Erepsin and that perhaps it was time to make a quick exit. Within moments, however, she found Erepsin down on his knees in front of her.

"I loved your brother as my brother," he said. "Brothers we were in every way. But I loved you not as my sister but as someone who would be far more wonderful than that."

She looked at him in complete disbelief.

"Your brother was truly my brother and he was my dearest friend. As I grew older, however, my thoughts, when I visited, were often of you. I knew that you didn't like me much and there seemed nothing I could do about it. But now, now that we're here and we've both lost everything and everyone, can't you reconsider? Can you not think differently of me?"

He placed the side of his head on her knee and at the same time took her hand off her lap and put it on top of his head.

"I'd even give up this whole city if I knew I could have you," he said. "Though I'd rather share it with you," he quickly added.

Georgiana felt a surge of compassion within her for the broken man who was now asking for her companionship and love. Her head whirled with this new declaration of affection that she'd just received. Erepsin's vulnerability touched her heart in a way that it had never been touched before and compassion for him welled up within her.

"Will you stay with me?" he said, lifting, turning his head and staring her in the eye.

When she hesitated he said, "Even if it is just as a friend?"

She paused, not knowing what to say. In that moment, Erepsin got up and walked up and down the room. Then he went to her again, got down on his knees, dropped his eyes and said, "I just want you to consider that we may at some point..."

"Erepsin," she cut in. "You misunderstand my silence."

She took in a deep breath to compose herself.

"You are a time bomb," she said, a tremor of fear in her voice. "A tick, tick, ticking bomb that has already gone off and you will detonate again, I just know it. I cannot stay around you. You're too dangerous to be with."

"But with you, I can reform," he insisted. "Can I not just have a chance to win you?" he added.

"That's not possible," she replied.

"Why not?" he responded, with anger in his voice. "Don't you have any feelings for me?" he enquired.

She did not respond but let out a sigh.

He lifted up his head again, feeling a sense of hope within him.

"Do you have any feelings for me?" he persisted.

She turned her face away from him but Erepsin was having none of it.

"Do you, could you, love me?" he said.

He stood up and moved to stand right in front of her face so that she could not look away. He cupped his hands around her cheeks and lifted her head to meet his gaze.

"Tell me," he said.

230

Georgiana eyeballed him, compassion filling her eyes for a person she'd tried for most of her life to stay away from.

"I," she said. Then again she hesitated.

"Yes," said Erepsin.

His eyes scanned her every movement as she stared back at him.

"I could never love any man who had betrayed the lives of so many people for his own gain," she emphatically stated, and pulled her face away from his hands. "All I feel for you is moments of compassion for someone who has wrecked himself and the lives of so many people who are connected with him. You have my pity, and you also have my disdain. Nothing more."

Erepsin stepped back, the cold reality of the situation dawning on him.

"That's the end of the matter," she said, dropping her gaze to the floor. "There is nothing more to say."

Once again Erepsin turned his back on her, knowing that the conversation was truly over and that his chance was gone.

Georgiana got up and dusted her dress with her hands, ready to leave. On the way out of the room she stopped by the dressing table and picked up the jet-black pillbox hat that Maltrisia had often worn. It was beautifully made, the hat's material and immaculate stitching oozed expense. She ran her fingers along its sides and felt the extravagant value between her fingers.

"Best throw that in the bin," said Erepsin, with tears in his eyes when he saw what she was doing.

To his surprise, however, Georgiana lifted it up to gaze at it for a little longer and then, standing in front of the mirror, carefully placed it on her own head.

"What are you doing!" Erepsin almost shouted, a tone in his voice that revealed the vulgarity of Georgiana's actions.

"It's my new identity," she replied, pushing her hair in place. "I'm reminding myself of who I am," she added. "I, like your mother, and like you, am a backstabbing traitor who gave up the lives of others in order to achieve my own goals."

Erepsin hesitated, not sure what to say next.

"My father," she continued in voice that was flat and lifeless, "would be ashamed of me and I must bear that shame. This hat that belonged to your most treacherous mother will be a constant reminder to me of my own treachery. I will wear it often, for the rest of my life. It is my badge of honour. A 'well done' to a girl who now has come face to face with her own true nature. I shall look beautiful in it. Beauty and treachery. Together they make such dreadful friends, don't you think?"

"You take yourself too seriously," Erepsin retorted, disdain etched across his face.

Georgiana didn't answer. After fixing the hat firmly on her head and making sure that she looked just right in it, she turned to leave the room.

"My offer still stands," Erepsin persisted, glancing at her just one last time.

Georgiana's delay in leaving was only for a moment to comprehend the sentence that had been spoken to her.

"You already know my answer," she retorted.

She walked straight to the door and left the room without looking back. This was goodbye; it was final and complete. Once she was gone and the sound of her footsteps had vanished from the hallway, Erepsin sat in the chair where she'd been sitting and wept.

Chapter 30 – Goodbye Uncle Jack

"How did you find me?" yelped Tristram.

"Liquid tracer," came the big man's reply. "Squirted you all with the hot stuff whist we were in the theatre together, before I took off in my pumpkin, if you remember!"

"You were shot!" declared Tristram, his voice trembling and surprised at the old man's strength.

"I was wearing body armour under my duffel coat," replied the big man. "You've given me a gammy leg, a very painful shoulder and multiple bruises, but that's nothing compared with what I'm going to do to you."

After a quick bop on the top of Tristram's head, the refined and sophisticated traitor, who normally knew just how to hold himself, flopped over and was left reeling. Uncle Jack grabbed him by the scruff of his neck.

"Let's see you get out of this, you weasel."

Pinning him onto the side of his pumpkin traveller, Uncle Jack pushed Tristram's hands between its outer bars and tied them behind his back. Then he did the same with his ankles. Seconds later Tristram came round to find himself helplessly strapped to the machine.

"What are you going to do?" he squealed.

"We're going on a journey," replied Uncle Jack. "You and me, together, imagine that! I shall be *so* glad of your company. Missed you I have, over these last few hours. You know, I think that today, somehow, we've really bonded in a unique way, don't you? So I've decided that we're going to be spending some good quality time together in a place that's far, far, far away."

"No!" shouted Tristram.

"Oh don't worry," replied Uncle Jack. "It won't be *just* you and me. I'm inviting lots of friends to come along as well."

Uncle Jack hobbled over to his pumpkin's open door and carefully lifted an item into his arms. It was wrapped in a finely woven piece of cloth. Slowly and gently he took the fabric away to reveal a square box with dials across its front.

"Recognise this?" he asked.

Tristram certainly did. It was one of Maltrisia's base stations.

"How did you get that?"

Uncle Jack carefully put the device down on the floor and leaned on the side of his machine in an unusually relaxing manner, taking the weight off his wounded leg and easing into a general conversation, as if about to deliver an interesting story round a campfire or an after-dinner speech at a gentleman's club.

"Years ago," he said, whilst pulling out his pipe, stuffing it with tobacco, striking a match down the side of Tristram's beard and lighting it up; he paused to puff out some clouds of smoke before continuing.

"I befriended a group of homeless orphans, who roamed the southern wastelands, just behind my house. They were a good little group of thieves when I found them. My pantry was a source of continuous food and we enjoyed exchanging insults as the years went by."

Uncle Jack paused a moment to think, and at the same time puffed some smoke from the side of his mouth, right into Tristram's face.

"Oh, I am sorry," he said, waving his hand to get the smoke out of the way and 'accidently' giving Tristram the odd facial slap whilst he was at it.

"I do apologise," he added. "Nasty stuff, getting smoke in your face like that."

Tristram whimpered a little more.

"There, there," said Uncle Jack, tapping him on the shoulder. He continued his story.

"Now, all these years later, those naughty, little, thieving boys are nearly grown up and, I must say, what an excellent group of undercover scavengers they have turned out to be. Their expert, pilfering fingers have been put to good use for me today, brought me one of your homing beacons right from underneath Maltrisia's nose. It's quite a prize, don't you think?"

Tristram said nothing.

Uncle Jack laid his head back on his pumpkin machine's outer framework, right next to Tristram's face, and looked up at the passing clouds.

"Very rare these boxes are, so I hear. In the right type of auction, I think they'd fetch a very high price. Not that I'm looking for money, you know. Dreadful stuff it is. The love of it is the root of all kinds of evil, so I hear. Rich or poor, I just like it when people can live life in peace with each other, don't you? Live in peace and quiet without bullies trying to take over and dictate what everyone else should think, say or do."

He closed his eyes for a few moments whilst the gentle movements of the late afternoon breeze let his words sink in.

"Now," he said, waking up and tapping out his pipe onto Tristram's chest. "We're going to put this devise to good use."

He bent over and picked up the cube.

"You can't shut down Erepsin's insects with it," said Tristram. "His code's different to the one we were using and you'll never figure it out. It could be anything."

"That it could," said the burly man, scratching his protruding stomach and playing along with the conversation. "But then again, I don't need that code do I. I'm not actually interested in shutting the insects down. That's *not* what this box is for."

"What are you going to do with it?" asked Tristram, his face ashen with anticipation.

Uncle Jack set the beacon directly on Tristram's chest.

"What are you doing?!" he yelped.

Pulling some rope from inside his pumpkin travel machine, he wrapped the thick chord round and round both the base unit and Tristram until they were fastened hard to each other.

"Now," he continued. "Let's you and I go on, go on... now, what's that word again?"

He paused for a moment.

"That word that those, delightful, innocent, rambling horticulturalists use to describe a purposeful journey towards a vague destiny. Can you remember what it was?" he asked.

No answer.

Uncle Jack stroked his long, silver beard a few times. Finally he stood upright on his good leg, as if the penny had just dropped.

"A coddiwomple!" he said, with glee in his eye. "That's it! Yes, let's you and I go on a jolly coddiwomple together. What a wonderful word that is! A coddiwomple, a coddiwomple, a coddy, coddy, coddy, womple. A coddiwomple. You know, the more I say the word, the happier I am."

Tristram groaned.

"And that's just what you and I are going to do. We're purposefully going off into the large, lonely desert, into the middle of nowhere, to a place of thirst and heat and wind and sand and more heat and more sand and more thirst. Then we're going to keep going and going and going! Purposefully travelling in a vague direction."

"No!" screamed Tristram, trying to break free from his bonds.

"Oh don't worry," said Uncle Jack. "It'll be alright, I'll be with you all the way!"

"Why can't you just arrest me and put me in prison?!" asked Tristram.

"Oh that would be boring," said the old man.

"I have rights," shouted Tristram.

"So did the people of Clearwash City," Uncle Jack pointed out.

"I demand a trial!"

"You can demand as much as you like, you're not getting one."

Tristram went quiet for a time.

"If you're going to do what I think you are, then you don't need me to be a part of it. You also don't need to sacrifice yourself either. Just put your machine on auto-park and let it go off into the desert and then put me on trial."

"Ah, well, there you touch on a delicate point," replied Uncle Jack. "This morning, when your soldiers were most rudely firing at my machine, they damaged some of its capabilities, one of which is the auto-park mechanism. So I'm sorry to disappoint, but I shall have to steer this thing right into the middle of the desert myself, can't afford the risk of it coming back now can we! Bit of a downer really, people do tend to die of thirst in that kind of environment, but hay-ho, such is life. So I have decided to do it myself and I've decided that you can come with me too, to share the adventure that is. I'm sure you're as thirsty for it as I am, or at least you will be within a few hours or so."

"No!" said Tristram again. "I demand legal representation! I'm not going with you!"

"That's not your choice," replied Uncle Jack, in a more serious tone.

Tristram recognised the change in the old man's voice and knew that his playful banter, no matter how irritating, was now over.

"Please don't do this," he said.

"You've left me no option," replied Uncle Jack. "As you've already admitted, you're a calculating person, aloof from the troublesome world of morality. A man with no moral inclinations holding you back from killing. So I can't go and leave you behind," he said. "That wouldn't be fair on the city."

The quiet that followed showed the immensity of the man's words. He knew exactly what he was doing and why. Uncle Jack held up a telescope to his eye and scanned the city square. He watched from a distance as Erepsin gave his speech from the palace city gates.

"What a silly boy he is," he said.

After Erepsin had gone inside the palace, the hymenopteran continued their preprogramed buzzing activity, looking for 'hits' across the city that matched Erepsin's list of wanted people.

"Now's the time," he said, more to himself than anyone else.

Uncle Jack turned some dials on the base station and got it ready to be turned on.

"Home call to all of our little friends," he said.

"You'll never get the signal out far enough!" Tristram stated, trying to discourage Uncle Jack.

"Ah" said Uncle Jack, "you're quite right. That's why I got my thieving little friends to get me these too," pointing into his carriage. "Don't you see?"

"See what?" asked Tristram, his whole frame was tied so that he could only look outwards.

"Oh you can't see them, silly me," replied Uncle Jack. "You're a little tied up at the moment."

He pulled one out and hobbled over to Tristram.

"They're booster stations," he said. "My grown-up marshland children have placed a whole line of them from the city centre up to the great reservoir. I've got a few more in my pumpkin. With all of these packed together, we should not only be able to boost the signal right across the city, but, when they're all turned on at the same time, there's such a surge of energy created around them that we could actually make popcorn in my carriage too," he added. "Would you like some popcorn for the journey?"

Tristram had had enough.

"Let me go at once," he shouted. "This is... you are ridiculous!"

"That's not very nice," Uncle Jack replied.

Sensing that it was time, the grey, bushy bearded man guided his machine back through the woodland in which he'd found Tristram. He ascended the hillside and parked it next to the city's empty reservoir. A stone's throw away stood his marshland children, now teenage lads who watched the old man from a safe distance.

"Thank you my good friends," called Uncle Jack, hobbling his way out of the pumpkin's open door.

A simple wave from the boys was all he got.

"You've saved this good city of ours," he added.

Looking on with sad faces and broken hearts, they clearly understood what Uncle Jack's plan was.

"Tell the good Lady McArnold Crispus Ken-Worthington-Brown, tell her, 'It's been an adventure!'"

The boys silently nodded their compliance with his last request.

Activating the beacon on Tristram's chest, Uncle Jack climbed back into his horseless carriage, closed the door and turned each of the booster boxes on. Within a couple of minutes swarms of insects raced across the city, like a great flock of birds, following the call to come home and ready to roost for the night.

"Here they come!" Uncle Jack cried.

One by one they began to descend out of the sky. Thud! Thud! Thud! Thud! The pumpkin shook a little each time a hymenopteran landed onto its metal structure; their main target being the box that was strapped to Tristram's chest. As the mass of hymenopteran drew closer and closer, the numbers that dropped out the heavens turned from ones and twos into tens and twenties, then fifties and hundreds.

Brace yourself!" shouted Uncle Jack.

Wave upon wave continued to fall, smothering the machine.

"Ahhhhhh," Tristram screamed, finding himself covered with the creatures.

Then, quickly disappearing from sight, his cries of terror were snuffed out underneath a multi-layered coat of silver.

"Off we go!" shouted Uncle Jack, putting his machine into a forward motion. This," he said, "is going to be one coddywooooopie of a ride!"

As his machine began ascending the city's eastern wall, he called out one last time.

"Clearwash City will never fall into the hands of insulant barbarians!"

That was the last that was seen of him, going over the wall, into the desert, carrying thousands and thousands, or what seemed like ten thousand times ten thousand of the hymenopteran; across the sands, towards the horizon and deep into no-man's land.

Chapter 31 – One Loyal Heart

The sky had cleared of the buzzing insects but Georgiana hardly noticed. Making her way across the city, she refused go home, she didn't want anything right now that was familiar. Instead, wandering in and amongst the broken-down buildings, gingerly stepping through and around scattered debris, she made her way to the north-eastern part of the city. At every street corner and down every avenue, a bewildered and stunned populace sought to get their bearings in and amongst the mess; finding which piles of dirt were once their family dwellings and where the boundary lines used to be for their land. Some couldn't locate anything, not even their back gardens, whilst others found much of their homes still intact. For a while Georgiana just stood, gazing about her at the heaps of rubble, whilst seeking to take in the meaning of the meaningless madness they'd all had to endure.

A couple of people walked passed her, recognised her, and walked on. Erepsin's declaration that she'd delivered the hymenopteran over to him hadn't gone down well. Wanting some privacy in the midst of the chaos, she decided to keep on moving to where there were less houses, less people and fewer piles of wreckage. Eventually she came to the canal, the now dirty and badly polluted boundary which marked the edge of the city's inner circle. Over the bridge she went, leaving the heart of the city behind, not looking anyone in the eye but keeping her head low and her focus on her walking. Somehow the further she went, the more she left the defilement behind.

Ahead was the road leading up to the city gates and to one side of the highway were some agricultural plots along with a small number of exclusive dwellings. Passing by a vineyard, she noticed a house with an extended walled garden. The home owner's daughter was known to Georgiana, a good friend from one of her city social groups. The residence was clearly empty, the family having fled the city with the earliest available convoy when Maltrisia first opened up her guns. A high, granite wall encircled the property and Georgiana followed its circumference, letting the tips of her fingers drag across the rough masonry, touching each nook and cranny within the crevices of each section of the stonework.

Eventually she came to a door, standing slightly ajar and giving an open invitation to enter. Pushing it back on its heavy hinges, she walked into a highly cultivated garden. Marbled pillars, dressed with winding foliage, stood in a line down the garden's centre. These supported the long and heavy wooden beams of pergolas from which matured, flowery canopies draped, creating a shaded, floral walkway of diverse, mingling colours. Finding herself amongst them, Georgiana wandered from pillar to pillar, stopping every now and then to lean on a loadbearing column and to gaze up at the carpet of life above her head. The explosion of colour was stunning, but it didn't penetrate and cleanse a guilty soul.

Eventually she sat on the floor, her back propped against the nearest pillar and her legs splayed out in front, exhausted from an hour or so of wandering. Warmed by the sunshine and shaded by the greenery, she felt she could hide in this abandoned garden forever, each keeping the other company. The garden needed her, she reasoned, having been so quickly abandoned without warning by its owners. She, however, also needed it. Having betrayed so many people, she required a friend who knew nothing of her past and a companion who wouldn't ask any questions. Yes, this would fit perfectly well. She closed her eyes and let the shade move across her face as the gentle breeze pushed its way through the leaves and flowers above her head. So she began her search for peace. Perhaps the beauty of a place can somehow penetrate and restore someone's soul?

A few minutes later the sound of footsteps disturbed Georgiana's solace. Stirring herself from her drowsy state, she looked up and was surprised to see Basil, standing at the far end of the marbled walkway. He gazed at her, pain in his eyes, disappointment on his face and an earnestness within him that would not leave him alone.

Georgiana sighed. "Was there no escape?" she asked herself. Now her secret garden was no longer a secret and it would find out all that she had done. Paradise lost in a moment, she knew her past was never going to go away. Walking over, Basil adopted a most awkward stance.

"It was, err, a very kind thing you did, when you gave up your life for me," he started.

Georgiana didn't answer.

Shuffling on his heels, Basil didn't quite know how to progress. After fumbling for a few moments, he just launched into what he had to say.

"But how could you do it!?" he asked.

Georgiana felt a wave of shame flood over her. Dropping her head, she still gave no reply.

"How could you do it!?" he asked again.

"I did not intend anyone to get hurt," she finally replied, a tremor in her voice, "let alone for anyone to die."

"Well die they certainly did," he firmly stated.

Georgiana turned her head away.

"You should have trusted us Georgie. You should have trusted that we would finish the job."

"I didn't think we were capable of succeeding," she replied. "It seemed impossible for us to win. Erepsin was the only way to guarantee getting rid of Maltrisia and getting my father back. How was I to know that he and his friends would betray everyone?"

Basil again shuffled on his feet, both compassion and frustration on his face for his young friend. He wanted to give her a hug, to say everything would be alright, but everything would never be alright. Changing his tone a little, to soften his accusations, he spoke slowly and clearly to make sure she took in his words.

"One loyal heart is worth the strength of ten thousand reckless men," he said. "And they were my friends," he added, his voice petering out in a painful whine.

Georgiana just stared at her legs, sprawled out in front of her in a most un-lady like fashion, both feet pointing up into the air as she sat slumped on the floor with her back leaning heavily on the pergola's cold marble pillar. Dignity was gone and she didn't care who saw it.

"I thought I was doing the right thing," said Georgiana, still trying to justify herself.

"Thought?" echoed Basil. "You knew it was wrong and you still went ahead with it!" he curtly replied. "If you hadn't interfered, hadn't given Erepsin the code, then those wretched insects would have stayed asleep. They wouldn't have killed Marcus and his friends. Marcus, might have been able to negotiate getting your father out!"

Georgiana felt those words like a knife enter her heart. It would be something that would play on her mind for decades to come. In wanting to save her father, had she been part of his demise? Had she lost him because of her own actions?

Basil bent over and tried to eyeball his young companion, something that he had tried to avoid when they first met just over a week ago. Now, however, his love for his friend and his feelings of indignation about her failure to protect their team compelled him to be as open with her as with anyone he had met.

"You cannot play the game of the heartless if you yourself still have a heart," he said. "You cannot compete by their rules. You cannot do the things they do. You cannot ask people to do the things that they do. You cannot walk with a snake and not expect to be bitten. A companion of fools comes to ruin. Everything you do must come from your heart. It is your conscience that decides how things are, not the wishful delusions of your head!"

Georgiana shifted uneasily and wished the talk would stop. It was like listening to her father all over again. "I've heard this rhetoric before," she said.

"It's not rhetoric!" snapped Basil, almost losing his temper. "It's reality and it's about time you learnt to live in it yourself!"

Silence lingered for a time. Both friends were so uncomfortable with each other, they didn't know how to move forward. Basil wasn't used to this type of conversation and bringing it to a sensible conclusion seemed beyond him.

"Your head and your heart must not disagree with each other. Have a heart and a head to match and people will follow you. They'll see right through you and trust you."

"Perhaps I don't want people following me," Georgiana replied.

"That's not your choice," said Basil.

"Not my choice?" she echoed.

"Not your choice!" he reiterated. He left it at that and walked out of the garden and back down the road.

Georgiana was incensed by the statement. She wasn't being pushed into anything and certainly wasn't having anyone tell her what to do. After waiting a short time to make sure that Basil had gone, she made her way out of the back door and onto the road.

Her house was now due south, perhaps twenty minutes walk away, but she wasn't interested in home. Instead she chose to wander through the rest of the posh suburb that surrounded her. To her disappointment, she found that other houses in this area had suffered war damage too. Through the ruins she went, picking her way between the bricks and slabs of broken rock. Eventually she came to a crossroads, badly shelled with dust and debris scattered everywhere. Amidst the rubble, a single signpost stuck up out of the ground, bent, warped and pointing towards the sky. 'The Old Manor House Walk' it read. She decided to follow the sign, knowing what the Old Manor House was, but never having ventured down that avenue before. Maybe it was deserted? Maybe she could find solace there? As she went, the sound of a baby crying gently floated in on the breeze. Faint and almost lost in the wind, it drew Georgiana on till she could see a newly renovated old building, almost set on top of a hill. The sign spanning the main driveway read, 'The Old Manor House'.

It was clear to see that the Old Manor had been damaged. Gingerly stepping over piles of rubble, Georgiana came to a what remained of the newly refurbished hotel. It had caved in on one side and debris blocked much of the entranceway. Georgiana picked her way through it, being careful as she made each step not to turn her ankles over as the ground often gave way under her feet. After slipping and sliding down the last bit of gravel, she walked into the entranceway and could hear that the baby wasn't too far away. She walked down the hallway and popped her head around the first door on her left. There, covered in bombshell dust and lying in and amongst the broken furniture was a young woman. She had recently given birth and was clutching her new born child. Not wanting to cause the mother any distress, Georgiana called out in a tentative voice.

"Hello," she said, in a friendly manner and took a couple of steps into the room to approach cautiously.

"Hello," she called again.

The young woman slightly lifted her head, her hair was thick with dirt but she seemed to recognise who was calling to her.

"Georgiana?" she called back. "Is that you?"

The young lady's voice was hoarse and tired.

She looked up, the relief on her countenance was clear to see.

"Yes it's me," said Georgiana, still wondering to whom she was speaking.

She walked right in to the room and approached the young woman.

"I knew you would come," said the young lady. "I knew you'd find us."

In that moment Georgiana recognised the sound of this young lady's voice.

"Emma!" she cried.

Georgiana rushed down the room and in moments was kneeling at her sister-in-law's side, tears streaming down her face.

"Oh Emma," she said, taking Emma's head into her arms and kissing her cheek. "How, how is it that you are here? You left the city days ago."

The two women hugged but Emma didn't have much strength to talk.

"I have a baby," she whispered. "He's a boy you know."

"Oh, he's beautiful," said Georgiana, completely at a loss as to why Emma was in front of her.

Seeing that the child was already suffering from the cold, Georgiana took the shawl from around her shoulders and wrapped the baby in it.

"Let's get you both out of here," she said. "Can you walk?"

"I don't think so," replied Emma.

"I'll get help," Georgiana replied.

"Please stay," she said, not wanting to lose Georgiana so quickly.

Georgiana looked at the state of her sister-in-law and knew that help was urgently needed.

"I shall be back before you know it," she replied. "I'm taking you both home," she added.

She hurriedly left the hotel, scrambled over the rocks and rubble and just over an hour later Georgiana was sat next to the bed in what was once her brother's bedroom and watched over Emma. Emma's face was ashen, her complexion pallid, dulled and her pale-grey lips told the tale that she didn't have much time to live. The babe was crying in the next room and one of the house servants was attending him.

"I've called him Scrub you know," Emma said, in a whisper.

"Scrub?" blurted Georgiana, through her tears.

"Yes," replied Emma. "Stephanus Cadmar Roberto Uriel Bannerman. The first letters of his name spell Scrub. I always feel that a gentleman should have a lowly nickname, don't you? It adds something to their gentlemanly status."

Georgiana wanted to say, "But shouldn't his last name be Pluggat-Lynette?" Something inside her, however, told her not to interrupt her sister-in-law.

"He's going to be a fine young man," Emma said.

"Yes he is," Georgiana agreed. "A fine young man indeed. I'm sure you'll be very proud of him and all that he will do and achieve in his life."

"I already am proud of him," she said, in a tired voice. "So delighted with my son," she muttered. "I know he will do amazing things."

The two women remained in silence for a few minutes, listening to Stephanus's crying and then the silence that followed.

"Emma," said Georgiana in a cautious voice. "I know you're tired, but I must ask you something. "

She hesitated just for a second.

"What is it?" said Emma, when her sister-in-law failed to speak out her mind.

242

"Do you know where my mother is?" she finally enquired. "I thought you'd both left the city days ago. I thought you were both safe."

Emma said nothing.

"Emma," she gently said again.

Emma took in a slow breath. Georgiana waited, not wanting to cause her sister-in-law any more distress than was necessary.

"I don't rightly know," Emma finally breathed out.

Georgiana felt her heart drop.

"We were being chased," she finally added. "There was a whole group of us. We were trapped."

"Trapped? Trapped where?"

"At the Old Manor House," she replied, "on the edge of Eastgate.

"Why were you still at the Manor House?" asked Georgiana. "I thought you'd left the city?"

"We had," she replied.

Emma signed and slowly told the story of their failed escape.

"When the war started, I was sitting with your mother on the front terrace, enjoying breakfast in the morning sunlight. It took us all by surprise. We watched in shock, horror and sheer disbelief as the first shells were fired. The city soon became ablaze with flames and we knew there was no turning back the tide this time. In fact, as soon as the guns started discharging, everyone around me scrambled to leave. We couldn't find you, and that just added to the chaos. People were running this way and that, I was so tired and didn't know what to do."

Georgiana watched Emma's eyes flicker as she painfully told the tale of their failed escape.

"The household left in two stages," she recalled. "The first group was the majority of the staff who, under your mother's instructions, hurriedly packed their things and left together, heading for the city gates to join the great caravan of refugees fleeing the violence."

Georgiana was to later learn that this large body of people left within the first few hours, among them the rich and famous; those who could afford to get out quickly and who took with them their friends and employees. The second group was far smaller, a rag-tag band of lowly people who fled in dribs and drabs, scattered across the desert in a disorderly manner.

"The poor people," sighed Emma. "They didn't know what was waiting for them."

"What do you mean?" asked Georgiana.

Emma, however, didn't seem to register her sister-in-law's question.

"Then Marcus arrived," she continued, "sent by your father to fetch something to do with the waterworks. Away he went for about an hour or so, then he returned to help us with our departure. He was told that you were missing so, initially, he and the people with him looked everywhere to discover where you might be. Your mother and I did not want to leave without you. Once I was finally ready, we tarried a while longer, as long as we could. We were both dismayed when Marcus finally got back from searching the gardens and local area to tell us that you were no-where to be seen. It was then that your mother, despite her great distress at the thought of leaving you behind, finally made the decision to take me out of the city. 'Tell my

243

husband to find our daughter at all costs,' was the last thing she said to Marcus, as we left. By that time, we'd lost over half a day's travel on the other people who'd gone before us, poor people," she added again.

"I don't understand," said Georgiana. "What's happened to..."

"Even when we were underway," said Emma, "our pace was slow. I felt so unwell and, knowing the baby was due any day, your mother told the carriage driver and the maid (who came along with us) to drive the horseless carriage at half pace, just a little quicker than walking speed in fact. We made our way down the estate's central drive and then through the outer circles of the city, keeping as much to the country lanes as possible. Through Eastgate we went until finally arriving at the city's main gates. From there we kept a steady pace as we followed the caravan trail trade route through the desert."

Emma licked her lips. "I need some water," she said.

Georgiana reached for a glass and the water jug from the bedside table, poured the drink, and helped her sister-in-law take a few sips.

"About three and a half days later," she continued, "we found ourselves at the top of a plateau with a clear view of the desert valley below; it stretched out for miles, towards the horizon, and in the distance we could see the mountains of Peleg – where the land divides in two and beyond which are the cities of Arabah. I'd heard about it so often as a child, the gateway to the trading cities of the north. With the sun getting lower in the sky, we initially thought it a most beautiful painted work of art. Beautiful, that is, until we caught sight of the rest of the people fleeing the city that'd gone before us, both the main group of refugees who'd left first and the stragglers who'd followed on. They were all gathered together, in a tight mass. We initially wondered why they were there, why they hadn't moved on across the rest of the arid wasteland. It was only then that we noticed a short distance ahead of them, their way being blocked by another band of people."

- -

"I need the monocular," called Lady Melanie to her maid.

After a few minutes of rummaging through the packed bags, the object was found and handed over. Peering through the eyeglass, Lady Melanie cast her gaze over the two bodies of people, camped opposite each other in a standoff that didn't seem to be going anywhere.

"Who are they?" asked Emma.

Lady Melanie examined the community of the people who were blocking the way. It was mainly made up of travel pods; portable homes that doubled up as mobile travelling machines, often used by international trade merchants on long and difficult journeys. Eventually her gaze rested on a national flag which flew from one of the metal structures.

"Oh," she said, taking in a sudden, sharp breath.

"What is it?" asked Emma.

"The Veles!" replied Lady Melanie,

"The Veles?" echoed Emma.

"Slave traders!" exclaimed Lady Melanie.

Emma's face fell ashen.

"What are they doing here?" she asked, a tremor in her voice.

"They've obviously been tipped off," commented Lady Melanie.

"By whom?" asked Emma.

"That remains to be seen," she replied. "It's certainly not an accident. From the size and structure of their camp, they've been waiting for a good few days."

"They knew this war was going to be happening?" asked the maid.

Lady Melanie nodded, still gazing over the people.

"Can we do anything?" Emma enquired.

"Not sure," she remarked.

"What about us?" Emma asked.

"We're not going anywhere," responded Lady Melanie, "except out of sight."

Moving the horseless carriage off the main track, they parked it in the shadow of a fallen rock. From there Lady Melanie continued to observe the stalemate in the valley below with Emma. The maid and coach driver sat next to her, all full of questions about what she could see.

"Can you recognise anyone?" asked Emma.

"Not in the foreign camp," she replied.

Taking her gaze back to the Clearwash City people, however, she slowly picked out person upon person who was known to her. Then,

"What!" she exclaimed. "What on earth is she doing here?"

"What is it?" asked Emma. "Who is it?" she enquired.

"Seleucia!" snapped Lady Melanie.

Lady Melanie pointed to the far right of the camp. There, amongst several waggons, was a small group of individuals, huddling and waiting for something to happen.

"Are you sure it's her?" asked Emma.

"Absolutely!" replied Lady Melanie. "See for yourself."

She handed the monocular to Emma and each person, in turn, looked across the camp.

"What is she doing here?" asked the maid.

"I'm sure we'll find out," replied Lady Melanie.

"Shouldn't we go down and warn the people," asked Emma.

"It's still half a day's travel to get down to the valley," replied her mother-in-law. "The journey downwards is an ever-winding road that continually turns back on itself. We'd be sitting ducks ourselves if she makes her move whilst we're on that track. No. We wait and see what happens from here."

"Is she going to make a move?" asked the maid.

"Why else would she be here?" replied the coach driver.

The question didn't need an answer.

On Emma's second turn of looking through the monocular she asked,

"What are those?" pointing to the carts and waggons which made up the perimeter of Seleucia's group.

Lady Melanie sharpened the prism's focus and gazed at the packing.

"They look like crates," she said. "There's quite a few of them."

245

"Strange that she should be so well packed when this war was meant to come out of the blue," commented the coach driver.

"Indeed," replied Lady Melanie.

"Shouldn't we warn them?" asked Emma, again.

"We can't risk it," she replied. "As soon as we're seen, we become targets ourselves. I have you and the baby to think about," she added. "None of us here, especially my grandchild, are going to become part of the Veles slave trade!"

Emma knew that her mother-in-law's words were final on the matter and, to be honest, she was quite relieved herself that nothing 'heroic' or 'stupid' was going to be attempted. How things would play out, however, left her feeling deeply sick.

Time went by with nothing happening except the stirrings within the Clearwash community. Arguments often broke out as they were obviously struggling to come to terms with what was before them. On more than one occasion white flagged scouts were sent out towards the Veles group, but each return from the discussions clearly showed that whatever they were offering on a monetary level, in exchange for safe passage, was rejected. Eventually, after some heated exchanges, the Clearwash City camp seemed to be astir. A portion of the refugees had clearly decided that, rather than face the slave traders, they would return to Clearwash City and face the war. Their group broke away and started the long walk back up the winding path which would take them from the valley up to the plateau.

The remaining collective of refugees quickly armed themselves for a fight. They gathered into groups, seeking to find some kind of strategy by which they might attack the Veles in several places along their line of blockade. Before they could even begin, however, Seleucia's team took their opportunity to mobilise. Some flipped open the cargo caskets on their carriages and within moments, out flew a small army of hymenopteran.

"What are they?" asked Emma.

She got no reply. The group of four looked on in horror as every person in the valley below and on the narrow mountain trail came under attack. Chaos consumed the Clearwash people as they fled in every direction. Many were stung and slumped to the ground. Others held up their arms in surrender and the humming, buzzing creatures seemed to understand what that stance meant. After the people cowered into submission, Seleucia and her team walked in amongst them, pushing and shoving individuals out of their way and triumphantly parading their prize to the Veles.

A delegation came across from the other camp and a payment was made in the form of a box, filled either with money or goods. Once the box was handed over, Seleucia and her team backed off, returning to their carriages and using a homing beacon to call the insects back to their storage space. As this happened, the Veles surged forward and pounced on the plunder, both on the valley people and those who had begun to escape on the trail. It was heart-breaking to watch. The weak and helpless were tied up and herded into groups, like cattle to be moved and sold.

"We have to return to the city!" exclaimed Lady Melanie. "There's no way forward here," she added.

"Can't we go round?" asked the maid.

"That would be an eight-day journey," she replied, "and we've only got provisions for another four days at best. Nor could we be sure that other routes are safe, they're probably blocked too."

Getting back into the horseless carriage, they quickly manoeuvred it into place to make the return journey.

"We need to start now so that we can stay ahead of Seleucia and her team," she added. "If they even catch a glimpse of us, then one release of those silver creatures and we're caught too."

That knowledge drove them on. Even with Emma's condition, the pace set for the carriage was as fast as Emma could bear. Eventually, however, they had to slow down as Emma found the constant side to side jarring movement insufferable.

For two days they journeyed back. As they went, Lady Melanie made regular watch checks to ensure that they stayed ahead of their potential pursuers. More stragglers coming out of Clearwash City met them on the road, seeking to flee the troubles that they wished to leave behind. These people they intercepted and either persuaded to turn back and accompany them or were advised to leave by a longer route, if they had the right amount of provisions. By the evening of the second day they had become quite a significant group of 'returners' who decided that facing their troubles back home was better than a lifetime of slavery.

Lady Melanie enquired about the progress of the war. They told of the stalemate that existed in the city and how there were breakaway groups who still wanted to pursue a violent outcome. They told of the hymenopteran storm that briefly happened, but which had remained subdued since its first recall. None of them, however, could give specific details of who was in charge and what was happening. All they could say was that it was rumoured that peace talks were now on the agenda but how they were to be facilitated and who would attend, no one quite knew.

As the evening faded into night, one of the watchmen on the hillside signalled to the group to come and join him. Gathering round, he pointed to a small set of lights that had appeared on the winding road behind them. As the minutes ticked by, the dots made steady progress following the trade trail and moved in their direction.

"Do you think it's them?" asked one person.

"Difficult to tell," replied Lady Melanie, though I assume it has to be. I can't see anyone else coming away alive from that ambush."

"They're still a long way off," said another.

"Very true," replied Lady Melanie. "But we'll have to be up extra early if we're going to stay far enough ahead of them. Four hours sleep only tonight," she added.

The statement was met with a few mumbles and murmurs but everyone knew she was right. No matter how tired they were, they had to get back into the city at all costs.

In the dead of night they began to stir themselves. It was cold. No fire had been lit to draw attention to their location. Shaking off their sleep and dusting off the night-time chill, they headed out once more, hopefully for the last time, to finally get home. After several short breaks, morning passed into mid-day and mid-day passed into late afternoon. Still they kept going, counting the minutes and hours that passed. Eventually they stopped at an area which was once rumoured to be a dried up river bed. Water flowing in the middle of a desert was considered to be a ridiculous thing by many, but its clear contours suggested that it used to be that very thing.

Lady Melanie held the monocular up to her eye and scanned the road back to the horizon. Finally she could see in detail those who were following.

"It is them," she confirmed.

Everyone mumbled their discomfort and displeasure at the news. At the same time, Lady Melanie could also see that Seleucia's group had made significant gains over the past hours. Hurriedly, they pressed on, though the dust that rose into the sky as they moved along was more than a tell-tale sign of their location.

"Let's hope they think it's a localised dust storm," she told their group.

Night would cover up this ever-present witness and it couldn't come too soon. As dusk approached, the road began to wind the last part of its snakelike trail through the mountain range and towards the high hills that looked out over Clearwash. Taking the lower road that circumvented these last set of slopes, the small company of people trudged onwards till they rounded what seemed to be the longest bend. Finally as the setting sun dipped beneath the skyline, they could see their city; the outline of the metropolis was the most welcome picture they'd ever seen. Now that the great capital was in sight, a general sense of relief filled their hearts, despite the anxiety of what was going on beyond its walls. Hope was but half an hour away. As its shadows lengthened with the ever-encroaching fall of darkness, steadily, steadily the city's form grew larger. Just outside the wall they came to a halt. Before them were the city gates, closed and locked to shut out the terrors of the night.

"Look," called someone from within the camp," pointing to an object that was moving skyward.

Everyone's gaze fixed on a small balloon which had inflated on the other side of the city wall. Up, up it went, taking to the sky. Propelled along by invisible rivers of exhaled breath, it quickly entered the deep darkness of the enveloping firmament and was welcomed by the white vapoury mists that inhabited the great expanse. Swishing and swirling its way through the clouds, the little object ascended the heights of the heavenly realms and, within moments, it was gone, out of sight, swallowed by the night.

A few minutes later, the city gates began to open in response to Lady Melanie's explanation to the gatekeepers as to who they were and what had happed to them. Bit by bit they cranked open as these ancient doors once again welcomed in city traffic. Their opening was encouraged by a young gentleman within their group who sounded a loud, 'whoopee' of relief.

"Quiet!" called Lady Melanie.

She looked back in desperation down the trail; the young man realising the enormity of his mistake. Silence still filled the air, a relief to everyone's ears.

"In you come," called the voice of the gatekeeper.

As they moved forward, however, from far behind down the trail, there came the sound of a buzzing frenzy.

"Quickly" called Lady Melanie.

The walk turned into a stampede for survival. Holding onto Emma's arms to help keep her steady, Lady Melanie ordered the carriage driver to pick up speed. It moved on through the gates and into the city. At the first possible turn off, she ordered that they leave the main highway. Going along a narrow country road they could hear behind them the cries of people who were getting stung. Their current path led in a steady upwards direction to what was affectionately called the Old Manor House. For a couple of generations it had been abandoned; in recent years, however, it had been given new life by a rich hotel owner. As they reached the outskirts of the manor courtyard, they stopped the coach. Lady Melanie stepped out and stood with her staff, looking across the hillside. From their vantage point they could see it was an impossible situation. Small swarms of the creatures were systematically making their way down each lane, across each field, swooping and stinging anyone who lay hidden or who tried to flee. The hotel was the only safe haven, but already there were swarms of hymenopteran at its front door.

"We're dead," said the coach driver. "We'll be found in a matter of minutes."

"There must be an entranceway at the back," Lady Melanie said to her two staff.

Even there, however, they could see buzzing insects searching, scanning, seeking out anyone that they might find.

"My daughter-in-law must be saved at all costs," she said, in a low tone.

"We'll need at least a couple of distractions to get her inside," replied the coach driver.

Looking at each other, they both seemed to know what needed to be done.

Turning to the maid, Lady Melanie said in a whispered tone, "I'm entrusting my daughter-in-law and unborn grandchild into your care. She gets into that hotel, no matter what the cost. Do you understand me?"

"Of course m'lady," replied the maid."

"What's happening?" called Emma from the carriage, not able to hear the discussion taking place.

They briefly got back into the transport and, after turning aside into one of the hotel's stables, Lady Melanie jumped out.

"Don't leave me," Emma implored her mother-in-law.

"I have to my dear," she replied. "The maid will see you safely inside."

She kissed Emma on the cheek and then signalled to the carriage driver to follow a narrow, one-way track that led off towards some trees at the back of the hotel. Lady Melanie took a horse from the stables and rode out onto the main road. From behind, there came a buzz of activity as she was spotted. She rode, full pelt, towards the main lawn at the front of the manor house and stopped when more insects barred her way. Steadying her terrified horse, Lady Melanie sat and stared at the swarming, buzzing hymenopteran that one by one gathered about her; their legs twitching and stings itching, waiting to make the kill.

"At least I'm well dressed for the occasion," she remarked.

With the tips of her fingers she stroked her horse's neck and with the other hand she slowly removed her hat, as if in resignation of her surrender and demise.

"Hold steady," she whispered to her steed.

Then, taking a firm grip on her horse's mane and, with a sudden waft of her hat in a circular motion above her head, she knocked the hymenopteran away and kicked her heels into the mare's sides.

"Come on!" she bellowed and charged on; drawing her insect pursuers after her, away from the hotel and off into the night.

"I didn't see her again," said Emma.

Georgiana sat in silence.

"The carriage driver took me and the maid to some trees, where we disembarked. Then he took the carriage to the far side of the field from where we were and deliberately sped up the side of the hill. The commotion of the machine's engine brought more insects after him. He was quickly stung in his shoulder. The last I saw of him, he was sitting in his driving seat, waving a stick in the air with his good arm to fend off the insects, whilst his machine went at full pelt over the top of the hill. The maid and I made our way to the courtyard at the rear of the manor house. Seeing that there was a back door, she quickly ran to it, tried it, and found it unlocked. Then she returned for me and walked me across the yard. Within ten paces of the door, however, we were spotted and a buzzing insect flew to block our path. It began to circle about us, I assume to be ready for the kill, but before I knew it, the maid jumped at the creature to pin it to the floor with her body. She cried out in pain, then shouted for me to run, so run I did. Once inside, I closed the door. I think they all planned to give themselves up to keep me and the baby safe. I'm so sorry," she said, with tears in her eyes. "There was nothing I could do."

Georgiana took her sister-in-law's hand and gave it a gentle squeeze to comfort her. "I should have been with you," she said, guilt etched across her brow. "I'm so sorry. If I had been with you, none of this would have happened."

"If you had been with us," replied Emma, "we wouldn't have been delayed and we'd have been captured by Seleucia, with the other people who left the city. Your absence, when we wanted to leave, saved us all."

Georgiana had nothing to say in response to those words. She just held her sister-in-law's hand and observed her frail body waning into nothingness.

"I have to go now," Emma finally conceded. "Look after Stephanus won't you. Promise me, you will look after him."

Georgiana looked on as her last family member faded in front of her eyes.

"I promise," she replied.

"Must sleep," sighed Emma. "I'm so tired."

Georgiana brushed her fingers through Emma's hair.

"Sleep well," she said, and kissed her on the forehead.

Emma lifted her face sightly to gaze at her sister and friend, then laid her head back, closed her eyes, breathed out her soul and was gone.

Chapter 32 – This Way Please Aunty!

Georgiana sat in her father's office and gently placed her hands on the arms of his leather backed chair, letting her fingers rest on the places her father had so often touched. On so many occasions she'd sat in that very place, waiting, waiting and waiting for him to finally enter his room; often with the singular purpose of 'having it out with him' when they'd disagreed on something in public and she needed to resolve the matter in private. Now, perched opposite the office's open door, she felt hollow and dull, knowing that on this, and every other occasion, he would not be turning up to talk.

From her vantage point, she could see right down the hallway, along which were the many entryways that opened into familiar rooms. The building, with its wood panelling, hand woven tapestries and rich velvet carpets, still held up its head to present itself as a place of grandeur, but amidst all of the beautiful décor was a noiselessness that hung everywhere, saturating the atmosphere and filling the house with the echoes of empty spaces. Together they chorused a song that 'all is not well'.

Home again she might be, with familiar furnishings, walls, doors, rooms and open spaces. Yet it was as if the heart had been ripped out of the place. No people and no promise of any. What she would have given for just one of them to walk in and say, "Hello!" Home had turned cruel, a reminder of absence; a noisy house gone quiet, a shell of familiarity deadened by silence. "Yes I remember you," she thought, but none of it made any sense anymore or brought her consolation. Without the people to fill it, it was pointless. Company makes a home, not its furnishings.

Stephanus' crying broke the quiet and his distressed noise was quickly subdued by the comforting sound of, "There, there, there," from his newly employed nanny.

A knock came at the door and the household butler answered it.

"I'm here to see Georgie," came a familiar voice.

"I'm sorry sir," began the reply, "but there isn't anyone by that name who lives here. Perhaps you could try…"

"Let him in," called Georgiana.

She left her father's study and went into the main lounge and sat down. A few moments later the butler arrived with Basil behind him. He was wearing smarter clothes than she'd ever seen him in, but colour-wise none of them matched.

"The gentleman called 'Basil'," said the butler, who quickly showed Basil in and then abruptly left.

Georgiana and Basil looked at each other for a moment.

"Won't you sit down," she politely asked.

Basil sat in the nearest chair, shuffled his feet and looked at his surroundings.

"Your father and mother kept a very tidy house," he eventually said.

"They loved it as much as I did," she replied.

Quiet sat with the two friends for a while, as the steady silence between them continued to grow, until eventually the mood was filled with the overpowering sense of sheer awkwardness.

"Err," said Basil, trying to start up the conversation. "I've come here to talk."

"I'm not sure there's much to say," Georgiana replied.

"I've come here to ask for your help," Basil finally said.

Georgiana stared at him and then realised that her fixed gaze was embarrassing her guest. Glancing around the room to find a place to sensibly put her eyes, she finally said, "Why would you want to do that? You know I'd let you down. You know what sort of person I am."

"I do know what sort of person you are," Basil responded. "That's why I'm here, asking for your help."

"You still trust me?" she said, in an almost contemptuous tone.

"I know what sort of person you are," Basil repeated. "You're as fallible as the rest of us, but you still want what is right."

"How do *you* know what *I* want?" she said, in a cynical manner.

Georgiana had no desire to do anything. She felt like dropping off the edge of the world and letting everyone else get on with living. For her, life was over. It was gone; living was nothing more than a waste of time. The only sensible way to exist was a permanent retirement from public life. For everyone else, life had many challenges, but not for her. Just existing from day to day with her own company would be the most difficult thing that she'd ever have to deal with.

"You still care enough to want us all to be free," said Basil.

Georgiana wasn't interested but didn't bother objecting to his words. She simply turned her head away to stare off into nothingness.

"And you have what it takes to get us there," he added.

"To get *us* where?" snapped Georgiana. "Who is this 'us' that you're talking about?"

Basil paused for a moment.

"I'm sorry," said Georgiana, coming to her senses. "That wasn't called for. Please do go on."

"I want you to gather those of us that remain and to lead us into a place where we can deliver a sensible and effective resistance to Erepsin and his new order of things," said Basil.

"Out of the question," she quickly retorted.

"I don't think it is," Basil cautiously countered, starting to find his feet in the conversation.

"I can't be your kind of leader," she said. Looking at her feet, she spoke in a cold, quiet whisper. "I can't guarantee you anything," she added, beginning to bear her shame. Shuffling in her seat to shake off the moment, she straightened her frame. "No-one would trust me anyway," she continued, trying to regain her composure.

"I'm not asking you to not make mistakes," replied Basil. "I'm not asking you to get it right. I'm not asking you to win. I'm asking you to take part. I'm asking you to lead and we will follow, whether our mission is a success or not. Success is not what I'm after, no-one can guarantee that. This isn't some kind of fantasy story where we all live happily ever after. There's no such thing. What we need right now is not success, but someone to follow. There are a huge number of self-promoting nincompoops out there who are starting up their own little resistance groups. They're full of so-called noble ideas, but they won't lift a finger to help once the real trouble starts."

"Have you not seen what I've just done?" said Georgiana. "Doesn't my betrayal of innocent people mean anything to you?"

"Of course it does," he replied.

"So why are you even talking to me?" she queried.

"Because your failure matters to you," said Basil. "I see it all over you."

Georgiana didn't like this window into her soul that had been opened nor did she necessarily agree with the conclusions that Basil was deriving from it.

"But I know you," he continued. "I know that once you've decided on a thing you'll stick to it to the very end, no matter what. You would have died for you own father if you could. Now I'm asking for the same devotion again, but this time for us, no matter what the consequences. If you can give us your heart, then that's all we need. If you lead, then we'll follow. If we go down, then we go down together. That's all that I ask of you and I know that you're capable of that."

Georgiana sat quietly. Basil could see that he hadn't won the war or words but his battle to get her attention was certainly making progress.

"I'm not ready for it," she said.

"None of us ever are," he replied.

Georgiana sighed. "We would need more resources," she said, trying to point out the obvious and put as many obstacles in the way as possible. "We don't have enough people," she said, "and as I've said, no-one would trust me anyway."

"I know a man," said Basil. "A good friend of mine from years ago. A professor of science he is these days. He'll be no friend of this 'Mr E' caricature that Erepsin's made up, that I'm quite sure of. We could go to him and his team and build a resistance group that way."

Georgiana sat in silence for a few moments.

"Ask me another time," she finally replied, putting off the moment of decision. "I'm not in the mood today for anything like this."

"Our city's unfolding story continues whether we're ready for it or not," said Basil, standing up and getting ready to leave. "You need to be a part of it," he added. "I'll make preparations for our trip."

Georgiana paused, she wasn't used to Basil being decisive and his recent mode of social intercourse continued to take her by surprise. Seeing that he was about to exit the room on the back of a decision that she hadn't agreed to, she lifted her voice in protest.

"I didn't promise you anything and I'm not about to enter into anyone's so called *story*," she countered.

"See you tomorrow morning then," replied Basil, ignoring her protest. "The next chapter is yours," he added, and with that he tipped his hat and left.

- -

Back in her attic, Lady Georgiana's silver pen flicked up and down as she finished adding the last words to fill up the page. She then blotted the text and put a new piece of parchment in front of her. Her open letter to the people of Clearwash City was almost half completed.

"Even with the loss of his hymenopteran, over the following months Erepsin took more and more power until his influence over the city populace was complete," she wrote. "His youth movement continued to gain momentum and finally the metropolis was bullied into submission. He did try and put right some of the trouble that the war had brought us. With the waterworks now out of action, no-one knowing how to turn it back on, we thought we were all doomed. One of the first things he sought to do was to restore the reservoir wall, whilst laying down pipes to deliver the water once the lake had refilled. He funded the project with the money left behind by the rich and wealthy, who'd fled the city during the war and failed to return; which some considered quite inappropriate and made very clear with their daily protests. Whatever your stance on the subject, however, and despite his large budget for the project, the technical challenges to fix the problem were too great for his skill and the city's water supplies were not replenished.

Daily visits to the reservoir kept us alive, once the wall was mended. However, after an initial filling from the annual storms, we watched as the water level continually went down and down. At one point it became so low, we thought the lake might have completely emptied. We most probably would have all perished if Erepsin hadn't, quite by accident, discovered his own private source of water; a source that he kept secret and secure for all of his rule. Through this hidden treasure, we were kept alive. Naturally, the price for this so called 'luxury item' (as he would phrase it) was an ever-increasing servitude that encroached upon our daily liberties. Bit by bit they were taken away, even to the point when just speaking out against his rule would initiate the action of immediate arrest. It was only much later, however, when the drought came and the reservoir completely dried up, that Erepsin finally got everyone completely under his thumb and so many of the city's people mindlessly accepted his regime.

Basil initially found it more difficult than he thought to get anyone to follow me. My failure had been so bad that it was years before I was trusted again. Nevertheless, through all of that time, he was a true companion and a more faithful friend I could not have asked for. Through him, and the man who we simply called, 'The Professor', I grew to love life again. Eventually there ignited within me a bid for our city's freedom. This tender glow was fanned into flame with each year that went by. Over the years I was able to reflect on our past events, to take from them the gems of wisdom that appear in the pressurised environment of life's refining fire. Dark times bring us to a place where we can appreciate the light when it finally comes. I also learnt to cling to my failures and not to let them go. Failure is a teacher like no other, a forthright companion you can trust who will not puff you up with notions of false grandeur but, instead, will be a constant reminder of your fallibility and your need to listen to others, to test everything, to not rush into your choice-making and to understand that even the most talented, intelligent and influential people can be, at times, completely deceived. You learn far more from failure than you do from success."

Georgiana sat back in her chair and rested. It had been a long morning's work. She felt, however, that something had been done to fill a gap that was now in place.

"So began the fight back against Mr E," she wrote. "Getting rid of Mr E, however, proved far more difficult than we could ever imagine. Yet, along the way, I made

255

peace with my past and became the person that I'd always wanted to be. Our final breakthrough came when we learnt to be a team, the most unlikely group of mismatched people, each in turn, playing the part assigned for them. And so we were brought to an initial place of peace and rest where, for many years, we enjoyed a general tranquillity and prosperity until, that is, the wolves came and the silence descended. Now, all that we had, we have lost again and there seems no way out of this den of iniquity. I cannot describe how..."

Lady Georgiana's pen jumped and scratched a line across the page as a stone shot through the back attic window. It bounced off the wall and rolled across the floor, settling near the fire place. Around it was a piece of paper. She quickly unwrapped it and read the scrawled message which said, "Escape to the kitchen and I'll be there. I'm entering from below."

Recognising the handwriting, Lady Georgiana hastily picked up her papers, exited the attic and hurriedly made her way down a back stairway to the servants' quarters. There she walked at a quick pace down the main servants' corridor and down a final spiral staircase to where the kitchen was located. All six members of her skeleton staff were there, sitting around the central table that ran down the middle of the room. At the end of the table was a chair and underneath that a rug.

Lady Georgiana quietened her surprised staff with a wave of her hand, moved the chair and lifted the edge of the rug. As she did, they were all startled by an explosion at the front of the house which shook the room, the kitchen utensils clattering together as they hung around the walls. Rushing to the kitchen windows, they could see the main gates at the front of the mansion had been blown open. Troops poured into the courtyard and then began the assault on the house. First the front door pounded, until it opened, then room upon room in the great building was systematically ransacked. Quieting her staff, Lady Georgiana pointed to the trap door that had been concealed by the rug. The butler undid the bolts which held it shut and, after doing so, found it being pushed open from beneath.

"It's alright," Lady Georgiana assured her staff, who obviously thought that troops were about to enter from beneath the trap door too.

The butler helped the trap door to open fully and through the hole popped the head of a young man. With great relief everyone recognised him and he waved the members of staff down into the passage below. There they were met by a young woman who took charge of them to show the way. Lady Georgiana was the last one to exit the kitchen. The young man watched her join him on the steps, looking steadily at her, smiling and grinning from ear to ear. His eyes were clear, a deep blue, and his face showed a person who was intelligent, mature and had a good understanding of what was happening around him. Lady Georgiana put her hand on his shoulder in a very familiar way and greeted him with a kiss on the cheek.

"Scrub!" she said in disbelief.

"It's Stephanus actually, Aunt Georgiana," came Scrub's reply, in a slightly corrective tone.

"So it is," replied Lady Georgiana, still trying to get used to her nephew's new manner of sensible, intelligent behaviour.

Stephanas held out his hand to her.

"Time to go Aunty," he said.

"Go where?" she asked. She shook her head in disbelief whilst taking his hand and descending the steps into the tunnel.

"Out of here of course," came Stephanas' answer, with a wink and a smile as if he were responding to a silly question.

She smiled her reply and disappeared into the darkness below.

Stephanus reached out and pulled the rug and the trap door back into place to disguise their exit. After descending the tunnel's steps, he held up a small lantern to light their way. The rest of the party had already vanished from sight.

"Yes, but where are you taking us?" she asked.

"You'll find out," he called over his shoulder.

As they walked, however, Lady Georgiana couldn't contain her questions.

"When did you get back and what are you up to?" she asked her nephew.

"What am I up to?" he echoed.

"Yes," she said. "What are you up to?" a sound of happy frustration in her voice.

He stopped and stared at her with a twinkle in his eye.

"Revolution," he replied.

"Revolution!" she reiterated.

"Of course," he said, with a smile.

Taking her again by the hand to lead her down the tunnel, he momentarily leaned in to talk face to face.

"Come on Aunty," he said with another wink. "We've got work to do."

- -

The Silence of Clearwash City

Book 3

Timothy J Waters

Sample Chapter: - Stephanus, Welcome Back

"Stephanus, Stephanus," called a voice.

The rich, deep sound floated out across the air and into the ears of the young man.

"Stephanus, Stephanus," it called again.

Scrub felt the words enter his mind; their weighty tone soothed his rushing thoughts, as if the words themselves were alive. Like a spray of fine particles of liquid love, they saturated his thinking and then flowed together down into his soul. Deeply refreshing, and yet despite this, his mind was still left hazy and muddled. Back and forth went his thoughts, again and again as he tried to make sense of them.

"Stephanus," called the voice to him once more. Scrub felt the hands that were placed either side of his head take a stronger hold. Thumbs pressed into his temple and the rest of the fingers pressed down onto his ears. "Stephanus," came the call once more, and the words washed yet more perplexity and confusion away. "You must forgive," the same voice came again. "Let it all go."

Scrub's mind was in a whirl. "Forgive who and what?" were his immediate thoughts.

Then he saw it. A bank of earth, covered in deep, lush green foliage that sloped steeply down to the water's edge. The place was familiar. As he watched, feelings bubbled up from deep within him. Emotions that he'd thought were lost and buried came rushing to the surface; anger, malice, unfettered hatred, bitterness and acute pain. All of these drove into his passions and rippled through them in a way that he could not control. He saw himself, not a boy but not quite a man – manhood just a short way ahead in the distance; a not-quite-yet adult but certainly no child, swimming through the water. Next to him was his aunty, Lady Georgiana Pluggat-Lynette. They swam together, racing each other across the lake. Already he was the stronger swimmer, and she knew it. He teased her with letting her take half an arm's length lead and then, with a sudden spurt of strength, he'd take it back again laughing at her protests. She wasn't used to losing to him and this turn around in their relationship was new, and somewhat unwelcome to her ego. He loved it, however.

To their far right a clunking noise resonated across the water. The flood gates behind the great turbine engines that sat at the lake's edge opened. Water gushed through them, causing the blades to rotate and chop at the water as they went. The city had used the water to create electricity for a long time. A little clunky and out-of-date now, they made a terrible din as they wound themselves up with the water's sudden flow. Stephanus and Lady Georgiana weren't in any danger. The suction from the water that flowed to the turbines was too far away and it was something they'd often seen. Lady Georgiana had, however, over the years, laid down the law to Stephanus that he could not swim close to the turbines, even when they were off. "If the doors behind them suddenly opened and the water flows through, you'll be sucked in and sliced to pieces," she once told him in his younger years when they first began to swim together. For some reason he'd always taken notice of this and not once had he given in to his desire to find out how things work by swimming towards them.

The twosome pounded their way through the water towards the shore. Finally they reached the water's edge, Lady Georgiana first and Scrub just behind her.

"You win again Aunty," said Stephanus, matter-of-factly slumping down onto the floor and not seemingly too out of breath.

"No I didn't," came her reply, as she sat next to him, resigned to the fact that all swimming victories from now on were conceded to her rather than won.

The two of them began to dry themselves off and found that just glancing at each other made them laugh at the silliness of the situation.

"I thought you swam rather well today," said Stephanus.

She playfully poked him in his side.

"I was just saying," he continued with a smirk. "Just saying that I thought you tried very hard today and that if you keep this up, you'll end up quite an ok swimmer, perhaps..."

"You're digging a very big hole for yourself," Lady Georgiana responded, a tone of caution in her voice that was playful and at the same time showed that her nephew was close to the edge of getting a thick ear.

"I know I am," Stephanus said, "spades and digging are my speciality," and with those words he threw his towel over his head to rub the wet out of his mossy blond hair, knowing that his aunty had no option but to listen to his current jovial blurting.

As she listened to her nephew's banter, saying how he had great hopes for her for the future if she continued to try hard, she understood that the teacher that she had been to Stephanus for so many years was slowly coming to an end. The teacher was at times, in fact, becoming the student, and it was all happening so quickly. Stephanus was growing up fast and this wasn't the only area in life that he was excelling in. Lady Georgiana had given him so much of her time, a dedicated life even, to bringing up her brother's son. Much of it she had endured at first, not being a natural mother to anyone, but these last few years she'd actually enjoyed, despite the difficulties that surrounded them both Stephanus had grown so well as a young lad and now, as a young adult, his personality had burst onto the stage of life. It was a pleasure to know him and this young man-in-the-making was going to be not only a success at whatever he put his mind to, he was also going to be a good friend, something that Lady Georgiana had not expected or predicted. This living revelation was something she was still getting used to, but one that was most welcome. The change that was taking place before her very eyes, however, that is the handing over of the reins so that he was more in control of his life, she still currently found a little unsettling. When she called the shots, what they were to do that day and what it was they were going to learn etc. that was fine. Now that he was better than her at so many things and his insights were deeper and sharper than hers, that wasn't so good, or should I say easy to swallow. You never know how a relationship will work out once it begins to change before it finally settles again. Stephanus' wit, which sometimes went quite close to the mark, was very clever and strong – but at least she knew there was always a smile behind it and the fact that he loved her, as if she was a mother to him, was enough to keep things in balance.

260

"So, you still haven't told me Stephanus. Why your friends have suddenly decided to call you Scrub?" asked Lady Georgiana. "Not sure that I like this new nickname."

Stephanus lay back on the bank, covering himself with the towel to keep the cool breeze from chilling him.

"Oh it's just a bit of fun," he replied. "They've just taken the first letter from all my names, "Stephanus, Cadmar, Roberto, Uriel, Bannerman, and put them together and you get Scrub, that's all."

This insight into the construction of 'Scrub' as a nickname caused a brief shadow to cross her face, remembering the words of her sister-in-law. She shook the moment off.

"Well I'm not sure that I like it," came Lady Georgiana's reply. Her tone was a little corrective. Perhaps she'd found a subject that she still had some power over and had unwittingly found herself expressing an opinion on something that she could control in their relationship again.

"Relax Aunty," came Stephanus' reply. "It's only a bit of fun."

"You're a Pluggat Lynette," she said. "Stephanus is a wonderful name linked to your Grandfather Lord Stephen. You'll be a lord one day yourself. I don't want people calling you Lord Scrub!"

Stephanus laughed.

"It's not funny," she said.

Stephanus looked at her and giggled and Lady Georgiana found she had to look away in order to maintain her serious composure on this matter, which didn't last very long.

"I'm just saying to be careful what you let people call you," she eventually said, when her giggles had stopped. "Those friends of yours are getting a little too familiar."

"Right you are Aunt," came his quick reply, meaning that he wasn't putting too much weight on her words. He got to his feet, picked up his shoes, bent over and kissed his aunt on the very top of her head and began walking up the bank. "Just going off to see some of my over familiar friends," he called back over his shoulder. "Thanks for the swim; I'll catch up with you after rush hour."

Lady Georgiana watched him disappear over the bank and then finished off drying herself down. She quickly pulled on and zipped up a full-length body suit over her damp costume and then put her all weather coat and boots on top to prepare for her walk back into the city. Next to them was a bag that contained an assortment of odds and ends that she'd meant to drop off at one of the city's flea markets that morning, but hadn't had the time to do so. So she picked up the bag as the next job to be done on her list before going home and getting properly changed. After rummaging through the bag to make sure that everything in there was of no use to her and she was happy to give it away, she sat for a little while longer on the water's edge just to take in the day. It was bright, as normal, but there was a refreshing breeze that had a cool nip attached to it that was unusual for the city at that time of the year. So she closed her eyes and rested in the moment.

"Help!" she heard a voice call. It carried across the water and Lady Georgiana sat up to see the splashing of arms and legs moving at high speed in all directions.

Whoever it was out there, they were in difficulty and already in a panic. She got to her feet and quickly ran up to the top of the bank.

"Stephanus!" she cried out, whilst taking off her boots and top coat. "Stephanus, help!" Without seeing if he had heard her or not, she ran down the bank again, zipping off her body suit and plunging into the reservoir's chilly water. Already tired from her swim, she fought against her floppy limbs and overpowered them with her determination and will to catch up with the person in difficulty.

After swimming a good distance she could see the distressed person clearly, a very young woman. She was slowly drifting over towards the area where the turbines were and getting caught in the underwater drag that would lead to her death. Lady Georgiana reached the middle of the lake and slowed down, distraught by the sight of the struggling person and at the same time not sure how far she could venture towards her.

"Help me," came the young woman's cry. "Help me," she called again.

Lady Georgiana swam further, spurred on by the woman's call, even though she knew she was entering a danger zone.

"Aunty!" she heard from somewhere behind her.

"Stephanus, help," she spoke over her shoulder as she continued to swim. His arrival was welcome. She heard him splash into the water and knew it wouldn't be long before he'd caught up with her. As she swam on she could feel the pull from the undercurrent take hold of her legs and getting stronger as it rushed her towards the turbines. She decided to turn her body round to face the opposite way and let the current pull her towards the woman whilst at the same time testing her strength in the water to swim against the current to ensure that she could still get back to safety. Very soon she was within three or four body lengths of the struggling individual. She quickly found, however, that she'd reached the point where she too began to struggle. It was taking nearly all of her strength to keep herself from being sucked in and, once that happened, she turned her face towards Stephanus and cried out to him.

"Stephanus, help me!" she cried.

Stephanus was already ploughing his way through the water towards his aunt and once he was close to her he let himself be pulled in by the current so that he floated next to her. Taking her elbow in his left hand, he placed his arm across her back and his hand around her waist and so began to swim her back to safety. With a set of strong kicks from his legs he managed to get them both free and back into safe water. Once she was in the middle of the lake he let go of her.

"Can you swim back from here?" he asked her.

"Yes," she said. Then, "No!" she cried when she saw him swim back towards the other swimmer in distress. "No Stephanus," she cried again, "the current is too strong for you!" but he didn't listen. He slid again in the water, being dragged by the current, till he was even closer to the woman than his aunt had been. As he drew nearer, however, he had to kick hard to keep himself steady in the water. He reached out his hand towards her.

"Can you grab my hand?" he called.

When the woman in distress saw that he was close by and had really reached the limit of his strength, she suddenly stopped her splashing about and just stood there, arms on hips and bobbing up and down in the water; not struggling at all and not, for some unseen reason, drifting off in the current either. Something hidden was holding her in place. Stephanus furiously splashed against the drag caused by the great turbines to keep himself on the same spot. The young woman smiled at him and enjoyed his helplessness.

"How?" said Stephanus, wondering what was going on, but was so out of breath by that time he could not say anymore. The girl put a couple of fingers to her lips and whistled. On the bank of the reservoir appeared a small group of people. Some ran across to steal Lady Georgiana's bags whilst others picked up a submerged rope and began to pull. As it became taut it lifted out of the water and in an instant both Stephanus and his aunty saw that the girl was attached to the other end. With each haul on the rope her friends began to pull her to safety. Once she could see he was stranded and drifting away from her, she waved a 'bye, bye' to him and continued being pulled towards the bank by her friends.

As she passed him, with a final spending of his strength, Stephanus lunged forward, reached out and grabbed her arm. His fingers locked onto her, like a limpet holding on for sheer life. Her immediate reaction was to pull away, but Stephanus' grip was firm. She struggled with him as her friends continued to pull her in. Stephanus held on to her and would not let go. She pulled her arm left and right, round and round, up, down, but still Stephanus held on. Then, to finally get away from him, she held up her hand, turned it into a fist, looked him in the eye and got ready to thump him. He stared into her face, knowing what she intended to do.

"Please," said Stephanus. "Please don't."

His call for pity struck a chord in her heart. A moment's hesitation went through her head as he returned her stare. She glanced over to see Lady Georgiana swimming over towards her, and panicked. She looked at her friends on the bank who were still pulling her in.

"Drop him!" shouted one of them.

Again she hesitated. In those moments of uncertainty her fist turned into a hand and then into a fist again.

"Drop him!" came a shout from the shoreline again.

"Please," pleaded Stephanus again.

She once more held her fist up and Stephanus closed his eyes and turned his head, ready for the impact. The conflict of conscience within her grew, but as long as Stephanus held on her escape was hindered. She dropped her fist once more and flattened her hand again but with the flat of her palm, she hit Stephanus squarely on the forehead. She looked at him, still clinging on, eyes tightly closed and ready for the next blow. Then her conscience snapped and she hit him again and again. Finally, to get herself free, she pushed his head under the water. Down he went, letting go of her arm at last and drifted off with both his hands flapping in the air above the water's surface. Up he came again, exhausted, injured in one eye and disorientated.

"Aunty," cried Stephanus, as he fumbled and slapped the water around him.

"Stephanus, I'm coming," she answered.

Lady Georgiana continued to swim towards Scrub who was now helplessly spinning in the moving current. Through the one good eye he had left he saw her come closer and closer towards the danger zone, the place of no return. There comes a time, however, when love is greater than fear. When love from the heart dictates everything, and not the reasoning of the head. Decisions are made in moments. For Stephanus, this was a straightforward choice. To save his aunty he took one last glance at her through the one eye he had left open and then, letting his head fall back into the water, dropped his arms and became still. Exhausted he rested and the current now had him.

"Goodbye," he said.

Off he drifted, picking up speed as every moment passed. The outcry of his aunty sent a chill through him but this was drowned out by the water that rippled over his ears and into his face as he bobbed in its flow. The sound of the turbines got louder and louder.

"I'm dead," he thought.

Choking, coughing, with his nose and mouth often filling with water, he knew he couldn't keep his head up for much longer. He raised his arm to wipe his face, but there wasn't any strength left. So he took a breath and rested his face in the water for the last time. The sound of the water over his head dulled everything as he went under. It was as if he had entered another world and the outside, where the real life existed, was barred forever. Through his open eye he could see, in the not too far distance, the hazy image of the turning metal blades and the open gates that were beyond them.

Then an arm grabbed him and pulled him close. A hand went under his head and, finding his chin, lifted it up. Out of the water he surfaced and moments later he found himself staring into the face of Lady Georgiana. Dismay filled his heart, understanding that they both now shared the same fate.

"I know," she said.

She pulled and wrapped his floppy arms around her shoulders and kicked with her legs to keep them both afloat for a bit longer.

"I love you Stephanus," she said, as she held his head close to hers. "You're the only son I have," she added, and kissed the side of his head.

Together they sped forward in the water, arms locked about each other and swirling in the current. The great turbines chopped the water, churning and frothing it up as the surging flood went through its blades. Twirling and almost spinning they shot forward and it would only be a matter of seconds before they were gone forever. The strength in Lady Georgiana's legs finally gave way and under they both went, she clung onto him, not wanting to let go, to share every moment of the last seconds of life that they had together; an aunty, who was finally a mother, perishing with her son.

"Clunk," the sound of the great doors behind the turbines that unlocked and locked the floodgates resonated as they finally went down and closed. The running river that drove the turbines around was instantly stopped and the blades slowed down. Lady Georgiana and Stephanus had moments to go and, despite the river that had dragged them on being contained, they still hit a slowly turning turbine right in the middle of one of its blades. With no water to push them through, the blade took them up and out of the water and tossed them off along the edge of the reservoir wall. Stephanus took the main force of the blow; in fact he was completely knocked out. His aunt too received a bleeding nose but resurfaced quickly.

"Stephanus!" she cried. And then she saw him a few feet away. Swimming over she turned his face upwards and pushed him towards the wall. There were service bars there that divers used to help inspect the wall and she quickly took hold of one, pulling Scrub towards her and trying to prop him up.

Passers-by had seen the event and within minutes Lady Georgiana found herself in the strong arms of the men who had plunged in to save her and her nephew. She made a couple of them take Scrub first and followed on with the help of another by her side till they reached the shore again. Stephanus' body lay still, lifeless on the bank of the river, his aunty wept over him. She thumped his heart and gave him mouth to mouth, but there were few signs of sustained life to comfort her. Like watching a silent movie, Stephanus still had a strange memory of seeing his aunty leaning over him as he was eventually picked up by those passers-by and transported back to his home. The family doctor and friends stood nearby, a waiting game of life and death. Several days later Stephanus came round. Lying on a bed and staring up at a ceiling that was unfamiliar to him, his first thoughts seemed cloudy and muddled. He was in a room with people in it, but that's all he knew. One of them eventually saw that he had opened his eyes.

"He's awake," said a voice, in great relief.

Suddenly his bed was surrounded by people.

"Stephanus," cried a familiar voice.

A lady's face moved into view just a few inches from his and he knew she was someone he had known for a long time. Feelings of comfort entered his soul as her kind eyes and gentle smile met his and her hand caressed his forehead, brushing his hair with a gentle touch.

"Stephanus," she said again.

He looked at her as his eyes blinked and he breathed deeply to stir himself.

"Lady Pluggat," he said, once he recognised her.

The lady seemed relieved that he knew who she was and could speak. It was a good sign, and everyone's relief was clear to see. The lady of the realm composed herself, wiped her eyes and smiled back at him.

"Now when did you ever call me that?" she said, a deep countenance of joy all over her face.

Her question puzzled him.

"That's who you are," he replied.

He half glanced around the room with semi-glazed eyes and briefly took in the gathered group of people who stood around the bed, but couldn't remember who they were or the place they were all in.

"Where am I?" he mumbled. "Who are you all?"

"Typical Scrub," said one of the young people, and there was a group giggle amongst them, a giggle that sounded like emotional relief from a bunch of friends who had been waiting for something good to happen and it finally had.

"We're all so glad you're well," another of them added. "You've been out for three days and we thought you were a gonna."

"A gonna," repeated Stephanus, in a voice that had the strength of a faded echo.

Stephanus closed his eyes and breathed a few more times and then opened them. Seeing the people around him he spoke again to the only face he knew.

265

"Lady Pluggat, who are these people?" he said.

"Oh Stephanus," she replied. "These are your friends."

He looked again at them but nothing of familiarity registered with him.

"Friends," he said once more, thoughtfully to himself.

The sustained puzzled look on his face brought a rush of compassion from the woman that he knew as 'Lady Pluggat' and she turned to speak to everyone.

"I think he needs to rest," she said. "You can all come again tomorrow when he's got some more strength."

After the room was emptied Lady Pluggat and another gentleman with a bushy beard sat next to the bed and talked to each other for a time, trying every now and then to include Stephanus in the conversation, to see if he wanted to add anything to it. Their voices were full of relief and their light chatter showed great emotion under restraint. Stephanus found it hard, however, to join in their chatter and was only picking up the meaning of some words in the sentences.

"I think he's a bit delirious still," said the ginger bearded man. "Probably super tired, poor boy," he added.

"Perhaps you should go and I'll sit and watch over him," replied Lady Georgiana.

"Yes, I think you're right," replied the man. "I'll come back tomorrow with some beer and broth."

"Just the broth will be fine," she said. "I don't want any of his brain cells burnt up by one of your home brews."

They both laughed and he left the room. Once he was gone the lady came back to the bed and sat on it. Stephanus closed his eyes as she continued to stroke his hair.

"Lady Pluggat," he said, in a tired tone.

"Rest now," she said. "And for heaven's sake, stop calling me Lady Pluggat."

Stephanus dozed off, wondering what else he would be calling her. He came round hours later, perhaps the next day even, to the sound of gentle talk. Opening his eyes he could see that Lady Pluggat was still in the room and a different gentleman was close by, sitting in an armchair and making polite conversation. They both stirred from their seats as they saw him become conscious.

"Hello," said Lady Georgiana.

"Hello M'lady," he replied.

She chuckled a quiet laugh at what he'd just called her, but he didn't know why.

"Where am I?" he enquired.

"Why Stephanus, you're in your bedroom," she replied.

He looked and looked, but nothing registered.

"Don't you recognise your own room?" said the man accompanying her.

Stephanus looked about him again, but nothing familiar came to his mind.

"No," he simply replied.

A worried look appeared across their faces and they exchanged glances of concern with each other before turning to Stephanus again.

"Do you know who I am?" said the gentleman.

"No," he replied.

"Do you know who this is," he said, pointing to Lady Georgiana.

"Lady Pluggat," Stephanus replied.

"I'm not just Lady Pluggat," she said. "I'm your Aunty, your Aunty Georgiana."

Stephanus just looked at her blankly, nothing making sense to him.

The man in the room said, "Stephanus, I'm your family doctor. I've been your family doctor all the days of your life. Do you really not recognise me?"

"No," replied Stephanus again.

"What about your friends from yesterday? Do you still not remember them or Basil who was with them too?"

"No," came Stephanus' eventual reply.

"Stephanus," said Lady Georgiana, in a gentle and concerned voice. "You must remember the good doctor and your friends, surely."

Stephanus hesitated and then said, "Why do you keep calling me Stephanus?" The question quite took them aback.

"Do you not know who you are?" the doctor said.

"Scrub," replied Stephanus.

"Scrub?" they both echoed together.

"That's right," said Stephanus. "My name's Scrub."

A haze sat in Scrub's mind, a damaged brain from lack of oxygen, a thinking that was dulled. Over the next few days he would ask,

"Where am I?" and sometimes,

"Who am I?" or

"What is happening and why are you all here?"

It wasn't a dullness that was the coming round from a bad night's sleep. It was a dullness that stayed and remained, like a persistent injury. All he could remember was that his name was "Scrub" and that this person with him, Lady Georgiana Pluggat-Lynette, was an important person in the city and that for some reason she wanted to be near him. In a single moment he had lost all of his friends and what was left of his family; nothing remembered and no-one to talk to. All he knew was that he was "somewhere" and beyond that he struggled to make sense of anything that happened around him and had to work hard to form words and sentences and conversations. His mind raced, and how he wished it would slow down; blocked in a way that he could not understand and, at the same time, opened so that he could think so many unstoppable thoughts.

- -

"Stephanus," the voice came again. "Stephanus, forgive them, forgive them from the heart."

"I can't," he replied, finally understanding what had been done to him and his aunt.

"You must," the voice continued. "It's the only path to your freedom."

Scrub thought and thought and thought. His mind raced to try to put all of the pieces together but the problem seemed too big to solve.

"Stephanus, let go," the voice said again, with great clarity and authority.

With these words all the swirling stopped. His mind was put on pause and froze in a moment of time. It was as if he could have a good look around his own brain. His emotions and feelings were suspended and he was somehow separate from them. He could see the anger, fear, betrayal, hatred even. He could see the sense of loss in

267

his own soul, the theft - not just of a bag of belongings stolen from the banks of a reservoir, but of living years of life itself; years where he felt useless and dumb, a lost and broken soul in a mind gone wrong and a continual puzzle game that he couldn't solve. A trapped maze, he finally saw the door that was set before him and the only way out was to leave behind the swirling mass of emotions that held him captive.

"Stephanus, come back," the voice rang out again.

For a brief few moments it was as if he was submerged in the reservoir water again. It was clogging up his lungs, filling his mouth and choking him. He could feel the heaving of his stomach and lungs as he gasped for a breath of air. He could clearly see the doorway to freedom in his mind's eye, but he was drowning as he tried to make his way out. There was the face of the girl who had lured them into the water; the sweet smile on her face as she waved him goodbye to let him drown. There too was the group of them, stealing a bag of nothings from the side of the reservoir and leaving them without a hint of guilt or concern. His mind wavered back and forth. His emotions came to life again and he could feel their grip gaining on his mind and soul. The doorway to freedom was closing and it would soon be gone.

Wheezing and moaning, he let out a call of pain from within that finally seemed to clear his inner self.

"I forgive them," he finally said. "I forgive them all," he echoed again.

Moments later he found himself back in the real world being sick at his own feet. He finished the coughing and choking and breathed in to steady himself, wiping his eyes, nose and mouth on his sleeve. There Scrub knelt, trying to see through blurry eyes where he was and who was speaking to him. An arm touched him on the shoulder and he stood up and looked round to see his aunty standing next to him.

"Aunty," he said, and they embraced and wept together. "I'm back," he finally said after many tears.

"So you are," came the broken voice of his beloved aunt.

Eventually Stephanus turned round from his aunt's embrace to look straight into the face of King Wash El Ami.

"Stephanus," said the great king, "welcome back."

- -

Keep an eye out for the next books
being written in this series:

The Silence of Clearwash City
The Ransom of Clearwash City
The Purge of Clearwash City
The Hope of Clearwash City

About the Author

Tim Waters stepped out onto his new literary horizons in the mid-1990s. He began to run annual "custard slinging" summer clubs with his wife for children aged 7-12 and, as a result, found himself writing short plays for the children to watch. After writing,

- Enter the Jungle
- Invading the Ocean
- Way out in the Wild West
- The Knights and Ladies of Camel Knot Court
- Search for Stone Valley
- Splash into Spaghetti

...he decided to write a play called "The Waterworks of Clearwash City." (The following year he wrote Surfing the Supernova). The young audience so enjoyed the waterworks wacky adventure that he decided to turn it into a book. Over the years Tim has developed and moulded the storyline into a mature text ready for people of all ages to read. Now he has written this follow up book, detailing more of Clearwash City's life and history.

As a bit of a perfectionist Tim loves to use words to paint pictures of the book's world by adding great descriptions, clearly illustrating the surrounding sights, sounds and smells. At the same time he makes every paragraph as tight as possible so that the story flows well, making it an easy read. It is this attention to detail that marks Tim's style.

His purpose as a writer is not only to craft an excellent storyline, taking your mind into an imaginary place that he wishes to share with you, but also to weave secondary meanings into his text to make a point on life itself. Words are the most powerful things in the world and the world itself is changed by them.

As a young child Tim's favourite stories were those written by Roald Dahl and C.S. Lewis and later in his teenage years by J.R.R.Tolkien. He also grew up on the comedy of Laurel and Hardy along with other classics such as Dad's Army. Somewhere between all of these, along with other childhood sources, are the many influences by which he has written his drama scripts and hence this book. He wants his fiction work to be available to all of the family so that each age group can appreciate his daft and hopefully interesting stories at their own level. Tim strives to write in such a way that each individual can take something unique away with them from their read and hopes that people can begin to pick up the secondary meanings in his text, whether a comic reference or a serious point made. It has taken years for Tim to discover his unique writing style and this second book represents his next stage of 'growing up' as an author. He hopes that his following books will take a little less time to write.

Tim enjoys being a husband and a dad. He likes watching Sci-Fi adventure movies, playing the guitar, watching films too young for his age, painting, drawing and dining out at 'all you can eat' buffets. It is not wise to play Monopoly with Tim as he turns

269

into a different person. Apart from this flaw in his personality, he's not too difficult to live with - and so he reminds his wife on a regular basis.

Tim really hopes you like this book and also looks forward to creating new reads for you as and when he can.

- - - - - - - - - - - - - - - -

To help Tim, could you please leave a review of this book
on Amazon where you purchased it.

- - - - - - - - - - - - - - - -

Georgiana's Attic

Georgiana's attic is the fictional hiding place of a wise and courageous heroine, Lady Georgiana Pluggat-Lynette. Surrounded by vintage treasures that remind her of happier times, she recounts on paper the exploits of a group of unlikely rebels. In their attempts to keep Georgiana's beloved Clearwash City free from tyranny they discover that friendship is the key to victory. You can find out more about Georgiana's attic and the items that are on sale there at
https://georgianasattic.com/

Printed in Great Britain
by Amazon

87702618R00159